PRAISE FOR *THE EXPEDITIONS*

"Beautifully written and outstandingly researched, Iagnemma's first novel is a keeper."   —*Publishers Weekly*

"Iagnemma's first novel is provocative, elegiac, and highly recommended."   —*BookPage*

"A stunning debut novel . . . intelligent and urbane yet also raw and unflinching."   —*Library Journal*

"Iagnemma's robust command of language creates an equilibrium between the two narratives, marrying the poetry of science with the promise of salvation."   —*Kirkus Reviews*

ALSO BY KARL IAGNEMMA

On the Nature of Human Romantic Interaction

I respect Assyria, China, Teutonia, and the Hebrews;
I adopt each theory, myth, god, and demi-god;
I see that the old accounts, bibles, genealogies, are true, without
    exception;
I assert that all past days were what they should have been;
And that they could no-how have been better than they were,
And that to-day is what it should be—and that America is,
And that to-day and America could no-how be better than
    they are.

—From *With Antecedents,* Walt Whitman

LAKE SUPER

Granite Island

Dead R.

Carp R.

Chocolate R.

Baptist Mission

Train R.

Pictured Rocks

Hurricane R.

Sucker R.

Silas Brush & Geo. Tiffin's

Intended Route

LAKE MICHIGAN

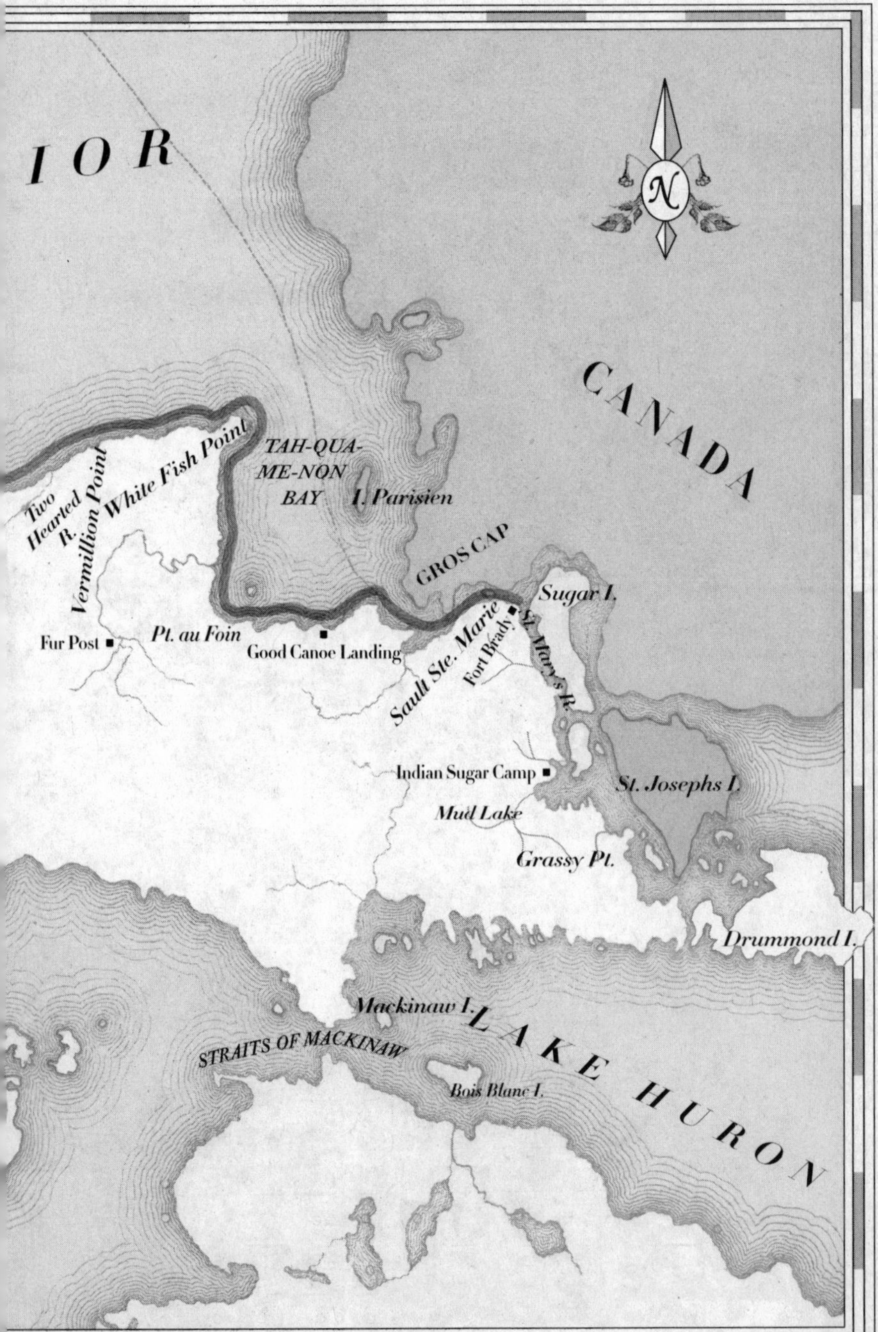
IOR
CANADA
TAH-QUA-
ME-NON
BAY
I. Parisien
Two
Hearted
R.
Vermillion Point
White Fish Point
GROS CAP
Sugar I.
Fur Post
Pt. au Foin
Good Canoe Landing
Sault Ste. Marie
Fort Brady
St. Mary's R.
Indian Sugar Camp
St. Josephs I.
Mud Lake
Grassy Pt.
Drummond I.
Mackinaw I.
STRAITS OF MACKINAW
LAKE HURON
Bois Blanc I.

The Expeditions

Part One

One

The appointment was at ten o'clock on Lafayette Street, on the city's west side, and Elisha stepped from his boardinghouse at six that morning into a gauzy gray mist. Draft horses slapped down the muddy street, hauling drays loaded with potatoes and cabbages. He strolled down the sidewalk to Jefferson Avenue, drank a mug of milk as he listened to a newsboy call out the morning's headlines: *White woman elopes with Negro servant to Windsor! Settlers burned alive in Shelby by savage Chippewas!* He felt a familiar nervous chill at the city's rush and clamor. The air smelled sweetly foul, like burning trash.

He walked down Jefferson to Woodward Avenue then up to the Military Square, where a group of men were unloading red lacquered trunks from a caravan of weather-worn buggies. A handbill tacked to a message board at the square's entrance read:

TRAVELING EXHIBITION OF FABULOUS BEASTS

L. GASPERI—ANIMAL TRAINER EXTRAORDINAIRE

SEE CAMELS FROM ARABIA—ELEPHANTS FROM SIAM—

LLAMAS FROM THE BOLIVIAN MOUNTAINS

ADMISSION FEE: ONE DIME

As Elisha watched, one of the men unlatched the door of a high-sided wagon and led a frail, shaggy camel by a rope knotted around its neck. The animal stepped gingerly, twisting its long neck to gaze at its surroundings. Elisha drew a notebook from his vest pocket and licked a stub of pencil, sketched the animal's head and oddly humped back. The camel's handler glanced over his shoulder and called, "Hey boyo, no free looks! Come back tonight, you want to see!"

Elisha started up Michigan Avenue into the Irish quarter and its cramped, hustling streets. At Sixth Street a group of women were singing choral tunes around a donation basket. He paused to watch them: two skinny, black-haired sopranos and a squat, sleepy-looking alto. The boy was sixteen years old and his thoughts were almost entirely of women: their hair, their powder smells, their fleeting glances on the sidewalk. Young women in shop windows and ladies in broughams and girls strolling arm in arm down the avenue. The alto cut her gaze to Elisha and he ducked away.

He hurried down Sixth Street toward the river, quickening his pace as he emerged at the wharf. He continued southward past a row of shanties until he came to a stagnant stretch of sedge and driftwood. Elisha pulled off his shoes and sat on a stone at the river's edge, careful not to muddy his trousers. He leaned forward and rested his chin on his knees. From his position he could barely hear the hoofbeats on Woodbridge Avenue, but despite the quiet Elisha could not settle his nerves. Pond skaters tickled among the sedge, their passage visible as faint dimples in the river's surface. A merganser coasted toward the boy then angled upriver. Elisha withdrew his notebook and sketched the scene, his thoughts slowing, the city's noise fading to nothing. He worked long after the bell at St. Anne's had tolled nine o'clock.

He rose feeling wonderfully calm. He started up Seventh until he reached Lafayette, then entered a shop with its window painted to read *O. Chocron, Clothier*. He purchased a five-cent collar from the frowning proprietor, then stood before a tall mirror and buttoned the collar beneath his chin, the stiff linen chafing his neck. His own figure in the glass annoyed him: the cowlicked hair, the high, pale forehead, the pockmarked cheeks without even a hint of beard. A frightened boy in a man's clothes, certainly not a fellow to be reckoned with, certainly not one to be entrusted with an important task.

He exhaled deeply and attempted a fierce smile, and for a moment the boy in the mirror disappeared.

Thirty-one Lafayette Street was a two-story mansion with broad double doors and a columned porch, an orange-tiled roof topped by a cupola. Elisha stood at the street's edge for some time. He had expected a surveyor's cottage but this was far grander, the home of a judge or senator. At last he straightened his cuffs and set his hat square, then mounted the steps and tugged the bellpull.

A tall Negro girl in a white apron opened the door, glanced at the boy's shoes and hat. "If you here about the expedition you haves to wait. Mr. Brush is busy just now."

Elisha nodded.

"Follow me." She led him into a dim study and motioned toward a velvet wing chair. "Don't you touch anything."

He nodded again. His gaze followed the girl from the room.

Blue linen draperies filtered the morning light and lent the room a petrified quality. A carved walnut desk sat in the corner, covered with books and scrolled maps, a pair of brass rulers. Beside the desk stood an oak bookshelf filled with leather-bound volumes: sets of Shakespeare, Milton, Gibbon, the spines looking as though they'd never been creased. Bragging books, Elisha thought, for displaying instead of reading. The room smelled of soot and candlewax.

He rose and paced before the marble mantel: three pink conch shells sat beside a rosewood clock; beside the clock was a gleaming brass instrument with a jumble of thumbscrews and vanes and eyepieces projecting from a circular base. Beside the instrument stood an angled block draped with red silk, displaying four gold coins bearing a man's profile in crude relief—Roman, Elisha figured, or Greek. He took up a coin and tilted it toward the window. The face was so worn that the only clear feature was the line of a mouth, which seemed to be etched in a wry smile.

Floorboards squeaked in the hallway and Elisha replaced the coin then perched on the wing chair. A man entered the room and the boy bolted upright.

He was younger than Elisha had expected, with long brown hair combed back from his temples, a clean-shaven jaw, watery blue eyes beneath a sharp brow. Mr. Silas A. Brush, surveyor and landlooker, hero of the Second War for Independence. The man's hand, when Elisha shook it, was rough as a corn husk. Brush said, "Well! You look barely old enough to dress yourself."

"I'm sixteen years old, sir."

Brush squinted at Elisha as if measuring the truth of his claim. He was wearing a black frock coat over a black satin waistcoat, a stiff black cravat. Pinned to the man's lapel was a pear-shaped sapphire. Like a minister with a wealthy wife, Elisha thought. The stone was the precise hue of Brush's eyes.

"I trust you're not aiming to join a storybook adventure. I will disappoint you by saying the expedition won't be any such thing."

Elisha nodded.

"Plenty of hard slogs through swamps, suppers of hog and hominy if we're lucky, beds of pine boughs and creation's finest dirt. Mosquitoes as big as walnuts. No whiskey or pussy for a hundred miles."

"Yes sir. I know, sir."

"You'll be ridden as hard as a borrowed mule. You'll lie down tired and wake up exhausted."

"Yes sir, I know. I'm not expecting any comfort."

The statement seemed to amuse Mr. Brush. "Then explain me this, young pup: why do you want to join the expedition?"

Because I'm flat busted, Elisha thought to joke, but paused when he noticed the sternness beneath Brush's grin. So instead he told the man the truth: about the creek behind his father's house in Newell, a narrow sandy trickle alive with limpets and water boatmen and fat darners, waxwings and wrens and prairie warblers, goldenrod and lilac and willow. As a boy he'd spent his days at the creek's edge, capturing minnows in his cupped palms to study their glassy scales, their wispy fins, their blank eyes. Other days he sat motionless for hours, until a swallowtail fluttered down to a puddle of sugar water at his feet. He loved the secret beauty of it all, the details that revealed themselves only after long inspection. The creek appeared simple but in fact was as intricate as a symphony. Elisha told Mr. Brush about the first specimen he'd collected, a gnarled brown shell that looked like a nub of tobacco; its odd shape made it seem like a hoax by God on unsuspecting scientists. He told Mr. Brush about the empty shelves in his boyhood bedroom, his desire to see them filled with examples of every species in the world.

When he finished speaking Mr. Brush offered a false smile. "Ambitious goal, wouldn't you say? The last man to collect every species was Noah."

"I don't expect to succeed, sir. Seems a worthy aim, though."

"It is not a worthy aim. It is a dream. I have no use for moon-eyed dreamers on this expedition." Brush's expression softened slightly. "Life is a practical endeavor, my boy."

"I understand that, indeed I do." Elisha paused. "I can shoot and handle an axe. I've read Say's and Nuttall's books a dozen times each. I can identify common trees and birds and the primary rocks, some minerals and gemstones—that sapphire on your lapel, for instance. I can tote as much as a packhorse."

The man chuckled, then rose with a sigh. He unscrolled a map on the desk and motioned Elisha over: Michigan's mittenish form divided by neat square survey lines, and above it the upper country, a hollow white sketch save for points labeled *Fort Brady* and *Sault Ste. Marie* at the eastern tip, a few rivers winding vaguely inland from the northern shore.

"A portion of the northern peninsula was recently gained by treaty from the savages, and our legislature is keen to learn what it holds. The land is rich in timber—that much is known. I assume you've heard reports of copper and silver and gold?"

"Yes sir."

"Well! We shall not be searching for copper or silver or gold. You do not build railroad tracks and locomotives and cannons from copper or silver or gold. You build them from iron. You see, my boy, *fortunes* are built from gold. But *nations* are built from iron."

Brush's tone reminded Elisha of an old schoolmaster, a rheumy pedant named Wilkerson. All responses to the man's questions were incorrect. He'd been fond of wielding a hickory switch on the class's younger boys.

"The expedition's secondary purpose is somewhat nebulous. The land office has attached Professor George Tiffin to the expedition. Professor Tiffin has theories about the savages—some notion about their artifacts, how they might explain the mystery of their origins. I suspect he is a moon-eyed dreamer."

Elisha nodded but said nothing.

"We shall depart from Sault Ste. Marie and canoe to the Chocolate River, here, then return on foot through the interior. We will measure topographical features, examine geological evidence, count timber—none of your minnow and butterfly nonsense. The journey will last twelve weeks. The wage is ten dollars per week, paid upon departure. You say you can shoot?"

"Shot a smoothbore flintlock since I was a boy. I can knock a hole in a watermelon at a hundred yards."

"A useful skill, should we be menaced by watermelons. You can handle an axe?"

Despite himself Elisha grinned. "I worked two winters in a lumber camp near Manchester—I believe we cut half the pine timber in New Hampshire. So I'm right friendly with both axe and saw."

"Are you a praying Christian?"

His grin froze. The true answer was clearly the wrong one. He said, "My father is a minister."

Mr. Brush grunted. He turned to the mantel, and as he did the breath emptied from Elisha's lungs. He had somehow disappointed the man. Now Brush would thank Elisha for his time, send him away with a stiff handshake. And then back to his boardinghouse room on Orleans Street, with its greasy window and fly-speckled shade, its smell of rotten fish. The boy wiped sweat from his brow.

Mr. Brush took up the brass instrument, handling it like it was made of glass. He offered it to Elisha with barely concealed pride. "Tell me, young fellow! How do you suppose this device might be employed?"

Elisha exhaled silently, turning the instrument over in his hands. There was an eyepiece oriented vertically between a pair of ruled vanes, a profusion of knurled knobs and spirit levels to adjust the eyepiece's orientation. He held the device to his chin and squinted along the vanes. He said, "I suspect it might be a tool for surveying. Or maybe navigation."

"And why do you suppose that?"

"You might sight along these vanes, use these knobs to adjust the eyepiece. And these spirit levels allow you to hold it true, maybe even if you're on a ship. The eyepiece might point at a star—you might measure the bearing to the pole star to figure your location."

"In fact, it is a compass that relies on the sun to determine heading. Do you see? It solves the troubles caused by ferrous minerals in the earth—they distract a magnetic compass needle. The presence of iron fouls their measurement."

"That socket clamp fastens it to a leveling stand," Elisha said. "And those verniers maybe correct for the time of day the measurement is taken. Yes?" Elisha grinned at the man as he returned the instrument. "It is a marvelous device."

"Thank you. It is of my own invention."

A stiff smile broke across Silas Brush's face as he replaced the instrument on the mantel. He moved to the desk and began arranging the scrolled maps, and without looking up he said, "Your jacket is filthy. And you are woefully inexperienced." He paused. "But you shall do. We depart from the long pier at dawn on Sunday. Bring a broad-brimmed hat and a pair of stout boots. Nothing else! Tell your girly friends you'll be back come August."

"I will! Be there on Sunday, I mean."

He stood motionless as Mr. Brush frowned at a map. The man seemed already to have forgotten Elisha's presence.

"Just one question, sir."

Brush stared blankly at Elisha. The mantel clock's ticking filled the room.

"I've heard stories about the Chippewas."

"What sorts of stories?"

"Stories like Alexander Henry's and James Smith's. That they might take a man's scalp or cut off his thumbs, especially if you trespass on their land. Trouble is, you don't know which land is theirs. Nor do they, sometimes."

Mr. Brush settled into the desk chair and closed his eyes. He was silent for a long moment. "Or they might slice off a man's eyelids, force him to watch his own wife be set afire. Or cut off his pecker, throw it to a pack of starved dogs while he's yet alive."

Elisha nodded. He clapped on his hat and ducked toward the door.

"Boy."

Elisha turned.

Brush motioned toward the wall behind his desk. A skein of loose black twine, like a charred perch net, was tacked beside the bookcase. With a shock Elisha recognized it as a scalp lock, dangling from a swatch of leathered flesh.

"There will be no trouble from savage Chippewas. That I guarantee."

On the sidewalk, in the sunlit drizzle, Elisha moved among a hustle of gentlemen and street vendors and ladies, amid the shouts of charcoal peddlers and airy clang of church bells, the smells of manure and smoke and coffee. He was almost too excited to breathe. He turned onto a side street and broke into a jog, then yanked the hat from his head and with a shout whirled it skyward. It skated far along the laneway, rising on an updraft before coasting slowly down.

A drunkard squatting in a doorway spat and called, "Hey! Don't dirty that fucking capper!"

Was this how bliss tasted? Of manure and woodsmoke and rot and roasting coffee? Elisha raced down the laneway and scooped up the hat, clapped it on his head. From the thrown-open doors of a corner church came a reedy chorus of praise.

He had come to Detroit after two winters in the forests north of Manchester, cutting white pine with an outfit of Swedes and Poles. The lumber camp existed in Elisha's mind now as luxurious sensations, devoid of imagery: the sharp scent of pine sap, the taste of smoky sassafras tea. The initial draft of morning air, so cold it made him sneeze. That first winter, he'd risen an hour before dawn to drive a team of Belgians down the snowy tote roads, a water tank's trickle turning the trails into belts of ice. Despite the wagon's jostling he often dozed, waking in startled confusion with the horses stopped, his breath clouding before him, the frozen reins limp in his gloved hands. Around him, snow-covered pines and birches and sugar maples slumped before a vast white sky. His calls echoed faintly then were swallowed by the forest.

The second winter Elisha gained promotion to the timber crew, cutting white pine that he figured to be two hundred years old by the rings on their table-sized stumps. Now he slept until dawn, hiked out to the cut beneath a chorus of grosbeak and chickadee. White-tailed deer froze as the men approached, then vaulted away. Afternoons, they stripped the felled logs then chained them into enormous pyramids to be hauled away by oxen. One afternoon a chain binding snapped. The sound was like a pistol shot; then a pyramid of logs collapsed with a groan, rushing toward Elisha and a young Polish teamster. Elisha dove away, his legs twisted beneath the timber, but the teamster was struck full in the chest, his toque knocked clear. The boy lay on his back as blood slid from his mouth. He was too frightened even to scream. The lumbermen lifted the pair onto a sled and rushed them to the bunkhouse, the Polish boy repeating a single whispered word: *Matka, matka, matka.* Mother. Elisha clasped his hand to comfort him. The boy died fifty yards from the bunkhouse.

Elisha laid up for two weeks, until the swelling in his knee diminished, then limped to the depot in Manchester and scanned the schedule board. Somewhere far away, he thought, somewhere warmer. Somewhere with women. He paid eighteen dollars for a seat on a train headed to Detroit via Syracuse, Buffalo, Cleveland, and Toledo. He carried a bundle with a spare pair of trousers and a change of underclothes. His coin pouch held two worn gold eagles. That first morning in the city he purchased a copy of the *City Examiner,* and that afternoon he knocked on the door of Alpheus Lenz on Woodward Avenue, who had posted an advertisement for a scientific assistant, no experience required, payment of three dollars coin per week. Elisha's shirt was stained from a long-ago bloody nose. His hair was matted and frayed.

Alpheus Lenz was a short, fleshy gentleman with curly blond hair and smoke-colored pince-nez spectacles. He squinted at Elisha's stained shirt, then reluctantly invited the boy into a study stacked with wooden crates. The crates, he explained, were filled with specimens that he planned to arrange in a cabinet of curiosities for public display. He asked Elisha to sit at a desk and write the words *Animal bipes implume* on a sheet of parchment. "How did you learn to write so beautifully?" the man asked, holding the paper close to his ruined eyes. Elisha thought to describe his father's nightly regimen: three verses of Scripture copied in perfect hand, any wavering characters causing the entire verse to be repeated. He said, "My mother taught school." Lenz hired him on to start that afternoon.

Alpheus Lenz showed Elisha how to pin butterflies through the thorax to cedar specimen blocks, there beside a screened fireplace, their shirtsleeves pinned up, sunlight slanting through the tall windows. Afternoons, Elisha penned title cards for specimens from Georgia and the Carolinas, Maine and Texas, the chiton shells like strange coins, the cave bats frozen as if in panicked flight. For reference he paged through Lenz's gilt-edged volumes: Say's *American Conchology* and *American Entomology,* Townsend's *Ornithology of the United States of North America.* Nuttall's *The Genera of North American Plants,* in green morocco binding. He admired the elegant logic of taxonomy: that everything in nature, no matter how varied or obscure, had a home in a single grand scheme. Weeks passed, the ripsaw calluses fading from his palms to reemerge as small nubs where his thumb pressed the steel pen. The lumber camp seemed to exist only as a dream, save for the deep, constant ache in his knee.

One Monday in August Elisha opened a crate to find it filled with broken shells—crushed, no doubt, during transport from Florida. He sifted through the sharp, iridescent fragments as a swell rose in his throat. It was the sole remaining crate in Alpheus Lenz's collection. Now Elisha would climb the stairs to the man's study, where Lenz would be dozing in a leather armchair, spectacles fallen onto his chest, a book splayed across his lap. Elisha would tell him about the crushed shells, and Lenz's eyebrows would furrow with the same irritated disappointment that Elisha now felt. Then they would walk together down to Woodward Avenue, and Elisha would stand in the bright morning light, dazzled, blinking. Alpheus Lenz would shake the boy's hand and say that he was deeply sorry, that there were no more specimens to catalog, and that he appreciated Elisha's diligent efforts, and that he wished Elisha the best possible fortune in every future endeavor.

It was possible to stay there, wasn't it? In that study, with its dusty blue light, the bookcases holding up the ceiling, the porcelain bust of Linnaeus looking like he might burst into tears. The row of pens, the inkwells, the blank parchment cards awaiting inscription. The insects and shells and plants and birds frozen on shelves, the cards below them penned in Elisha's hand. Surely there were as many specimens in the world as there were sheets of parchment. The study's empty shelves seemed a pitiful admission of failure.

It was possible to stay in that room forever. Wasn't it?

. . .

That Thursday night Elisha opened the front door of his boarding-house to find the stairway dark. He lit a splint and made his way to the second floor, judging each footstep with drunken precision. He had spent the evening in a saloon on Franklin Street at a table near the fire, reading and sipping from a flask of whiskey. In his pocket was a paste-board pamphlet: *Language and History of the North American Indian Tribes,* by Professor George D. Tiffin.

At the print shop on Jefferson Avenue he'd found a dozen of Tiffin's works: *On the Physiognomy and Racial Equality of the American Negro. Receipts for Growing Vegetables of Prodigious Size and Quality. An Examination of the Hebrew Language and Its Bearing on the Question of the Unity of Races. A Simple and Effectual Cure for Consumption.* Elisha had pointed at the Indian pamphlet then waited impatiently as the proprietor fetched a stool and retrieved the volume from a top shelf.

"That'll be me someday," Elisha said. "My books will be on your shelf, lined up next to Professor Tiffin's."

"And what makes you think a body will want to read your writings?"

"Because I aim to write on scientifical subjects—I'm joined up on an expedition with Mr. Silas Brush to the state's northern peninsula. You'll read reports of it in the newspapers soon enough!"

"My best congratulations." The man slid the volume across the counter. "Remember me for an especial discount."

Now, outside his room, he worked his key in the lock as a sigh drew his attention to a man's form sprawled in the hallway: his neigh-bor, an Italian named Vecchione. Vecchione had come to Michigan from a farm town in Abruzzo because he'd heard there was gold in the territory. Lucky fellow, Elisha thought, drunker even than me. Vecchione had shaved, and in the dim light his face was as bronzed and craggy as a Chippewa's.

An image formed in Elisha's mind of a childhood journey with his father to Boston, to view an exhibition of tame Iroquois braves: the Natives had squatted on a raised platform in the Boston common, smoking clay pipes and wearing tattered turkey-feather headdresses, staring dully at the clustered men and women. The braves' faces, Elisha remembered, had looked like crumpled leather masks. He'd buried his face in his father's trousers but the faces had remained in Elisha's mind all that month. Years later they reappeared in his dreams.

In the room, he lit a candle then slumped to the floorboards. In three days he would be on a steamer headed to the northern peninsula; the notion caused his stomach to flutter. There will be specimens everywhere, he told himself, insects and animals and plants and fish— he might encounter a new species, have his name immortalized in Linnaean taxonomy. *Pinus stonus. Coleoptera stonus.* But his thoughts kept returning to the Iroquois's face.

He fetched his notebook, tore a page from it and dipped his pen. He wrote *My dear Mother,* then crumpled the page and flung it toward the room's corner. A mouse's rustle answered from the darkness. He tore a second page and smoothed it against the floor, his chest tightening in a familiar knot of guilt and love. At last he wrote:

May 30, 1844

Dearest Mother,

    I pray this letter finds you in good health, as it leaves me. I write these lines from the city of Detroit, having today won a place on a scientifical expedition with Mr. Silas A. Brush to the state's northern peninsula. Do not worry for my safety, as Mr. Brush has guaranteed there is no danger, whatever, from savage Natives. Know that I am daily taking solace in prayer.

    I would explain my disappearance from Newell and my absence these past years, but any words I might write seem pale shadows of my true thoughts. Know that not a day has

passed that I have not dreamed of home. Mother, this country
is more mean and solitary than I had ever imagined. In my
dreams Newell seems part of a different world entirely.

Is the bantam cock with the injured comb still alive and
ruling the chicken yard? Have you kept at growing the
Chinese vines on the trellis behind the privy? Dear Mother,
I have missed you with every part of my heart. My mood is
lifted only by the hope that I might see you again, very soon.

My fondest greetings to Father and Corletta.

I remain, forever,

> Your dearest loving son,
> Elisha Stone

He blotted the ink then stared at the page, his calm sentences a
strange counterpoint to the ache in his chest. He thought to strike the
lie about taking prayer then decided to leave it be. A lie to ease another's worries couldn't be entirely sinful. Elisha folded the thin sheet
in four then held it to his lips. How long had it been since he'd written
to his mother? Fifteen months, during the train ride to Detroit from
the forests of Manchester. He'd been homesick and miserable, there in
the frigid rail car, and at the Buffalo station he'd nearly gathered his
belongings and boarded a train back east, toward Newell. But the motion of his hand across the page had been enough to temper his un-
happiness. He'd finished the letter then torn it into squares, let them
flutter like snowflakes to the carriage floor.

But now the ache in his chest refused to diminish. You were a boy
then, he told himself, and you're a man now. So act as a danged man.
Outside, the clock on the Thompson Bank tolled nine o'clock. In
Newell his father would be slouched in a rocker beside the fire, eyes
closed, a half-written sermon on his lap. His mother would be humming a quiet melody as she doused the lamps. Elisha had once measured the distance from Detroit to Newell on a map and found it to be

seven hundred and twenty miles. A mouse skittered along a baseboard and he shrank deeper into the corner.

Seven hundred and twenty miles, of forest and lake and darkness and snow. Elisha wrote the address of his father's house on the folded sheet, then slipped the letter into his vest pocket, next to his heart.

Two

Reverend William Edward Stone placed his hat on the dining room table and wiped a slick of sweat from his neck. Not yet eleven but already the sun shimmered above Newell and the damp meetinghouse yard. It had rained that morning, the storm's thrum waking the minister to a smoke-gray dawn shot with silver veins of lightning, but now the clouds were dissolved and sunlight spangled on the meetinghouse's high windows. Such ridiculous, extravagant splendor, Reverend Stone thought. If the Lord ever displayed vanity it was during moments like this, these heart-lifting flights of beauty.

Rain had seeped through the rotted shingle roof and lay pooled on the dining room floor. He stepped over the puddle and sat at the scrubbed pine table, and a moment later Corletta, the hired woman, emerged from the kitchen with a platter of fried ham and stewed green beans and milk biscuits. He thanked her and murmured a blessing over the meal, then reclined in his chair and gazed idly out the window. From the dining room he could see past the meetinghouse and chicken house and whitewashed privy, down the treeless hillside to the creek and Baptist church. New Hope, with its portico and brass weathercock and oak pews, its six-hundred-pipe Appleton organ shipped from Boston. The church was quiet now, but lately on warm afternoons its choir would practice with the front doors flung wide, the organ's raspy bass rolling uphill to the minister lying sleepless on his bed. The melodies had at first pleased him but soon piqued his annoyance; they felt like a pious show of strength, a taunt. The Baptists were winning new followers in Newell every hour, plucking them like wildflowers from the thicket of unbelievers. Soon New Hope would be too small to seat its congregation.

He ate a biscuit and scrap of ham but found he had no appetite. From the kitchen came a harsh scrape of iron against iron: Corletta preparing to black the cookstove. Often she sang while she worked, simple workaday or Bible-story chants, and the minister found himself awaiting her breezy voice. She was a virtuous woman but not religious. Once he had drawn out her beliefs and the result was a disappointing muddle of Scripture and superstition.

The scraping stopped and Corletta appeared in the doorway. She frowned at the clotted grease on the minister's plate. "Something wrong with your lunch, Reverend Stone?"

He began to speak but was seized by a cough. He clapped a handkerchief to his mouth until the spell faded. "No, nothing. I'm weary from yesterday's services—I am sure my appetite will return quick enough."

Her gaze lingered a moment, then fell with an expression of vague shame. She stepped back into the kitchen. Reverend Stone glanced at the handkerchief to find the gray linen flecked with crimson blood. The absurdity of his furtiveness struck him: concealing the blood from Corletta, when she was the woman who laundered his handkerchiefs. He was filled with sickly amusement. Then Corletta reappeared and took up his plate and fork. The minister smiled at her, then stared hard at her retreating form.

Lately Reverend Stone had begun feeling a queer conviction that he could see the color of other people's souls. That if he stared deeply enough, he could see a person's soul hovering about them as a pale, colored nimbus. Two months ago, on the morning of his sixty-first birthday, he'd been delivering a chipped hewing axe to the smithy for grinding when he'd been overwhelmed by the notion that if he gazed at William Lawson he would see the man's soul as a faintly hued mist. Lawson hunched over the anvil, truing a warped pry bar. The minister stared, transfixed. A dusty gray haze grew around Lawson's shoulders, like ash consuming a burning page. Reverend Stone's throat constricted. He lost his grip on the axe and it clattered to the floor. Without a word he rushed from the shop, hurried to the parsonage and lay motionless on the bed, his heart drumming as though he'd run a sprint.

The color of souls. Purity, he suspected, was white as January snow; the violent and corrupt possessed scarlet or ocher colorations; sinners of the flesh fell among the infinite shades of gray. What was the color of his own soul? Reverend Stone hadn't yet chanced to observe himself, and for that he was grateful.

He took up his hat and crossed the humid yard. The meetinghouse was an old clapboard building with a steeply pitched roof and squat tower and open belfry, low granite steps leading to a weathered front door. In need of whitewashing yet again, Reverend Stone noted. A dim chill surrounded him as he stepped inside. The meetinghouse smelled faintly of mildew. He shook the wet from his brogans then climbed the back stairs to the vestry, where Edson, the deacon, was bent over a paper-strewn desk figuring sums in a ledger. Edson was a wide, clumsy young man with a shock of corn-tassel hair and thick spectacles that lent him a false appearance of intelligence. Four scratched-out sums showed at the bottom of the page.

Edson smiled and shook a pinch of blotter powder over the ledger. "Discouraging news from the collection."

"A difficult week. There is a torpor in the air, Edson. Do you feel it?"

Edson nodded uncertainly. "I meant to ask you: did you hear any commotion last night? There's a fox troubling the chickens. This morning I found the chicken house nearly dug under."

Reverend Stone settled into a chair beside the desk and clasped his hands behind his head. "Well, our old friend mister fox! Corletta will be unhappy if there are no chickens to stew."

"I mended the planking. I hope it will hold."

Reverend Stone nodded. " 'The natural body is an obstruction to the soul or spiritual body.' Do you believe that statement to be true, Edson?"

Edson stared, motionless, at the minister. From the road outside a clap of hoofbeats rose then faded.

"I have often wondered what is meant by that passage. *Obstruction*. A strange choice of words. Yes?"

"Maybe it means that only after death is the soul truly freed. Maybe that's what is meant by obstruction."

Edson had been raised in Maine, a potato-farm boy with a deep, simple faith that Reverend Stone both scorned and admired. The minister saw him as a child, saying grace over supper at a coarse sawbuck table by the glow of a tallow stub, the pitiless Maine wind prying at the door. Edson had come to Newell when he was fifteen years old.

"Tell me, Edson: would you say that passage contains heresy?"

The young man reddened. "No. No, I don't believe it does."

"But our natural body was formed by God! If it obstructs the spiritual body it must be deeply flawed. How could the body, created by Him in His own image, be so imperfect, Edson?"

"Nothing He created is imperfect."

Reverend Stone's gaze fell to the pen lying atop the blotter, then traveled to Edson's ink-stained fingertips. Edson folded his hands and placed them in his lap. He said, "Or maybe the author is referring to the natural body's wants—the sinful wants. They could be viewed as an obstruction."

"Perhaps. The sinful wants of the natural body obstructing the sublime aspirations of the spiritual body." Reverend Stone tapped his index finger against the desk. "Troubling thoughts, Edson. Good, troubling thoughts."

He noticed a clothbound volume half-hidden by papers at the desk's edge, and picked it up: Milton's *Paradise Lost*. "Excellent, Edson! We must resume our literary discussions. We must contemplate whatever meaning you might find in Milton."

"If you think that's best," Edson said stoically.

"Oh, I do. Milton is brimming with troubling thoughts."

He rose to leave, then Edson said, "I'd hoped we might speak. About the coming Sunday."

Reverend Stone paused.

"You'd mentioned some while back that you were feeling withery." Edson drew a breath, then continued. "Of course, you seem perfectly well, but if you have a need for—"

"You would like to preach this Sunday."

Edson nodded. "I've been sketching a sermon. I hope you don't mind."

"What is the topic?"

"Geology and religion. Would you like to hear a piece?"

Reverend Stone relaxed back into the chair. From beneath the ledger Edson drew a sheet of paper filled with loose, slanting script. He cleared his throat.

"There is much argument of late on the complementing natures of geology and religion, especially with regard to mineral evidence of the great deluge. It is fully agreed that geology and religion shine with new and peculiar beauty in each other's light, and cannot obscure or destroy one another. Yet doubt often lurks beneath the cloak of geology, and all the sciences. This doubt is cause for gravest concern."

"You need not be a scientist to feel doubt."

Edson glanced at Reverend Stone. The minister said, "Go on, go on."

"Geologists correctly claim that every happening follows certain chains of causes. Thus, some hold, the entire world's workings might eventually be explained. But man is capable of observing only the lowest, and crudest, links in the chain, whereas God exerts his influence on a higher level, one entirely hidden from our observation. The peril for a geologist lay in believing he has discovered the meaning of an entire happening, when he has merely discovered the last, and simplest, cause in a grand chain."

"Interestingly phrased," Reverend Stone said. In truth, he was struck by Edson's eloquence. Perhaps he had underestimated the young man. That, or Edson had flourished without the minister's notice, his light hidden beneath a bushel basket. I could disappear, Reverend Stone thought, and the congregation might continue under Edson. Might thrive.

"There's just a bit more." Edson smiled nervously. "We know that the waterwheel is driven round by gravity—but what, then, is gravity? We know not. Men shall never divine the true nature of the world's essential processes; and thus to claim that the Lord created the world, then allowed it to function freely and without command, is a form of infidelity, and one deserving great wariness."

"Again, interestingly phrased." Reverend Stone rose to depart. "I am sure the congregation will find it enlightening, despite the fact that there is not a single scientific gentleman in Newell."

"You received a letter—or, one arrived for Mrs. Stone." Edson gathered the desk's papers into a sheaf. He riffled through the papers, then set them down and slowly opened and closed the desk drawers. He paused with his hands spread over the desk; then he said, "Aha. Yes." Edson reached to the far corner of the desk and lifted his wide-brimmed hat to reveal a letter. "Here it is now."

Without looking at it, the minister slipped the letter into his trouser pocket. He nodded to Edson then descended the stairs and stepped from the meetinghouse into the warm yard.

Grackles were huddled in the rhododendron bushes, and as the minister approached they ascended in a single black ribbon and wheeled toward the parsonage. The grackles' shrill song and the creek's distant mumble augured the coming of summer, and for this the minister said a silent prayer of thanksgiving. It had been a relentless winter that had turned people inward on themselves; bitterness had hung in the air like soot. The words of his sermons had echoed over rows of pallid faces then tumbled unheard to the stone floor. For the past several winters Reverend Stone had struggled toward spring like a swimmer toward a distant shore; this year, though, he feared that the change of season would not bring relief. He felt exhausted, his spirit as heavy as water. And then there was the blood in his throat, the taste of his body trying to unmake itself. The blood's appearance some months ago had terrified Reverend Stone, but now its presence was numbingly familiar.

He descended the hillside to the creek edge, momentarily nostalgic for his first days in Newell: he had been a young man of thirty-one, suffused with hope. His darkest sin was pitying the congregation members for their failings. He'd felt God's grace as nearly palpable, a certain thickness in the meetinghouse air. Glorious, light-filled days. Reverend Stone hiked his trousers and sat on a mossy oak stump and withdrew the letter from his pocket, and with a shock recognized his son's script.

He unfolded the letter against his knee and read *Dearest Mother,* and was struck by the beauty of his son's penmanship. *Dearest Mother,* he read again, then traced his fingers over the faint indentations where his son's pen had pressed. The letter was puckered with moisture, and Reverend Stone held it to his nose but could not discern a scent.

He rose and hurried southward along the creek, head bowed, his mind filled with toneless clamor. He passed the mill bridge and the Spillman stables, then slowed his pace as a memory surfaced: a bone china platter lying shattered against oiled oak floorboards. Smell of goldenrod and privy, drone of cicadas and a woman's far-off call for her daughter. Heat. His thirteen-year-old son crouched at the edge of this very creek, attempting to conceal himself in the rushes. Inside the parsonage the boy's mother lay beneath two woolen quilts, her forehead the gray-white of a boiled egg. Her cough echoed through the empty house. Reverend Stone stood on the creek bank, shouting, his cheeks gone crimson with anger. The boy stared out at his father then closed his eyes.

He unfolded the letter and read it again, refolded it carefully and placed it in his breast pocket. He was stricken by an urge to see the boy, an ache that seemed equal parts love and remorse. He had not seen his son since Elisha had vanished one Sunday in July, nearly three years earlier; Reverend Stone had tracked the boy as far as Worcester before he'd lost the trail. Who was he now? Still a liar and petty thief, a Sabbath day runaway who'd emptied the meetinghouse's collection basket? Or grown into a man, with whiskers on his chin and weariness for the world's beauty? His father's son, then. Of course he could be nothing else.

A breeze rippled in from the south, bringing a scent of mud and high, chirping shouts. Downstream, three children squatted at the creek's margin, two towheaded but one dark, like Elisha. Reverend Stone watched their frolic for a long time, then at last wandered back upstream, ascended the hillside and entered the meetinghouse.

He called, "Edson?" Dust motes swirled before the sunlit windows. He climbed to the gallery and took a seat in the rearmost pew. An empty meetinghouse: the building felt holiest when it was free of bodies and voices, when it was filled only with sunlight and silence and the mossy smell of rain. It was near to prayer, this silence. Reverend Stone closed his eyes and said a prayer for guidance, then pushed every thought from his mind and sank into the silence.

He woke with a start at a polite, feminine cough. Prudence Martin stood at the pew's end, hands clasped before her. Reverend Stone stood, stifling a yawn.

"Mrs. Martin. I hope you're well on this admirable day."

She curtsied. "I'm awful sorry to trouble you, Reverend Stone. I asked after you at the parsonage and Corletta said you might be here." She paused. "I hoped I could get your counsel. About my husband."

Prudence Martin was a nervous, mole-like woman, eyes narrowed in a squint and small hands worrying the fabric of her skirts. She had once contributed a significant sum to the congregation, and within days all of Newell knew the amount of her largesse. Her husband was a wheelwright who dozed, eyes half-open, through every service.

"Matthew Martin."

Prudence Martin nodded.

"Please, sit down."

She perched on the pew's edge, her gaze darting to the minister's tousled hair. Reverend Stone straightened, smoothing his shirtfront against his chest. She was not a pleasant woman, he decided. Soul the color of weak tea.

"He hasn't been to meeting for nigh upon seven weeks. I'm sure you've noticed."

"I will call at your home this week, to speak with him. Sometimes we all need to be reminded of the importance of faith's rituals."

"That's not the primary trouble. He's been studying on pamphlets by William Miller. He went to a revival in Springfield last Sunday and that's who they were preaching on, William Miller. It's all he wants to talk about, Miller and his prophecies, and he don't care about a thing else."

The minister noticed with distaste a rime of dirt along Prudence Martin's jaw. Strange, he thought, how much pleasure people drew from the admission of sin. As though the act itself was nothing compared to the confession and inevitable penance.

"I'm familiar with Reverend Miller's writings. He has made a peculiar reading of the Book of Daniel."

Prudence Martin nodded. "My husband selled our silver and sent Miller the money. And yesterday he spent thirty dollars on muslin for ascension robes. Thirty dollars." She leaned toward Reverend Stone, her voice taut. "He believes what Miller says about October and the last day. He believes it in his heart."

"Does your husband ever speak about the last day? Does he ever describe it?"

She nodded once. "Near daily."

"What does he say?"

A flush bloomed on the woman's cheeks and washed across her forehead. "He says the righteous shall gather on the hilltops, to witness the new millennium. And there will be riotous voices and war with the saints, and a dragon."

"A dragon."

"A crimson dragon with seven heads, with crowns on its heads. And a beast like a leopard, with the feet of a bear and mouth of a lion. And he says the righteous—Reverend Miller and his followers—will stand amidst the chaos but they shall not be harmed. He says there will be a new Jerusalem, where the righteous will dwell alongside God as neighbors, just as we're neighbors to the Boyers."

Reverend Stone closed his eyes and frowned. He knew Prudence Martin's words by rote, from Revelation, but it unnerved him to hear them from another's mouth.

"And he says I will be thrown amidst the unbelievers and murderers and liars and whores, and cast down. And I will burn in hell. Forever." Prudence Martin sobbed, a sharp, surprised gasp, then buried her face in her hands.

Reverend Stone reached toward the woman then hesitated, imagining her bony form shuddering against his shoulder. He touched her elbow, her skin startlingly warm beneath the threadbare homespun. He searched for a comforting verse of Scripture, but instead found an image of his son in the dim parlor, reading aloud from Psalms, his voice a soft high cadence, a song.

"Tell me, Mrs. Martin: is your husband afraid of the last day? Or is he made glad?"

Prudence Martin looked up, her lips trembling. Wildness shone in her eyes. "He says he's glad, Reverend Stone, but I know he's afraid. I can feel it. He's dreadful afraid."

Good, the minister thought. He should be afraid. Reverend Stone rose, and the woman rose slowly with him. "I will speak with him soon. You must pray for your husband, Mrs. Martin."

"I do. I pray daily for him."

"It's a challenge to stay the right path—even an upright man like your husband can find himself astray. He may spend hours in prayer and contemplation, then fall prey to a moment's weakness. He may live for years in purity and good intentions, then one morning wake to find himself...confused."

Prudence Martin stared at Reverend Stone. Her right hand kneaded the seam of her dress.

"Read on the Psalms, Mrs. Martin. 'Why art thou cast down, O my soul, and why art thou disquieted in me? Hope thou in God, for I shall yet praise him for the help of his countenance.' "

"I'll dwell on those words," Prudence Martin said miserably. "I reckon there's nothing else to do."

Reverend Stone murmured a farewell, then followed Prudence Martin to the meetinghouse door. Outside, the sun lay half-hidden behind the western hills, orange and scarlet streamers rising in the chalky sky. He watched the woman trudge down the cider mill road, a column of dust trailing her like a phantom. When she'd disappeared he returned to the parsonage and took off his jacket and brogans, sat at his bedroom desk with the folded letter before him. Only when the light had failed completely and he was surrounded by darkness did he think to light a lamp.

He woke shivering in the moonlit dark. His clothes felt greasy against his skin and his forehead was damp with sweat, even in the night's chill. Reverend Stone groped atop the side table for a phosphorus match, lit a candle stub and watched the room flicker into existence. He rose from his bed and shut the half-open window, dulling the crickets' creaking, then sat at the desk with his son's letter and a tin of McTeague's Patent Toothache Medication. He placed four brown tablets under his tongue. He set the tin on the desk, beside the letter and whale-oil lamp. Tin, letter, lamp—the arrangement seemed somehow ceremonial, like objects on an altar. The tablets tasted of bitter herbs.

He removed his collar and unbuttoned his shirt then waited for the numbness to creep over him. When it did, the feeling was like a velvet mask against his face, a tickle in his lips and eyelids that slowed his blood to a thick trickle. He felt deliciously warm. He fumbled four more tablets from the tin and placed them under his tongue and leaned his head back and closed his eyes.

When the surge quieted Reverend Stone picked up the letter and read the date: May 30, 1844. Ten days previous. His son was likely in the far Northwest by now, amid foreigners and half-naked savages. The minister tried to recall Elisha as a very young child, before he'd grown solemn and distant, but he could summon only certain details. The mud-colored hair. The clear blue eyes, his mother's eyes. As a child he'd been exuberant, delighted by life, but as he'd grown older this quality had vanished. What was the pitch of his voice? In his mind's eye Elisha spoke, but the voice belonged to Edson.

Reverend Stone read the letter again, then placed it in a drawer. A moth fluttered near the candle, its wingbeats a soft patter. Outside the crickets' song grew louder, as if in alarm. The minister took up the candle and a whiff of smoke caught his throat, and he coughed until his chest pinched and the rasp turned wet and thready. Without looking at his palm he wiped it on his trousers. He shuffled through the kitchen to the back door and stepped out into the restless night, waiting for the dark to coalesce into familiar forms: the squat chicken house, the pump like a stooped old man, the sharp roof of the privy. To the east, Newell was asleep, its men and women dreaming of wealth and distant lands. Good people, he thought. We are all good people, absurd and lovely. We are all God's children. Reverend Stone understood suddenly that he must leave Newell and go to his son, to tell the boy about his mother's death. The notion pierced him.

He heard a rough scratch, like a boot scuffing pebbles. The sound paused then resumed, quickening to a steady pace. Wingbeats burst from the chicken house. Beside the house, a pair of brilliant eyes flashed then disappeared. The fox. Reverend Stone stood motionless, listening to the chickens' uneasy warble. He backed through the doorway and padded to the lumber closet, and from the back of the closet door he lifted an antique Springfield flintlock and tattered shot bag. He loaded powder and ball and primer then moved back through the kitchen and stepped out onto the wet grass. The scratching quickened and paused, quickened and paused. Reverend Stone glimpsed a smudge of motion and he raised the musket to his shoulder and sighted down the barrel at what he thought was the fox. The scratching stopped. Sweat rose on the minister's forehead and hands and he tightened his grip on the gun. He waited.

He stood that way for a long time, until the night was quiet save for the rhythmic chirping of the crickets.

Three

Sault Ste. Marie was a garrison town set between wide, white-flecked straits to the north and a swampy cedar thicket to the south. Elisha and Mr. Brush arrived at noon on the *Catherine Ann* and took rooms at the Johnston Hotel. They were to stay four days, to purchase supplies and await Professor Tiffin's arrival. That first afternoon the boy sat on the hotel porch, sipping ginger beer and sketching the half-breeds and Natives that passed on the muddy road. The edge of the white world, Elisha marveled. He could not stop grinning. It seemed impossible that they were but three days' voyage from Detroit.

By dusk he had summoned enough courage to leave the hotel, so he started past a mercantile and Baptist mission and bowling parlor, a leather goods shop, a saloon with shattered windows. The buildings were sturdy but in poor repair, the paint peeling and windows grimy. Outside a shop called Indian Curiosities, a bald, elderly Chippewa lay sleeping in the dirt. He was dressed in a breechclout and filthy broadcloth shirt. A string of saliva ran from his slack mouth. The sole full-blood Native in Newell, Joseph Gooden, lived in a white frame house and dressed in store-bought clothes, attended Baptist services every Sunday, though Elisha supposed he couldn't properly be called Native anymore. A town Native, perhaps, as opposed to the true Natives found here. Two species of the same race.

He continued through town to Fort Brady. The picket gate was closed; a bored-looking sentry leaned from a blockhouse window and called, "Tomorrow at sunup!" Elisha waved to the man then followed the fort's perimeter to its western side, where an encampment of shanties and bark lodges were laid out, Native and half-breed women tending cookfires as children ran shrieking along the water's edge, a thin yellow dog darting among them. A man's laughter rose then trailed away. The air smelled deliciously smoky. Elisha slowed his pace to survey the women: they were tall and slender, dark-haired but fair, handsome in a coarse, foreign way. A different species again from the town women in Detroit.

Some ways past the encampment Elisha came to a low hill topped with tiny bark houses. What in the world, he thought. He kneeled before one of the dwellings, then froze as if gripped by icy hands. They were Chippewa gravesites. The houses were meant to shield the graves from scavenging animals. Elisha stuffed his fists in his trouser pockets and hurried back toward town. In the slaty light Fort Brady's pickets loomed like castle walls; above them the garrison flagpole was a black needle. He thought he had never been more grateful for such a sight.

The next morning Elisha rose early, gathered some biscuits and cheese and his notebook and Professor Tiffin's pamphlet, then set off to explore the swampland south of town. To his disappointment he recognized every birdcall: mostly warblers and brown creepers, a few cedar waxwings. He paused for lunch in a mossy clearing and opened Tiffin's pamphlet at random.

For example, we learn in Chippewa legend that the god of sleep is called *Weeng,* and has numerous tiny, invisible emissaries armed with *puggamaugons* (war clubs). At night these invisible spirits sneak into bedchambers and search for lying-down persons. On finding one, they ascend his forehead and smite the skull, thus inducing sleep.

Readers will doubtless recognize *an identical image* in Pope's creation of gnomes, in his *Rape of the Lock.* More interestingly, we find similar apparitions in the *hosheewa* of Mongol myth, as the esteemed Professor Linden of Harvard has noted in his *Survey and Notes on*

Ancient Mythologies. In fact, if one inspects the known corpus of Native mythology, with an eye toward similarity of image and plot, one finds a great share of myths similar to our most familiar stories. Most notably, we find parallels to many Native myths *in the Old Testament itself.*

Elisha went on to read about the Native story of creation, in which a flood covered the world, drowning every creature except a great sea turtle, or *Mikenok,* upon whose back men stood and were therefore saved. He flipped to the final chapter. Professor Tiffin's rhetorical style mimicked that of a laborer driving piles.

In this work I have proven, through logical examination of Native myth and language, that FIRSTLY the Native race shares *undeniable similarity* with Christian forebearers once located in the region of Judea. SECONDLY I have presented argument that a community of these *ancient Christians* migrated by land and sea to our country's far northwest, and begat the "savage" Natives that are today so *shamefully persecuted.*

The connexion of the White and Red races is a significant, though perhaps not quite conclusive, stride toward proving the unity *of all races of Man.* For if the Master Craftsman saw fit to create White and Red men from a single source, then He undoubtedly acted similarly with the Black man! And thus it is inevitably true, and *morally certain,* that all Christian men—White, Red, and Black—are *equal before the Lord,* and deserving of every freedom and right dictated by Natural Law.

The summary continued for several pages, followed by an appendix detailing the route ancient Christians might have followed during their migration to America: from Judea across the Caspian Sea to Russia, then overland through Bering's Straits to Canada and down across the territory. Why not? Elisha thought. Odder journeys had surely occurred.

He ate a biscuit and retraced his own journey, from his father's house in Newell to Springfield, by rail to Worcester and Lowell then by coach to Manchester. Strangers had regarded him with curious pity. He'd struggled to conceal his fear. And then by sleigh into the snowy forest to the lumber camp. He'd felt anxious and homesick, over-whelmed by dread. He wondered if the ancient Christians had felt the same way.

He returned to town near noon. Back at the Johnston Hotel, he unlocked his door then paused with a hand on the latch. The neigh-boring room's door was ajar. Elisha called, "Professor Tiffin?" He knocked, and the door swung open with a groan.

A steamer trunk sat open on the floor, its contents strewn about: a folded shirt and rolled felt hat, a heap of small canvas sacks, a rock hammer and ruler and battered writing case. On the bed lay a closed journal: Professor Tiffin's scientific fieldbook. A tingle crawled through the boy. He called, "Professor Tiffin? *Hello?*" Elisha entered the room and took up the book.

It was a plain ten-cent journal bound with cheaply tanned calfskin—purchased new for the expedition, Elisha realized. Its pages were empty of observations and measurements, hypotheses and theories. He riffled through the book, and as he did a sheet of onionskin flut-tered to the floor. Elisha held it toward the window so that sunlight filled the page.

June 9, 1844

My Dearest Dear Heart,

   Now I am gone from the city where you laugh and walk and sleep, and your absence fills this ship the way a thousand men could not. Not even the memory of your smile can lift my heart. My spirits are *laid low* without you.

Do not forget to deliver thirty *Vegetables* to Mason and Crane, ten *Consumption* to Benjamin Stover (Randolph St.), twelve *Schooling of Children* to L. Thacker. Also be aware of the following debts:

Thirteen dols. to Soward
Eleven dols. twenty to Pierce
Twenty dols. fifty to Isaac Rowland
Sixteen dols. to Wm. Rowland
Five dols. to Jos. Rowland

Please do not overfeed Biddle as you are wont to.

I will return with wonderful news that will *change our lives.* My dear, my soul—*che-baum,* as the Chippewas say. These days without you stretch forward like an eternity. My only consolation is a dream of return—to your voice, to your lips, to our bed.

> I am, now and forevermore,
> Your deeply devoted,
> G.

Elisha replaced the letter feeling vaguely ashamed. He turned to depart but was drawn to a small framed portrait lying on the bed. It was a miniature painting of a Negro woman sitting on a carved wooden armchair, a lace shawl over her shoulders and white-gloved hands clasped in her lap. Behind her stood a plump, pasty man with orange muttonchops. He was dressed in a black frock coat and ruffled shirt and striped waistcoat, an opera hat. Wedding clothes. The sight confused Elisha; then he understood that she was the Dear Heart of the letter. The white man's right hand rested on the Negro woman's shoulder. A serene smile lay on his lips.

A clatter of silverware rose from the dining room, and Elisha froze. He moved to the doorway: muttered conversation, a clink of glass, the first whistled notes of "Fanny Gray." He turned back to the trunk and withdrew a shaving kit, a pair of woolen socks, a pocket compass, a Hebrew lexicon in chipped black boards. Beneath the lexicon was a parcel wrapped in oilcloth and bound tightly with twine. He turned it over in his hands. It was the size of a Bible, though rounder and heavier, lacking a book's crisp rectangular form. He picked at the knotted twine.

Footsteps rose on the stairs. Elisha shoved the parcel and lexicon and socks and shaving kit into the trunk and ran to the door. He stepped quietly into the hallway, and as he did a man appeared on the stairs holding a tumbler half-full of whiskey. He arched his eyebrows at Elisha.

"Good afternoon."

"Good afternoon."

Professor Tiffin sat heavily on the hall bench. He was stouter than his portrait's likeness, with an infant's creamy skin and squint eyes and soft, sagging chin. Coarse orange muttonchops marked his cheeks. The man was sweating and his shirtsleeves were pinned at the elbows, exposing hairless forearms and fingers like steamed sausages. He tugged at his stained collar.

"I resent the mundanity of town life—I much prefer the variety of a city like Detroit. I witnessed a Siamese elephant there last Monday. An exceedingly interesting creature: size of a steam locomotive, yet it could rise onto its hind legs for hoecakes. An Italian fellow rode it like a horse, just rode it along neat as can be. Far slower than a horse, however."

"I suppose it would be."

"Yes, on account of its colossal size requiring significant arterial pressure to induce motion of its limbs. It is physiologically impossible for such an animal to move rapidly." Professor Tiffin removed his hat, exposing a pink scalp fringed by damp orange curls. He scrutinized Elisha as he rubbed his forehead. "And how did a healthy young fellow like yourself get joined with our humble expedition?"

Elisha had imagined the man as a stooped, older gentleman in a high-buttoned vest and pince-nez spectacles, his brow wrinkled by years of contemplation. Instead he looked like a lounger in a Woodward Avenue billiard parlor. Elisha said, "I read your pamphlet, *Language and History of the North American Indian Tribes*. It's why I wanted to join the expedition."

Professor Tiffin hooted, settling deeper onto the bench. "You will have me blushing!"

"And I aim to identify a new species this summer—a fish or plant or insect, anything. I want to be a scientist, like you and Mr. Brush."

"You have your terminology misapplied, young fellow! We have a word in the sciences for men like Mr. Brush: we call them *toilers*. They are skilled professionals, adept at gathering specimens and running survey lines and executing sketches—but this is not the work of the scientist. Combining observation with hypothesis—synthesis, *suntithenai*—do you see? Drawing conclusions from a corpus of knowledge, to produce a greater truth. That is the prize. Do you understand?"

"Yes sir."

"You see, facts are like rocks. They are dead. Ideas are like trees. They possess the ability to grow. Facts are useless except in service of an idea." Professor Tiffin drank off the whiskey then handed Elisha the empty glass. "Toilers do, of course, serve a vital purpose. Science requires these people, much as a complex clock requires each minute screw."

Tiffin's manner reminded Elisha of his favorite uncle, Lawrence, who would visit yearly from Boston when Elisha was a boy. Lawrence's first business upon arrival was to haul Elisha onto his knee and pluck a penny from each nostril. Professor Tiffin was swaying slightly, as if on a rolling ship; then Elisha understood that he was drunk.

"So, my healthy young friend! What would you like to be: a scientist, or a toiler?"

Elisha grinned. "Both. I'd like to learn from both Mr. Brush and yourself, if that's possible."

"You don't recognize the significance of this expedition, do you? Our discoveries this summer will twist the nose of the entire United States!" Tiffin tapped Elisha on the knee. "Your grandchildren will be discussing this expedition. Your grandchildren's grandchildren. And et cetera."

"I'm very honored to be on this expedition, Professor Tiffin, truly I am. I admire your ideas deeply. You're a great scholar of the Native people."

The man belched softly. "I wish I had a hoecake. I am near starved in this funny little town."

Elisha said nothing. The word *suntithenai* lingered in his mind, accompanied by a pang of gloom; it seemed a symbol of how little he knew. As a child he'd been indifferent in the schoolroom but a scholar in the creek behind his father's house. And what had he learned? The feeding habits of fox sparrows. The differences between stone flies and dragonflies and mayflies. He'd spent his days knee-deep in the chilly water, the sun's hot stare on his neck, gathering specimens and executing pretty sketches. A budding young toiler at work.

Professor Tiffin was regarding Elisha curiously. "Go now, take some fresh air. Go on. I am told it can be invigorating."

Elisha hurried down the corridor. He was still holding the man's empty whiskey glass. As he reached the stairs Professor Tiffin called, "Young fellow! What is your name?"

"Elisha Stone."

"Elisha Stone! I shall teach you to be a scientist this summer. By expedition's end you will be teaching me!"

He spent the afternoon lying on the beach near the fort's pickets, watching Native fishermen navigate the straits in their flimsy bark canoes. They surged through the foaming water, a steersman guiding the craft while a second Native dipped for fat, wriggling whitefish. The boy was at first enthralled by the men's dexterity but soon grew irritated. He envied them the simplicity of their task: no ideas or synthesis, just a canoe and a net and a river full of fish. He wished he had his sketchbook.

At six Elisha returned to meet the hotel supper bell, and as he passed the parlor he heard Mr. Brush's voice. He glanced through the open door: Brush and Professor Tiffin were sitting beside each other on a settee, Brush stiff-backed while Tiffin hunched forward with his chin in his hands. They were staring across the room.

A woman was sitting beside the fireplace. She was dressed in half-breed garb, a blue strap dress and calico scarf. Her hair was the color of a crow's wing, black overlaid with a glossy blue hue. Her cheekbones were sloped like a Chippewa's but her forehead was high and broad, her nose dotted with reddish freckles. She was gazing intently at the two men.

"Her knowledge is not the point in question," Mr. Brush said. "It is solely her gender. A woman of her stature cannot bear a fully loaded pack." Brush bowed toward the woman. "With all respect, madam."

"It is a commonly accepted fact, proven by no less an eminence than Dr. Samuel Mitchill, that Native women have heartier constitutions than white women. Edwin Colcroft describes Chippewa women completing portages while bearing ninety-pound bales of furs. Catlin describes similar feats performed by pregnant women."

"She is but half Native."

"I can bear as much as any man," the woman said suddenly. Her English was tinged with a French accent. "More than some, even."

"And regardless, we have no other possibilities to consider." Professor Tiffin sighed. "Her husband is *absent*, you see. Every healthy voyageur is departed for the summer. It's only soldiers and drunk men in this funny town, and we *must* depart!"

"Your language," Mr. Brush said. "We are in the presence of a lady."

The woman turned to the window. Outside lay a dusty strip of road and beyond it the beach, the straits, then the Canadian shore with its bright, tiny cabins. She studied the scene with her lips pursed. It was as though she wanted badly to speak but did not know the words. Elisha guessed that she might be twenty-two years old.

He stepped into the parlor. Neither Mr. Brush nor Professor Tiffin noticed his presence; then the boy cleared his throat.

"Ah, young Elisha," Tiffin said. "Let me introduce Madame Susette Morel. She is the wife of Monsieur Ignace Morel, the voyageur I engaged to guide us this summer. He was to sail with me from Detroit, however he never came aboard. Apparently he is nowhere to be found."

Elisha smiled at the woman. Her eyes were the color of peat. A faint white scar, like a chalk streak, ran along her jaw. Susette Morel nodded stiffly to Elisha then turned back to the men.

He sat on a stool and attempted to study an engraving above the fireplace. It was a scene of Canton harbor crowded with junks and schooners and Chinese fishing boats. Elisha's gaze moved back to the woman's scar. She was older, he decided, twenty-five or even thirty. A tobacco pouch was knotted to her sash. Beside it hung a beaded knife sheath.

"I propose we travel without a guide," Brush said. "We will pack twenty pounds extra weight each, rely on the Bayfield chart for reference. It is incomplete but likely adequate. With all respect to Madame Morel, it would not be proper to travel in mixed company. This is not a pleasure tour."

"You will not find the image stones without a guide." The woman edged forward. "They are located far inland, through a very big swamp. They are impossible to find unless you know them. You need a guide."

"Well! In that case we will enquire at a Native village about their location. Natives living nearby will no doubt know the whereabouts of these precious stones. We will engage a trustworthy savage to lead us the final distance."

"A trustworthy savage!" Professor Tiffin gasped in feigned astonishment. "Do you suppose such a mythical creature exists?"

The supper bell rang. Immediately footsteps moved across the ceiling and down the stairway, accompanied by muted conversation, a burst of laughter. A heavyset gentleman glanced into the parlor and said, "Hurry or you'll lose your chance!" The kitchen door shut with a bang.

"Perhaps we should continue over supper," Elisha said quickly. "We'll compromise better with food in our stomachs. And then we could hear more from Madame Morel."

"In fact, we are settled." Mr. Brush rose and bowed to the woman. "Madam, I thank you for your patience."

"We are not settled!" Professor Tiffin jerked upright, his nose nearly grazing Brush's chin. Their difference in height seemed to startle Tiffin. He said, "Hear me now, friend: We will not find the image stones without a skilled guide. We will certainly not find them with a crude map and our good intentions. Now, this expedition's commission authorizes me to engage a guide, and Madame Susette Morel is the guide I have chosen to engage."

"This expedition's commission was drafted by a shallow-brained clerk in the land office in Detroit. It can be amended to account for unforeseen circumstances."

"If you do not agree with my decision, you are not obliged to join me on the expedition!"

"I am the sole recipient of all appropriations. Without my presence you will not be paid." Mr. Brush smiled impassively. "If you had arranged your affairs more carefully, we would be negotiating with this woman's husband. We would not be involved in this gander pull."

The men stared at each other with expressions of polite distaste. Susette Morel strained toward the pair, fists clenched in her lap.

"I am prepared to leave in two days' time. Myself, this fine woman as our guide, and young Elisha Stone as an assistant." Tiffin turned to the boy. "Yes?"

Heat surged to Elisha's face. He nodded once.

Mr. Brush shook his head as the smile faded from his lips. For a moment he looked old and tired, his eyelids heavy and slack. To Tiffin he said, "You would have been better served staying in Detroit, waiting for your imaginary guide to appear. You seem ill-suited for practical work."

Outside a musket cracked and echoed, followed by a distant cheer. Supper at the fort. Susette Morel looked from Mr. Brush to Professor Tiffin to Elisha. She seemed as though she might curse the men or burst into tears.

She said, "Merci beaucoup, thank you very much," then rushed from the parlor.

He spent the next morning pacing along the straits west of town, then walked a roundabout path back to his hotel room and stripped off his clothes and lay on the bed, his thoughts adrift among images of Susette Morel. Her hair was liquid black, her cheekbones smooth planes. Her skin was suntanned but freckled, a mixture of Native and French, but when she spoke she was neither Native nor French, nor American.

Elisha could not decide if she was beautiful. It was her foreignness that confused him, her accent and strange clothes. As though the idea of beauty was being described to him anew. The boy trailed a hand down his chest, tried to will himself toward sleep. After a while he rose and scrubbed his face with cold water, then dressed and took up his hat.

He stepped into the mercantile and Hudson's Bay Company post and Indian curiosity shop, scanning the few female faces, then hiked eastward toward the fort. The picket gate was open and a group of soldiers were tossing quoits beside the blockhouse. Inside, Native men sat in a ring outside the Indian Agency, conversing in low tones. Elisha walked a circuit of the grounds, stepped inside the sutler's and hospital. Susette Morel was nowhere to be seen.

On a whim he peered into the Catholic church. A service was in progress. A handsome priest with a shock of black hair stood before an

assembly of white women and soldiers and a single, somber Chippewa.
" 'I am the living bread which came down from heaven,' " the priest
said, " 'and if any man eat this bread he shall live forever.' " His
English was marked by a German accent. " 'Except ye eat the flesh of
the son of man and drink his blood, ye have no life in you.' " The
priest repeated the scripture in halting Chippewa and the Native nodded silently. Elisha wondered what the man might make of such a lesson.

He spied the woman at the edge of the Native encampment. She
was sitting outside a small log shanty, mending a fishing seine that was
draped around her like lace skirts. The shanty's window was hung with
oiled parchment, its door propped open to reveal a table and pair of
chairs, a stained pallet on the floor. A gray chemise hung like a ghost
on the wall. Beside it was a carved wooden crucifix.

The sight startled Elisha. The cabin was no better than a Native
lodge, with its bark walls and dirt floor and smoke hole hacked in the
roof. The Chippewa blood dominating the white, he figured. He ventured a few paces forward then took out his notebook and pencil. He
sketched the woman's face in profile, her forehead and taut lips and
long, Roman nose. She was beautiful—of course she was beautiful. A
beautiful woman living in a dark, comfortless shanty at the country's
edge. He glanced up to find Susette Morel regarding him impatiently.

Elisha clapped shut the notebook. "I was sent to find you! I would
like to apologize for the confusion at the hotel yesterday evening. And
for not offering you a proper supper, at least."

The woman looked back to her mending. "I do not require any
apology. I know how to cook a proper supper."

"Still. I pray you'll accept my regrets. It was a poor showing on our
part, truly it was."

Susette Morel said nothing. Elisha watched her work the frayed
cords, running a shuttle between the split sections then drawing them
tight with twine. Her fingers were as cracked and weathered as dried
tobacco leaves. He attempted a smile then scratched his jaw. He could
not formulate a clever comment.

"I also came to ask if you could depart as early as tomorrow morning—to act as the expedition's guide, of course."

Her fingers stopped moving. "He changed his decision?"

Elisha understood that she was referring to Silas Brush. "You don't need to worry about Mr. Brush—I'm planning to discuss with him tonight. Or else Professor Tiffin and you and I will go on our own, just the three of us. I bear some influence on these men, you see. I am the assistant scientist and surveyor."

Susette laid the seine at her feet and gazed warily at Elisha. "He said I was not strong enough to bear a pack in the forest. He was interested in engaging my husband only."

"As far as I can see your husband's not here. And we absolutely need a guide. So!"

Elisha cringed at the false jauntiness in his tone. He watched Susette Morel absently smooth her skirts, the wool as patched and mended as the fishing seine. A flicker of excitement seemed to pass through the woman. She said, "What about payment?"

"You'll have to negotiate with Mr. Brush—I'm not in charge of matters financial. My job is to identify animal and mineral and plant specimens, form ideas and hypotheses." Elisha was suddenly aware of his shabby bowry and worn trousers and shirt; then he wondered if such things mattered to the woman. "Where is your husband, anyway?"

"Montréal, or Rainy Lake. Or Detroit."

"And why didn't he join up with Professor Tiffin, like he promised?"

The question was impertinent but the woman merely shook her head. "My husband makes his own choices. I cannot explain the choices he makes."

She set down the seine and rose, still fussing with her skirts as though to calm her nerves. Elisha could not decipher her expression: at once excited and wary, courteous and remote. She was nearly as tall as the boy. She stepped toward Elisha and despite himself he leaned toward her.

"What shall I tell Mr. Brush? If the terms are not acceptable I could try to negotiate—I could speak with Mr. Brush on your behalf."

Susette Morel smiled, exposing small white teeth like kernels of corn. "Tell him I can depart tomorrow."

Elisha nodded.

"I will need payment when we reach the image stones. Full payment."

"That should be acceptable—it *will* be acceptable! I'll speak with Mr. Brush tonight."

"You will need pork and grease and rice and flour. Kegs of powder and shot. Plenty of salt and sugar and coffee. You have all this?"

"Mr. Brush has arranged it all, don't you worry." Elisha grinned. "Professor Tiffin aims to study Chippewa artifacts—he believes that Natives are descended from ancient Christians. That's why he wants to study the image stones, to link them to the ancient Christians. He believes that Natives and white men and Negroes belong to the same equal race. He's written pamphlets on the subject."

Susette Morel was staring at Elisha as though he was a specimen in a cabinet of curiosities. A faint smile grew on her lips.

"I speak a little French, from school—bonjour, bonsoir. Je vous prie, madame."

The woman laughed. "Je vous *en* prie."

"Je vous en prie! Of course. Parlez-vous français? Qu'est-ce qui se passe?"

She moved another pace toward the boy, and Elisha's grin faltered. "You are nervous," Susette said softly. "Why are you so nervous?"

He turned and stumbled toward the fort a few paces, then stopped. "Be ready to depart tomorrow at dawn! This'll prove to be one of the great scientific expeditions of the age—your grandchildren will be discussing it!"

The boy cursed himself as he hurried away. Dang it all, anyway. A thing isn't worth a whit if it don't make you nervous.

·   ·   ·

The dining room at the Johnston Hotel was narrow and low, the table laid with chipped earthenware and surrounded by mismatched chairs. A vase of desiccated irises stood at the table's center. The wallpaper showed a faded scene of Cornwallis's surrender to Washington at Yorktown. Elisha sat across from Mr. Brush as the sullen proprietor brought out dishes of roast whitefish and venison and fried pumpkin, potatoes and stewed greens. Professor Tiffin was nowhere to be seen.

A flushed, heavyset man with a spade beard sat at the table's end. He wore a blue velvet waistcoat and satin cravat, a pearl brooch crowded by diamonds. A gold watch chain lay across his belly. He was a businessman from Boston, he told the proprietor, come to inspect the region's mineral prospects. The man did not acknowledge Mr. Brush or Elisha.

"I find that the richest deposits are in fact the simplest to locate," the man said. "I have a particular talent for such matters—I have been called a *diviner nonpareil* by my satisfied associates. Do you see this chain? I personally selected the claim in Georgia from which this gold was taken." The man forked two venison steaks and a mound of greens onto his plate. "It is a magnetic phenomenon, you understand. I quite literally *feel* the presence of minerals beneath my feet. I may someday write a pamphlet on the subject."

Elisha watched Mr. Brush drain a glass of whiskey then pour another. He seemed to be struggling to hold his tongue.

"Copper, gold, iron, and silver just waiting to be carted away—and yet today I observed a dozen red nigger savages sunning themselves on the riverbank, with nary a care." The businessman tittered. "Small wonder their state is so wretched! I wonder if they are employable even as mine hands. We may have to import good Cornish stock to this territory."

Brush rose as the proprietor placed a wedge of cherry pie on his plate. He said, "Gentlemen," then stepped from the room.

Elisha waited a moment, then excused himself and followed Mr. Brush to the parlor. He found him sitting in a wing chair beside the fireplace, staring out the window, a newspaper open on his lap. When the man noticed Elisha he took up the paper with a snap.

"Pardon my abrupt departure. It stank of fool in that room."

"Sir, I—"

"You can quit with the sirring. There's no need to be a lickfinger."

Elisha nodded. "I wanted to discuss with you about the woman from yesterday, Madame Morel. I believe she should accompany us as a guide."

"She is a half-breed, and married. I trust you have no designs on her virtue."

For an instant Elisha heard his father's voice, its crisp note of warning and disapproval; then he saw a smirk curling the edges of Brush's lips.

"Of course not! I just don't relish the prospect of slogging through a cedar swamp without a guide. We'll lose plenty of time. We might never even find the image stones."

"You are listening to Professor Copper Knob too closely. His precious pebbles are not the expedition's first purpose." Brush jerked his head toward the dining room. "Fools like him are more pressing concerns—speculators tramping through the territory before the government even knows what the land holds. That fat chuff wouldn't know gold from a trickle of piss down his trouser leg."

"But surely Susette Morel's presence would aid us in dealing with Chippewas."

"Aid us."

Something in the man's tone caused Elisha to remain silent. Mr. Brush folded the newspaper and reclined in the wing chair.

"Let me educate you about dealing with Natives, young fellow. I ran survey all through the state of Indiana as a younger man. This was 1818—you were not yet even a notion. Indiana is flat terrain, a few rivers and lakes, some forest but no thick swamp—easy work, save for the Miamis. They'd sold their land that summer but word hadn't quite reached the outer tribes. They were powerful suspicious of white men with chains and telescopes and compasses tramping over their land. They saw all the measuring and calculating as a sort of witchery, you see.

"We had with us a guide named Little Frog. He was no bigger than a turd, cheerful for a savage, with a reputation for hard work. He had claimed to be a half-breed when we hired him. But he'd lied. He was full-blood Potawatomi. Our fifth week out we were running chain along the Kankakee when we saw cookfire smoke that Little Frog figured to be a Miami raiding party. He became as fidgety as a woman, hemming and hawing about turning back. We posted night sentries, part to calm the man's nerves and part to shoot him if he ran off. The next morning the poor fool could not bear his pack. I thought he might melt from fear. That afternoon we decided to cross the Kankakee, and when we reached the river's middle ten Miami appeared in dugouts, their faces painted like Satan himself. There were but four of us. They'd have shot us down if we even raised a shout. They dragged Little Frog into one of their canoes, then they disappeared upriver."

Mr. Brush was quiet for a moment. "We found Little Frog three days later, some six leagues upriver. His stomach was sliced open and he was lashed to a tree with his own innards. His scalp lock was cut away. His face and chest were nigger black, like they'd rubbed him with gunpowder. The crows had plucked out his eyes and the poor fellow's face was no longer even human, just a mask with holes ripped through it. We buried him there beside the Kankakee."

Silence lengthened between them; then the businessman entered the parlor, sucking his teeth. He strode to the window and drew a deep, theatrical breath. As if to himself he said, "Copper and gold and iron and silver. Whip me if I'm wrong!"

"Now. About this woman. We will hire her on, on the logic that a half-breed guide is better than none at all." Mr. Brush stared at the businessman's back. "And if we delay any longer, the fat chuffs of the world will be out before us."

"I'll find her. I'll have her ready to begin tomorrow morning."

Elisha rose to depart, and Mr. Brush called after him, "Since how long have you carried that limp?"

The boy froze. "I don't hardly limp."

"A crippled assistant, a nancy-boy partner, and a half-savage Catholic woman for a guide." Brush closed his eyes. "I suppose this is one of His trials."

"Though not an arduous one."

The man chuckled wearily. "We shall see."

Four

The man had fallen asleep before the train departed Albany, and some miles later his head had lolled sideways and come to rest against Reverend Stone's shoulder. He was foreign-looking, his brow holding traces of German or Dutch, and his suitcoat was mud-spattered but tailored, his shoes cut from thin cordovan leather. An itinerant salesman, ostentatiously displaying his good fortune. Or putting a brave face on failure. The man's breath smelled strongly of peppermint. Reverend Stone wondered idly what he might be selling.

The train had stopped often between Springfield and Albany, traveling a few slow miles before the steam whistle hooted and the locomotive shrieked to a halt. Then the doors were thrown open, a rush of cool air bathing the car as men departed with haversacks and trunks while other men shouldered aboard. At each stop Reverend Stone placed his valise on his seat then stepped down to the platform, brushing soot from his sleeves as he studied the quiet towns: Westbridge, Carroll, Fall Valley, Humberton. He'd seen the names on maps but never imagined the places themselves; the sight of their meetinghouses and banks and barbershops and town greens brought trills of childish delight. He yawned, affecting a distracted air.

In Garton he'd boarded the train to find his valise missing and a heavyset stranger slouched in his seat, squinting at a broadsheet. Reverend Stone cleared his throat. When the man didn't glance up he said, "Pardon me, I believe that seat was in use."

The stranger raised his eyes with a grave expression. "How do you reckon that?"

"My valise was on it. I left it on the seat when I stepped out for air."

The man held Reverend Stone's gaze until a prickle of annoyance rose in the minister. He surveyed the half-empty car: a few bored faces were turned toward the scene. A young peddler had appeared in the aisle, offering his tray of newspapers and cigars and peanuts. Reverend Stone shook his head but the boy didn't move.

"Every fool knows you don't leave your valise just setting out. Especially not at a depot."

"I left it to keep my seat while I took a breath of air. As I told you."

"I saw naught but a bare bench. I would have noticed a valise just setting out."

"But you *must* have seen it. A sheepskin bag, brown."

The man slapped the broadsheet to his lap. "There wasn't no valise nowhere! I didn't take it myself, if that's what you mean to say!"

"Of course not, pardon me." Reverend Stone hurried to the door and stepped down to the platform. Across the road, a hatless man carrying a sheepskin bag was climbing the stairs of the Pierce Bank. The minister jogged across the road to the bank, mounted the steps two at a time. He paused, gasping, then opened the door and laid a hand on the man's shoulder.

An idiot woman dressed in trousers whirled around and shrieked, "Remove your *smutty* hands from me!" then smashed the bag against Reverend Stone's shoulder. It was a ratty sackcloth satchel, nothing at all like the minister's valise. He said, "Pardon me, I've made a mistake, I believed—"

Just then the train whistle sounded. Reverend Stone backed through the door, apologizing, then turned and sprinted toward the depot. The conductor called *Ho!* and the engine chuffed. The locomotive jolted forward. Reverend Stone shouted as he ran toward the gentlemen's car. The conductor waved, grinning, the door propped open with his boot. The engine churned faster. At the platform's edge Reverend Stone seized the handrail and slung himself through the doorway, flush against the conductor, and the man whooped.

"Decent pace for a fellow your age!"

He slid into a vacant seat and stared furiously out the window. Someone had snatched the valise from his seat, tucked it beneath their jacket as they strolled away. At that moment some chiseler was fingering his cravat and handkerchiefs, rattling his tins of toothache medication. Reading Elisha's letter. Sweat trickled down the minister's cheeks. It all seemed very obvious.

He closed his eyes to still his restless thoughts, but they ran stubbornly to the few occasions of the valise's use. From his father's home in Chicopee to the seminary in Cambridge forty years ago. From Cambridge to Newell five years later, his heart buoyed by optimism. From Newell to Saratoga Springs on his wedding tour, Ellen in the coach beside him, her lips pursed with nervous excitement, her fist pressed against his thigh. Joyous times. Beginnings and endings. Reverend Stone wondered which of the two the current occasion might be.

Now he slipped a hand into his trouser pocket and withdrew a half-empty tin of medication and fold of bank notes, moving stiffly so as not to disturb the fellow resting against his shoulder. He counted thirty-three dollars: perhaps enough to take him past Detroit, if he was miserly. The minister mentally figured the cost of a new valise and shirt collar and change of trousers, quickly realizing that he'd have to go without. Three days from home, he thought, and already I have lost everything I own. He supposed it was plain to everyone that he was a country greenhorn.

The man beside him muttered sleepily, then jerked upright. He said, "Apologies."

Reverend Stone tucked the bills into his pocket. "None required."

"My jay." The man rubbed his face, blinking. "I'm fairly well put out. I could probably sleep through to San Francisco if we went that far. Do you know where we are now?"

"Somewhere past Albany."

"Then I'd have been woked anyway by the conductor. The line ends in Buffalo."

The man offered his hand and introduced himself as Jonah Crawley, his voice holding a drawl that might have been a foreign accent or simple drowsiness. He said, "I don't suppose you have a bit of niggerhead."

"Even if I had, I wouldn't now. My valise was stolen at Garton."

The man's weary face betrayed only mild interest. "That so?"

Reverend Stone nodded. An urge for conversation had grown in him. "It was my own fault, partly—I left the valise on my seat while I stepped out for air. I should have kept hold of it. I'm not accustomed to this sort of travel, you see. I have come all the way from Newell, Massachusetts, bound for Detroit. I am traveling to meet my son."

Jonah Crawley yawned. His teeth were stained a rich, marbled yellow. "That so?"

"He's not aware that I am coming—I've not seen him in three years now. I suppose he will be quite surprised to see me."

"I expect you have a pretty nice speech prepared."

The minister nodded. In truth he had not considered what he might say when he found his son. He would tell the boy about his mother. And then . . . what? Stern questions about the boy's disappearance, his whereabouts the last years? Or breezy chitchat about Newell, news from the congregation and Corletta and Elisha's childhood friends. The possibilities were awkward, incongruous. In his mind's eye Elisha was thirteen years old, his hair tousled and fingernails crusted with creek mud, his arms outgrown his shirt cuffs. Reverend Stone could not imagine him as a young man of sixteen.

"I'm sorry to hear about your cold luck," the man said. "Folks of the itinerant variety don't seem to have much regard for the welfare of others."

"Why do you suppose that is?"

Jonah Crawley blinked, as if surprised by the question. "Well, I suppose some of them are running away from trouble. Sometimes that trouble was deserved. They're moving toward what they hope is a better place. Usually it ain't."

"I don't believe itinerants are more callous than most. Lack of regard seems a common enough trait."

The man grinned. "You must be a constable. That's a fairly uncharitable judgment of folks."

"Not at all! I only mean that men are occasionally careless—they forget to be governed by their conscience."

"I prefer to ignore my conscience," the man joked. "It gives me the feeling of being a decent person."

"And that is important to you? Feeling like a decent person?"

Crawley stared hard at the minister. "Of course it is."

The man turned away, rubbing stiffness from his neck as Reverend Stone watched him sidelong. He tried to recall the last time he'd had a conversation with a stranger. A gruff but inquisitive tin peddler who'd knocked at the parsonage door eight months ago, a year perhaps. The man had finally admitted his belief in the doctrine of immaculate conception with a solemn, regretful air. Reverend Stone had bought a pair of ornate bull's-eye lanterns, out of pity for the fellow.

"Milton allowed Satan to be touched by conscience. 'Now conscience wakes despair that slumbered, wakes the bitter memory of what he was.' Yes? Of course Satan ignored his conscience's guidance. Decent folks are guided by reason and governed by conscience—they cannot help but strive for goodness. Some even argue that conscience is what civilizes us, separates us from Negroes and savage Indians. It's not an unsound argument."

"You should consider fashioning your ideas into a sermon. I'm told circuit riding can be lucrative." Jonah Crawley slouched in his seat and closed his eyes.

Reverend Stone turned to the window, unexpectedly wounded by the man's dismissal. Outside, twilight had seeped over a prairie stubbled with stumps. Where were they? Somewhere in New York, between Albany and Buffalo. Cutover country. The minister imagined a horde of men grunting at crosscut saws, their beards stippled with sawdust. Flattening the landscape, removing any place to hide. He fumbled in his pocket for the tin of medication then placed three tablets under his tongue and closed his eyes.

He was a coward, wasn't he? Abandoning his home, running westward with a farewell wave. That previous Sunday, when he'd announced his departure to the congregation, the meetinghouse had filled with brittle silence, as though no one believed he would truly depart. That, or they did not believe he would return.

The minister wondered, as his thoughts uncoiled and slowed, if he would ever find his son in this vast, empty territory. An image formed in his mind of Elisha's face pinched with fear as he sat in prayer, his bright blue eyes dulled by hopelessness. The boy's faith was feeble. He possessed a coward's heart. He's my son, Reverend Stone marveled, so much my son, so much myself.

He leaned toward the window until his forehead brushed the cool glass. He felt a sudden, desperate affection for the town he had left. Already Newell seemed vague and distant, like a beautiful dream half-remembered upon waking.

It was past midnight when the train arrived in Buffalo. The depot was a cavernous brick building lit sparsely by gas lamps, and possessed of a bleak, funereal air. Haggard hotel drummers moved among the disembarking passengers, holding placards printed with bucolic names: *Cascade House, River View Inn, Verdant Falls Hotel.* Baggage handlers heaved trunks and suitcases and valises onto the platform, the men's shouts echoing in the lofty building. A few faded handbills fluttered on an announcement board.

Reverend Stone stood empty-handed, surveying the scene. He approached a drummer smoking a sour-smelling cigar, holding a placard that read *Elysium House—Choicest Views of the Falls!* Reverend Stone's throat twitched and he drew a breath to subdue the cough. He said, "How much do you ask for a night's stay?"

"Depends on the room. All's I have vacant now are rooms with views of the falls. Those cost one dollar extra."

"It's nighttime. I cannot see the falls."

"Come morning you'll see them. Unless of course it's raining."

A tug at his elbow; the minister turned to find Jonah Crawley standing beside a young woman in a dingy yellow cape. Crawley said, "I know all the finer hotels in Buffalo. Let me offer you a piece of advice."

"Mr. Crawley! How wonderful to see you again."

The man grinned. "My daughter, Adele. She was riding in the ladies' car."

The girl curtsied. She was pale and narrow-shouldered, her green eyes holding a clouded, distant cast, as though she was preoccupied with a grave decision. She might have been twelve or she might have been sixteen. The minister offered her a benevolent smile.

"These chuckleheads would have you believe their shacks border the falls for a dollar a night. Trust me, they don't. I know a place that's near enough to hear water kissing rock, and it won't empty your pockets."

"I would be obliged," Reverend Stone said gratefully.

He followed the man around the depot to the avenue. Jonah Crawley rapped on a buggy frame to wake the sleeping hackman, then helped his daughter aboard. Reverend Stone seated himself across from the pair. The carriage jerked forward. Buffalo's streets were deserted, the awnings drawn and shopfronts dark save for an occasional lit-up saloon. They passed a theater and surgeon's college, an opera house with white stone columns and a lofty dome. A pair of steeples loomed behind the blocks of row houses but the minister could not gauge the denomination.

He turned from the window to find Jonah Crawley staring into Adele's blank gaze, as though they were engaged in a wordless dialogue. Crawley patted the girl's hand; then she glanced warily at Reverend Stone. Her expression embarrassed the man. Jonah Crawley said, "No need to offer me compensation, Reverend! I'm merely trying to aid a fellow traveler."

The minister dug a finger in his pocket and produced a quarter dollar. "Thank you kindly. Please."

Crawley tucked the coin in his waistcoat. "Some of these hotels are owned by Jews, some by Catholics. You need to be careful where you lay your head."

"And the proprietor of the hotel tonight?"

"He's a good wet Baptist."

The carriage turned down an alleyway lit by saloon windows. Reverend Stone smiled mildly at Jonah Crawley but said nothing. A dull, unnameable urge gnawed at him. He would buy a tin of medication tomorrow morning. The thought lingered in his mind until he forced it away.

They rolled to a halt before a two-story hotel with a sagging porch and unpainted front door and missing shutters. The signboard was so weathered as to be unreadable. Crawley said, "Here we are now."

Reverend Stone studied the building before opening the carriage door.

"You should try to temper your expectations," Crawley said. "That's the traveling life."

Reverend Stone said nothing. He mounted the steps then glanced back at the waiting buggy. "Are you not unloading your trunks?"

"We're staying farther up toward the falls. This lodge will do you just fine but it's a mite characterful for my daughter."

The minister raised a hand in farewell as the carriage rattled away. He knocked softly at the door; eventually it opened on a man holding a lantern that threw just enough light to shadow his eyes. He led Reverend Stone up a back stairway and pushed open a room door, dipped a rush into the lantern and passed it wordlessly. Reverend Stone said, "Obliged," and closed the door, tossed his hat on the floor and shucked his jacket and trousers. The rope bed-frame sagged as he crawled beneath the quilt.

Wind rose from the street and howled through the loose window frame, the sound holding a vaguely human quality. As he listened the howl coalesced to a moan, emanating from the room next door. The moan repeated: a sweetly falling note, an aria of loss. He wondered about the nature of the woman's grief.

For some months after his wife's death Reverend Stone had found himself contemplating the sorrow of others. Grief, it suddenly seemed, was all around him: in his bedroom, on Newell's green, in the fallow tobacco fields, each stone and sapling shadowed by loss. He found himself wondering at the depth of other folks' grief, his thoughts accompanied by startling rushes of affection for his fellow sufferers. It seemed natural that grief should marry folks in shared misery. But instead the minister felt terrifyingly alone.

She had fallen ill on the third Sunday in March: her first coughs echoed through the meetinghouse during his sermon, and he'd shot a quick, irritated glance from the pulpit. That evening at supper the cough slid from her throat down to her lungs, bringing a liquidy rasp and bright, spidery threads of blood. Reverend Stone's thoughts crumbled at the sight; he was stricken by the memory of his meetinghouse scowl. Ellen's expression was one of shame, and poorly concealed horror.

He prepared her bedroom as if for a wedding-week stay, a pyramid of songbooks and novels and literary journals beside the bed and a platter of sugared bannock cakes on the side table. Beside the platter lay a wadded handkerchief stained with rust-colored sputum. Reverend Stone pulled a rocker alongside the bed and read Scripture interspersed with Dickens and Irving, unable to look at the handkerchief. The room's air tasted foul, poisoned. He felt as muddled and removed as a man in a dream.

To distract themselves they compared memories of the first Sunday she'd appeared in Newell, sitting straight-backed in Lemuel Butler's pew, her lace-collared dress drawing flinty stares from the congregation's women. Everyone in Newell knew she was a Boston girl, sent to board with her father's family. The minister's sermon that morning seemed directed only to her, so often did he glance her way. She recalled that his words had concerned Luke's description of the temptation of Jesus in the desert, and the vigorous force of temptation in everyday life, and at this they both smiled, Ellen pressing a hand to her lips to keep from raising a laugh.

Temptation. After the service, in the sodden meetinghouse yard, he'd moved among other members of the congregation, avoiding Lemuel Butler's clan. They stood patiently in the chilly rain, waiting to introduce this young woman, Ellen Butler. She was just nineteen years old, to his forty-two. Finally there was no one left but himself and the Butlers and a pair of stray hogs snuffling along the road edge. When she was presented to Reverend Stone he said, "Next Sunday I may ask you up to the pulpit beside me, so folks won't have to crane their necks."

She offered an exasperated grin. "I pray by next Sunday the novelty will have worn thin."

"You underestimate the regularity of town life."

"In Boston I was told that wasn't possible."

Lemuel Butler introduced himself uneasily into the conversation, commenting on the stoutness of the stray hogs and his fine early crop of sweet corn, a notice in the Springfield *Intelligencer* about a new moral primer available at the print shop, and did the minister recommend this new text or should they remain reading the old to their children? Reverend Stone paused, his thoughts aswirl. He said, "Yes, both."

What did we know? Reverend Stone wondered now, half asleep. The view from the belfry of faraway thunderheads. The taste of blackberry preserves passed from Ellen's lips to his own. The words to "The Girl in the Homespun Dress." He mumbled a scrap of half-remembered lyrics: *Across the slippery river rocks, a blue-eyed girl with auburn locks.* Ellen's eyes were cornflower blue, her hair an oaky auburn. He closed his eyes, intoxicated by the memory. She wore lilac water on her throat and breastbone. Her nose was marked crosswise by a thin white scar. Her feet canted outward when she walked, giving her a broad, boyish gait. She'd told him during their courtship that it was one of her several mannish qualities.

One morning seven months after the wedding he had awoken to a hail storm's thrum on the roof, and then she had appeared in the bedroom doorway, nightclothes gathered around her waist, a heaviness about her lips. The light held a rounded, silvery cast, lending her sight an ethereal quality. Her warmth had covered him; then she'd murmured in his ear, "Wake wake wake my dear husband wake." He'd feigned sleep, savoring the moment. She whispered, "When you awaken I will drain you dry."

We loved too much, Reverend Stone thought now. Not connubial love, or chaste love: they'd loved urge and sensation and pleasure, beyond the point of modesty. Surely it was sinful to love so much. At crucial moments he'd been reduced to a bare outline of himself, his mind overwhelmed by touch and sight and smell. When he woke the next morning he felt choked with guilt, shocked and embarrassed by the memory of his ardor. As Adam must have felt, the morning after the fall.

Reverend Stone's mind lingered over the memories, like fingertips drawn to a bruise. Her fierce brow and tugged-down frown at moments of severe pleasure. Her sighing laughter breaking the bedroom's silence. The pepper-rich smell of her hands, her long fingers. Her patient grin as she watched him shed his trousers.

That last evening he had returned from an errand at the apothecary to find Ellen's bed empty, her nightclothes crumpled on the floor. She was in the kitchen, dressed in housecoat and bonnet, scrubbing the floor with a soapy rag. He smiled, attempting to mask his surprise. "I figured you were saving your strength for pickling season. You're yet two weeks early."

"If I laid there one more moment I would've died of tedium."

He thought to make a joke then held his tongue. He took the rag from her hand and said, "Sit. Leave it for Corletta."

That night she sat across from him at the supper table, picking at potato and broiled pork while Reverend Stone talked about the creek's parched state, about a new milliner opening shop in town, about a notice posted for a runaway slave with six toes on each foot. He ate with strained heartiness, clattering his fork against the plate to obscure the sound of Ellen's shallow breathing. She stood abruptly, a crust of bread in her mouth. She stepped toward the bedroom, then with a look of shocked discomfort sat heavily on the floor.

He laid her on the bed and covered her legs with a quilt. Her jaw had slackened, the skin clinging to her cheekbones like wet cotton draped over rocks. A thread of saliva slid down her chin. She coughed, a ragged jag, and when the worst of it ended he kissed her, his tongue sliding between her cracked lips. She tasted of sour blood. Of death. Reverend Stone's heart surged with panic. Love is as strong as death—how often had he counseled a member of the congregation with those words? Each occasion, he realized, had been a lie. He hurried to Corletta's quarters and sent her to fetch Dr. Powell, and when he returned to the bedroom Ellen's eyes were fixed on the open window.

He stood motionless in the bedroom's thick silence. A breeze lifted the curtain edges. He found himself holding his breath, then realized he didn't want to fill his lungs—as though breathing might force time forward, and not breathing might somehow hold it back.

Now Reverend Stone jerked awake to a moan from the room next door. He closed his eyes, grasping after the fading images. Where was Elisha in his memories? The boy had disappeared some three months earlier, but still Ellen had set a plate and knife and fork at supper every night, as if expecting him to rush through the door, his hair smelling of pollen and knuckles creased with dirt. Reverend Stone remembered praying for the boy, his thoughts clouded by anger. He wondered if his son could sense, wherever he was, that his mother was gone. Surely a person could feel such a thing. Surely he didn't need to be told.

The moan rose again, and with a shiver the minister realized it wasn't a cry of sadness. It was a man and woman, together. Mumbled voices rose then trailed to a harmony of laughter; then a man's heavy footsteps crossed the floor. Reverend Stone stiffened toward the sound. A trunk lid thumped shut. A bed frame groaned. The minister's heart was smothered by tenderness, for these blissful strangers. Go forth in ignorance, he thought. You have my blessing.

He had stepped into trousers and laced his brogans the next morning when he noticed the yellow stains covering the bed quilt. He surveyed the small hotel room: gaps between the scuffed floorboards were packed with clay and pebbles. The ceiling was cratered and split. The window was smeared with greasy handprints, so that the sun's light held a filmy, liquid cast. Reverend Stone scratched a row of bumps along his wrist, a reminder of the bedbugs in the filthy pallet.

He descended to the parlor to find the hotel's proprietor reclined on a settee in a soiled linen shirt, reading an almanac. Without looking at Reverend Stone he said, "Ninety cents. Specie, if you please. I apologize for the lack of washing water."

"Your establishment is filthy."

The man looked up with an expression of cautious disbelief. He laid the book over a knee. "I aim to clean the rooms regular. It ain't no one else but me."

"Then you might consider taking on assistance. Your rooms are filthy. Your patrons are inconsiderate—I was kept awake much of the night by their carryings-on."

The proprietor stared at Reverend Stone as if probing for a hint of levity. "I can't always vouch for other folks' decency. And I can't afford to turn folks away on account of their inconsideracy—I'd be worse off even than I am, if I did."

"You should be less concerned with money if it means forfeiting your respectability."

"I wish respectability filled my stomach. It don't."

"That logic might someday cost you dearly."

The man offered a wan smile. "I'm waiting on the day I can afford to improve my logic. I would like that mightily."

The door creaked open and a woman in a red pelisse and pink poke

bonnet stepped into the parlor, followed by a man in a dusty teamster's coat. She arched her eyebrows at the proprietor as they passed
through the room. Reverend Stone listened to their footsteps rise on
the staircase, the man's mutterings answered by a girlish giggle. With a
mortified start the minister realized he was in a house of low repute.

"It's a hard location for a hotel, what with all the competition. I
can't afford to turn away paying customers. I pray you can sympathize."

Reverend Stone fumbled ninety cents from his trouser pocket and
laid the coins on a lamp stand. He supposed he was a laughable sight:
a minister in the parlor of a grimy bordello, complaining about the
quality of his night's sleep. He said, "I will leave you to your reading."

The proprietor took up the almanac and stared miserably at its
pages. "I thank you for that. Have a grand time in Buffalo."

The *Lake Zephyr* was an elegant side-wheel steamer with a long, low
bow and slender smokestack, a wheel-box painted with yellow stars.
Faded burgundy streamers wound around its railings. An American
flag hung limply from the bowsprit. Reverend Stone purchased a
steerage ticket to Detroit via Ashtabula and Cleveland for four dollars,
then walked to the pier end, watching herring gulls wheel about the
hurricane deck. It was nine o'clock; the steamer would depart at three-
fifteen. He felt pleasantly bemused at the prospect of empty hours in a
strange city. The *Lake Zephyr*, he noted, smelled faintly of yeast.

He strolled to the frontage road and hired a carriage, told the
driver to stop at an apothecary then run a scenic course up to the falls.
The buggy jerked forward. At the druggist's Reverend Stone purchased five tins of medication, then hurried back to the carriage and
placed two tablets beneath his tongue and slumped against the
cracked leather upholstery. He considered stopping at a meetinghouse
to inquire about the Baptists' progress in Buffalo, then decided he
would rather remain ignorant. Shopfronts and drays and merry yellow
omnibuses swam before his eyes.

Some time later he noticed a thrum rising around the horses' hoof-beats. The carriage stopped, and the sound enveloped him like thunder. He stepped from the buggy into a moist breeze and started toward the crowded prospect. He recalled a description of the falls, from a newspaper report of a marriage tour to Buffalo: an infinitude of water, the earth's purest display of His awesome hand. Reverend Stone quickened his pace. The thrum swelled to a roar.

From the prospect, the falls curved away in a great arc, wisps of spray peeling from the cascade as it sluiced downward, the water the color of an old woman's hair. Far below, mist billowed over shadowy black rocks. From a distance the water appeared barely to move, like draperies ruffled by a breeze. Reverend Stone leaned out over the wooden railing. On the lower river, a miniature steamer churned toward the falls' base then vanished into the mist.

He stepped back from the prospect feeling vaguely disappointed. One of creation's great marvels, he thought, and I'm unhappy it is not greater. He dismissed the notion but a haze of displeasure remained. Beside him, young couples stood arm in arm, grinning at the falls or whispering in each other's ears or giggling with delight. For a moment Reverend Stone wished he could follow Jonah Crawley's blithe advice and temper his expectations. It seemed a simple enough route to happiness.

Back at the pier, he boarded the *Lake Zephyr* and found standing room against the steerage deck railing. The steamer was crowded with peddlers and soldiers and wary-looking immigrants, families hauling saddlebags and gunnysacks and rope-bound trunks, sailors lying drunk against the engine house. A child with tangled black ringlets stamped like a sentry around a rickety bureau. A Methodist preacher bawled above the din. Reverend Stone thought, I am now one of these itinerant sorts. The idea held sharp, illicit appeal. Just then Jonah Crawley and his daughter Adele passed, the man hauling a trunk's fore while the girl struggled with the rear, a stick of peppermint clamped between her teeth. Reverend Stone called the man's name and raised a hand.

"Reverend Stone!" Crawley dropped the trunk with a startled grin. "Are you quitting Buffalo? You've just arrived!"

The minister smiled at Adele. She took the candy from her mouth and curtsied expressionlessly. He said, "I'm headed on to Detroit. I suppose I would have passed Buffalo altogether, if I could have—though then I would have missed my viewing of the falls."

Jonah Crawley's grin blossomed into a smile. He was a difficult man to gauge, Reverend Stone thought. He might be a schemer or simply a harmless fool. Crawley said, "I trust you found your accommodation comfortable enough."

Reverend Stone offered a placid nod. "Do you frequent that establishment yourself?"

"You said you were searching for cheap accommodation, Reverend. You must admit, the room was dog cheap. If you like, I can make similar arrangements for you in Detroit. I can offer several hotels of my highest approval."

"I think I shall rely on providence in Detroit."

Crawley's expression betrayed a note of hurt. "You should come to one of my daughter's performances while you're in the city. We'll be set up somewhere in the Irish quarter. I'll let you in half fare."

"What sort of performance?"

"My daughter is a spiritualist medium." He laid a hand on the girl's bony shoulder. "She has a talent to converse with those who've passed."

Reverend Stone leaned toward the girl. Her eyes possessed a weary, womanly quality, and her cheeks and brow were marked by a scatter of pockmarks, tiny seeds flung by the wind. He said, "Tell me, young lady. What is the mood of those who've passed? Are they happy to be disturbed from rest?"

Adele shrugged. "It depends on the folks. Most seem to enjoy the occasion—my sense is that purgatory ain't the most sociable place. Though some are plain rude."

"What about those who are not in purgatory? Can you contact them?"

"Indeed. I can contact anyone who's passed."

Reverend Stone nodded. A rash of heat crawled over his skin.

Jonah Crawley said, "You're not angry that Adele thinks heaven isn't sociable, are you, Reverend? That's not what she means to suggest."

"With all respect, I have trouble allowing that the contact is genuine."

"Reverend Stone! You don't believe the deceased want to be heard?"

The minster's gaze moved past the pair. A boil of anger had risen in his chest. He said, "The dead have passed to a place that is unreachable to the living, Mr. Crawley. They desire nothing this world might offer. Nothing at all."

Crawley scowled pleasantly. "I allow that some girls are nothing more than low liars, selling copper in the name of gold. But not my daughter, Reverend Stone. I assure you. She has a sincere gift."

A steam whistle sounded; then a chorus of shouts as the engine groaned to life. The *Lake Zephyr*'s smokestack sighed. A crowd had assembled along the waterfront, waving handkerchiefs in farewell as the engine built steam, and as the steamer slid away a barefoot boy ran sobbing to the pier's edge. He waved his boater furiously, then flung it toward the departing ship. It spun out in a yellow streak then settled on a swell.

Adele Crawley turned to the minister, her large green eyes staring straight through him. "It's a gift, Reverend Stone. I converse with the dead."

Five

They set to loading the canoe at dawn, kegs of gunpowder and pork belly and dried peas, sacks of flour and coffee and rice and lyed corn, bags of salt and sugar and saleratus, rifles wrapped in oilcloth, Mackinaw blankets for trade, a parcel of soap and matches and tacks and cooking gear, tents and hatchets and files. A moment's confusion; then the scientific instruments were located and stowed, Mr. Brush chuckling at his forgetfulness, his laughter echoed by Professor Tiffin and Elisha and Susette Morel. Giddiness spread like a vapor through the party. The sky lightened from indigo to a brilliant blue. The straits were a gleaming, empty turnpike stretching westward.

At last Mr. Brush settled himself in the canoe's stern. The craft was long and slender, a yellow moon painted on its hull, and as Professor Tiffin stepped into the bow the canoe lurched beneath him. He yelped, steadying himself, then took up a paddle and hefted it curiously as Susette and Elisha took their places. The craft jittered on the rippling straits. Mr. Brush called, "On my mark—*we are off!*" and as one the party's paddles dipped into the water. Professor Tiffin hooted as they surged toward the horizon. I do not deserve this good fortune, Elisha thought. I do not deserve this life. He felt swollen with gratitude that was near to tears.

Ring-billed gulls screamed toward the canoe then banked away. The beach was yellow sand dotted with dune thistle, edged by red cedar and maple and mountain ash. Elisha paddled with his gaze fixed on the passing shoreline. Within an hour the straits began to widen, and suddenly they entered the open lake, rollers tumbling out to the horizon's black thread, the sky a vast blue sheet pricked by stars. Fat, fleecy clouds floated over the plain of water.

The party stopped paddling and let the canoe bob on the swells. "It must be a curse to be born in a land so beautiful," Mr. Brush said. "The rest of creation must seem dismal by comparison."

"Tahquamenon Bay!" Professor Tiffin shouted. "I have been told that voyageurs pause here to make tobacco offerings to their spirits, to ensure a safe journey. It is a Native myth, or perhaps a Catholic one. Is this true, Madame Morel?" The man swiveled to face her as the canoe rocked crosswise. "Est-ce vrai?"

Susette was dressed in the previous day's clothes, along with a blue scarf trimmed with rabbit fur—a lucky talisman, Elisha figured, or perhaps her sole piece of finery. Her hair was freshly washed and fell in a thick black braid down her back. The boy wanted to press it like a scrap of silk against his cheek.

"It is not necessary," she said. "Let us continue."

"Nonsense—we shall pause so you can make your offering."

"Come now," Mr. Brush said gently. "The lady can make her own decisions. There is no need to ridicule her beliefs."

"Nothing could be farther from my aim!" Tiffin said. "I am simply curious to learn if the practice descends from the Native rather than the French tradition. It is a burnt offering, you see, a way to appease their great spirits and celebrate their departure. The tradition likely dates back to ancient times—in fact, some Native tribes make burnt offerings of animals, just as the ancient Hebrews did. I personally have observed firepits containing burned bone shards. Interestingly, in many cases the bones were unbroken—just as dictated by Hebrew law, that no bone of paschal lamb should—"

He broke off as Susette untied the pouch at her waist and withdrew a stub of tobacco, fire steel and flint and wad of tow. She turned her back to the breeze and cupped the tow. She struck a spark into it and blew gently until a small flame rose, then she pulled the tobacco

into shreds and set it afire. She held the smoking stub over the gunwale and mumbled a few quick phrases, then crossed herself as she
tossed the tobacco into the lake. The scrap floated on the shallow
swells.

"And now we are protected!" Professor Tiffin shouted.

Part Two

One

They paddled through mornings of damp heat and high, tissuey clouds. Their course skirted the shoreline, which varied from stony breakwaters to pocked sandstone faces to belts of smooth, sugar-white sand. Beach grass riffled like whitecaps in the breeze. Terns and sandpipers whistled at the water's edge. At noon the party put ashore for lunch, Elisha gathering driftwood for the fire while Susette stirred peas and rice and pork belly into the cookpot. The boy's neck was sunblistered, his palms rubbed raw from paddling. Mosquitoes hovered in a haze along the beach.

Despite his discomfort Elisha felt buoyed by a happiness that felt akin to grace. It was like being in Alpheus Lenz's study, he thought, that same gorgeous calm, the bookcases replaced by tall white pines, the specimens replaced by the creatures themselves. Lunch finished, Elisha assisted Mr. Brush in measuring latitude and temperature and barometric pressure, then accompanied the man on a quick mineral survey. The soil was siliceous sand mixed with loam, Elisha learned; the rocks were basalt trap and hornblende and sandstone and graywacke slate. He scratched notes in his fieldbook and labeled mineral specimens and blazed bearing trees, scrabbling to keep pace as Brush strode ahead. The man whistled a jaunty marching song, allowing Elisha to track him even when he disappeared among the trees. He was as relaxed and content as a man at a town fair.

The survey complete, Elisha returned to camp to find Professor Tiffin reclined beside the cookfire with a volume of Scott. The man rose with a groan and motioned for Elisha to follow him up the beach, beginning a discourse on glacial upheaval or fossil dispersion that quickly digressed to a litany of complaints. His trapezius muscles were strained from paddling. His buttocks were calloused and sore. Susette's breakfast preparations were excellent but her suppers too powerfully seasoned for his palate. He would trade his grandmother's eyeteeth for a veal steak and a gill of whiskey. Elisha nodded in commiseration, but somehow this only deepened his pleasure.

On the third afternoon from Sault Ste. Marie Elisha was sent on a hunt, and was passing through a grove of Juneberries when a loud scraping rose from the brush. A tall, slope-shouldered bear rose on its haunches not fifty yards distant. The animal was silky black, its small head dusted with wood chips. Elisha tore open a cartridge and fumbled with a cap as the bear pawed its face; then as he raised his rifle the bear turned and shambled away. Elisha's shot splintered bark from a distant pine. He sat on the forest floor until his legs stopped shaking. Then the boy shivered with relieved laughter.

On the fourth afternoon from the Sault Elisha was strolling with Tiffin when the man spied a bone-thin mongrel splayed near the forest edge. The dog lifted its head as they approached, the effort seeming to consume all its strength. Its muzzle was stuck thick with porcupine quills, its head swollen to the size of a melon. Its leaden eyes tracked Elisha. "The inflammation is severe," Professor Tiffin said, touching the animal's neck. "We must shoot the poor beast at once." Elisha charged the rifle and Tiffin laid the barrel against the dog's ear; then he lowered the hammer with a sigh. He sent Elisha to camp for a piece of stewed pork, then laid the softened meat on the dog's tongue.

Elisha soon realized that this was the expedition's routine: mornings spent paddling along the lakeshore, afternoons spent surveying with Mr. Brush or walking with Professor Tiffin or hiking alone through the forest, his rifle at the ready. Evenings, they relaxed around the cookfire as Susette served mugs of peppery stew. Brush and Tiffin had discovered a topic on which they agreed: politics. They were both for the annexation of Texas, both agreed that His Accidency the President was a hooligan and disgrace. Both agreed that the Michigan legislature contained more rats than the Detroit River. Professor Tiffin cackled, his laughter loud in the black night. Fireflies flashed at the forest's edge.

Elisha grinned at the men's conversation, all the while watching Susette Morel. How were her afternoons spent? Fishing for lake trout or gumming the canoe's seams, preparing the evening meal. Dreariness, Elisha thought; but she moved briskly among the men, saying little, the trace of a smile on her lips. Elisha longed to speak with her but could think of nothing to say.

On the fifth morning from Sault Ste. Marie Elisha rose at dawn to a gray sky and swirling northwest wind. The lake was whipped into dirty green peaks. His morning drowse hardened into disappointment, at the prospect of waiting out the weather. At the water's edge Mr. Brush sat on a boulder, bent over his fieldbook, occasionally glancing up from his writing to frown at the lake.

Elisha took up his own fieldbook and moved a few yards up the shore from Mr. Brush. He dipped his pen and wrote:

June 16, 1844

The shoreline is here composed very pleasingly of siliceous sand mixed with various multicolored stones, including hornblende and jasper and agate, and interspersed with dense tufts of beach grass. Sea crows and sandpipers and plovers can be found ducking for food at the water's edge, or nesting in scrapes on the yellow sandy beach. Some four rods inland the forest begins, first as a verdant stand of beech and red maple and striped maple, then interspersed with a few small hemlock, the canopy so dense as to nearly extinguish the sun's light. Gazing outward from the forest's edge, Lake Superior spans the horizon like a great blue bowl, its waves lapping the shore with remarkable vigor, as if it were not a mere lake but instead an immense open sea stretching to farthest China, or beyond.

He blew the ink dry, pleased with his first effort at description: it seemed to capture the essential nature of the place. Elisha began sketching a view of the beach and shorebirds and choppy lake; then he sensed a presence beside him. He looked up to find Mr. Brush squinting at his open fieldbook.

"Love letter to your girly friend?"

Elisha closed the book. "Just describing the region. So that I might remember it when the expedition's ended."

"An oil painting would serve you better in that regard."

"I can't paint. Though neither do I have the proper words to describe the landscape."

"A body can learn the proper words." Mr. Brush squinted out at the lake, nodding as if in confirmation of some fact. The man's hat was neatly brushed, his boots polished to a black gleam. "Well! I am curious to read what you have written."

Elisha offered the fieldbook and Brush paged to the most recent entry. The boy stared nervously out at the lake. A loon called, the sound like an infant's wail. Bad luck birds, Elisha thought, a bad omen for the evening's weather.

At last Mr. Brush grunted. "You have a sharp eye for particularity. That is good. However you spend far too much effort attempting to capture the region's beauty."

Elisha nodded uncertainly.

"There are infinitely many ways to describe a thing's beauty, young man—and so beauty is difficult to describe *precisely*. However, precision is our aim! You must aim to be precise and all-seeing. An all-seeing scribe, recording the most interesting details of God's creation."

"But wouldn't the scene's beauty be considered interesting in the—"

"Beauty is the realm of poets and painters. Of *penniless* poets and painters." Mr. Brush laughed. "Perhaps I am a poet myself!"

"I'd like to read your entry. If I may."

The man hesitated; then he offered the boy his fieldbook. It was a green leather-bound journal with the initials *SB* stamped in gold leaf on the cover. Elisha turned to the second page as a shiver of excitement passed through him. He read:

June 16, 1844

Site loc apprx 3.5 mi N Pt. au Foin (Bayfield). 46° 33'. Large granite boulder on shore bears N 10 E. Elm, 14 in. dia, bears N 57 W. Beech, 24 in. dia, bears N 42 W.

Metamorph, mainly quartz (spc 0), sandstone, slaty hornblende (1), imperf. talicose slates (2), some argill. Veins of alum-slate, similar E Penn. Silic pebbles, some carnelian (3), chalcedony (4). No comp defl.

Soil silic sandy to sandy with silt loam. Poor. Terrain flat, dry, suitable Ry.

Timber primly beech & sug map, some wht pine—appx 9,500 bf per ac. 90–120 ft high, 3 ft dia avg. Moderate.

Elisha turned the page to find it blank. He said, "But you've barely described the region at all!"

The man smiled indulgently. Blue-black stubble shadowed his jaw. "I have described rock formations that are often found near iron-bearing minerals—and thus they are *interesting*. They are one of the interesting details of God's creation."

Elisha shut the book, disappointed by Brush's logic. The man had described an important mineral specimen; yet there was no description of the region's loons or lake trout, Juneberries or black bears. And though Brush was certainly correct about detail and precision, it seemed heartless to ignore the region's beauty. He said, "But what about the remainder of the scene?"

Mr. Brush clapped Elisha on the back and turned toward camp. He called over his shoulder, "We shall leave that for the painters!"

The storm arrived that evening as low streaky thunderheads thrown over the forest like an ink-stained quilt. Raindrops spattered against the canopy; then a torrent began that stung a man's skin and rose in a mist from the forest floor. Mr. Brush and Professor Tiffin and Elisha and Susette hurried to their tents, ducked beneath the oilcloth flaps. They gazed at one another across the smoldering cookfire. Elisha said, "Do you suppose the—" but the sky flared white and thunder ripped above them. The sound was like virgin pine splintering beneath an axe.

Elisha realized with a thrill that he'd been wrong: this was not like Alpheus Lenz's study. Not the slightest bit. Lenz's study was silent and warm, a shrine to contemplation; this was thunder and storm clouds and hunger and fatigue. A practical endeavor, as opposed to a theoretical one. It seemed fitting that Lenz's specimens were stuffed and lifeless. Lightning flickered again; then a flame winked in the distance.

"I propose a toast!" Professor Tiffin called. He leaned forward and raised a flask into the downpour. "To the intrepid members of this expedition! And to knowledge, my sullen paramour—may she surrender her most intimate secrets, without shame or moderation!"

"Your language," Mr. Brush said mildly. He chuckled as he tipped his flask.

Susette had kindled a low fire beneath her tent's cover, and now she ladled out steaming mugs of whitefish stewed with rice and wild onions. Rain drummed against the oilcloths. As they ate the men discussed Lake Superior's possible origins as described in Scripture; at last Mr. Brush suggested that Tiffin read a few verses. The party laid aside their empty mugs, nestled deeper into their bedrolls. Like a family around the hearth after harvest day, Elisha thought.

"Exodus seems fitting for this evening. A long journey through a dark land—yes?" Professor Tiffin swallowed a sip of water and cleared his throat.

He read about the wilderness of Sin and manna from Heaven, about the murmurings against Moses and water from the rock. About rest on the Sabbath, and war against the Amalekites. About Jethro and Aaron and Zipporah, Gershom and Eliezer. Elisha closed his eyes, overcome by a pleasant fatigue. He felt soothed by the tale's familiarity.

But as Professor Tiffin read on the boy's mood soured. It frustrated him—for why should he feel unhappy, here at the country's edge with a scientist and surveyor and a strange, lovely woman? He was surrounded by beauty and nature's rarest mysteries. He half-expected to awaken and find it all a dream. Then Elisha recognized the sour feeling as homesickness.

There had been many such nights, before his mother's illness: firelight, murmured Scripture, raindrops tapping at the windowpanes. But after she fell ill the house quieted. Evenings passed in silence, Elisha and his father drifting like spirits through the empty rooms, startled by one another's glimpsed presence. His mother was shut away in the bedroom, too weak even to see her son. Her cough pulled time forward in a sickening lurch.

Elisha spent his days at the creek behind the parsonage, at a willow-shaded bend thick with pollen and mudminnows. Afternoons, he walked to Joseph Eliot's dry goods shop and purchased a penny's weight of boiled sugar. He loitered at the candy counter until the man stepped into the storeroom; then the boy stuffed a carrot of tobacco into his trousers and hurried from the shop. At home, he huddled behind the chicken house and pulled the tobacco into shreds, set the fragments alight and watched them burn. He felt dull and vacant, lifeless, like a sleepwalker moving through an empty town.

One afternoon Elisha waited until Eliot turned away, then he leaned across the counter and palmed a bone-handled Barlow knife. As he reached the shop's door a man said, "Son?" Joseph Eliot was standing at the storeroom entrance holding an empty coffee sack. He approached the boy and pried open Elisha's hand, scowled at the knife.

"I'm very sorry. It's for my mother."

The man moved as if to speak; then he clamped his mouth shut. "She's very ill."

"I know she is." Joseph Eliot gripped the boy's shoulder and steered him out the door. "You get along home now. Get."

Three days later Elisha was back at the shop. Eliot watched him with an expression that was equal parts irritation and sorrow. Elisha dawdled at the candy barrel. He asked for a half-penny of licorice, then spilled a fistful of coins across the plank floor. The man knelt with a sigh, and as he did Elisha snatched up a yellow silk hatband and stuffed it into his trouser pocket. Joseph Eliot rose and slowly untied his apron. He took Elisha by the elbow and led him from the shop, then across the town green. The boy's limbs felt numb. He could not form a thought.

Reverend Stone was a long time answering Eliot's knock. When he opened the door his hair was disheveled and collar unbuttoned, his thumb stuck into a thick volume: *The Old Curiosity Shop.* He had been reading to her. Joseph Eliot said, "I apologize very sincerely, Reverend Stone. However we have a matter to discuss."

In a nervous mumble Eliot explained what he had seen: the Barlow knife, the yellow silk hatband, the carrots of tobacco gone missing whenever Elisha visited the shop. Reverend Stone nodded, his expressionless gaze moving from Eliot to his son, then back to Eliot. At last he said, "Thank you, Mr. Eliot. Truly." He ushered Elisha inside and closed the door.

He stood with his hand on the door latch. He looked anxious but exhausted, his red-rimmed eyes searching the boy's face then trailing to an absent stare. It was as though he did not recognize his only son. At last he drew Elisha into a loose embrace. The man smelled of old, rank sweat. He kissed the crown of his son's head, then without a word stepped into the sickroom and gently closed the door. Elisha heard his voice resume its murmured narrative.

That night the boy gathered a spare shirt and comb and tin mug into a bundle, took a loaf of bread and chunk of salt pork and some cheese from the pantry. The house was quiet. He stood at his bedroom window, staring at the meetinghouse glowing white in the moonlight, the privy's shadowy form, the pear trees gesturing toward the chicken house. In the next room his father lay asleep, and Elisha wondered if the man would even notice his own son's absence. He smothered a bitter sob. He wanted to kick down the bedroom door, burst in on his father and shake the man awake. Instead Elisha opened the window, then stepped through it and started down the Springfield road.

Where had she been? Elisha wondered now. It was as though his mother was being hidden away, as punishment for some unknown sin. He could not understand it. She must rest, his father had told him countless times, turning Elisha away from the closed bedroom door. Your mother is exhausted. Go now. She mustn't be disturbed. She mustn't ever be disturbed.

When his father left the parsonage, Elisha would pad to the bedroom and press his ear against the closed door, try the doorknob. Locked. He would hurry to Corletta's room, then follow the woman down the hallway, watch silently as she unlocked the door. His mother lay beneath a thick quilt, her skin clammy and pale. She smiled weakly. Elisha would pull a chair beside the bed and present his most recent sketches; she would take up a pencil and show him how to use shading to create depth, how to draw a viewer's eye to the finest detail. Finally she would hold the drawings close, point out Newell's citizens in the thrushes and toads and bumblebees. There was Aeneas Weatherspoon in a mantis's bony elbows, Edson in a dung beetle's blunt brow. Elisha himself in a wiry red squirrel. She laid a hand on the boy's knee and closed her eyes. Her breath smelled of sour milk. Stiff, bloody handkerchiefs lay wadded on the side table. At last Elisha kissed his mother's cheek and slipped from the room, fetched Corletta to lock the door. In his own room he curled on the bed and stared at the empty ceiling. He lay there for hours, until at last he fell asleep.

A punishment, then. Elisha knew his father was disappointed in his weak faith: Reverend Stone had compared him endlessly to Newell boys who had heard the call. One boy in particular, James Davidson, had shocked the congregation by walking stiffly down the meeting-house aisle during a sermon, then dropping to his knees with a fevered cry. For weeks there'd been talk of sending him to seminary in Cambridge. Reverend Stone had gone three days without speaking to his son; finally he told Elisha that he should be mortified. The son of a minister, yet lacking any trace of God's will.

Elisha had confronted Davidson that afternoon in the town green. The boy was sitting against an oak tree eating a pear. Elisha asked, "How did it feel?"

"Did what feel?"

"The vision. Or whatever it was. Your fuss during the sermon."

Davidson giggled, pear juice running down his chin. He said, "Like this."

He rolled to his knees and cried out, with precisely the same pitch and quaver as in the meetinghouse. Elisha stared, aghast. James Davidson rose and placed the wet pear in Elisha's palm, then ran across the green.

Now the boy started at a nearby rustle from the forest. He waited, motionless, but the sound did not repeat itself. Perhaps, he thought, I'm not homesick at all—perhaps this gloom is simply a product of the weather. Immediately he understood the thought to be false. He crouched deeper into his bedroll. Outside, rain whispered through the spruces. He thought, this is a scientist's life: hours spent alone in a dark forest, or alone in a musty library, or alone on an endless lake. A man's only companions were his voice, his instruments, the rain, the dark. No one explained the world to a scientist. He found answers only in nature, or in himself.

That's a rich one, Elisha thought.

They set out the next morning despite a marbled sky and cold spray gusting off the lake. Elisha bent over the paddle, his lips pursed to stop their trembling. To distract himself he counted each paddle stroke until he reached one hundred, then began anew. A hundred strokes closer, he told himself each time. To what he didn't know.

Susette began to sing. Her voice wavered on the first notes then dropped to a low, pure tone, a choirgirl's tone. The song was more a chant than a true melody, every fourth paddle stroke marking a phrase; as she sang the party's pace fell in with hers.

> *Mon canot est fait d'écorces fines*
> *Qu'on pleume sur les bouleaux blancs;*
> *Les coutures sont faites de racines,*
> *Les avirons, de bois blanc.*

Something about a canoe, something white. Elisha felt a twinge of regret at his poor French.

> *Je prends mon canot, je le lance*
> *A travers les rapides, les bouillons.*
> *Là, à grands pas il s'avance.*
> *Il ne laisse jamais le courant.*

Rain had started as a drizzle, and with Susette's singing and the lake's gauzy spray their passage was strangely beautiful, as though they were paddling through a cloud. After some time the rain stopped and Susette fell silent.

"Madame Morel, don't quit just because the rain did."

She glanced back at the boy but said nothing. He bent forward and said, "You have an awfully sweet voice."

"You claimed to speak French, but I did not hear you singing."

Elisha chuckled nervously. The presence of Mr. Brush and Professor Tiffin made him feel awkward and furtive. "Yes, well. My singing is worse even than my French."

"I was told there are many French in Detroit. My husband told me this. He said that there are many voyageurs living there. That a person might hear French in the street every day."

"Indeed, you can. There are French barbers and French tailors, a man named Chocron. The Berthelet market is owned by a Frenchman. I suppose I haven't yet spent enough time in Detroit to practice my French—I'm from Newell, Massachusetts. That's where I was raised."

"I have never been in Detroit. I would like to see it someday."

"You should visit! I could show you the Berthelet market and the French tailor—though of course your husband likely knows their locations. But if he doesn't I could show you both, together. We could make a tour, just the three—"

Susette had stopped paddling. Elisha followed her stare to the horizon, where a gray shape slid through the mist. As he stared, the shape materialized into a canoe.

"Ahead."

Professor Tiffin's paddle paused, dripping. The canoe was three hundred yards distant, near enough to see three hunched forms in a vessel that was too small to be a bateau or canot du nord, but was closer in size to a Native bark canoe. Elisha strained forward. A chant rose from the distant craft.

"Are they voyageurs or Natives?" Elisha asked. "Are they Sioux?"

"Chippewas, on their way to the Sault," Tiffin said. "Hopefully they've fresh meat of some sort—we can trade for tonight's supper."

"Start ashore," Brush said. "We shall let them pass. If they want trade they can come to us."

A moment's silence; then Tiffin said, "There is no cause for alarm—we're too deeply into Chippewa territory to encounter Sioux. And even if they are Sioux, they certainly won't trouble a party of white men."

Brush dug hard and the canoe swung shoreward. He took up an oilcloth-wrapped rifle from the canoe bottom and propped it between his legs. He said calmly, "Elisha, ready a rifle."

"You need not be worried." Susette's voice held a note of strain. "They are not meaning trouble."

Brush grunted as the canoe coasted toward a narrow shoreline scattered with plover. It was just a strip of stones beneath a sandstone cliff, as poor a landing site as they'd yet seen. He said, "We should be prepared, whatever the case. We are indefensible in this damned canoe. Pardon my language, Madame Morel."

"How do we know if they mean trouble?" Elisha asked. He took up a rifle and removed the oilcloth. From his shot bag he withdrew a cartridge but did not move to set the charge.

"Put away your blasted rifle," Tiffin said. "You will only provoke them! There are thirty thousand Chippewas in this territory. What, precisely, do you mean to accomplish?"

They skirted a massive boulder then angled back toward the beach, and as they bottomed on a swell the canoe lurched with a sound like a door dragged open. Plover rose in a flutter. Mr. Brush called, "Step out!" and jammed his paddle against a submerged rock, the canoe rolling sharply, water spurting through the split planks. The party swung over the gunwales, the surf a frigid shock at Elisha's chest. Together they hauled the craft shoreward, Professor Tiffin stumbling on the slick lakebed, Susette groaning at the load.

"Drag it up the beach. Carefully!"

Tiffin staggered up the steep beach, his muttonchops pearled with water. Mr. Brush eased the canoe onto its side, quickly untied his pack and withdrew a scrolled cloth, unfurled it to reveal a faded American flag. He draped the flag over the canoe's bow, just above the gashed planks.

They watched the Natives approach. The craft was but fifty yards from shore, near enough to make out the angular silhouette of the foremost paddler's hat. The other paddlers were bareheaded. Elisha took up a rifle and wiped the hammer dry, in his nervousness dropping the percussion cap. Susette touched his arm and the boy started.

"You need not be frightened."

"I'm not frightened."

The woman held his gaze a moment then turned to the landing canoe.

The Natives splashed into the shallows and hoisted the craft, laid it atop a patch of stones some thirty yards distant. They started up the narrow beach. They were led by a tall, light-skinned brave wearing a tattered three-cornered hat and a scarlet cloak clasped by a medallion. He looked to be near Mr. Brush's age. Behind him were a pair of like-looking braves wearing breechclouts and leggings and ragged calico shirts, their hair smeared with grease, their skin the color of sand. Brothers, Elisha figured. The taller brave's left arm canted outward, as though it had been broken. The smaller brave's eyes were ringed with black paint. He stared at Elisha.

"Bojou," said the first Native. His medallion bore the likeness of John Quincy Adams.

"Bojou," Susette said. She began to speak, a language that sounded like the German that Elisha had heard in Detroit's dining halls, though muddied somewhat, the consonants drawn to a soft slur.

"What are you saying?" Mr. Brush asked sharply. "You are to say nothing except through translation of Professor Tiffin or myself."

"I simply greeted them. I told them you are Americans. I said you have been sent by your Great Father the President to the far end of the lake. I told them you are here as friends."

The first Native answered in a rasp, his expression calm to the point of boredom. His gaze lingered on Mr. Brush.

"They are Chippewas, from the Dead River band. He wishes to trade fish and deer meat for flour and tobacco."

Elisha exhaled, a shiver of relief running through him. Of course they wished only to trade. Flour and tobacco. Of course.

"Tell them we would be gratified if they would accept a small gift." Tiffin fumbled open his pack and removed a carrot of tobacco, held it aloft with an unctuous grin. He placed the tobacco at the first Native's feet. "And tell them we will gladly accept whatever meat they might have, in exchange for more tobacco. Unfortunately we cannot spare any flour. Tell them we are as brothers to them!"

The Chippewas listened to Susette's translation, then looked to one another in silent conference. They paced back to the canoe, scuffing across the pebbly beach. Mr. Brush took a rifle from the canoe and placed it at his feet.

"They are not meaning trouble," Susette hissed. "Put away your rifle."

The braves turned, each with a pair of fat whitefish held through the gills. Pink blood washed over the greenish scales.

"The meat—tell them we would actually prefer the venison." Professor Tiffin sighed. "No matter!" He withdrew a second carrot of tobacco and placed it with the other. The first Native stared at the offering.

"It is not enough," Susette said. "He is not satisfied with the trade."

"That is all we will offer," Brush said. "Tell the big buck. Now."

The first Native spoke for a long while, his voice flat, his expression unchanged throughout the speech. Elisha studied the other braves: they shared the same low brow and broad, humped nose. Brothers, or cousins. Elisha wondered if the first Native was their father.

"He says we should turn back to the Sault. He says there have been Sioux war parties all along this shore during the past days. He says they have killed three Chippewas in the past days and taken two more as prisoner. He says that if we make him a present of whiskey and gunpowder they might come with us for some days, to protect us against the Sioux."

"You tell him that we can protect ourselves far better than they." Mr. Brush took up the rifle and laid it across his arms.

Before Susette could speak the braves tensed as if to sprint, and the first Native stepped toward Mr. Brush. Susette uttered a rapid string of syllables as Professor Tiffin raised his hands, shouted "Ahnowatan! Stop! *Ahnowatan!*"

"Don't gesture with your rifle!" Elisha tried to calm the tremor in his voice. "They take it as a threat!"

"You damned fool, you will have us killed!" Professor Tiffin dragged a keg of pork from the canoe and opened his folding knife, pried up the lid. He withdrew a thick cut of side meat and shook it at the Natives, smiling desperately. "A gift, please! Some excellent pork!"

"That is far too much," Brush said.

Tiffin seized another carrot of tobacco, laid the pork and tobacco before the first Native. He said, "Madame Morel, tell him we would be grateful if they would guide us for the next days. Tell him immediately."

Before Susette could speak the first Native mumbled a short phrase. She said, "They want whiskey and powder. Not meat."

"Listen to me now," Brush said. "You tell him that this parley is ended. You tell him that if he troubles us a moment longer, white men from the fort will arrive with as many rifles as the trees in the forest. You tell him he will be driven from his fishing and hunting grounds, and his family will starve. Tell him now."

"Do not say any such thing!"

"Tell him now." Brush's words were clipped by rage. He shifted the rifle in his grip, and as he did the Chippewas dashed to their canoe, the first Native's hat tumbling from his head. Susette shouted as Professor Tiffin stepped forward with arms outstretched, shouting *Ahnowatan! Brothers!* The Chippewas ducked behind the canoe and reappeared with muskets at their shoulders. Elisha fell to one knee and leveled his rifle at the smallest brave. He felt so weak that he feared he would drop the weapon. The Chippewa muskets looked to be antique fowling pieces, though at close range Elisha knew their age would matter little. If they fired a volley it would be a terrible scene indeed.

Susette spoke. Her voice was calm and measured, the tone of a mother reading Scripture to a child. Elisha stared into the smallest brave's eyes: they were black-ringed like a raccoon's, betraying a tension bordering on panic. His musket was aimed at Elisha's stomach. Beside him, the taller brave stood with a musket laid across his twisted arm, as though on a gnarled tree limb. Susette continued to speak, and with a rush of relief Elisha understood that she was saying far more than Brush had intended.

At last she stopped speaking. The silence was broken by a seagull's chatter. The first Native muttered a short phrase.

"They will depart. They will not trouble us. Put away your rifles."

A vision rose in Elisha's mind of the party laid out along the beach like cordwood, blood washing over the gray stones. He prayed that he wouldn't be sick. Susette stepped toward Elisha and yanked his rifle barrel down. "Now! Let them depart."

"I am going to address them," Tiffin said. "And you are not to interfere."

"Do not say anything foolish." Mr. Brush had not lowered his rifle.

Professor Tiffin's face was beaded with sweat. The first Native's musket was trained on his chest. "Tell them I am seeking news of their ancestors, of their grandfather's grandfathers. Tell them I will learn of their ancestors' great acts of courage, and that I will tell the entire land, and that their Great Father the President will be awed, and that white men will treat them with respect. Tell them they will be given gifts of fine land, and gunpowder, and whiskey, and tobacco, and they will never want for food. Tell them."

Susette spoke for a long while. The first Native uttered a few words, then as one they lowered their muskets and stowed them inside the canoe. The first Native crossed the beach, his stare fixed on Mr. Brush, and took up the pork and tobacco, then fetched his hat and dusted it off before settling it on his head. He walked slowly back to the canoe. The Natives hoisted the craft into the shallows and swung gracefully aboard, then set to paddling. Within moments the canoe had vanished into the white mist.

Susette said, "He wishes you success."

Two

In Detroit Reverend Stone took a windowless room on Miami Avenue and collapsed into bed, his throat torn to wet shreds, the ceiling blurring before his eyes, his ears feeling like they were stuffed with tow. Sleep washed over him, his waking hours obscured by feverish daydreams. On Saturday he pulled himself upright and stepped slowly down to the street. Sunlight pierced his eyes. He stumbled along the sidewalk as if dragged by a team of horses.

The surgeon was a cheery bewhiskered Englishman wearing a black linen coat stiff with bloody stains. He ushered the minister into a makeshift operating theater in his parlor, seated him in a highbacked chair fitted with leather straps. The floor was strewn with sawdust. The surgeon laid two calloused fingers alongside Reverend Stone's neck. The man grunted. He said, "You feel set to burst."

"I suffered a coughing spell on the steamboat. I felt—" Reverend Stone paused. "I felt as though I was ascending into the heavens."

The surgeon chuckled. "I suspect you'll remain earthbound for some hours yet. Is this a common occurrence?"

Reverend Stone thought to tell him about his visions of souls, the ghostly colored nimbuses. "No. It is rare."

The man squinted into Reverend Stone's ears, pinched his earlobes. "Besides the consumption, I would hazard you have a touch of milk sickness. It's an illness of the nervous faculties, symptomized by spells and paleness and morbidly strong arterial excitement. It can cause weakness, queer sights—over time it can cause a crippling of one's mental powers." He straightened. "Of course if you are interested in a professional diagnosis I can supply one, for two dollars."

"I don't think that will be required."

"Then." He cuffed Reverend Stone's shirtsleeve and from a coat pocket withdrew a leather thong, cinched the minister's arm. He tapped the crook of his elbow until a thick blue vein rose like a worm beneath the skin. The surgeon turned to a sideboard and a tarnished pewter tray filled with instruments. A moment later Reverend Stone heard the quick scuff of a blade being stropped.

Outside the window, a hatless Native stood talking to a ruddy Irish constable, their peculiar accents audible in the quiet room. Every nation of the world, Reverend Stone thought, here at the country's edge. The notion confused him somehow. He glanced at the surgeon, and as he did an airiness lifted him, a pink haze surrounding the man's form. Reverend Stone drew a sharp breath.

"Now, then." The surgeon tapped the minister's arm. He pressed a steel lancet against the vein, and for an instant the split skin showed; then a scarlet line welled and thickened. Blood slipped down Reverend Stone's forearm and spattered on the sawdust. He watched for a moment then turned away.

"I'll take just enough to settle your pulse." The surgeon turned to his instruments, whistling a lilting child's tune: "Pop! Goes the Weasel."

Reverend Stone wondered, as the seconds passed, how much blood it might take to calm his heart. He imagined his lips turning gray, his fingers stiffening as sawdust clotted around him, the surgeon whistling all the while. A strange euphoria overtook him. *The natural body is an obstruction to the soul or spiritual body.* Reverend Stone wished he had a tin of tablets, then realized he didn't need them.

As blood drained from his arm the minister felt as though his body was rising from the chair, up to the parlor ceiling, then through it into the cloudless blue sky.

He felt strong enough that next Monday to emerge onto Miami Avenue, the sidewalk slick with rain, buggies slapping down the wide clay street. The sky was an iron-gray sheet. A sweet, loamy smell hung in the air.

He walked to the Grand Circus and watched traffic swirl around the fountain, then closed his eyes and listened to the wagons' jolt and creak and clap, the click of horsewhips, the shouts of hackmen in French and German and country English. The din of commerce. Boot heels thundered on the sidewalk planks. Detroit was a hundredfold louder than he'd expected. He continued along Macomb Avenue, past a silversmith and druggist and crowded gambling hall, a grocery, a brick Presbyterian church with its doors propped open. The sidewalks were teeming with newspaper sellers and laborers and ladies in crinolines carrying silk parasols. At State Street, the Catholic Orphan Asylum stood beside the Protestant Orphan Asylum. Reverend Stone grinned at the sight. He was filled with wonder at the city's rush and vigor.

Hunger pangs prodded him. He bought an ear of corn wrapped in newsprint from a Negro sidewalk vendor, unwrapped the *City Examiner* and surveyed the day-old stories. Congress appropriating two thousand dollars for the purchase of shoehorns. The steamer *Atlantic Star* catching fire and exploding while at dock in Baltimore, killing dozens of cattle. Summer snowstorms wreaking chaos in London. Fifty crates of raisins received and for sale at Z. Chandler's. Reverend Stone rubbed grease from his fingers on the paper's edge. The stories seemed as eccentric and irrelevant as fiction.

He scanned the back page for news of steamboat departures, and his eye caught on a notice entitled "Delusions." It read:

Our country appears to be sadly affected with delusions just now, the consequences of which are quite frightful. How are we to account for this? We will not venture an explanation. One thing is certain, however. Profligate and designing knaves too frequently seize upon these delusions as a means of livelihood, and inculcate false doctrines, such as the new clique of Millerism. This sect has attracted of late a great number of converts from other faiths, most notably at the recent revival in Monroe.

Even here, Reverend Stone thought, at the edge of civilization. The thought was troubling but offered a hint of comfort. We are all of us the same, even the Natives and Irish and Jews and Chinese. He wadded the paper and dropped it beside a hog snuffling in the gutter.

At the Military Square Reverend Stone asked a hackman for directions to the public land office, then followed the instructions to Woodward Avenue and a two-story stone building with white columns flanking an outsized door. Inside, he paused to regard the baroque, shadowy ascension scene painted on the ceiling: The artist had endowed Jesus with a tense grimace as he reached toward a spiky, radiant sun. It was as though Christ was afraid of being impaled by sunbeams. The overall effect was one of grotesque comedy.

The surveyor general's office was located on the second floor, at the end of a long marble hallway. The door was painted to read *Charles A. Noble*. Reverend Stone tugged at his shirtsleeves and straightened his hat while a voice inside the office murmured, "Thirty west, township forty-five north, section fifteen, Joseph T. Smithfield. Range thirty west, township—"

He stepped inside and the voice paused. A man wearing a boiled shirt and green-tinted spectacles looked up from behind a desk. At the room's rear, a sober-looking man sat with his feet propped atop a low bookcase, one hand tucked into his waistcoat, his shirtfront spotted with tobacco juice. A robe of flesh swaddled his neck. The office smelled strongly of vinegar.

"Mr. Charles Noble?"

The man squinted at Reverend Stone. His brows formed a single thatched hood above deep-set eyes.

"I would like to discuss a scientifical expedition that I believe was commissioned under your authorization."

"And which expedition might that be?"

"It is directed by Mr. Silas A. Brush, to the northern peninsula. I suspect it departed Detroit some three weeks ago."

Charles Noble worked a quid in his cheek but said nothing.

"My son is a member of the expedition. Elisha Stone."

Noble swung his legs down and turned to a rolltop desk. He flipped open a large logbook and licked his thumb, began slowly turning pages. Reverend Stone moved a step forward and the bespectacled man's expression tightened.

"Yes," Charles Noble said, "Elisha Stone, packman and general scientific assistant. We are agreed that your son is joined to an expedition directed by Mr. Silas Brush and Professor George Tiffin. A good fellow, Silas Brush. A uniquely philanthropic individual."

"I would like to know their intended route. I am on an urgent errand to locate my son."

From the street below came a cornet's melodic tunings, then a snare drum's rattle and a child's squeal of laughter. A parade was assembling. Reverend Stone glanced at the bespectacled man: his expression had softened to a curious stare, his eyes barely visible behind the colored lenses.

"Now. What you are proposing is difficult."

"Why is it difficult?"

Noble slapped the book shut. "Many people are waiting to see what Mr. Brush will discover in the northern territory. The possibilities are illimitable: timber, rich farmland, minerals. Already there are rumors of copper and gold. Knowledge of his route might well inspire land speculation."

"I am not at all interested in what the expedition might discover. My only aim is to locate my son. Certainly no one besides myself is concerned with that knowledge."

Charles Noble chuckled as though indulging a child. "You would not be the first father to trade on his son's name, Mr. Stone."

"Reverend Stone."

"Pardon?"

"Reverend Stone. That is my common address."

Noble dribbled a dark stream into a tarnished brass cuspidor beside the desk. He glanced at the bespectacled man; the man smiled faintly, then turned to the ledger on his desk and scratched in the margin with a dry pen.

Reverend Stone felt as though he was playing a game in which he did not understand the rules. He ignored the feeling and smiled pleasantly at the two men. Charles Noble remained expressionless, fingertips tapping the logbook.

"My sincere apologies," Noble said finally. "It is a violation of statute to offer details of an expedition's route before its completion. I hope you can sympathize."

"I can offer my word before God that our discussion would remain private."

The bespectacled man spoke in a reedy, gentle voice. "How might we be certain you are who you claim? With every respect, Reverend Stone, we've seen dreadful bad behavior from speculators."

The minister drew a worn Bible from his breast pocket and passed it to the man. He swallowed hard to quell a cough. "That is my inscription, in my hand. William Edward Stone."

The bespectacled man appeared unmoved. "So it is."

Outside, a brass band struck up a march that rose above a choir of children's shouts and a charcoal peddler's hoarse call. Charles Noble paced to the open window. He shook his head, his fleshy neck wobbling. "We cannot offer details of an expedition's route, whatever the circumstance. It's the nature of men to be greedy—surely I don't need to advise you of that. I have seen men forfeit their honor at the faintest whiff of money."

"Have you?"

Noble scowled at the minister. "I have seen it firsthand! Just last month one of our surveyors was found falsifying timber reports, so that an accomplice could purchase the choicest lots. The accomplice was a wealthy gentleman but the poor surveyor could barely afford tobacco. Now they are setting together in jail. I imagine they have some right interesting discussions about greed."

The march faded as the brass band set off toward the river. Charles Noble stuffed a hand into his waistcoat. "Now. It is nearly impossible for us to provide details of your son's route."

"Nearly impossible."

The man turned to the window so that Reverend Stone could not see his face. "As I said, it is astonishing what effect money can have on men."

Reverend Stone nodded uncertainly. The bespectacled man looked away, fiddling with an inkwell. With a start the minister realized he was expected to offer the men money. A bribe. Heat rushed to his cheeks then coalesced in a knot at his throat. He clapped his hat on his head and said, "Thank you both for a remarkable discussion."

"You are welcome to call at any time," Noble said. "Any time at all."

Reverend Stone opened the door, then paused with his hand on the knob. To the bespectacled man he said, "You should be ashamed of your activities."

The man did not look up from the ledger.

"Both of you should be ashamed of your un-Christian activities. It is a disgrace. A disgrace to this city and a sin against God."

"Why, Reverend!" Charles Noble's voice was hollow with resentment. "Are you suggesting some form of impropriety? For if you are, I can assure you it exists solely and completely in your own imagination!"

"You know profoundly well what I am suggesting."

"Then I pity you, sir, for owning such a wicked imagination—and as a man of God, no less!"

Reverend Stone thought to respond then recognized the gesture's futility. He would accuse Charles Noble, and the man's taunts would turn bitter and scornful, his face grow crimson with fury. Noble would stride to the door and command Reverend Stone to leave, and the minister would be alone in a strange city, rootless, waiting for a son who might never return. The thought exhausted him.

He turned without a word and hurried down the long hallway, his heels echoing on the polished marble. Reverend Stone thought he had never heard a lonelier sound.

Detroit at sunset was quieter and more handsome than its daytime counterpart. Golden light lay draped against the city's steeples and signboards and wide shop windows. Shadows lengthened like silhouette cuttings from news vendors and stevedores. The river brightened, then burst into a ribbon of glimmering spangles. Reverend Stone wandered from Woodward Avenue to Michigan then out to the immigrant neighborhoods, with their billiard parlors and flimsy houses and crowded saloons, voices pouring from every open window, children squealing at play along the gutter. His son had likely walked these same cluttered streets. The thought was accompanied by a deep, familiar ache.

He had never understood why Elisha had left Newell. The boy had been melancholy during the months before his departure—though no more melancholy, Reverend Stone supposed, than any boy whose mother lay on her sickbed. Yet even as a child Elisha had been difficult to gauge. He would sing, wide-eyed, throughout Sunday morning services; yet when the bell rang for afternoon services he was nowhere to be found. At sunset Elisha would slip through the parsonage's back door, his pockets filled with muddy pebbles, and Reverend Stone would scold the boy, watch him retreat slump-shouldered down the hallway. He understood his son's impulse toward solitude; what he could not understand was his lack of faith.

Other boys his age had heard the call. James Davidson had stumbled down the meetinghouse aisle one Sunday, and the next week made a profession of faith before the congregation. Oscar Phelps at a tent revival in Springfield, crawling on his knees to the candlelit platform as the crowd wailed. George Lowrie whimpering in the middle of Mill Street, his face drawn in fear and awe. Shiny red apples lay scattered at his feet. Later the boy explained that a divine wind had overwhelmed his senses.

Reverend Stone had always assumed that his son would follow him, first to the seminary in Cambridge then to his own congregation in a town like Newell, to his own worries about collection plates and Baptists and unbelievers, his own unwritten sermons. But when Elisha prayed he seemed filled with fear. The minister watched the boy, mumbling silently in his dim bedroom, his shadow a dark slash against the wall. The sight filled Reverend Stone with guilty confusion. He could not comprehend how he had failed his son. And he could not comprehend how his son had failed him.

He spent the next days inquiring at boardinghouses with the faint hope of stumbling onto Elisha's past dwelling. He took lunch in a rude dining hall, shoulder-to-shoulder with German laborers. The meat was greasy and ill-cooked but delicious. Afternoons, he bought a mug of bitter coffee and walked along the quay, fingering the coins in his pocket. Nineteen dollars: enough to buy passage on a steamer to Sault Ste. Marie, but then . . . what? He had no map or guide, no notion of the boy's whereabouts. Reverend Stone allowed himself to consider the possibility of paying Charles Noble. The man would demand forty dollars, perhaps fifty; the minister might find day labor, or borrow money from the local congregation. The thoughts sat uneasily in his mind until he pushed them away.

On the Thursday after his arrival in Detroit Reverend Stone emerged from the dining hall onto a crowded sidewalk, and in the shadow of an approaching figure felt a glint of recognition. As the man passed he realized it was Jonah Crawley.

He hurried beside the fellow. "I seem to have no trouble locating you in a crowd. It must be a strange form of magnetism."

Jonah Crawley seemed genuinely pleased. "Reverend Stone! Again a pleasant surprise! I trust you found suitable accommodation in the city?"

The minister smiled, thinking of his bare, windowless room. "Suitable enough, compared to my last."

"You'll find Detroit to be a bit rougher-hewn than Buffalo. The trouble of course is foreigners—Germans and Irish, mainly. Italians, too. It's a wonder my daughter and I accomplish any civilized business."

"Do you?"

Crawley's expression fell momentarily. "There is a strange amount of loss lingering over this city. Our enterprise tends to thrive on loss."

"As does mine."

"Then we are alike. As I figured all along."

The man offered his hand as a farewell gesture, and Reverend Stone said, "I wonder if you might care for a dram?"

Crawley's face registered a note of surprise. "Why, I can't imagine why I wouldn't."

Jonah Crawley led the minister to a small, empty saloon where they stood at an oak bar strewn with sand, facing a mirror speckled near to blackness. Crawley chatted about the immigrant problem while Reverend Stone drank a glass of cider. The trouble, apparently, was not a surplus of foreigners but rather a lack of regulation on which religions might be legally practiced. Irish Catholics found assimilation near-impossible while their English Protestant brethren had no trouble whatever. Similarly he had never met a Norwegian who was not bright, hardworking, cheerful and industrious, and all of them good Protestants with a loathing for things Romish. Jonah Crawley rapped his knuckles against the bar for emphasis, downed a shot of whiskey. He seemed the sort of man who did not require a partner to hold an enjoyable conversation. Finally Reverend Stone interrupted to ask after his daughter, Adele, and the man paused. "What about Adele?"

By way of response Reverend Stone found himself telling Crawley about Elisha. About the boy's quiet watchfulness. About his days spent roaming the creek edge, alone, instead of frolicking with other boys. About his lies regarding school, his theft from the Sunday collection and mercantile, his mussed, empty bed one May morning. About the letter arriving three years later, its regretful tone unlike anything Reverend Stone might have expected. Finally he told Jonah Crawley about the public land office and his conversation with Charles Noble. Crawley tried unsuccessfully to stifle a guffaw. He rubbed his hands together.

"I see the dilemma! Luckily one easily solved."

"I am not inclined to solve it the way Noble suggests. No decent man would." Reverend Stone immediately regretted the righteousness in his tone.

"What will you do otherwise? Await your boy's return to Detroit?"

"I don't know that he will return. I plan to travel to the northern territory, to inquire after the expedition—surely someone must know their route."

Jonah Crawley scrutinized Reverend Stone as if examining a banknote for counterfeit traces. He could not seem to remove the smile from his face. He said, "Perhaps I might speak with Charles Noble on your behalf."

"I would never suggest you do that."

"I might do it anyway, to satisfy my curiosity. And then you might offer me consideration, as a measure of your gratitude."

Reverend Stone's heart fluttered with excitement. "I am staying at Mrs. Barbeau's on Miami Avenue. I expect I will be in the city only a few days more."

Crawley drained his glass and squinted at the empty bottom. "Well, then. Perhaps we'll speak yet again."

The men stepped from the saloon into a soft drizzle, the sun shining brilliantly despite the rain. The street was empty save for a Negro porter asleep on his feet outside the Commander Hotel. Crawley pulled his hat brim low and said, "I wonder do you have any engagements this evening?"

Reverend Stone nearly laughed. "Nary a one!"

The man turned up his collar as he paced backward down the sidewalk. "Come to 23 Sixth Street! Second story, above the sweet shop. You'll see something truly astonishing. That I promise!"

Reverend Stone raised a hand as the man disappeared down the street. He started toward his boardinghouse, and as his elation faded it distilled into something darker, melancholy muddled by guilt. He decided to attribute the feeling to the weather.

He paced the damp room until sunset, then stood in the dark awhile listening to rain tap against the windowpanes. On the pallet lay a cheap edition of Catlin's *Letters and Notes on the Manners, Customs and Condition of the North American Indians;* Reverend Stone had read a passage describing a corn-planting ritual, in which a squaw dashed through newly sown fields at midnight, naked and howling, her chemise dragged behind her through the soil. The description had unnerved him. Reverend Stone had riffled through the pages then tossed the book aside.

He rose and located his brogans and jacket and hat, then made his way down to the dark street. He walked down Miami Avenue to Grand River, then followed an alleyway that opened onto a courtyard smelling of night soil and rotten cabbage. A bareheaded woman wearing a ragged cloak watched him from beneath an awning. Reverend Stone nodded to her, and without smiling she hiked her skirts above her stocking tops. He turned quickly away. He hurried down Fort Street and walked several blocks to Sixth. He was in the Irish quarter now, with its saloons and churches, its brightly painted houses crowded like rows of teeth. A man's rich tenor spilled from an upstairs window, singing "The Minstrel Boy."

A signboard leaned beside the door of number 23, displaying a sodden broadsheet.

THE RENOWNED & PRODIGIOUS MISS ADELE CRAWLEY

SPIRITUALIST MEDIUM

CONTACTS THE DEARLY DEPARTED WITHOUT FAIL

NEW YORK—BOSTON—LONDON—PHILADELPHIA

Reverend Stone stepped inside and ascended a creaking stairway to the second story and a closed wooden door. Murmured voices seeped through the doorframe. The sound was like that of an anxious mob awaiting a verdict. As the minister listened a tapping began, followed by a woman's pained cry; then the crowd's drone rose to swallow the cry. He slowly opened the door.

Adele Crawley sat at a small table in the room's center, her white-gloved hands flat on a black tablecloth, candlelight shadowing her closed eyes. She looked to be nearly asleep. Across the table a Negro woman in a high-collared dress sat with her fists clenched at her throat, eyes wide with fear, sweat gleaming on her gaunt cheeks. Figures filled the large room, crowding the women. The air was hot from the crush of bodies.

"Pray ask about the housen stuff. Ask about the mirrors and the nice combs and the pearly earbobs."

Adele Crawley's lips parted as though she were about to speak. Veins wound down her forehead like rivers on a faded map. A quick, muffled tapping emanated from the floor, followed by a single loud rap. Adele's brow tightened. "He says he can see them."

"Tell him the pearly earbobs! Ask him are they in the keeping room or in the parlor. Pray ask him!"

The crowd jostled toward the table, their whispers growing to hushed shouts. At the room's edge a man scrabbled onto a windowsill for a better view. A soft tap rose from the floorboards. The sound was like a touch from velvet-gloved knuckles. "He says they are in the parlor."

The woman whimpered, "Oh my Lord my Lord my sweet Lord."

"He is fading now."

"Ask him about the nice combs! Tell him the nice combs from his mammy's stuff! Pray ask him, please!"

"He is becoming fainter before my eyes. He is waving farewell now. He is smiling." Candlelight flickered over Adele's waxy skin. Her eyelids fluttered, then slowly opened. She withdrew her hands from the table and placed them in her lap. "He is gone."

The Negro woman slumped forward as a pair of men rushed from the crowd. She stamped her feet and wailed, a forlorn keening. The men hauled her upright and ushered her past the minister and out the door, mumbling low consoling phrases, a barefoot Negro boy trailing behind. Her screams echoed in the stairwell. Reverend Stone's throat twitched and he bent to still the cough. When he straightened Adele Crawley was staring at him.

"Reverend Stone. Please."

A tall, hatless Irishman stepped to the table and shouted, "I's next on that docket! You swore you'd take as come, and I's here nearly—"

Adele silenced him with a shake of her head. She turned back to Reverend Stone. The crowd parted, and the minister felt himself tugged and pushed toward the room's center, voices urging him forward, a young girl yanking at his trouser leg. He approached the table and sat across from the woman. He smiled at Adele Crawley as he would an infant.

"Would you like to converse with her?"

The minister cocked his head.

"Your wife. Would you like to converse with your wife now?"

His smile faltered. The girl's eyes glistened with pleasure. He said, "I would. Of course I would."

Foolishness. Now she would stamp the floorboards with her heel, utter platitudes vague enough to please a legion. Reverend Stone scanned the crowd for Jonah Crawley, but outside the globe of candlelight the room was dark. Foolishness and blasphemy. He recited a silent prayer of contrition.

Adele Crawley closed her eyes and said, "I was near to you in earthly life, my dear, and am nearer still to you now." The girl's expression tightened; then a wave of fear seemed to pass through her. The crowd pressed toward the small table. The room smelled overpoweringly of bodies. At last Adele relaxed to blankness.

"I see her now. She is very beautiful. So young, and so very beautiful. She has the most beautiful blue eyes."

She is guessing, Reverend Stone thought. She has guessed Ellen's eye color, nothing more. Sweat slid down his back.

"She yearns for you."

"How do you know?"

"She is telling me. She says that she yearns for you and she does not blame you."

A breeze caressed Reverend Stone's cheek, and for an instant he thought he might faint. "There is no reason for her to blame me."

"She does not blame you and she says neither does your son blame you. He forgives you your selfishness. He knows it was borne from love."

The minister's throat drew taut. "Stop."

"She knows you are greatly frightened. She says you must quiet your fears. You must trust in His guidance of your journey, and quiet your fears."

Reverend Stone stood, the chair scraping the floorboards. The crowd hushed. "Stop. Stop saying these ridiculous words."

"She says she feels wonderful where she is. She is consumed with love, completely."

"Stop. Please."

"She says her cough has vanished utterly."

Reverend Stone's stomach fell away. He sagged into the chair. A faint smile curled the corners of the girl's lips.

"Her cough is vanished and she is consumed with love. She wants you to know that she feels wonderful. You may ask her a question, if you'd like."

Adele Crawley's eyes skittered beneath their lids. A woman in the crowd cried, *Lord bless this child!* then a hiss stifled her words.

"Ask her . . ." Reverend Stone licked his parched lips. "Ask her about Elisha. Ask her where he is."

A rattle started in the floor then rose to the table, the candle flame shuddering as the sound sharpened to a *tap tock tock tock*. Reverend Stone jerked his hands from the tabletop. Adele slowly cocked her head, as though nodding toward sleep. "She sees him in a dark place. He is in a dark place among strangers, and it is not his home. He is awful far from home."

"Ask her if he is well."

Outside a whip cracked, then a horse whinnied sharply. The crowd closed around the table, a hip bumping Reverend Stone's shoulder, a hand brushing his neck. Adele Crawley leaned forward as if straining to hear. "He is not among the dearly departed. But she is concerned for him. He is in some sort of danger, from other men. She is very deeply concerned."

"Ask her who the danger is from! Is it from Natives, or his companions? Ask her."

"She cannot see the man's face. It is a white man. It is not a Native."

"Ask her what the—"

"She is fading now. She is drawing away."

"Ask her if he is happy!"

"She is waving farewell and drawing away. I can see nearly through her. She is so very beautiful, her beautiful blue eyes."

"Tell her I mourn her daily," Reverend Stone whispered. His face tingled with numbness. "Tell her I am sorry. *Please.* You must tell her!"

Adele Crawley opened her eyes. "She says she awaits you."

Three

The party canoed along a leafy shoreline, the weather dry and cool, the sun's warmth on their shoulders. To Elisha the lakeshore resembled the coast of Massachusetts: knobs of granite bearded with widow's-cross, framing long, sandy strips of beach. Thick fringe of hobblebush below columns of beech and yellow birch and red maple, grading upward to a string of low hills. Elisha paddled absentmindedly, distracted by the scene's beauty.

Sheldrakes and loons skimmed alongside the canoe. The loons darted toward the craft then ducked beneath the lake's surface, reappeared ten yards distant with a call like a child's whinnying laugh. Elisha had seen loons behave likewise at the millpond in Newell, though there the birds' actions seemed driven by terror. But here the loons' behavior matched the region's joyful nature: it was as though they'd glided into a forgotten corner of Eden.

He recalled an essay he'd read in the Springfield *Intelligencer*, claiming that red Indians gradually lightened in complexion when exposed to white society. Their demeanor and character, the author claimed, were likewise improved. The essay's logic was simple: that a Native's complexion became paler due to decreased time spent outdoors; that his character was elevated by the comforts of civilized life. Now Elisha imagined a Chippewa brave standing in Detroit's Grand Circus, amid manure and heaped-up slops and rushing carriages, deafened by shouts and clanging bells and whining street organs, choked by dust and smoke. The essayist was wrong, Elisha realized. Natives could only become more savage when exposed to civilization.

They had encountered Chippewas twice during the previous week. The first was a canoe following them for an hour at dawn then disappearing, only to reappear when they put ashore for lunch at Vermillion Point. Elisha had moved beside Mr. Brush, nervously monitoring the man's reaction to the approaching craft. A sour-looking brave disembarked with a graybeard mongrel at his feet, followed by a squaw with her hair cropped short and a cradleboard strapped to her back. The cradle was filled with black feathers. The brave offered a haunch of rancid venison in trade for whiskey or gunpowder; Professor Tiffin gave the man a carrot of tobacco and a neck bone for the hound then sent him away. Later Susette explained that the black feathers indicated the death of an infant. The poor woman was in mourning.

The second encounter was a Chippewa camp laid out along a horseshoe inlet. A half-dozen lodges lay like black shells on the grassy beach, Native women moving among them while a group of men breakfasted around a cookfire. Smoke rose from the fires in shimmering threads. As the party's canoe approached, a few braves emerged from the lodges and stood at the lake edge. It was the Yellow River band, Susette said, her husband's grandmother's band, at their summer fishing ground. At this Professor Tiffin stopped paddling, said, "Would you like to pause for a visit?" The woman shook her head.

That next afternoon they made camp at the edge of a burned-out birch forest. Susette staked the tents then fetched a kettle of water, hauled out sacks of peas and rice; Professor Tiffin prepared himself a mug of tea then started westward down the shoreline. Mr. Brush leveled his telescope and fixed on a nearby peak. Elisha recorded the inclination in Brush's fieldbook, then assisted the man in measuring barometric pressure.

The tasks complete, the boy took up his own fieldbook and wandered eastward, pausing to scrutinize pebbles of hornblende and smoky green agates. Seabirds floated like bits of ash over the lake. Some ways up the beach he came upon a huge, knobbed boulder that was sheared flat along a vertical face, as though it had been cut by a chisel. Parallel grooves ran like scars across the face.

It was igneous rock streaked with flesh-colored veins of feldspar. Elisha compared the boulder's characteristics to those of granite: mottled gray-white appearance; large, coarse pores; too hard to scratch with the tip of a blade. But how to explain the grooves? A pleasant eagerness stirred inside the boy. He opened his fieldbook and wrote:

June 22, 1844

Here at the lake's edge there is a most intriguing granitic boulder, with diameter equal to that of a carriage wheel, and parallel gouges along a vertical face to a depth of one-quarter of an inch, at an angle of approximately 20° with the horizontal. The grooves suggest the action of irresistible force, such as waves— yet how might water create such sharp relief? For surely waves would tend to polish a surface, rather than score it. Thus another mechanism must be at work.

Perhaps Professor Agassiz's theory of glacial action might be here in evidence? The grooves might have been formed by the vast power of a glacier, inexorably surging north-eastward. The thought of such unyielding power is at odds with the tranquil sublimity of the scene, where the serenity of the lake and idle frolic of sheldrake and loon lead one to imagine that there is no force on Earth greater than the breeze on one's cheek, or one's own breath.

Elisha read over the description with gathering impatience. Mr. Brush would disapprove of his dreamy suggestions of beauty; Professor Tiffin would scoff at the mundanity of his observations. The description contained neither facts nor ideas, just a jumbled amalgam of both. As a scientist he made a decent writer of travel narratives.

He shut the fieldbook and started back along the beach. The sun had shifted behind a veil of clouds, and the day's light was wintry and diffuse, as though filtered through a frost-coated windowpane. As

Elisha neared camp he saw Susette sitting cross-legged beside the cookfire. She was hunched over a magazine.

The boy approached quietly. When he was ten yards distant the woman looked up, then shoved the journal aside and took up a long spoon. The magazine appeared to be a tattered *Godey's Lady's Book.*

"That must be a pretty good issue. You've read it nearly to shreds."

She pinched pepper from a cotton bag and sprinkled it into the cookpot. A hint of color had risen to her freckled cheeks. "It is a fine issue. I bought it in Sault Ste. Marie before we departed—I look at it only when there is no more work to do."

"I don't mind a bit if you look at the magazine! Nor do Mr. Brush or Professor Tiffin, I suspect. They'll be happy no matter what, so long as the stew is hot and the fire stays lit."

Susette's expression tightened as she stirred the cookpot. She tasted the stew then added another pinch of pepper.

"Shall I read to you?"

Her stirring paused. Surely she doesn't have much English, Elisha thought, maybe a winter or two at a French Catholic schoolhouse, learning the catechism by rote from a foreign priest. Maybe she'd learned how to write her name, maybe just her mark. Her reading skills were likely no better.

She handed him the magazine. It was open to a page of watercolored illustrations of women's capes and collars. Elisha said, "This one?" Susette nodded. He knelt beside her and cleared his throat.

" 'Number two is a collar à la Vandyke. It is of guipure lace, and fastened with a knot of ribbons. Neck ribbons are a distinguishing peculiarity of the season. They are worn of very bright colors, usually embroidered, and tied close at the throat. The square flat knot, usually called a "sailor's tie," is most fashionable. It is suitable for a dinner dress, or for a small evening company.' "

He glanced at Susette as he turned the page. She had been more sociable of late, engaging in suppertime chatter about the weather and their course; Elisha had begun to wonder if her warmth was directed toward him in particular. But now she sat straight-backed, peering out at the lake. She seemed to be feigning indifference while listening intently.

It's her Native blood, Elisha thought, bringing forth an emotionless Native demeanor. White women seemed simple: they smiled when they were happy and frowned when they were sad. But Natives were as stony and inscrutable as sleepwalkers. He could not imagine what the woman might be thinking.

"This next page is just an essay about points of etiquette at the theater. Shall I skip ahead?"

She shook her head. "Read it, please."

"Then. 'Several queries regarding proper modes of demonstrating approval at the theater have been submitted to us for decision. We must strongly insist that loud thumping with canes and umbrellas, in demonstration of applause, is decidedly rude. Clapping the hands is quite as efficient, and neither raises dust to soil the dresses of ladies, nor hubbub enough to deafen them. In Europe such a display would be frowned upon, if not outright mocked.' "

Susette was absorbed in the narrative, the spoon frozen above the cookpot. Elisha asked, "Have you ever been to a theater?"

"My mother," she said, resuming her stirring. "She went twice to the Pearl Theater on Queen Street in Toronto. She saw British actors play *As You Like It*."

"*As You Like It*! That's a good one—one of the best, actually. Rosalind and Orlando and Duke Frederick, and Touchstone and Jaques and all the rest. And Rosalind dressing up as Ganymede to court Orlando, and accidentally wooing Phebe. And then the end in the forest with the weddings and the songs."

"Yes. My mother told me the story."

"Of course," Elisha said quickly. "I haven't seen the play, either—I've just read it, on account of my own mother. She's partial to Shakespeare—I've read nearly all of his plays due to her. She's still back in Newell, Massachusetts."

"My mother is in St. Catharines. She is half Canadian. She's as white as you."

Elisha nodded. Susette's hair was unbraided and lay draped over her shoulders, the tendrils at her throat like a beautiful necklace. With her loose hair and leathery hands she could pass as a Massachusetts farm girl, sun-browned after the tobacco harvest. Or a farm girl stolen into Chippewa captivity, raised to forget her own language and customs. Despite the notion's absurdity a tingle of excitement moved through Elisha. She might have been seized from her mother in St. Catharines, brought to the Sault and forced to marry against her will. Elisha might be her rescuer to civilization.

An image rose in his mind of him and Susette entering the meeting-house in Newell arm in arm, every head turning as conversation quieted then ceased. Their footfalls echoed in the cavernous room. From the pulpit Reverend Stone stared down at the pair, agape. The image pleased Elisha. In white society Susette would be viewed as a Native; in Native society she was no doubt viewed as white. Neither of two, the hybrid's curse.

"I will go to the theater soon," Susette said. "In Detroit there is the Rogers Theater on Woodward Avenue. In Buffalo the Cascade Theater on Clinton Street."

"With your pay from this summer you can go as often as you please. Every night for a month, even."

Susette smiled. "Perhaps I shall."

"You must tell me if you go in Detroit. I'll likely be staying in a boardinghouse near Woodward Avenue—we could go together, see *As You Like It*."

The woman's smile quivered, a barely perceptible tremor. Wildness flashed in her eyes. She took the magazine from Elisha and looked away.

"If you sit in the wrong part of the theater there are rowdies and single men. I could escort you, show you the safe places to sit. People would believe I was your husband and wouldn't trouble you. Wouldn't trouble us, I mean."

He understood that he was acting brazenly but could not stop himself. A beautiful woman traveling with a party of men, without her husband—it was inexplicable, no matter if she was white or Native or half-breed. Without looking at the boy Susette resumed stirring the cookpot.

"Perhaps." Her voice betrayed a hint of emotion. "Perhaps I will go in Detroit."

He moved close to her and took up the metal spoon. He tasted the stew: whitefish with peas and wild rice, flavored with smoke and pepper. Elisha's hands were trembling. He was overwhelmed by a desire to touch the woman. He said, "Tell me the Chippewa word for tobacco."

"Why?"

"Because I am curious." He smiled awkwardly. "I am curious about your people—or your mother's people, I suppose."

She regarded Elisha without speaking.

"Just as you are curious to learn about the theater," Elisha continued in a rush, "I am curious to learn about your people. I have never met a Chippewa woman, and I figured perhaps—"

"Asemaa."

"Asemaa! What about . . . what about the word for canoe?"

"Jiimaan."

"Jiimaan. Jiimaan." The boy turned the soft vowels over in his mouth. "A beautiful word."

Susette fingered the worn *Godey's Lady's Book*. "There are many words that are not beautiful. Just as in English, or French. Chippewa has no special beauty."

"Well. I don't believe you."

"You must."

"Love." He touched the woman's wrist. "What is your word for love?"

A shout rose from down the beach and Elisha bolted upright: Professor Tiffin was running toward them along the lake's edge. He was waving what appeared to be a specimen pouch in the air. The man stumbled in a wash of surf, then with a hoot he hauled himself up and continued forward.

Susette rose, her gaze fixed on Elisha. The two were very close; he smelled her breath and her hair's pungent grease. The boy's breathing caught. Susette shook her head, and as she did her eyes dulled, as though a light inside them had flickered out.

"We have no word for love," she said, then moved past Elisha toward the lake's edge.

The drawing was of a man, a hollow-faced figure with upraised arms and jagged hair. A plume rose from the man's mouth and snaked toward a large dome with a flag at its peak. Beside the dome was a row of eight parallel grooves, and beside the grooves was a web of curved lines, like veins, spreading across the curling scrap of birch bark. The lines were traced in a rich red pigment that might have been cherry juice or ocher, or blood.

"Remarkably serendipitous!" Professor Tiffin said. "I was strolling along the lakeshore beyond that outcrop, not two hundred yards distant, searching for a petroglyph that Colcroft described in *Chippewa Researches*. I was scanning the upper rock face—the petroglyph is reportedly located fifteen yards above lake level—and I happened to glance down. There it was! Trussed to a bough staked into the ground, plain as pudding. I had nearly trampled it underfoot."

"What do the figures represent?" Elisha asked.

By way of response Tiffin sighed with pleasure, rubbing the soles of his bare feet. He was seated cross-legged beside the cookfire, the birch-bark scroll on the sand before him. The man's nose was sunblistered and peeling, his muttonchops grown to carroty tufts. Behind him Mr. Brush reclined against a pack of stores, absorbed in oiling his rifle.

"In fact, the message is simple to decipher. Observe: a figure of a man with a banner streaming from his mouth, as if in proclamation.

Next, an image of a Native lodge—likely a Midewiwin medicine lodge. These curving lines, here, represent streams or rivers. And these grooves are a temporal counting method, describing the passage of days or weeks. Thus, it is an announcement to passing Chippewas that a medicine lodge is being constructed near a particular river, and that all are invited to attend the ceremony in five days' time."

Susette passed mugs of steaming stew, and Professor Tiffin swallowed a spoonful then puffed to cool his mouth. "My dear woman," he said, "would you agree with my interpretation?"

"I do not know. My mother never wrote with drawings. She had French."

"Precisely!" Tiffin said. "You see, the Chippewa people have lost the ability to communicate with symbols—and thus they have no written record of their own history. Imagine! They cannot answer the most fundamental questions: How did you come here? When did you come here? And why?"

"Please excuse me." Mr. Brush rose with his mug and started down the beach. The day had darkened beneath a scrim of clouds, and now a breeze swirled in and flared the cookfire. Lake Superior's swells were tipped with greenish foam.

"A marvelous scroll, truly. The pigment is astonishing—a mixture of hematite-rich clay and pine sap. Quite indelible." Professor Tiffin turned to Susette and whispered, "Madame, your culinary preparations are delicious, however *perhaps* you could employ a bit less pepper."

"But surely not all Chippewas have forgotten their language," Elisha said. "Otherwise no one could have written that message."

Tiffin grinned condescendingly as stew rilled down his chin. The sight amazed Elisha: the unkempt hair and clothes, the vagabond manners; yet with it a confidence near to arrogance. He was like a court jester, the boy thought, or a wise fool in one of Shakespeare's comedies.

The man dipped a second portion of stew. The Chippewa people, he explained, use pictographic writing for mundane communications;

however they also employ pictography to maintain the historical record. These writings are recorded by members of the Midewiwin, a mystical society—a sort of Native Masonic order—who etch historical narratives on scrolls and stone tablets, which they bury in sacred locations. Over time the Midewiwin have dwindled in numbers, and the locations of the buried tablets have been lost. And thus the ancient historical record has vanished.

"I have read about buried tablets," Elisha said. "The one in Albany, a few years back. And the one in western Virginia—the broken tablet with the prayer carved on its face."

"The Grave Creek tablet!" Professor Tiffin's cheeks were pink with excitement. "The Grave Creek tablet is mere pottery, my boy—this summer we will unearth tablets describing the history of the Native people *after the deluge*. They will explain the Chippewas' connection to the ancient Christians, and the mystery of their arrival to America! We will discover a Native Genesis, if you will!"

Mr. Brush had returned to camp during Tiffin's monologue and stood with arms folded, listening. Now the man snorted. "A Native Genesis! That is simply too rich."

Tiffin froze with the mug at his lips. "As you are no doubt aware, the question of the origins of the Native people is rather crucial. Smith and Harlan have written on the subject. Constantine Rafinesque as well. Though perhaps you've been too busy collecting pebbles to notice."

"You are suggesting that howling red savages are the lost sons of Moses! Natives *have no religion*—they are incapable. The nearest a Chippewa ever comes to Christ is when he passes a church en route to the saloon!" Mr. Brush nodded to Susette Morel. "I refer only to full-blood Natives, Madame."

Tiffin turned from Brush and addressed the flickering cookfire. "Your mind is fouled by bigotry. A pathetic condition for a scientific gentleman."

He is not intimidated by the man, Elisha marveled. Brush had been with Brown at Sackets Harbor during the Second War for

Independence; Elisha imagined him shouting orders from horseback above a smoky field, his soldiers motivated by fear rather than affection. Nervous, as Elisha was, at the prospect of disappointing the man. Tiffin was either very brave or very foolish.

"Mr. Brush, Professor Tiffin," Elisha said, "why don't we all simply abide each other's opinions. Maybe both of you—"

"I refuse to pay you any more mind," Brush muttered. "That our legislature is financing your efforts is enough to put me off supper." He tossed his mug into the empty cookpot and Elisha started at the clatter. "Well! I will spend my days analyzing this region's topography and timber and mineral evidence, and you will hunt for buried treasure. In that case I propose a wager: at the expedition's conclusion we will independently submit reports to an impartial authority in Detroit—say, the Young Men's Society—and ask them to judge whose work is of greater value to science."

"Excellent! The loser will publish a notice in the *City Examiner,* apologizing for squandering public funds. We shall wager our scientific reputations."

"I would prefer you offer something of value, but so be it."

Tiffin stepped around the cookfire, his trousers shifting to reveal a ragged tear, a seam of floury skin. Brush bent forward with a tight smile, a lick of hair fallen loose from his oiled coif.

The two men shook hands.

They paddled past the Two Hearted River and Sucker River into a range of high, steep dunes. The party spent an afternoon measuring the peaks' heights, then climbing the highest dune to achieve a vista. Ospreys watched them from deadwood logs half-buried in the sand. The terrain was yellow siliceous sand mixed with nuggets of hornblende and limestone; the rocks were glassy volcanic fragments and variegated mounds of sandstone. Elisha dutifully recorded his observations, allowing himself a single painterly description: of quartz pebbles the size of pigeon's eggs littering the beach.

Susette shot a brace of fat wood ducks and spitted them over an open fire. Mr. Brush and Professor Tiffin toasted her health with mugs of water, their previous day's argument seemingly forgotten. Despite Elisha's attempts at conversation Susette said little, her attention fixed on the roasting birds. *She understands everything,* he realized: *my daydreams, my ridiculous desires.* He knew he should apologize for his brazenness but the notion left him heartsick. He retired to his tent without finishing supper.

That next morning they came into a region of sandstone cliffs streaked with pink and violet and deep, bottle-glass green. These were the Pictured Rocks, according to Tiffin, the colors caused by chemical reactions of lichens with minerals in the stone. Swallows flitted among cliffside nests. Each man reached for his fieldbook while Susette steadied the canoe, singing, *"A la claire fontaine, M'en allant promener..."* The wind was still, the sun barely strong enough to warm the skin. They sketched rapidly, Tiffin brushing his scene with watercolors; finally the three presented their work to Susette for jury. She grinned, declaring Professor Tiffin's drawing the finest, though only for his access to paint. Mr. Brush said nothing, rubbing his jaw to conceal a smile.

They had been among the Pictured Rocks for an hour when the lake grew suddenly restless. Sooty cumulus clouds lay heaped to the west. A drizzle began that slid beneath Elisha's waxed cape and set his teeth to chatter. Waves chopped against the canoe's bow.

The party doubled their pace, searching for a landing site among the cliff walls. A vague, vaporous column moved toward them; then the rain thickened to a downpour and thunder crackled overhead. "We must land immediately!" Tiffin shouted. "We will be swamped!" Water sluiced over the gunwales. Elisha dug with the paddle, his shoulders burning, his throat gripped by fear. Behind him, Mr. Brush grunted at every stroke. The canoe rolled and Tiffin shrieked with terror.

"There!" Brush steered the canoe toward a stretch of low shoreline between the cliffs. It appeared to be the entrance of a river. Tongues of lightning flickered over the forest. When the canoe neared the river's entrance Mr. Brush leapt into the lake, waves licking at his chin, and then Elisha and Professor Tiffin and Susette splashed beside him, groaning as they hoisted the canoe over a sandbar and into the placid river.

They sat on the riverbank for a long while, hunched against the rain. No one spoke. Elisha rested his head on his folded arms, over-whelmed by fatigue. At last Professor Tiffin said, "We might have, perhaps..." His sentence trailed to silence.

The river was umber-colored and smelled sharply of balsam. They glided past rows of pine stumps, the sawn faces like grave tablets in a cemetery. Some ninety yards upstream they came alongside a clearing with five split-log cabins set in a half-circle around a small frame house. A bare flagpole stood beside the frame house's door.

It was a white man's camp. The party landed the canoe then stood motionless, as though confused by the sight; then Mr. Brush rapped at the frame house's door and called, "Hello in there!" Silence; a hermit thrush's call. Brush knocked again, then stepped back and stamped at the door's edge. It swung wide, smacking the inside wall. Professor Tiffin stepped past him into the house.

Inside it was warm and stank of musk and smoke. Susette lit a splint to reveal a low room dusted with ash, shriveled herbs hanging from the ceiling joists, a charred backlog crumbled in the fireplace. Above the mantel hung a tin-framed print of King George. In the far wall was a single small window, the bull's-eye panes opaque with soot.

"Abandoned fur post," Brush said. "This must have been the com-mis' house." He toed a mound of beaver pelts beside the door. "These must not have been worth the burden of transport when they de-parted. Or else they departed unexpectedly."

"I remember a fur post here," Susette said. "It was the Hudson's Bay Company. I do not know why they departed."

"You are insinuating that they were massacred, but I do not care," Tiffin said to Brush. He moved to the woodbox beside the hearth and rooted inside for kindling. "I propose that we dine immediately. I am near starved."

"Someone has laid us a banquet."

Brush nodded toward a sawbuck table in the corner. A plate and knife and mug sat before a pewter platter that appeared to be draped with a mink's pelt. Then Elisha realized it was the remnants of a meal, lumps of meat or fish furred with black mold that had crawled over the platter's lip onto the table.

"Pay that no mind," Professor Tiffin said. "The fact that they were untidy does not mean they were scalped by rabid Chippewas. Elisha, fetch some water while I kindle a fire."

Susette prepared a quick meal of fried pork and corn mush and they fell to eating, sitting on beaver skins around the hearth, their grease-smeared faces flickering in the firelight. When the last bit of mush had been mopped up Professor Tiffin sighed, blotting his brow. "My dear woman," he said softly. "Your cookery skills would put Hestia herself to shame. Perfectly seasoned."

The man rose with a groan and ventured into the room's far corner. "Silver and red fox, fisher . . . black bear, by jay. Our host was a tolerably good trapper!" He took up a splint and ducked into a low storeroom, reappeared holding an earthenware jug. Tiffin twisted off the cork and brought it to his nose. "Whiskey! Indian whiskey, but whiskey nonetheless!"

"Curb yourself," Brush said. "That is home-brewed mash, for Natives. If you're lucky you'll only go blind."

Professor Tiffin took a sucking pull on the jug. "My sweet darling dear. Oh! I have missed you severely!"

"We may as well make camp," Elisha said. "These skins are likely the softest beds we'll see until September."

"Dickens!" Tiffin shouted. "Scott! Hemans!" He was kneeling beside the window, the splint illuminating a low bookshelf. The man's voice rose to a strangled pitch. "Pope! An entire library! English and French!"

He gathered an armload of books and spilled them before the hearth with a gleeful cackle. Elisha took up the jug and drank: the liquor was weak but seasoned with fiery red pepper. He coughed, blinking back tears.

"Is there Shakespeare?" the boy asked. "How about *As You Like It*?"

"A splendid choice! But unfortunately...here, instead we have *A Midsummer Night's Dream*. Even more appropriate! Madame Morel, you sit beside me, here. We shall read alternating parts."

The woman hesitated; then she sat beside Tiffin on a pile of skins. Elisha passed the jug and she sipped deeply, wiped her mouth with her wrist. She offered the jug to Mr. Brush; he scowled, then tipped it back and swallowed two long gulps. He gasped.

"Begin here," Tiffin said. "Act two, where Oberon encounters Titania in a wood near Athens. I shall read Oberon. You shall read the role of Titania."

She tilted the book toward the fire. "Titania. 'What, jealous Oberon. Fairies, skip hence. I have forsworn his bed and company.' "

"No, no—you don't announce who is speaking, you simply speak. And project your voice, as if to an enormous audience, like this." Professor Tiffin cleared his throat. " 'What, *jealous Oberon!* ' "

" 'What, *jealous Oberon!* Fairies, skip hence! I have forsworn his bed and company!' "

Elisha was frozen, mortified. Susette's reading was halting but clear, her pronunciation nearly perfect. In his mind's eye he saw himself kneeling beside her, reading like a schoolmaster from *Godey's Lady's Book* while she sat patiently. He swallowed a pull of whiskey. My good Lord, he thought, I am a fool.

" 'Tarry, *rash wanton*,' " Tiffin said. " 'Am I *not* thy lord?' "

" 'Then I must be thy lady! But I know when thou hast *stolen away* from fairy land, and in the shape of Corin sat all day, playing on pipes of *corn*, and versing love to amorous Phill...Phillida.' "

"Phillida, yes. Excellent!"

Pleasure flickered over Susette's face. She took up the whiskey jug and her eyes met Elisha's. She held his gaze as she drank.

The boy thought he had never seen a woman as lovely. Susette's color had risen, and in the firelight her skin was as burnished as an old penny. Elisha turned away, humiliated by his ardor. She was married and older and half Native; he was lonely and childish and a silly white fool. Above the mantel, King George's image regarded him with a disdainful smile. Then it occurred to Elisha that Susette had allowed him to read to her. That afternoon on the beach, when he'd asked to read her *Godey's Lady's Book:* she could have told him she read perfect English, sent him away with a scowl; but instead she'd offered him the magazine. She had sat quietly beside the cookfire, listening as Elisha read. Perhaps he was not such a fool.

" 'Why art thou here, come from the furthest steppe of India? But that, *forsooth,* the bouncing Amazon, your buckskinned mistress and your warrior love, to Theseus must be wedded, and you come to give their bed *joy* and *prosperity*!' "

" 'How canst thou thus *for shame,* Titania, glance at my credit with Hippolyta, knowing I know thy love to Theseus?' " Tiffin cackled again. "This is where it becomes rich! 'Didst thou *not* lead him through the glimmering night from Perigenia, whom he ravished? And make him with fair Aegle *break his faith,* with Ariadne and Antiopa?' "

Susette read about Oberon's forgeries of jealousy, of the wind pulling fogs from the sea to cover the land, of the seasons becoming mixed and confused. Of oxen straining at their yokes and green corn rotting in its husk. Her voice softened as she navigated the unfamiliar names. She read about a young boy, son of a mortal woman who'd died in his conception. " 'And for her sake do I rear up her boy,' " she said. " 'And for her sake I will not part with him.' "

She concluded the speech with a pained expression. "What happens to the woman and boy?"

Professor Tiffin closed the book. "Perhaps we shall learn that tomorrow."

A contented silence, broken by the fire's pop and hiss. At last Mr. Brush said, "I never cared overmuch for that play. The notion of fairies in the forest is too foolish to seriously consider."

"Not all stories need be serious," Tiffin said.

"They do need to be true, in some manner."

"Your idea of truth seems fixed in the literal. A story can be true without mirroring common life."

Mr. Brush's grunt was a grudging concession of the point. He unlaced his boots and placed them on the hearth, rolled his spare shirt into a pillow. With a sigh Professor Tiffin did the same. Susette rose, steadying herself on the mantel, then gathered the supper plates and stepped outside.

Elisha felt as though he were swimming in air. He stood, and the whiskey dragged him off balance. Professor Tiffin laughed. "Easy now, my healthy young friend!" Elisha took a sip of whiskey then moved to the open door, listening for Susette's quiet singing: *A la claire fontaine, M'en allant promener*... The chanson from that morning, a song about a beautiful fountain. Along the riverbank, black pines were silhouetted against a starry black sky. A barred owl called, the sound like a pup's whine.

He stepped out into the night. Susette was squatting at the river's edge, scrubbing the plates with sand. She rose at Elisha's approach, grinning drunkenly. *"Midsummer Night,"* she said, "I must write to my mother, she—" Elisha took the woman by the shoulders and kissed her on the mouth.

She stiffened, shoving the plates against his chest; then her body yielded. Her lips parted, the tip of her tongue touching the boy's teeth. She tasted of whiskey and salt. Elisha felt as though he was falling. He gripped her shoulders, her neck, her back, his hands running down her spine to her fleshy hips. Susette whimpered, tugging at the boy's hair. She twisted away and the plates clattered in the dirt, then she took Elisha's hand and hurried around the house's side, pulled him down to a patch of bare earth, whispered, "Here, this way, this way." The woman's breathing was shallow and fast. She turned away and rose onto her knees and forearms, reached behind herself and drew her skirts over her waist.

A shock arched through Elisha. The woman's back glowed like marble, the dimples above her bottom like twin kisses from a chisel. He touched the root of her spine and she groaned, grappling blindly behind herself. He fumbled with his trousers and with a jolt he was inside her. His lungs felt as though they would explode. He gasped, "My love—" then Susette shoved against him with a grunt. Elisha sensed himself on the edge of control. Susette drove the boy into her and he froze, trying to remain utterly still; then with a cry he emptied himself.

She pitched forward like she'd been struck. The woman lay motionless for several long moments, the rhythm of her breathing matching Elisha's; then she rose and slowly brushed the dirt from her skirts. Her cheeks shone with tears. Elisha touched her shoulder and she jerked away; then she rushed past him to the riverbank and gathered up the supper plates, ran to the door. She turned to Elisha. "I am sorry," she whispered hoarsely. "Please, I am so sorry." She stepped into the lit-up house.

"Queen Titania returns!" roared Tiffin.

Four

He had fallen into something of a routine, spending mornings at the quay sipping bitter coffee as he watched schooners nudge toward the pier, then walking up Franklin Street past the dance halls and rattrap hotels. Reverend Stone nodded to ladies in crinolines and Scottish stevedores and grubby charcoal peddlers, asked if they'd seen a boy of Elisha's description. The men squinted; the ladies offered apologetic smiles. He wandered from Beaubien to Saint Mary to Michigan to Cass, then back to the quay while the sun sank to an orange knot, the last ships approaching as the evening whistle offered an oboe hoot. Men watched from the pier, hands thrust in their trouser pockets, but despite their shared indolence no one spoke. A city of strangers. The thought did not entirely displease Reverend Stone.

Nights, he found himself back on Franklin Street. It was a narrow clay track lit by puddles of lamplight, loud with ill-tuned fiddles and crowded with Irish and Negroes and laborers and lawyers. The men were dirty-faced, drunk, their shirtfronts muddied and hats askew. Reverend Stone leaned against an awning post and feigned impatience as he watched them move from saloon to bowling parlor to brothel. He had never seen such a concentration of sentiment: bitter arguments and laughter and regretful stares and declarations of false love. Were there a meetinghouse and cemetery, Reverend Stone thought, Franklin Street would contain the breadth of human emotion.

He had seen seamy city blocks during his years in Cambridge, but only from the vantage of a passing buggy. Now he lingered on the street itself, studying the men's faces as they passed, smelling their whiskey breath. The most common expression was joy. A delicious reveling in transgression, the truant boy's thrill writ large. Reverend Stone wondered for the thousandth time why so much joy might be derived from sin. The question was accompanied by a familiar note of confusion: it seemed evidence of a fundamental error on His part.

That Saturday Reverend Stone was caught on Franklin Street during a cloudburst that left gentlemen cursing and ladies scurrying for the nearest awning. He stepped into a low wooden saloon. Inside, the day's light was swallowed by gloom, wood smoke rolling from a squat fireplace, the windowpanes caked with soot. Pairs of men sat at round tables, filling the air with the slap and rattle of dice. The room stank of fish oil and tallow, and the faint ammoniac stench of horse piss. A teamsters' haunt. No one looked up at Reverend Stone.

He found standing room at the bar and a creased *Evening Clarion*, ordered a glass of cider. The barman whistled "Hey, Betty Martin" as he flicked a dirty rag over the row of bottles. In Newell Reverend Stone had taken his daily cider at John Hensley's, but he had forgotten the excitement of an unfamiliar tavern. He shook open the newspaper, frowning to stifle a smile. Some time later he called for another cider, and as he did he glimpsed himself in the bar mirror: he was dressed in his traveling clothes, homespun dungarees and a worn linen shirt, and his appearance was that of a kindly old tobacco farmer come to market. The sight was startling, and oddly liberating.

He'd nearly finished the second cider when a man leaned beside him and said, "Care to rest your feet?" He was tall and pink-faced, his hair hanging in snowy ropes, white mustache tinted brown with tobacco juice. He introduced himself as Leander Clarke. Reverend Stone followed him to a table near the fireplace, jammed the *Evening Clarion* beneath a wobbly leg. The man sucked the fringe of his mustache as he withdrew a deck of cards.

Leander Clarke explained a version of brag with a blind first bet and suicide kings as floaters, nickel ante, the only curb to raises being a man's courage. Before Reverend Stone could protest Clarke said, "Of course, we may as well play for honor alone. I expect you saw Tuesday's comet."

"I did not—I read a description in the *City Examiner*. Did you see it yourself?"

"A wondrous sight! I was standing outside my privy when it passed. My first thought was from Psalms: 'The heavens declare the glory of God, and the firmament sheweth his handiwork.' " Leander Clarke grinned. His teeth were black, nuggets of anthracite nestled in puckered gums. "And imagine—it appearing on the very day Reverend Miller predicted! Ante up."

Reverend Stone hesitated, then drew a nickel from his pocket. He said cautiously, "I have heard debate about the proper material for ascension robes. What is your view?"

"Only muslin will suffice. Muslin of the primest quality, with no tassel or lace nonsense. A body wants to be clothed in his finest raiments when the Bridegroom appears." Clarke grinned again. "Raiments are garments."

"Yes," Reverend Stone said. "I know."

The man was a Millerite. The minister had read of Reverend Miller's ninety thousand followers, but had ever encountered only one: Prudence Martin's husband, Matthew. An image rose in Reverend Stone's mind of Prudence Martin's bloodless lips stumbling over words from Revelation in the meetinghouse in Newell: a crimson dragon with seven heads, a beast like a leopard, a new Jerusalem. Unbelievers and liars and whores cast into hell. Reverend Stone cleared his throat. He said, "I have read that Reverend Miller demands significant donations from his followers. He would not approve of your losing money at a game of chance."

"I don't hardly see that I'm losing. Raise one."

One dollar. Reverend Stone checked his cards: pair of deuces with a floater, a low prial. He pushed a dollar toward the pile of coins, then took a long draft of cider to quell his guilt.

"Reverend Miller has proofs," Clarke said. "Numerical proofs, calculations from the Bible. From Daniel. He figured the date of Judgment by five different means, and every one yielded the identical result: October 22, 1844. Less than six months nigh."

"The Book of Daniel was not meant as a tool for calculation."

"I was taught as a nursling to read the book with openness and scrutiny. Just as Reverend Miller has done." Clarke spat on the floor. "Raise two."

Reverend Stone examined Leander Clarke: the man seemed possessed of a blunt intelligence that might easily tend to cruelty. So he was not a mindless follower, then, one of the multitudinous flock—likely he considered himself far superior. A backwoods apostle, Daniel in one hand and bowie knife in the other. Surely the man was bluffing.

"Fold," Reverend Stone said.

He ordered another cider as Clarke raked the coins to his chest. Rain rapped against the barroom windows. As they played the man spoke about Miller: How he'd been a simple onion farmer when he heard the call. How he'd forfeited his farm to roam the country and awaken souls. How he insisted to his followers that he was nothing more than a wretched, lowly messenger. Leander Clarke's voice was a deep monotone, uninflected by his erratic play: nervy bluffs mixed among cautious strings of folds. Within an hour the minister was down two dollars and ninety cents.

"I am acquainted with some of the man's writings," Reverend Stone said finally. "And his pamphlet—what is it called, *The Tuba?*"

"*The Trumpet.*"

"Of course." The minister smiled. "Reverend Miller is a learned fellow, no doubt. I am afraid, however, that his zeal has led him down a misguided route. The Bible is not a storehouse of riddles."

"What about the comet? How would you explain it, passing on the very morning Reverend Miller predicted?"

"The comet was a natural phenomenon. Explainable with scientifical reason."

Clarke spat and wiped his mouth. "And who are you to declare? How can you be certain the Lord won't come in October? The book says we know not when he shall return, that he is like a master of a house returning from a dreadful long journey, that he may cometh at midnight or at the cockcrowing or in the morn. And that he will come without warning, so we must not be sleeping. *We must not be sleeping! We must watch!*"

"Of course," Reverend Stone said quietly. "I did not intend offense."

Leander Clarke's brow was a hard furrow. The man checked his cards, and Reverend Stone noticed his fingers trembling—from nerves, or from whiskey. Around the saloon were traces of violence: shattered glass near the fireplace, a wide-bore shotgun propped behind the bar. Screams had echoed in this room. Shouts and accusations. The smell of horse piss was sharp and sour.

"You sincerely believe the last day will occur in October?"

Leander Clarke paused before he spoke. "I sincerely believe it might. And I don't intend to be on the losing end of that wager. Raise two."

Reverend Stone thumbed forward two dollar coins then immediately regretted the action. He studied his cards as a flush rose to his neck: three deuces, a fine hand. He understood that, were he to win, he might have enough money to pay Charles Noble.

Excitement flared in the minister then was instantly smothered by shame: paying an extortionist with gambling winnings. Sin in service of sin. Leander Clarke peeled a card from the leathery deck, raised another dollar. Reverend Stone's stomach fluttered. He drew a gold half-eagle coin from his trouser pocket and set it carefully in the table's center. Five dollars.

"Ho! Now we're sincere!" Clarke flipped a half-eagle into the air and caught it in a fist, slapped it on the table. *"Call."*

The minister slid two cards from his hand and turned over the remaining three: deuce of spades, deuce of clubs, deuce of hearts.

"Reverend William Miller thanks you for the generous donation."

Leander Clarke scraped together the coins with a low whistle. His hand showed three nines.

Reverend Stone nodded automatically as the barroom's noise faded to a hum. He gazed at the tabletop, its rough grain carved with initials and faceless figures, marked by treacle-colored stains. He felt strangely listless. He thought to take up his hat but could not recall where he'd laid it. The door—of course he'd hung it on a rack beside the door.

"Listen to me now." Leander Clarke was staring at him. "You are lost. I hear it in your voice. I hear your lostness as clear as a piano note. I hear your voice then I think about Reverend Miller's voice, and I know that if you heard him speak a single sentence, a single word, you would be found. His words are truth. The truth is in his voice. It trumpets from him."

Reverend Stone nodded. Dryness crept into his throat.

"When he speaks, I feel drawn apart from myself. We all do." Leander Clarke smiled painfully. "When he speaks, I feel . . . I feel my soul rise from my body and float away."

Reverend Stone fumbled away from the table. Heat washed through him and pushed every sound from the room. The saloon seemed to lurch. He leaned against a chair and coughed, his stomach twisting into a rope.

"Hey. Hey. Do you need air?"

He stared at Leander Clarke: fleecy white light lay draped over the man's shoulders, as though he was enrobed in sunbeams. The light sharpened, then blurred.

"I'm fine," he stammered. "Thank you."

"You should have that cough inspected," Clarke said. "I know a good surgeon that can aid you. Drain just enough blood to settle your temperament."

A metallic taste rose in Reverend Stone's mouth. He spat on the floor and turned away.

Leander Clarke gripped his elbow. "What will you do when the last day arrives? Will your family be prepared? Will *you* be prepared?"

"You should be concerned with your own preparations," Reverend Stone said. "Do not waste your worries on my family. Do not waste your worries on me."

"But I shall worry about you," Leander Clarke said softly. "I shall pray for you."

He spent the evening walking Detroit's outer streets, Atwater over to Orleans up to Elizabeth then back to Grand River, the city yielding to farmland that stretched to the horizon like a flat, black lake. The creak of sidewalk planks and click of horsewhips gave way to a cow's mournful lowing, a whisper of windbreak poplars. Reverend Stone felt reckless and deeply ashamed. He thought to purchase a bottle of cider but suspected that would only worsen the feeling.

Sometime past midnight he returned to his shabby boardinghouse on Miami Avenue, lit a candle stub and paced the small room. He did not want to sleep. Again he figured his finances: he had spent four dollars on the room and suppers, another dollar on hackney cabs, a few coins for shoeshines and coffee and tablets and a half-dollar on the Catlin book. And then nearly ten dollars lost at the saloon. Now he had but three dollars, eighteen cents. He stacked the coins on the side table.

He woke at dawn to a smoky purple sky. His head ached. He stepped down to the street and walked to the Berthelet market; the scene was one of quiet commotion, farmers unloading bushels of carrots and potatoes and asparagus, street vendors setting up their stalls, a water wagon sprinkling the dusty road. Reverend Stone purchased a mug of coffee and a large red apple, picked a *City Examiner* from the gutter and irritably scanned the headlines. A notice about the comet, reporting various scientific observations recorded in New Haven and Cambridge. A second notice, discrediting Reverend Miller's predictions. The editorialists seemed alarmed, though they tried to mask their concern with a third notice entitled "Comets and Women."

Comets doubtless answer some wise and good purpose in creation; so do women.

Comets are incomprehensible, beautiful, eccentric; so are women.

Comets shine with peculiar splendor, but at night appear most brilliant; so do women.

Comets confound the most learned when they attempt to ascertain their nature; so do women.

Comets and women, therefore, are closely related; but as each are inscrutable, all that remains for us to do is view with admiration the one, and love to adoration the other.

Despite himself Reverend Stone felt cheered by the notice. He crumpled the newspaper, annoyed by his own fatuousness.

A meetinghouse stood across the square from the market. It was a slender whitewashed building set between a jeweler's shop and a garish lavender brothel. Reverend Stone stared at the meetinghouse as though at a mirage. With a feeling of relief he climbed the stone steps.

The minister was a plump, avuncular fellow with a bald pate encircled by silvery curls. At eight o'clock precisely he said an invocation then led the congregation through a lined-out recitation of "Raise Him Up on High," followed by readings from Mark and John. Then he slowly ascended to the pulpit and surveyed the assembly with a lugubrious scowl.

"Religion is not a theory, but a *desire*. We contemplate God and faith, and we reach various conclusions—and this constitutes our *theory of religion*. Yet men are religious because they possess *religious natures*, just as they are moral because they possess *moral natures*. From Psalms, verse seventeen: 'As the hart panteth after the water brook, so panteth my soul after thee, O God!' "

A cough echoed through the meetinghouse; then a rustle of crino-line and a pew's wooden creak. The minister spread his arms wide. "No man feels the *desire* for religion at all times; many feel it only when low, or disheartened. Just so with the desire for food: we eat only when hungry. This is one of faith's *great challenges:* man is not drawn to religion by his knowledge of its *value,* but only by his *desire* for it, and the uneasiness this feeling creates."

He leaned forward over the pulpit, his eyes squeezed shut. "The spring of *all human activity* is the *unease* that accompanies *desire!*"

A frustrated thespian, Reverend Stone thought, an actor without wig or greasepaint. He imagined the man recounting the parable of the sower in a winking singsong, the story of Exodus in a gaslight pantomime. Rolling baritone for Moses, reedy quaver for Pharaoh. Reverend Stone frowned distastefully. The pews, he noted, were full to capacity.

"Not all human desires reside on the surface. Indeed, the very *defi-nition* of *progress* is the awakening of new and higher desires! The de-sire of religion is the highest desire of our nature—yet before it can be experienced the soul must be *awakened,* through self-inspection, self-activity and self-culture, but most directly through God's *divine* and *loving* aid. Again from Psalms: 'My soul *thirsteth* for God, for the *liv-ing God.*' All of us, every one of us in this meetinghouse, must strive to maintain this thirst."

The pipe organ drew a raspy breath and the congregation began "Voices Raised to God." Reverend Stone sang, "We raise our voices to you, O Lord...." His gaze moved from the choir loft's scoured benches to the treadworn aisle runner, the thickly varnished candle-holders, the cobwebs like exquisite moldings in the corners. The tall, bright windows ribboned with rain. How odd, he thought, to be sit-ting in a pew among strangers, unburdened by responsibility. With only music and sunlight and the Word. How beautifully odd.

He began the next hymn feeling weightless: like sunlight, like mu-sic. He was filled with grace—the understanding pierced him, so that he momentarily lost the music's rhythm. *This land of holy people...*

Reverend Stone sensed doubts gathering but he raised his voice to quell them. A flutter began in his stomach that mimicked the organ's tremulous notes. Each chord vibrated with pleasure.

The hymn ended and the minister led the congregation in the Lord's Prayer, then said a brief benediction. The pipe organ drew another breath. Reverend Stone proceeded up the aisle as if in a waking dream. I am near it, he marveled. I am within it. Bright husky chords surrounded him.

He opened the door and stepped into the warm morning, and waited for the congregation to follow him.

The minister's name was Howell, a Maryland native come west ten years earlier to be clear of the Catholics of that state. Reverend Stone sat across from him at a small Chippendale table in the parsonage, cups of sassafras tea and a plate of sweet cherries between them, the room's air musty and close. The man's eyes were jaundiced, the whites tinted yolk yellow. With a sigh he unfastened the top button of his trousers.

"You have a superior congregation," Reverend Stone said. "Very upright and quick-seeming. I noted their attentiveness to your excellent sermon."

"We are commonly regarded as the city's cream," Howell said. "Though of course it's a struggle to convince them to tithe. We sponsor an idiots' asylum and a Magdalene society, to reclaim prostitutes to virtue. We recently purchased a five-hundred-pipe Stansfield organ, which you were graced by this morning."

"In Newell there is severe competition from Baptists. We've lost near thirty souls in the past year alone."

Howell wheezed out a laugh, rubbing his gleaming scalp. "Oh, it is everywhere the same! Baptists. Lutherans. Universalists. Catholics. Friends. Moravians. Millerites, for mercy's sake. You can't swing a stick in this city without walloping a Millerite."

"So I've found." Reverend Stone nodded vigorously. "You are doing superior work. It's clear to even a casual observer."

Howell's laughter faded to a prim smile. The expression seemed calculated to express both pleasure and irritation. In the room's corner, a massive clock stood with its hands frozen at noon and three, its face painted with a side-wheel steamer trailing smoke and greenish spray. Beside it hung an oil portrait of a man with reddish curls winding like grapevines over his lapels. The man's eyes were colored expertly, lustrous white pools softened by patience and compassion. With a start Reverend Stone recognized it as Howell as a young man.

"I am curious," Howell said. "What has brought you to this stimulating city?"

"As you said so incisively this morning: the spring of all human activity is the unease that accompanies desire. Lately I've felt uneasy."

Howell said nothing as he unfolded a clasp knife and speared a cherry. Reverend Stone continued, "I am on an urgent errand to locate my son, Elisha—he's joined a scientifical expedition to the northern peninsula."

"The northern peninsula is enormous! You are more likely to encounter a howling red savage than you are your boy." Howell chewed wetly. "I have heard news that the Catholics are busy infesting the territory with missionaries, sent direct from Rome. Their tactic is to pour poison into the ears of dying savages, promise them everlasting bliss if they agree to be baptized." He spit a pit over his shoulder. "Apparently the technique is ineffective. Even savages are too clear-thinking to fall sway to popery."

Reverend Stone edged forward in his chair. "I have an opportunity to obtain a map of my son's route. And I aim to hire a guide when I reach Sault Ste. Marie—I'm no woodsman, but I imagine an experienced Native or half-breed could locate the boy's party with little difficulty."

Howell shrugged. "Still. Seems a fool's errand."

"But a necessary one." Reverend Stone rubbed his chin, and with a shock of embarrassment felt a bristle of stubble. He had forgotten to shave. "There is a matter I had hoped we might discuss. The matter of a loan."

"We are a poor congregation."

"Of course. Yes." Reverend Stone felt the beginnings of a cough tickle his throat. "I was robbed on the Buffalo train. A thief took my clothes and valise and nearly all of my money. It has been only through severe hardship that I have sustained myself thus far. However I have not enough to continue my journey."

"Your journey," Howell said wearily. "It seems that everyone is on a journey. I don't mean to wax metaphorical—I mean that in the literal. One day a fellow is your neighbor and the next he's a dust cloud on the Toledo road. It's the nature of the country, I suppose." He stared at Reverend Stone. "How old is your son?"

"Sixteen. Born twentieth of November."

"Sixteen is a significant age. I expect your son will have changed in ways you cannot imagine. Perhaps you mightn't even recognize the boy."

Reverend Stone had contemplated the thought many times, but it irritated him to hear the possibility raised by a stranger. He began to speak but Howell said, "I recall my own sixteenth year, my first year in Baltimore. First year away from my father's farm. When I closed my eyes at night I could still smell the privy." Howell smiled into his teacup. "Many nights I wanted to rise from that boardinghouse bed and run clear to Catonsville, with only the shirt on my back. I never did."

"I suspect Elisha has felt a similar urge—to return to Newell. To return home. But he yet hasn't."

"No. Of course he hasn't."

Silence stretched between the men, punctuated by an apple vendor's muted shout; then they raised their teacups and drank. Reverend Stone studied Howell's face: the flaccid eyelids and pitted nose, the cheeks dragged down to jowls. The youth of the portrait had vanished, replaced by his weary father. It must have been painted at seminary, Reverend Stone thought, when he was still a homesick farm boy, full of earnest passion. The minister imagined Howell to be near his own age, and he wondered if the man was married or widowed, if there were children nearby. If he still entered the meetinghouse with cool excitement, a feeling of returning to a lover's room. We might be brothers, he thought mawkishly. He sipped the cold tea.

"Have you considered petitioning the governor?" Howell said. "He would doubtless make special provision for your circumstance. Help you locate your map, et cetera."

"That would take months. This is a matter of weeks. Of days."

"Or you might consider inquiring at one of the city's benevolent societies. I could refer you. Some support could be quickly arranged."

Reverend Stone leaned forward. "Of course I would not be troubling you if less burdensome methods existed. I would hire out as a day laborer but I seem to lack useful skills. Our training leaves us ill equipped for matters financial."

The minister's throat tingled and he reached for the teacup; then he stayed his hand and let the cough rise. His chest convulsed, the jag bending him double, his eyes straining as if to burst. He turned away from Howell and covered his face. When the spell faded Reverend Stone dried his eyes and looked up at the man. His throat felt scraped, raw. His mouth tasted of blood. "Please," he said. "I beg of you."

"There is no need to beg," Howell said miserably. He rose and unlocked the clock case, withdrew a worn leather purse and untied the strap. He poked through the purse's contents and fingered out a coin, then another.

" 'Let none admire that riches grow in hell; that soil may best deserve the precious bane.' "

The man stopped counting and stared at Reverend Stone.

"*Paradise Lost*," the minister said. "Volume one."

Howell resumed counting, his mouth pinched in a line.

"I shall repay you the moment I return to Newell. I'll send banknotes by post with appropriate interest—I pray that is acceptable."

The man set the coins in the table's center then wiped his hands on his waistcoat. He stared past the minister, out the fogged window.

"You are blessed," Reverend Stone said. "Thank you."

"Yes," Howell said. "Now go."

He wove down Beaubien Street among the pedestrians and sidewalk window-gazers, the coins like lead shot in his pocket. At the druggist on Larned Street Reverend Stone purchased six tins of toothache medication, and as he exited the shop placed three tablets under his tongue.

Relief trickled through him as he hurried toward the river. He wanted to shout with joy. The sun was shielded by flat-bottomed clouds, but as Reverend Stone passed the Confidence Bank the clouds nudged eastward and the day brightened. Carriages and dray horses and hotel drummers and news vendors were shadowed in flat, hard light. The city swarmed around him.

He had come to admire Detroit: its vitality and haste, its blunt edge of menace. Surely anything was possible here—the city seemed the antithesis of Newell, of New England. A trio of French boatmen stamped past singing a coarse chanson, then fell silent as they approached St. Anne's. An elderly charwoman squatted at the gutter, poking through heaped-up trash with a walking stick. It was the sense of rebelliousness, he realized, the lack of concern with meeting windy ideas of civilization. A pleasant restiveness grew in Reverend Stone: he was a man in a strange city with a pocketful of coins. He wandered from Larned over to Randolph Street, and as he passed the Excelsior Hotel he heard his wife's voice.

Reverend Stone froze. A door slammed, then a cat yowled in the distance. He drew a breath, his chest feeling as though it was burdened by stones. He strained toward his memory of the sound.

He had heard Ellen's voice often in Newell, a rising inflection in the bank or crowded meetinghouse, on an empty sidewalk. It was easy to explain away—a misheard snatch of conversation, wind hissing through bare December branches—but logic did nothing to thaw the freezing shock. Then the wash of murderous grief, of guilt. The back of his neck gone damp with sweat. Reverend Stone wondered if his wife's voice was meant to be punishment or a small, fleeting reward. Usually it seemed equal parts of both.

Now he sat against an awning post and stared blankly at the buggies rolling past. He smelled lilac and rain-wet leaves. They were in a buggy and Ellen was singing, *Home, O home, O happy hillside home.* It was October, the maples like orange torches along the roadside. Elisha's voice braided with his mother's: *Home, O home, O cozy sweet refuge.* Reverend Stone luxuriated in the memory, wondering all the while if it was merely a hopeful dream: his wife singing, his son beside him on the driver's bench, the wide endless road, the maples. No. Of course it was not merely a dream. His heart churned, a thick pumping that finally settled to nothing. At last he rose and dusted off his trousers.

The public land office was closed when he arrived. He stepped into the street and peered up at the second story: Charles Noble's window was shut, the draperies drawn. Reverend Stone rapped on the broad door and listened for answering footsteps. Then he remembered that it was Sunday—the office would not be open until morning. He knocked again and pressed his ear to the polished wood.

He started up Woodward Avenue toward Mrs. Barbeau's boardinghouse and his airless room, then stopped. He backtracked to Jefferson Avenue. The minister passed Italianate mansions and sturdy brick cottages, an Episcopal church, the Michigan garden. A bored-looking constable at the garden gate nodded at Reverend Stone. Dusk was approaching, the sun a low shimmer, the June air dense as oil. He passed down an alleyway beneath rows of strung-up laundry, then emerged onto Franklin Street. Across the road was the teamsters' saloon.

Inside, the barroom was smoky and hot, the tables surrounded by cardplayers. Leander Clarke was nowhere to be seen. Reverend Stone moved to the bar feeling mildly disappointed. He ordered a glass of cider and paid with a gold half-eagle, and as he awaited his change he noticed the man beside him scowling; then the man tapped his elbow.

"Lonnafellalevy, wouye?" The man's Irish accent was so thick as to be unintelligible.

"Pardon?"

"A levy. Loan us a levy. For a whiskey."

The man sat hunched over an empty tumbler, dull-eyed, his head shaved as though for a bleeding. Reverend Stone said, "I am sorry," and took up his change.

"I sees that half-eagle. Ye's got plenty. Be Christian, stannus a dram."

Reverend Stone hesitated; then he nodded to the barman and laid two half-dimes on the bar. He moved near the door and scanned the handbills tacked to an announcement board: an animal trainer showing camels from Arabia and elephants from Siam at the Military Square. A sixty-dollar reward for runaway Negroes returned unmutilated to Mr. Edgar Wallace of 77 Jefferson Avenue. A recovered atheist named J. Dover describing his glorious return to Christianity in a lecture at the Young Men's Society. Reverend Stone finished the cider and ordered a second glass.

He drank it with a bowl of gluey beef stew as he fingered the coins in his pocket: likely enough money for Charles Noble and a guide in the northern peninsula, perhaps even enough for a pair of sturdy boots. Guilt gathered inside Reverend Stone but he forced his thoughts elsewhere. He found himself wondering if it was possible to live without faith.

He had weighed the question at seminary as a study in abstraction, but now he considered it as a practical matter: no mornings spent at the meetinghouse, no nights consumed by sermons. No disappointment in others' failings. No guilt. A looseness in the world's workings, a lack of heft and texture, a feeling of uncontrol. A vision of life as an ornate, peculiar drama. As a young man Reverend Stone had considered himself a vital member of the universe, part of a supreme struggle; now the notion seemed as childish as a fantasy.

His faith had weakened, he knew, after Ellen's death. The shame of this fact continuously troubled him. He was not bitter or angry—he understood that death was as natural and necessary as birth—yet when Ellen passed Reverend Stone had found himself wondering if he'd fallen prey to some crucial misunderstanding, some misapprehension of His nature. He had always viewed God as a loving force, merciful and gentle; yet perhaps he had not comprehended the fullest meaning of His love. Weeks passed into months, his prayers yielding little solace, his thoughts tumbling into an endless, empty well. It was as though he was too exhausted to meet faith's challenge.

Now Reverend Stone drank another cider then stepped out onto Franklin Street, the night cool and moonlit, the sidewalk glimmering with broken glass. On a whim he started east, toward the river. Laundry fluttered like ghosts above the warped laneways. An infant's wail rose from an open cellar door. As he passed a lamppost Reverend Stone sensed a presence; he glanced back to see the shaved-headed Irishman strolling beside a second man. Reverend Stone nodded to the pair then turned quickly away.

He turned down a familiar-seeming alleyway. He counted twenty paces then looked back: the men entered the alleyway, silhouetted by lamplight. Reverend Stone quickened his pace. Coins jangled in his trouser pocket. He began to run, hat clapped to his head, brogans slapping the waxy clay. He turned to see the two men sprinting, then with a lurch the minister stumbled to his knees and elbows. He scrambled to his feet as a cry caught in his throat. The city seemed suddenly deserted.

He veered westward and in the distance saw a streetlamp like a lighthouse beacon in the gloom. Franklin Street. He would burst among the revelers, breathless and pointing, and a crowd would shield him with fists readied. Reverend Stone gasped, his lungs feeling slashed by razors. A fat mustachioed man stepped from a carriage house holding an urn of night soil. The minister shouted, then pain jolted through him as his legs jerked sideways and he slammed to the ground, the smell of manure suddenly sharp. He rolled onto his side among a blur of shadows. He squirmed to his knees but a kick knocked him flat and robbed his breath. Reverend Stone looked up to see the mustachioed man step into the carriage house and shut the door.

A boot stamped his wrist and the tendons wrinkled. Hot needles tingled beneath his skin. Hands gripped his lapels and the shaved-headed Irishman gasped in his face, his breath thick with spittle.

"Stannus a dram, ye stingy bastard!"

The minister flung both fists, felt the man's nose yield sickeningly. The Irishman huffed. The second man hissed *Down! Down!* as he struck the minister in the kidneys. Pain corkscrewed up to Reverend Stone's throat. My good Lord, he thought, preserve me. He looked up: the Irishman's mouth was bearded with blood. He drew back quick as a rat and punched the minister's face.

He closed his eyes and the night's silence grew to a hiss. Boot heels scuffed his shoulder, levered open his ribs. He tucked his knees to his chest as a crushing weight settled over him. The breath slipped from his lungs. The minister's ankle was speared and the bones shifted. Preserve me, please. Reverend Stone covered his face with his hands.

He seemed to drift away from his body: he felt the blows land but only vaguely, waves against a distant shore. Hands rooted in his pockets and he moved to stop them, felt his fingers bent away. A man's face was close to his: peering at him, breathing, saying nothing. Someone patted him on the head.

And then it was quiet and he was alone, there in the muddy street, curled like a sleeping child.

Five

Morning light showed the commis' house to be smoke-blackened and littered with hare droppings. Elisha woke late, the sun a yellow smear on the window. Gray ash crusted the backlog. Professor Tiffin lay against a mound of skins with his shirt untucked, reading an octavo volume with a tattered pasteboard cover: *Travels in the Interior of Africa,* by Mungo Park. He grunted to acknowledge the boy's presence, then slipped the book into his trouser pocket. They stepped out into a stumpy clearing surrounded by red maple and arborvitae and hemlock, the ground spongy with moss, the river slow as sap. Elisha figured the time to be near nine o'clock.

By day, the fur post held an air of faded optimism: scabs of whitewash flecking the frame house, shattered windowpanes like gap teeth on the log cabins' faces. A collapsed privy beside a heap of trash wood, near a garden patch gone to weeds. Around them the forest was strangely silent. To Elisha it seemed as though every living thing was asleep or had disappeared.

Mr. Brush was squatting at the riverbank beside the overturned canoe, arranging a pile of stores. Without looking up he said, "Your half-breed is vanished."

"Vanished to where?" Tiffin said.

"Her fishing gear is gone. So is one of the oilcloths." Brush hefted a keg of pork, gave the tin mugs a merry rattle. "She took some pork and rice. At least she left us the canoe!"

"She is off fishing for your lunch," Professor Tiffin said curtly. His eyes were heavy-lidded, ringed with violet moons. "She took pork and rice for her own breakfast."

"She has never gone fishing without notice."

"Then bless her independent heart." He pulled the Park volume from his pocket and slumped on a pine stump. "She will return by noon, I guarantee. We shall wait."

Elisha fixed a breakfast of coffee and leftover corn mush, some mottled cheese found in the storeroom. Images from the previous night seized him: Susette squinting at *A Midsummer Night's Dream,* her calloused fingers underlining a word; his hands moving down the woman's knobby spine, her dress wrinkling beneath his grip. He shaved specks of sugar into the coffee, his excitement tempered by guilty unease. And then the plates clattering in the dirt, her cheeks shining with tears. Her apology. And now Susette was nowhere to be found.

He longed to see the woman but was terrified by the prospect of what he would say to her. Did she love him or was she simply lonely? That previous night, when she had apologized, Elisha had heard her words but could not understand their meaning. It was as though she'd been speaking a foreign tongue.

He should be the one to apologize, of course; and yet *she* had led him into the darkness, *she* had tugged her skirts up over her waist. She had fallen as far and as fast as he. Elisha realized that Susette's actions nohow lessened his own guilt; they simply joined both of them in sin. He stewed over the thought as his coffee grew cold.

The three of them waited through the morning, Professor Tiffin occupying himself with Mungo Park and Indian whiskey while Mr. Brush completed a series of timber density calculations. Elisha paced along the riverbank, unable to settle his thoughts. At last he took his fieldbook and a pocket compass and started inland. He followed the river past a caved-in beaver dam and a ford that smelled of deer, then down through a patch of orange touch-me-nots that burst like confetti as he brushed past. Swamp cabbage and turtleheads and golden cowslip lined the river's margins, the wildflowers' beauty offset by the swamp cabbage's thick stench. Elisha checked his bearing with the compass, then headed westward into the forest.

Beneath the canopy it was quieter, the river's mutter silenced, his footfalls hushed by a litter of spruce needles. Elisha felt for a moment the sort of melancholy that seemed to fascinate poets: a gorgeous aimlessness, a sense that nothing he might do would matter a cent. And with it a conviction of being alone in the universe. He supposed the feeling was the opposite of prayer.

The sensation evaporated as he hiked deeper into the forest. Waxwings whirled overhead, a pair of yellow streaks dodging through the understory. The mating dance, nature's fascinating shamelessness. Elisha wondered why it was that some species' mating habits were complex and cloaked in mystery, while others needed no such artifice. The waxwings called, a pennywhistle chorus. He found himself humming, "*A la claire fontaine, M'en allant promener...*" Perhaps I am wrong, he thought—perhaps there is less to fear than I expect. He felt thrillingly alive, like a man who'd discovered a vanished country.

He sat against a hemlock and opened his fieldbook, but could not focus his mind to serious observation. Finally he wrote:

June 26, 1844

Along this pleasant amber-colored river are many ginger-orange touch-me-nots, with small triangular serrated leaves and flowers shaped like small trumpets. A beautiful flower, but strange: its seed husks burst quite explosively at the barest touch, scattering seedlings in every direction. In this manner it achieves reproduction.

This strategy is remarkable but certainly imperfect—for what if I had not chanced to pass along the riverbank this morning? Who, or what, would have scattered the seed? A sparrow or hare or deer, purely by providence—and so perhaps touch-me-nots tend to thrive at feeding locations of these animals (the nearby ford smelled strongly of deer musk). Regardless, it seems ill-advised to rely on another species for one's own survival.

Particularly ill-advised to rely on humans, Elisha thought. Humans were skilled at cutting down, burning up, gouging out; not the opposite. Touch-me-nots would not fare well in Newell or Detroit.

Another highly curious plant present along this river is the swamp cabbage, whose foul smell is doubtless intended for some purpose, most likely to ward off insects that might feed on its fleshy purple leaves. In contrast, the cowslip's cheerful yellow flowers perhaps serve as welcoming beacons to passing bees, who might feed on them to facilitate reproduction. In sum, nature seems inclined to bestow one of two gifts: the gift to attract, or that to repel.

With plants as with people, nature's cruel chance—for surely there was no logic behind the choice of gift. Were there, the ugly and cruel would die off over time, and the beautiful and kind would remain. But that was not the case at all.

Increasingly I find myself here, among immense white pines or at the lake's crystalline edge, in a state of pleasant yet profound confusion. Nature's questions do not, at first glance, appear as questions at all: it is only upon reflection that her paradoxes appear. Then one wonders how anything at all—plant, animal, insect, bird—manages to thrive. And yet here this forest stands, in deep and solemn harmony, requiring nothing but sun and wind and rain for its own survival.

Better, Elisha thought, though still entirely lacking in precision. And nowhere describing anything new to the world—no new plant or animal or insect or bird. Or idea, for that matter. Elisha sketched a shriveled bracken frond, then with a sigh dragged the pen across the page. He closed the fieldbook.

He started eastward toward the river. Clouds had joined in a pasty white layer, so he hewed closely to the compass bearing until he reached the river, then turned northward past the deer ford and collapsed beaver dam. Elisha quickened his pace as he neared camp. He entered the clearing to find Mr. Brush squatting on a stump with his fieldbook open across his knees. A mineral specimen lay between the book's pages.

"Out practicing your painterly technique, were you?"

Elisha was taken aback by the man's stern tone; then Brush grinned and motioned the boy over. He said, "I was conducting a timber survey not two hundred yards due west. I recorded a bearing with my solar compass, however when I recorded the same bearing with a magnetic compass the two readings differed wildly—the magnetic compass's needle skittered like a beetle. Now! Why do you suppose that might be?"

"I don't know."

"Think for a moment, my boy! Why?"

Elisha glanced past Mr. Brush: the frame house's door was propped open, coughs of smoke trailing from the chimney. The party's packs and kegs and instrument cases were laid out around the flagpole, as if in preparation for departure. Susette and Professor Tiffin were nowhere to be seen.

"Perhaps you erred in your measuring process," he said. "Perhaps the magnetic compass was poorly leveled."

"Iron, of course! The compass needle's magnetism was distracted by ferrous ore deposits near to the ground!" He took up the mineral specimen. "I discovered an ore outcrop that had been exposed by a windfall pine. The ore was literally entangled in the tree's roots."

Elisha turned the specimen over in his hands: it was a shaly pewter-colored stone shot with thick maroon veins. He scratched at it with a thumbnail, then rubbed it across his shirt cuff. It left a reddish streak. He smiled weakly. "Susette," he said. "Has she yet returned?"

Mr. Brush held the boy's gaze for a long moment. "She has not," he said, taking the mineral specimen from Elisha. "She has not and I expect she won't ever return. Your friend Mr. Tiffin is inside the house, consoling himself with whiskey. A damned pathetic sight."

Elisha hurried across the clearing feeling faintly nauseated. He stepped inside the house then stood motionless as his vision adjusted to the dimness. A voice called, "Young buckra Elisha! Welcome to the maison de merde, also known as the house of shit!"

Professor Tiffin lay sprawled on a throne of skins. He was barefoot and shirtless, a book stuffed into his trouser waistband, one arm cradling the whiskey jug. With a thumb and forefinger he rolled a rabbit pellet before his eyes. "Fascinating beast, the snowshoe hare. Are you aware that it changes color with the season—that it is snow-colored in winter, and shit-colored in summer? A capital example of nature's capital genius!"

"Susette is gone?"

"Gone, gone, gone." He flicked the pellet toward the fire, fluttered his fingers like a bird's wings. "Vanished like a squalid caricature of a Native. Like a lying, shiftless, heathen red nigger."

"Perhaps she's fishing at the lake edge—have you taken the canoe upriver?"

"I have been upriver, downriver, cross-river." Tiffin blinked furiously then looked away. "A half-breed Catholic bitch, who should not have been trusted in the first."

"Mind your language, Professor Tiffin."

"Brush was correct about the woman. I was wrong."

Frustration welled inside the boy. "She'll return—she *must* return. We'll wait one more day. I'll search the riverbanks and up along the lakeshore. Mr. Brush can scout the forest."

Professor Tiffin exhaled in a moan; then his entire body sagged, his shoulders slumping and head falling forward. He looked like a child's string puppet that had been cast aside. He laughed softly. "Who will guide us to the image stones? We are near to them, my boy. We are very, very near."

Elisha felt an urge to shake the man. Of course this was a mistake—Susette was pacing among the nearby pines, confused, the clouds causing her to swap west for east. She would wander into camp at dusk, hungry and abashed, and the men would tease her while she devoured a bowl of stew. And then whiskey, Shakespeare. *A Midsummer Night's Dream.*

Yet even as Elisha thought this he realized that Susette would not return. She was likely hiking eastward along the lakeshore, or paddling in a Chippewa canoe toward the Sault. At that moment she was imagining what she'd say to her husband: about her departure with the expedition, about her early return. The notion sickened Elisha.

"There is yet hope." Tiffin drew the book from his waistband and struggled upright. "Our dear friend Mungo Park, in deepest, blackest Africa, several days' journey from Pisania. Listen:

> Whatever way I turned, nothing appeared but danger and difficulty. I saw myself in the midst of a vast wilderness, naked and alone, surrounded by savage animals, and men still more savage. At this moment, painful as my reflections were, the extraordinary beauty of a small moss in fructification irresistibly caught my eye.

"Surrounded by jackals and flesh-eating tigers—yet he is comforted by a scrap of moss." Tiffin smiled sadly. "Quite beautiful."

"Yes. It is beautiful."

"There is more.

> Can that Being, thought I, who in this obscure part of the world brought to perfection a thing which appears of so small importance, look with unconcern upon the sufferings of creatures formed after his own image? Surely not. I started up and traveled forward, disregarding both hunger and fatigue, assured that relief was at hand. And I was not disappointed."

Neither of them spoke. The fire popped, embers jumping like lightning bugs then fading to nothing. Elisha said, "So. Let us pray we have as much good fortune as Park."

"Mungo Park was drowned at Bussa," Tiffin said. "So let us pray we have more."

Professor Tiffin and Elisha set off the next morning in a chill dawn rain, the canoe riding high through a windy chop. As if in harmony with the foul weather the craft began to leak, a trickle at Elisha's feet that grew to a steady seep. Tiffin pulled toward shore, cursing providence in general and Susette Morel in particular. Elisha paddled with his head down, shivering. He felt a grave, disorienting sensation of having failed, but not knowing how.

The boy kindled a driftwood fire then gummed the canoe's seams. Lunch without Susette was a makeshift affair: water set on to boil, then lyed corn and peas and a strip of pork belly tossed into the cookpot. The resulting soup was ill cooked and flavorless. They ate without speaking, crouched beneath a fly tent. Susette Morel had vanished; Mr. Brush was back at the fur post completing a detailed mineral survey. Professor Tiffin had proposed to paddle ahead to a Chippewa camp and engage a new guide, then return to the fur post in three days' time. Now Tiffin stood, his head brushing the low tent. He said, "I believe I have forgotten to bring powder and shot!" Elisha smiled, as if at a poor joke; then he realized the man was serious. It occurred to him that they were woefully ill equipped, even for this brief journey.

Storm clouds lightened then dissolved as they passed the Miner's River and Train River, Professor Tiffin shouting their location as he squinted at the Bayfield chart. Near dusk he spied the Chippewa village. It was a thicket of lodges set beside a stream, rows of cigar-shaped canoes strewn along the beach, a woman's laughter and a dog's yip and the *thock thock thock* of hatchet blows drifting over the water. A group of braves lay in various postures of repose near the water's edge, muskets propped beside them. Professor Tiffin raised both hands and hollered, "*Bojou!*" The braves sat up without returning the greeting.

"He believes we should wipe them away, slaughter them," Tiffin said. "Or exile them to the far forgotten corners of the United States." Elisha understood that the man was speaking about Mr. Brush. "The Christian way is to raise them up! To improve them morally and spiritually, you see, offer them entry into the civilized world. To instruct them in mechanics and agriculture and the rule of law—of course you agree."

Elisha grunted at the paddle but said nothing.

"Silas Brush would not admit even that Indians are human beings—he considers them a unique species, distinct from white men and Negroes! Imagine: if Natives are distinct from white men, then they are not descendents of Adam, and thus are not inheritors of original sin. It is utterly contrary to Scripture! And consider the case of half-breeds, such as Susette: is the poor woman half-saved, or half-damned? Analysis of the spiritual state of quinteroons and octoroons requires higher mathematics!"

Professor Tiffin twisted around and laid a hand on the boy's arm. "You must choose."

"Choose what?"

"Choose whom you intend to follow—Silas Brush or myself. I have seen the man instructing you, crowding your brain with minutiae. You simply cannot be trained by both him and me—your mind cannot abide such radical discord."

Elisha stopped paddling and the canoe rocked crosswise over a swell. He could not determine if Professor Tiffin was serious. He leaned away from the man but Tiffin tightened his grip.

"Of course I choose to follow you. Of course."

"Excellent fellow." The man nodded solemnly. "Then we shall achieve this summer's successes together."

Tiffin stepped into the waist-high shallows and started toward the braves, arms outspread, speaking a halting mixture of Chippewa and English. The Natives hesitated; then they splashed into the lake and shouldered the packs, helped Elisha hoist the canoe and set it gently ashore. They looked to be near Elisha's age, though taller and thickly muscled. They stank of deer grease.

"Bojou," Tiffin said again. He spoke a few words in Chippewa, then said, "We are Americans. We would like to trade. *Trade*." The braves remained expressionless. One of them spoke a single syllable and Tiffin said, "Yes, yes, oui." The brave turned and started up the beach.

The village was larger than it had appeared from the lake, three dozen bark-covered domes in a grassy clearing, Native women working at tanning frames while a group of young girls looked on. A smell of smoked venison seasoned the air. Professor Tiffin and Elisha followed the braves through the lodges, past a sour-looking Chippewa smoking a clay pipe; his gaze tracked the pair as they passed. Elisha looked back to find the man squinting after them.

We're in American territory, the boy told himself. The fact failed to calm his nerves. Chippewa men and women milled about the village, dressed in leggings and woolen breechclouts, trade shirts and cotton dresses: Natives in white men's clothing, living on land they no longer owned. Their presence seemed bleakly absurd. The children's shrieks unnerved Elisha.

The brave ducked into a lodge, emerged a moment later leading a squat, bald Native wearing a ratty pea jacket and striped broadcloth leggings. Black metal cones hung in wreaths from the man's ears. He introduced himself in broken French as White Wing, then extended an open palm toward Tiffin and Elisha. "Pour faire du troc. Oui?" His earlobes wobbled as he spoke.

"Oui," Tiffin said, "faire du troc."

White Wing led them toward the village's edge, past a group of braves working at the skeleton of a long lodge. One brave bowed a sapling into an arc while another lashed it with roots to the lodge frame. White Wing glanced back at Elisha, nodding as if to calm the boy. "Heureux," he said. "Troc. Bon."

The Native settled himself beneath a tall, solitary elm and motioned for the pair to sit opposite. From his seated position Elisha was faced with the interior of a nearby lodge: skins and pine boughs were laid around the dim perimeter, a low cookfire in the center trailing ash. A man was tending the fire. With a start Elisha recognized him as the Native that Mr. Brush had threatened during the expedition's first days. The man sat heavily beside the cookfire.

Professor Tiffin placed a carrot of tobacco before White Wing, and the Native said, "Sugguswau, fumons." He seemed acutely proud of his command of French. He withdrew a long reddish pipe and packed it slowly. His lips were puckered and grooved, shriveled by years of smoke. He drew a thick puff then gestured toward the cardinal directions, offered the pipe to Professor Tiffin. The man smoked then passed the pipe to Elisha; he sucked the wet pipe stem and hot smoke entered his lungs. The boy coughed harshly.

"Nous cherchons un guide," Tiffin said. "Pour nous escorter vers l'intérieur des terres. Nous payerons avec de l'argent et du tabac."

"Guide? Pas commerce?"

"Nous sommes des scientifiques. Scientifiques—nous recherchons des informations. Nous voulons un guide. Notre guide précédent nous a quitté. Nous pouvons vous payer avec de l'argent et du tabac."

White Wing took up a pebble and tamped the tobacco. The man's silence agitated Professor Tiffin. "Nous faisons un voyage important," Tiffin said. "Envoyés par notre Grand Père le président."

The Native's reply was broken by long, moody pauses. Professor Tiffin responded rapidly; then White Wing grunted. "Difficile. C'est tout." He drew on the pipe and puffed sharply skyward.

"I explained that we would like to engage a guide," Tiffin said to Elisha. "He suggested it was possible, however when I described the image stones he claimed not to know their location. He is lying. He does not want us to visit the image stones."

The Native fastidiously tamped the tobacco. He seemed to regard the presence of Tiffin and Elisha as of minuscule importance compared to the proper draw of the pipe. Were he a white man, Elisha thought, he might be a bank bookkeeper with watch chain and pincenez spectacles, slowly checking his arithmetic while an impatient patron looked on. White Wing drew on the pipe and closed his eyes with pleasure.

"There is an event tonight—a feast dance, or perhaps a Midewiwin ceremony. That lodge is being constructed in preparation." Professor Tiffin tugged at his shirt collar. He was perspiring despite the day's coolness. "This man is lying! He would prevent us from visiting the image stones!"

A Chippewa woman had entered the lodge opposite, and now her conversation with the brave rose to shouts. He spat into the cookfire; then his glance landed on Elisha. The boy froze. The brave said something and the woman stared out at the boy.

"I explained that our aim is to assist his people, by studying their glorious history," Tiffin said. "He claims not to understand. He does not want to aid us, at all."

The brave stepped from the lodge and squatted beside White Wing, mumbling in the man's ear. White Wing removed a particle of tobacco from his tongue. "Où votre frère?"

"He is speaking about Mr. Brush." Elisha's tone was deliberately calm. "This is one of the Natives from our parley near Point au Foin— the brave with the scarlet cloak. Mr. Brush nearly shot him."

Professor Tiffin's expression flickered; then he smiled stiffly. Elisha said, "Tell them Brush returned to the Sault. Tell them he deserted us, along with our guide."

Tiffin addressed the Natives in crisp, measured French. Elisha understood the words *man* and *forest* then lost the sentence's thread.

White Wing wheezed around the pipe stem. He spoke a phrase in Chippewa and the brave's glare deepened; then the man offered a grudging nod. Professor Tiffin reached into his pack and placed a second carrot of tobacco before the men.

"I informed them that Mr. Brush is wandering among the pines,"

Tiffin said, clambering to his feet. "I explained that we sent him into the forest this morning to hunt beaver, despite the fact that beaver appear only at night. I told them he is likely now hollering about the vanished canoe. Come, we must go. Immediately." Professor Tiffin bowed to the Chippewas then turned away.

They hurried among the lodges. A hunting party had returned, four young braves clustered around a pair of does trussed to travoises while women bent over the animals with skinning knives. A drum's hollow thump rose from the village's outskirts. To Elisha the scene seemed familiar yet sharply strange: a Chippewa version of a frontier town on militia day. Natives paused to watch them pass.

At their camp on the beach Elisha raised a fire while Tiffin paced with a flask of Indian whiskey. "They will ruin me," he repeated. "They will ruin me, both of them. They will ruin me utterly." Elisha did not know how to comfort the man. He busied himself with staking the tents and gathering driftwood, fixing a meal of panbread and fried pork. The day's light faded to a smear of stars. The drumming grew louder. At last Professor Tiffin dropped the flask and with a wheeze sat beside the cookfire. He stared at his mug for a long while before setting the food aside.

"Did you ever dream you would find yourself in such a circumstance? At the edge of the white world, without a guide, a profound discovery just beyond your grasp?"

Tiffin was drunk. Without waiting for Elisha's response he began a rambling monologue about his wife. Her name was Minerva. He had met her in Buffalo at the Hudson Street fish market some seven years ago. Her grandfather and grandmother had been slaves in Savannah but her mother and father were free in Buffalo. He had been stripped of his pew in the First Congregational Church for marrying a Negro. She was the most beautiful woman God had yet formed, her skin the color of cocoa, her lips as sweet as maple sugar. Her elder brother had been killed in a sugar factory in Manhattan, her younger brother had been killed in the Second War for Independence. He would someday stroll into the First Congregational Church with Minerva and their children, take their seats in his pew and smile at the minister. The minister's name was Howell. He owned slaves in Savannah.

Tiffin's tone was flat, as though he were narrating the misfortunes of a stranger. Elisha felt a tug of sympathy for the man. Minerva was the woman in the wedding portrait that Elisha had seen in Sault Ste. Marie, when he'd entered Tiffin's room at the Johnston Hotel. He tried to recall her face: beautiful for a Negress, with high, proud cheekbones and a delicate nose, an expression of grave determination. As though she understood that her marriage would be both a blessing and a severe trial.

A wailing chant rose from the village, and Tiffin cocked his head like a pointer tracking game. "The ceremony," he said. "It is beginning." He swallowed a pull of whiskey and hauled himself to his feet.

"What are you intending to do?"

Tiffin started toward the village. Elisha called again, "What are you intending to do?" Then he rushed after the man.

Cookfires glinted like wildflowers among the empty lodges. At the village's edge a bonfire threw globes of light into the sky. The drumming grew to a loud pulse. A dog bayed, plaintive and wolflike, then a child began to cry. The air smelled of tobacco smoke and burning hair. Tiffin stumbled forward, groping before himself like a blind man. They emerged at the massive elm, and then they were in the midst of the ceremony.

A cold shock gripped Elisha. An open-ended lodge stretched before them, crowded with braves and old men and women and young boys, their faces streaked by shadows as if with war paint. A bonfire as tall as a man burned near the lodge's end. White Wing sat beside the fire, smoking his red pipe, pea jacket buttoned to his throat. Before him a brave scuffed in the lodge's center, naked save for a beaded breechclout and leggings. The brave's face was painted with red stripes, and an otter-skin pouch was slung across his chest. His chant rose to a falsetto then dropped to a low mutter. Dust billowed from the brave's tracks and glared pink in the firelight. His eyes were pinched shut, as though he were struggling through a terrible dream.

"A Midewiwin ceremony." Professor Tiffin's voice was an awed whisper, a drunk man startled to sobriety. "Most likely it is the last night of an induction ceremony, in which the public views the initiates. This brave is an initiate! He is singing an incantation, he is saying— What is he saying?—'I take life from the clear sky.' Something... 'The spirit is coming into my body.' Yes."

The brave's voice pitched like a kite in a gale. He stepped with stiff precision, bending double then throwing his head back, running forward in a dash before slowing his pace. Tiffin strained forward, among a row of children. A Native woman cradling an infant glanced back at him.

"We should not be here," Elisha murmured. "Please, Professor Tiffin, I beg you—"

" 'The spirit has dropped medicine from the clear sky. I have the medicine in my heart.' "

Elisha could not drag his eyes from the brave. The man's body glowed, sweat shimmering on his neck and chest, strands of black hair scrawled across his face. He was the howling red savage of countless engravings, the image Elisha had feared as a child. A feral-looking dog ran into the circle and snapped at a cloud of smoke. The man did not open his eyes.

" 'I have the medicine in my heart. Listen! I have the medicine in my heart.' "

White Wing stood with a fist held to his lips, tracking the man; then the brave suddenly screamed, his arms thrown wide as though he'd been shot. He collapsed in a sprawl as a cry rose from the crowd. The dog feinted at the fallen brave. After a moment the Native rose, eyes closed, and resumed scuffing around the fire.

Professor Tiffin edged toward the lodge's center. Elisha grabbed the man's wrist but he twisted away, stumbled into the firelight. He stood petrified, mouth slack; then he staggered forward in imitation of the dancing brave.

A howl went up and two braves were upon Tiffin, one brave wrenching his arm while the other collared his neck. Tiffin screamed. They dragged him thrashing in the dust toward the lodge's far end. Elisha ran around the gathering's perimeter, his chest tight with fear, and saw the braves hurl Tiffin down to the dirt. The sound was like a sack of meal dropped onto a stone floor. He rolled to his knees and a brave kicked him in the stomach. Elisha cried, "Arrêtez! *Please!*" A brave stomped Tiffin's back and the man crumpled, moaning. The second brave drew a skinning knife, and Elisha threw himself across Tiffin's body and raised a hand. "Please, *arrêtez*! I beg of you!"

The brave seized Elisha's throat and screamed in his face. The boy twisted away with a whimper. He scrambled beneath Tiffin and hauled the man to his feet. Blood welled from Tiffin's forehead and seeped across his nose. He lurched toward the circle but Elisha locked his hands around the man's chest and dragged him stumbling into the darkness. Tiffin smelled of vomit and whiskey. The braves shouted after them.

"I have the medicine in my heart," Tiffin said.

"I know you do. Shush now."

Elisha staggered through the empty village, ignoring the man's mumblings. At the lake's edge, he eased Tiffin down beside the cook-fire. The man's head lolled forward; then he groaned and touched his swollen cheek. He stared thickly at Elisha. "I am sorry, my boy. I am so very sorry."

"I know you are. Shush."

"You must help me. You *must*."

"I will."

"Susette Morel is vanished—I cannot engage another guide. We may not ever reach the image stones. Do you understand?" Professor Tiffin searched the boy's face. His teeth were marked with blood. "We are alone now, the two of us. You *must* help me."

Tiffin reached for the boy but Elisha pushed his hand away. "You have to curb yourself! Quit your drinking and your foolishness with the Chippewas. You—"

Elisha broke off. For it was his own fault that Susette had left—this trouble was a product of his own drunken foolishness. He thought to tell Professor Tiffin about his encounter with the woman, then realized it would solve nothing.

Tiffin struggled upright. "We will continue onward tomorrow, the two of us. We have the Bayfield chart and plenty of stores. Providence will keep us."

"We must return to the fur post. To fetch Mr. Brush."

"Silas Brush is a fine woodsman—he will manage. We must continue onward! We will explain our circumstance when we return to Detroit—that we were threatened by enraged Chippewas and barely escaped with our lives! It is nothing less than the truth."

Elisha said nothing. He could not look at the man.

"You must help me, my boy. You *must*."

Elisha rose and took up a mug. "I'll fetch some water. Don't go anywhere."

He hurried into the darkness and squatted on the riverbank, waiting for his breathing to settle. He felt queasy with fear. Two days ago I was lying beside a fire, he thought, listening to Shakespeare. And now I am here. Shouts rose from the ceremony. Elisha returned to camp to find Professor Tiffin slumped beside the cookfire, asleep.

He drew a blanket over the man then watched his chest slowly rise and fall. The drumbeats' pace was that of a panicked heartbeat. Elisha fetched the rifle, then realized they had no powder or shot. Desperate laughter bubbled inside him. He rummaged in the stores for a hatchet, crouched against a boulder with it hugged against his chest. I will sit awake until dawn, he thought. The notion filled him with grim determination. Beside him, Professor Tiffin snored raggedly.

An aurora had spread across the sky, ghostly greenish clouds shot with amber ribbons. The colors pulsed as if in time to the drumming. Elisha recalled a passage from Ezekiel, about a whirlwind come from the north, a vast cloud, and a fire unfolding itself with great brightness. And out of the fire's midst the color of amber. Ezekiel, the angry prophet, with his vision of Magog, his valley of dry bones. Elisha wondered what the Chippewas might make of such a display. Augury, he supposed. A symbol, of good or ill.

And they shall know that I am the Lord, he thought. And I shall destroy the foreigners and the enemies of Judah.

Overhead the sky trembled and flared, as though stars had exploded and darkness would be no more.

Six

He woke with eyes closed, the shadow of an anxious dream darkening his mind. Where was he? Clap of hooves and wagon wheels, a church bell's clang. A boy's voice singing out, *Tyler's excesses exposed! Read every shocking word!* A mouse's rustle. He felt queasy, weightless. He did not want to open his eyes.

When he did, Reverend Stone faced a blurred version of his boardinghouse room: an airway filled with sun, a crumpled hat perched on the bedstead, a torn, mud-smeared jacket sprawled on the floorboards. A pitcher and chipped basin on the bedside table, beside a washrag stiff with blood. Reverend Stone reached for the pitcher and a hot splinter drove into his ribs. He wheezed sharply.

He stared at the mottled ceiling and explored the geography of his pain. His wrists and ankles were stiff, the joints scraped raw. His legs were scored with welts. The fingers of his right hand were kinked, the nails crusted with blood, and the entire arm was numb as wood. His throat was bruised. Reverend Stone touched his cheek to find the skin stretched and swollen, hot beneath his fingertips. It felt like a mummer's mask pressed against his face.

He raised himself to an elbow and sponged his neck with the bloody rag, then fell back, exhausted. Howell's money was gone. Reverend Stone thought he might be sick. A moment later he woke: the sun had shifted lower, the street noises become sparse and indistinct. The supper hour. Hunger pierced him; he rose and ate a crust of bread, chewing slowly. Visions of mud and fury crowded his mind, but he closed his eyes and drew a long breath and prayed a muddled appeal for forgiveness. Forgive me my weakness, O Lord, and my courtship of sin. Forgive me my scorn and suspicion of others. Forgive me my greed and my doubt in Your providence. Forgive me my pride. Accept my failings, Lord, and deliver me into Your grace. Reverend Stone repeated the petition until the words vanished. Then he lay listening to the sound of his own breathing.

He rose feeling superbly calm. He walked a few stiff turns around the room, fetched the Catlin book and a half-empty tin of toothache medication then reclined and fumbled five brown tablets into his mouth. He paged through the book, glancing at pictures of dour Natives dressed in beads and skins, their hair arranged like spurting fountains. His eye caught on a mention of the Great Spirit, their childish notion of God.

> I believe that the North American Indians have Jewish blood in their veins, though I would not assert (as some would) *that they are Jews,* or that they are *the ten lost tribes of Israel.* However Indians, like Jews, believe that they are the favorite people of the Great Spirit—and they, like Jews, seemed destined to be dispersed over the world, and scourged by the Almighty, and despised of man.

Along with the Catholics and Millerites, Reverend Stone thought. At least they are not alone. His eyelids and nose began to tingle, his breathing to thicken. He read on.

> The pious missionary finds himself here, I would venture, in an indescribable confusion of vice and ignorance, that must disgust and discourage him. And yet despite this I have ever thought, and still think, that the Indian's mind is a beautiful blank, on which anything might be written, if the right mode were taken to do it.

An image formed in Reverend Stone's mind of a schoolhouse slate covered with scrawl: She sells seashells on the seashore. Able was I ere I saw Elba. He grinned painfully.

Voices rose in the corridor: a man arguing with the proprietress. Then a rap at the door and Mrs. Barbeau's muffled voice: "Open up this door. You've a visitor claims to know you."

Reverend Stone rose gingerly and unlatched the door. Jonah Crawley stood in the hallway, holding a straw hat and wearing a corn-yellow waistcoat and maroon jacket, his hair oiled into a cowlick. His offered the minister a confused stare. "Good jay. What's become of your phiz?"

"Mr. Crawley," Reverend Stone croaked, "what a fine surprise. Come in, please. I fear I can offer little by way of hospitality."

Crawley stepped into the room as if into a smallpox pesthouse. He glanced at the ceiling and warped floorboards and flattened tick, then his gaze returned to the minister's face.

"I'm afraid there is just the one stool," Reverend Stone said. "My Empire chair is gone for repair." He attempted a smile and pain flared across his cheek. He sat heavily on the bed.

"Well. My goodness." Crawley produced two gnarled red apples from a jacket pocket. "I've brought these but I don't figure they're much use to you, what with all that swelling." He set the apples on the bedside table then took up the pitcher, filled an ironstone mug. He offered it to Reverend Stone with an encouraging nod.

The minister's throat felt like it was lined with flannel. When he'd finished drinking he asked, "Do you by chance have a mirror?"

Jonah Crawley chuckled. "I don't, lucky for you! You look like— my gracious—like fresh beefsteak on a butcher's counter. No: ground beefsteak. I guess you fared worst in the exchange?"

Reverend Stone recalled a flailing blow, a crush of bone beneath his fist. A shameful thrill rose in him: He had fought. He had passed the coward's trial.

"I suppose that is true."

Crawley chuckled again, then scanned the room and motioned grandly. "Well! It's finer than it looks from the street, at least. Though from the street it looks like a Neapolitan bordello. Pardon the expression."

"Just strolling through this part of the city, were you?"

Jonah Crawley dragged the stool beside the rickety bed. Through the slender airway came a riot of snuffling squeals, a call of *chuk chuk chuk chuk:* a hog reeve walking his rounds. He said, "In actuality, I'd hoped to ask your guidance on a certain matter. And I have brought you something. A gift."

"A gift?"

He reached inside his waistcoat and produced a folded sheet of cream-colored vellum. He opened it to a large square, offered it to the minister. "This is for you. A gift."

Reverend Stone angled the sheet toward the light. A drawing of an animal covered the page, a stag or antelope with spidery hairs dangling from its back labeled *Two Hearted* and *Dead* and *Yellow Dog*. It was a map of Michigan's northern peninsula. The hairs were rivers, the animal's horns a curving spit of land. Notes were penned along the peninsula's northern coastline: *Rapids, Portage Route, Indian Sugar Camp, Good Canoe Landing*. A thick black line wandered from Sault Ste. Marie westward along the coast, then down inland and back east, a notation reading *Silas Brush & Geo. Tiffin's Intended Route (approx)*. In the map's corner a compass rose was sketched in the form of intertwined trumpet vines.

"What in a Wednesday is this?" Reverend Stone whispered.

"Your boy's route, drawn by Mr. Charles Noble himself—as near as he could figure, anyway. It don't look to be especially precise, I know. I pressed for more particulars but that's all he claimed to know."

Reverend Stone's lips trembled. He brought the vellum close to his eyes. "How can we be certain it is truthful?"

"Oh, I'd wager it's truthful enough. Men like Noble generally tell the truth when there's no more to gain from lying."

The northern peninsula's eastern tip was dense with river and trail markings, regions of swampland and marsh, but the interior was blank save for a few scattered crosses: *Baptist Mission. Fur Post. Abandoned Fur Post*. Elisha's route wound through the heartland, a stone flung through empty space. Reverend Stone lay the map on his chest. He said, "Mr. Jonah Crawley. I am indebted."

"No, I wouldn't term it such." Crawley ducked his head as a pleased grin spread over his face. "I wanted to assist you, Reverend Stone. Purely that. Of course, I hoped you might want to assist me in return. But you've no obligation."

The minister said nothing.

Crawley straightened on the stool. "You see, I would like to be married."

"Mr. Crawley! My sincere congratulations!"

"I'm not a deeply prayerful man, but I want to be married proper. For my bride's sake—I want her soul to be in the pink of health. Mine's too far lost for concern." Crawley grimaced as he pinched the brim of his straw hat. "That was meant as a joke. Of course I don't mean that."

Reverend Stone sensed that the man had not finished speaking. Jonah Crawley's gaze was fixed on the sun-filled airway. "Adele, you see. She is not quite my daughter. She is my betrothed. We've meant to be married for some while, but never managed it." Crawley wiped his face with both hands. "She is with child."

Reverend Stone nodded as a prickle raced over his scalp. He could not find a single thing to say. Adele Crawley, with her pockmarked cheeks and weary, womanly eyes. Perhaps it was plain to everyone except himself that the two were a pair. His country greenness was showing yet again.

"How old is Adele?"

"Sixteen. No—fifteen."

"And yourself?"

"Thirty-seven." The man blinked rapidly and turned away.

"Well. Mr. Crawley." Reverend Stone found himself worrying the map edge. He set it down to avoid fraying the vellum. "You have no doubt identified your sin: lying with a woman before matrimony. 'Let every man have his own wife, and let every woman have her own husband.' Yes?" He leaned forward to peer into the man's face. "Under such circumstances I'm afraid I cannot join the two of you. I am truly sorry."

Crawley nodded.

"What creed is the girl? And yourself?"

"Adele's Methodist. Myself the same, I suppose—I've heard them preach as much as any other." Crawley pursed his lips. "I did not intend to lie with her, Reverend Stone. It was merely a traveling arrangement at first, sharing a bed. Purely thrift."

A wave of nausea rose in the minister's stomach, and he swallowed hard to subdue the feeling. He needed a tablet. He said, "Tell me. How did you come to be with her?"

Jonah Crawley sighed, a long whistle. When he spoke his voice was tinged with wonder: Adele Grainger had saved his life. He had met her three years ago in Paducah, Kentucky, traveling at the time, an itinerant salesman of Indian herbs. The remedies he sold were ground nettles mixed with tobacco and powdered manure, with a sprinkle of whatever was handy. For cholera cures a pinch of wood ash. For ague a trace of dirt, damp with horse piss.

His partner was a violent half-breed Chickasaw named Thomas Coldwater, who drummed business in a ragged eagle-feather war bonnet and leggings, spent his earnings on claret and opium. Crawley had been raised in a temperance house but quickly adopted Coldwater's habits. Entire days disappeared, Crawley waking in strange cities at midnight, the half-breed muttering beside him and the horses near starved. He felt anxious and miserable, overwhelmed by fear, as though he were living beneath a raven's black shadow.

They worked their way from New York down through Pennsylvania and Maryland then on into the prairillons of Virginia. Rheumy old women came to them. Spotty young men. At first Crawley was startled and delighted that folks would buy their wares; then his delight faded. Girls bearing wheezy newborns. Shaky folks of every age. Dyspeptics and consumptives and yellow-eyed malarials. Gentlemen and whores and darkies. The country was everywhere sick, everywhere dying. Folks handed Crawley worn half-dollars and blessed his name, then solemnly accepted a bag of shit.

One morning in Big Lick Crawley rose at dawn and stepped from the wagon with his old flintlock pistol. He was naked save for his boots. He walked a circuit around the touring wagon then squatted in the mud and shoved the pistol barrel in his mouth. It tasted of clay and bitter metal. Above him the sky swarmed with ravens, their stench fouling the air, their wingbeats deafening. He realized that it wouldn't matter a cent if he pulled the trigger.

So he did. The powder flashed and sizzled, the rusted hammer snapping uselessly. Crawley laid the gun down and curled into a ball. Thomas Coldwater found him there hours later, whipped him awake with a Negro lash. Crawley feigned drunkenness to avoid the half-breed's mocking questions.

They traveled together for three more years, through the Carolinas and Georgia and Alabama then back up north, the raven's shadow ever near. They had been three days in Paducah when he was awakened by a rap on the wagon frame. He poked his head through the gate flap: a sallow, barefoot man stood beside a green-eyed girl with freckled cheeks and knotty red hair. The girl was prison pale, her hands trembling with fever, her chemise hanging like a scarecrow's cloak.

The man spoke. His girl was ill in the lungs, a pneumoniac disorder. The town surgeon had bled her near empty. A slave root doctor had given her sticks to chew. Neither had helped. He needed some strong herbs. He feared she would die.

She had been so lovely, standing wide-eyed in her pink chemise, fingernails gnawed to nubs. Crawley shook Thomas Coldwater awake, asked him to mix a real remedy, a Chickasaw remedy, at any cost or trouble. The half-breed blinked at him. Finally he laughed. "No such thing as real. Stupid white coot."

Crawley told the girl to come back that night, then set to making his own remedy. He boiled sprigs of comfrey root and tansy and elecampane, added horehound and creosote and a dollop of honey. His spirits blackened as he watched the mixture bubble. His life was lies. He knew no trade, had no particular skill save for making pleasant conversation. His Indian herbs were shit and dirt and lies, his life was lies. He added five grains of Thomas Coldwater's opium to the thick mixture. Then he added five more grains and a slug of claret.

She returned alone that night in a mizzling rain. Crawley had clipped his beard, brushed his coat and hat and steamed his shirtfront, and for good measure combed the tails of the mangy Cleveland bays. When the girl tapped at the wagon frame his appearance caused her a moment's confusion; then with a flourish he produced a phial.

She flushed deeply. "Please accept my sincerest apologies," she said. "I've no coin to buy your remedy. I can offer you a séance in barter."

"She peered inside me," Crawley said. "I can't describe it otherwise. She summoned my dead grandam in conversation, but mainly she was speaking to me. About my loneliness and fear. About my lies. She told me I'd been running up and down the country to avoid something that was chasing me. She was right."

And then the girl left. The next morning Thomas Coldwater woke in a sulk and bridled the horses, pissed on the cookfire. They drove on to Metropolis then Midway, Crawley misplacing his memories of the girl among fevered daydreams. Two weeks later in Golconda, Crawley at midnight laid eighty dollars coin beside Thomas Coldwater's delirious form, then saddled the smaller bay. Eighty dollars was nearly all the money he possessed in the world, but he considered it a bargain to be rid of the man.

He spent much of the trip back to Paducah considering what he might say to the girl. That he was lost and seeking directions to Golconda. That he was verifying the effectiveness of his remedy. That he needed to speak with his dearly departed sister Alma. Kentucky rolled before him, the lush green hills like crumpled satin. That he had dreamed of her every night for fourteen days. That he loved her beyond reason and beyond the confines of his puny heart.

Her father's house stood at the end of a grist mill road. It was a dogtrot cabin with a single window hung with parchment, a stick chimney warped near to collapse. The day was hot and a teasing breeze rose from the south. Crawley rubbed his face with creek water and gathered a spray of oxeye daisies, smoothed his shirt and hair, buffed his muddy boots. He rapped on the cabin door.

The girl opened the door. Her cheeks held a ripe tint; her shoulders were thicker and softer, less birdlike. Her expression moved in an instant from wariness to confusion to glee. She covered her mouth and squealed. "I prayed and you came! Good holy God."

"The raven's shadow disappeared—I've not seen it since." Jonah Crawley shrugged. "And that is how she saved me."

A swell of emotion had grown in Reverend Stone, far out of proportion to the story's sentiment. He said softly, "You should've quit her while you might have."

"I tried to, with all my soul. We were chaste for eleven months, until the day she turned fourteen." Crawley shook his head. "I am sorry, Reverend Stone. She is my tonic, that girl. She is my life."

The minister turned toward the wall to avoid facing the man. Jonah Crawley was thirty-seven years old to Adele's fifteen; when Crawley was forty-one the girl would be nineteen. Nearly the same ages, Reverend Stone thought, that he and Ellen had been when they'd married. And so perhaps he and Jonah Crawley were more alike than he had imagined. Crawley was worried only for Adele's happiness. He understood her presence in his life as a gift, inexplicable and undeserved. He believed their future together to be limitless and full of light.

"Do you love Adele, Mr. Crawley?"

The man nodded. "With every particle."

"Do you love her as deeply as you love the Lord?"

Jonah Crawley stared at the minister. "It's different, Reverend Stone. A different sort of love. Surely."

"It is, yes. It has a certain texture, and warmth. And with it a sense of fragility. A fear that it might someday...disappear."

Crawley rose with a defeated sigh. "I understand if you can't marry us, Reverend Stone—most ministers wouldn't. The days will go on. Not being married will just make us a little more damned."

He set his hat upon his head. "Oh—there's one more thing." He patted his waistcoat pocket then withdrew a stoppered phial of yellow-green liquid. "For that cough of yours. An old Chickasaw remedy."

Reverend Stone took the phial in both hands. He had no faith in herb medicine but nonetheless felt a deep bloom of gratitude, a chambered part of himself opening outward. He thought he might begin to weep. He set the phial on the bedside table, his fingers trembling. What is happening to me? he wondered.

"Don't drink it all at once, you'll get the sprays. Take half now, half tomorrow morning."

"Thank you, Mr. Crawley. Truly."

Crawley touched his hat brim as he opened the door.

"Arrange a place for tomorrow at noon," Reverend Stone called. "Please. I will be honored to marry you and Adele."

The ceremony was held in the upstairs room of Anders Lund's saloon, a lawyers' haunt with garish crimson wallpaper and a plaster replica of Michelangelo's *David* propped in the corner. An organ grinder squatted on a three-legged stool before the fireplace, studying a picture magazine. Beside him was a table transformed by pine boughs into a makeshift altar. Jonah Crawley sat stiffly at the bar, dressed in a sky-blue jacket and waistcoat, a yellow silk cravat blossoming at his throat. When Reverend Stone appeared in the doorway Crawley jerked upright and took the minister's hand. His white cotton gloves were damp with perspiration.

"We're ready to begin anytime, Reverend. I thank you again."

"You will need a witness, of course." Reverend Stone nodded toward the organ grinder. "Is he agreed to the task?"

"He is. Cost me two dollars extra." Crawley laughed abruptly, his breath sharp with whiskey and onions. Then he became serious. "Does it matter that he don't speak English?"

Reverend Stone smiled to calm the man. "I will need to speak with Adele for a short while. Alone."

"Of course. She's just in the storeroom."

The minister passed behind the bar to the storeroom and knocked softly. A voice said, "One moment," followed by a rustle of fabric and a chair's loud scrape. Adele Grainger opened the door.

She looked so frail. She wore a yellow satin Trafalgar dress trimmed with crepe, white kid gloves with ivory buttons, a white lace fichu knotted loosely at her breast. Her hair was twisted into sugar curls and garlanded with orange blossoms, the flowers wilting on her powdered forehead. She looked like a girl playing dress-up in her mother's wardrobe, and Reverend Stone imagined her standing in the rain outside Crawley's wagon three years ago, penniless, her hair in knots and fingernails worried away. Adele squinted at Reverend Stone's swollen face but said nothing.

"Goodness me. Am I the lucky first to admire your radiance?"

She glanced shyly away. "These gloves are the same old ones I wear for séances. The fichu I found in a rich lady's gutter on Beaubien Street, just cast away. The dress is precious, though. It was my mother's when she married my daddy, God rest her soul."

"How wonderfully fine." Reverend Stone paused to lend gravity to his next statement. "Young lady. Do you understand the significance of the matrimonial covenant?"

The girl nodded, her green eyes unblinking.

"You understand it as a lifelong joining between husband and wife, ordered toward their happiness and toward the procreation of children, that no man may put asunder?"

She nodded again. She was strangely calm, more old woman than young girl. She nudged an orange blossom higher on her brow.

"I was certain you did. I simply felt that I must ask."

Reverend Stone grinned awkwardly as several long moments passed. A barman passed the open door, yawning as he tucked a shirttail into his trousers. He took up a tumbler and poured a measure of green liquor, then with a sigh drank it down. At last Reverend Stone said, "Tell me. How do you do it? Your . . . talent."

Adele shrugged. "I merely listen. Though often it's not listening as much as watching those who remain. They tell you plenty about the departed without saying a word. It's engraved on them."

"And the table?"

"Well, yes, the table." She bit her lower lip to hide a smile. "The table is primarily for theatrics—I rigged it myself, quite cleverly I believe. Folks expect a show when they pay a quarter dollar." She looked up at the minister. "But the spirits are genuine, Reverend Stone. Some of us possess a gift for the spiritual. You and I are similar in that way."

He thought of his visions of souls, the ghostly haze that appeared and disappeared without reason; then he realized the girl was speaking of his vocation.

She leaned toward Reverend Stone and took his hand. "You have suffered a loss, but you mustn't let yourself feel guilty. It's common for a person to feel guilty when they suffer loss. The two are boon companions."

He said nothing.

"Mr. Crawley helped me to surmount the loss of my mother. He cured me of my guilt and sorrow, my black feelings. He showed me how to aid people with my gift, how to cure them of their own sorrows, their own black feelings. He would not let me feel guilty, not the littlest bit. And now I am famous."

Reverend Stone smiled vaguely. "You are a wise girl."

"I know."

Adele Grainger reached into her handbag and withdrew a closed fist, opened it into the minister's palm: a tarnished silver chain fastened to a loop of rawhide. The hide was dimpled and scored, as though it had been chewed to relieve pain. She said, "For your journey. It's from my daddy's brogans that he wore all through the Indian wars. They kept his luck for nearly three years. He had a ball pass through his hat brim but he marched home, safe as a salamander. He's living still."

Reverend Stone draped the chain between his fingers. A lucky talisman: it was an inappropriate gift, but nonetheless he dropped it into his vest pocket. "Thank you, Adele. I pray it keeps me as well as it kept your father."

"As do I. And there's this—for your service today." She pressed two gold eagle coins into the minister's palm.

"Now, that is far too generous."

Adele shushed him as she closed his fingers around the money. "Mr. Crawley and I are indebted far beyond two eagles. And besides, that's just a lazy night's work on Sixth Street."

Reverend Stone thanked the girl, then excused himself and stepped out into the barroom. He touched Jonah Crawley's elbow and said, "Now," and the man's face fell slack. He fluffed his cravat and tugged down his shirtfront, signaled to the organ grinder. The man dropped the magazine with a hiccup and cranked his instrument. A wheezy chord rose and thickened to a strong, clear melody: "A Mighty Fortress Is Our God." Reverend Stone moved to the fireplace, smiled at the bemused barman. A moment later the storeroom door opened and Adele appeared, her skirts flared, a square of white tulle veiling her face. She clutched a bouquet of oxeye daisies.

"Good holy God," Crawley said.

She hurried toward the altar, then as if recalling an instruction slowed her pace. A smile trembled on her lips. She glanced from the minister to the organ grinder to Jonah; then her smile steadied.

They stood before Reverend Stone at the altar as the organ sighed to silence. Adele's smile had vanished. Droplets of sweat slid down Crawley's forehead. A shout rose from the saloon below, followed by laughter and a man's mincing falsetto. Jonah Crawley squeezed his eyes shut and heaved a sigh. The girl took his hand.

"We are gathered to join in marriage Mr. Jonah Crawley of Yonkers, New York, to Miss Adele Grainger of Paducah, Kentucky, and if anyone present has objection to this union let him speak."

Silence; then a groan escaped the organ grinder's instrument. Crawley smiled nervously.

"Jonah Crawley. Do you promise before God your unending love and constancy, your devotion and support, for better or worse, for richer or poorer, in sickness and in health, until parted by death? Do you promise this though you might be brittle in temper and low in spirit, though you might be burdened with sorrow and doubt, though you might find faith a dark and narrow path?"

"I surely do. Of course I do."

"Adele Grainger. Do you promise the same?"

"Indeed I do."

Was this how I appeared? Reverend Stone wondered. A stooped, nervous man beside a radiant young woman? That morning in the meetinghouse, he remembered, the gallery had been filled with crying infants, and the sound had been as satisfying as music. By March Ellen would be pregnant with Elisha.

"Adam said, This is now bone of my bones, and flesh of my flesh, and she shall be called woman, because she was taken out of man. Therefore shall a man leave his father and his mother and cleave unto his wife. And they shall be one flesh. And it shall be good, and blissful, and true." Reverend Stone smiled. "My dear friends. It is with profound pleasure that I bond you in matrimony. Go forth together in His service, and may your days be long together upon this great, green earth."

A squeal escaped Adele. Jonah Crawley's cheeks were wet with tears, his jaw trembling as though he might be sick. He lifted the girl's veil. She blinked, her eyes clouded with fear and longing, an achy fullness of joy. Jonah Crawley touched his wife's chin and kissed her softly on the lips.

Part Three

One

They canoed eastward on a riffled gray lake, Tiffin sprawled across the gunwales as he described an idea that had emerged in a recent dream: that perfectly spherical pearls might be formed by continuously rotating pearl-bearing mollusks in an underwater device. Centrifugal force, he explained, would smooth the distribution of nacre about the pearl's seed, and continuous agitation would induce prodigious growth. Elisha said little, struggling against a swirling breeze. Professor Tiffin's cheek and lip were swollen taut, his forehead filigreed with dried blood. He had not protested when Elisha had steered the canoe east that morning, toward the fur post and Mr. Brush. Finally Tiffin drifted off to sleep, his hat tumbling to the canoe's bottom. By nightfall they had traveled only two leagues.

They set out the next morning at dawn and by midafternoon had come to a familiar umber-colored river. They followed it past pine stumps budding with root sprouts, bayberry and shadbush blooming in swollen clumps, slender red maples poking through the mat. Death and renewal, the forest rebirthing itself. A marsh hawk skimmed over the knobby tract. Two hours later they reached the circle of split-log cabins and the naked flagpole. Mr. Brush was sitting on a stump before the commis' house, whittling a tent stake. At the river's edge stood Susette Morel.

"Welcome!" Tiffin scrabbled over the canoe's side and splashed toward the woman, arms outspread. "Welcome back, my dear madame, welcome! One hundred thousand welcomes!"

Tightness gripped Elisha's throat as he landed the canoe. He could not look at Susette.

"It appears you were correct," Brush said dryly. "She claims she was lost. Ask her. She claims she was gathering herbs for supper and misremembered the camp's location."

"You were lost and now are found! And so we are reunited!" Tiffin seemed to be resisting an urge to hug the woman. At last he seized her hand and kissed it. "And we are utterly thrilled, all of us!"

She stood ankle-deep in the river, skirts gathered at her knees, holding a skillet. Her cheeks were flushed and wisps of loose hair lay pasted across her forehead. She smiled politely at Professor Tiffin; then her gaze shifted to Elisha. To the boy's surprise he was overcome by anger.

"Seems odd," he said. "How does a body become lost such a short distance from camp?"

"The sun was hidden by rain clouds. I lost my direction. It can happen like that in the forest, no matter the distance from camp."

"I suppose we're expected to take you at your word."

"I expect nothing at all."

"No matter, no matter!" Tiffin clapped his hands. "I propose that we continue onward at the first glimmer of dawn, after a hearty supper! No offense, young fellow, but your cookery skills are a fair stripe lower than our dear madame's."

"Your face." Mr. Brush squinted, leaning toward Professor Tiffin. "You have been attacked."

"No matter!" He threw open the door to the commis' house. From inside he called, "A celebratory toast! Where is my beloved whiskey jug?"

"This discussion is not ended!" Brush waited, lips pursed; then he flung the tent stake away and snatched up his rifle and shot bag. To Elisha he said, "I will be back in one hour. I feel the need to shoot something."

Elisha watched the man vanish into the forest. He felt suddenly exhausted, as though the tiniest movement would overwhelm him. He could not understand whether he should run to Susette or run away. She took up a cookpot from the riverbank and rinsed it; then she threw it tumbling away. She sobbed, a thick gasp. She looked as shocked and mortified as a child.

"My dear," Elisha whispered. "I am so sorry. For my behavior—for what occurred the other night. *Please.* I am so very sorry."

"There is no need to apologize," Susette said. "I am the one who chose—"

"A celebratory toast!" Professor Tiffin appeared in the doorway with the jug held aloft. "Come, both of you—we must celebrate the joyful reuniting of the party!"

At Tiffin's insistence supper was an elaborate affair, broiled lake trout and venison steaks, wild greens stewed with liver and kidney, flour biscuits with gravy and gills of Indian whiskey for toasting Susette's health. The cabin was quiet save for the clatter of pans and Tiffin's cheery instructions to the woman. Wind sluiced down the chimney and flared the fire, sent puffs of ash over the hearth. Professor Tiffin, as he ate, recounted their excursion to the Chippewa village.

"It is a large encampment of perhaps two hundred souls, quite attractively situated beside a fair-sized stream. The location was doubtless chosen for its fishing opportunities, as there was of course no evidence of land cultivation. We were granted an audience with a chief named White Wing. Do you know the man?"

Susette shook her head. She was seated near the hearth, her back to Elisha.

"A curious fellow. Solemn in the extreme, like many of their chiefs, and possessed of a subtle stubbornness. Earbobs the size of chestnuts, I suspect as an indication of his warrior status. I explained the purpose of our expedition, and he confirmed that, indeed, a narrative exists of the origins of the Chippewa people. He was reluctant to reveal any details—only elders of the Midewiwin society are privy to such knowledge."

Tiffin set down his plate and tugged his frayed whiskers. "That night, however, I secretly observed a Midewiwin ceremony. An initiation ceremony, I believe, with ardent singing and music-making, the form of which strongly recalled certain rites of the ancient Hebrew people. I observed—"

"You were attacked," Brush said. "Did that occur during your tea party with Mr. Wing?"

Tiffin dismissed the comment with a glance. "A minor misfortune—I stumbled over an exposed root. To continue, I observed Midewiwin elders reading from stone tablets that appeared to contain pictographic transcriptions of their ceremonial songs. The brave undergoing initiation was chanting an incantation, which I inter—"

"And in your excitement, you stumbled numerous times over an exposed root. A natural explanation for the bruising on your face."

" 'Mock on, mock on, 'tis all in vain.' Young Elisha can confirm every detail of my account."

"Can he?"

Elisha stared into the fire, avoiding Mr. Brush's gaze. He wished Professor Tiffin would stop lying.

"We are near to the image stones," Tiffin said. "Very near. I expect that quite soon I will unearth written accounts of the origins of the Chippewa people, which will resolve forevermore the question of the unity of races—and, of course, secure my victory in our wager."

"Secure your reputation as a fool, you mean." Brush shoved his plate away. "This expedition is becoming as ridiculous as a bull with teats. Pardon my language, Madame Morel."

A tense silence settled over the cabin. Mr. Brush arranged a pair of grease lamps on the table, opened his fieldbook and frowned at the pages. Professor Tiffin strode to the bookcase and took down a volume, threw himself with a huff on his throne of skins. Sapwood popped and hissed in the fire. Susette gathered the supper plates, and as she moved toward the hearth Elisha said, "Let me assist you. Please." He hoisted the cookpot from its trammel, then followed the woman into the night.

Clouds had gathered in thin, low layers, violet and indigo against a black sky. Night animals skittered through the brush. Elisha followed Susette to the riverbank, then knelt beside her as she sprinkled sand over the plates. An ember of anger burned in his chest. Despite it he felt drawn to the woman, like a compass needle toward iron.

"We nearly engaged a new guide, figuring you wouldn't return. Lucky for you Professor Tiffin is a terrible negotiator. Otherwise you'd be swimming back to the Sault right now."

Susette glanced toward the cabin door. "Lower your voice."

"I can understand why you ran away. What I can't understand is why you came back. Can you explain me that?"

"I told you this morning. I became lost in the forest, because of the clouds. This morning I found my way back to camp."

"You did not become lost in the forest," Elisha hissed. "You ran away. You ran away without even a farewell, because you felt as guilty as I did for doing what we did. But then you changed your mind and you came back."

"The sun was hidden and I lost my direction—you do not believe me, but it is true. It happens even to my husband."

"Your husband. There. At least now you've said the word." Elisha seized a plate and scrubbed roughly. "You don't have to explain yourself. Seems you'd want to, but I guess a woman like you—"

"You know nothing!" Susette threw the platter into the sand. "You are a frightened little boy! You claim you are a scientist when you are nothing but a packer, you point your rifle at Chippewas when they want only to trade! You talk like a man but you act like a frightened boy, and now you think—what? What do you think you know?"

Elisha was frozen, wordless. Susette turned away and he said, "Forgive me. I am sorry."

She began to sob in sharp, dry coughs. Elisha touched her wrist, suddenly unsure of how to comfort the woman. She is right, he thought, I am a frightened boy. He pressed his lips to her shoulder and her scent was achingly familiar. She looked at him with an intensity that momentarily startled the boy.

"I left because I was afraid," Susette said. "But I returned because I am not afraid anymore."

"I don't get your meaning."

The woman was silent for a moment; then she drew a thick breath. "I cannot return to the Sault."

"Because of us. Because of our union." Elisha took both of her hands in his. "I admit that I feel very guilty about what happened. But I—"

"Sometimes I deserve it, I say something bold or I raise my voice. Then I do not blame him. I deserve what he gives to me."

"What who gives to you?"

She shook her head. "I try very hard but I deserve it. I do. I am bold and I deserve what he gives to me."

"Susette—who are you talking about?"

She shook her head again, her cheeks shining with tears. A thin whine escaped her throat.

"Susette, my dear." Elisha drew the woman to him but she pulled away. "You must tell—"

"I do not blame him for the strap or the switch or the cinder tongs. But other times it is too much. He is drunk and it is too much." Susette's words fractured into choking sobs. "When he is drunk he cannot feel how much he hurts me. He cannot feel when it is too much."

Elisha said nothing.

"He has a fiddle. He takes the bow of the fiddle and he uses it inside me. Do you understand? He uses it inside me and tells me terrible things. I am a dirty chienne, a cunt, a whore. I am a dirty whore and I deserve to be treated like a dog. He hurts me."

Elisha was numbed by the woman's words. "Please, Susette."

"Our cabin is one room and there is no place to go. He hurts me and then he plays his fiddle. He plays a song for me, 'La Belle Susette.' I lay on the floor and listen to him play, and there is no place to go."

"Stop. Please." He drew the woman close and she buried her face against his neck. Elisha stroked her shoulder as the night's sounds melted away. He felt lifeless, his senses dulled and confused. He pressed his lips against the woman's hair and closed his eyes.

An image rose in the boy's mind of Susette's cabin in Sault Ste. Marie: a dirt floor, a flattened pallet, a soiled chemise like a stain on the wall. A single small window, a wooden crucifix. He remembered thinking that it was no better than a Chippewa cabin, a case of savage blood dominating the white. The memory sent a chill through him. Elisha moved to speak but could not. His heart throbbed and he was mortified by its intensity.

"Is there no one for you there? Your mother, or a sister..."

His question trailed to silence. Susette drew away from the boy and wiped her face. "My mother is in St. Catharines. My sister is dead. I have no one at the Sault except my husband."

"I will help you."

She nodded, blinking back tears.

"I will help you—we'll go somewhere, together. We'll go to Detroit, take a room in a boardinghouse on Woodward Avenue. I know a man named Alpheus Lenz who might give me work as a specimen cataloger. We can stay there for a while and you'll be safe. We can go to the Rogers Theater—we can see *As You Like It*!"

A tearful smile flickered across her face. "You are a sweet boy."

"Or we'll go farther, to New York or to Massachusetts. We can go to Newell, where I was raised. My mother and father are living there still. We can go there and live in a proper house, with some land for crops. We can raise beans and squash and you won't ever have to worry about your husband, ever again."

"You are a sweet boy, but I cannot go to Detroit or Massachusetts. I wish that I could, but I cannot. I cannot go anywhere that—"

Just then the cabin door creaked open. Susette squeezed Elisha's hand, then clattered the supper plates into a stack. Mr. Brush's shadow darkened the doorway; then the man cleared his throat and spat.

"You are a sweet boy," Susette whispered. "But that is not how you will help me."

They remained at the fur post until noon the next day while Mr. Brush cataloged mineral specimens and copied field notes, recorded a few last measurements of the compass needle's deviation. Elisha wrapped ore samples in specimen pouches, penned a date and location on each pouch's bottom. Professor Tiffin paced along the river's edge. At last they loaded the canoe and started downriver through damp, feverish heat, a warm breeze rippling the river's surface. "A song," Tiffin urged Susette, "to pace our efforts!" The woman began a listless chanson.

Sparrow hawks circled overhead as the canoe entered the lake. They paddled past the Miner's River to the Train River, Elisha recognizing the streams from his journey with Professor Tiffin. The forest was a mixture of white pine and hemlock and beech and sugar maple; the coastline was fine siliceous sand studded with granite boulders. They encamped at dusk and ate a supper of bean stew and panbread then collapsed around the fire. Elisha woke before dawn from a dream of menacing pursuit. The party set off at first light, and at noon arrived at the Chippewa village.

The encampment was quiet, just a few women moving among the lodges, a pair of Native boys fishing at the lake's edge. Gray smoke hung in a veil over the village. Without pause the party portaged over a sandbar and started upriver. The Native boys boarded a canoe and paddled alongside, offering fresh, fat whitefish in exchange for tobacco. They were twelve years old, perhaps thirteen; Elisha recognized in their gestures a restrained eagerness, of young boys engaged in men's business. With a word Susette sent them away.

Red ash and sycamore appeared as they canoed inland, the forest growing shady and chill. After some time the river quickened to a white-flecked rush; then Mr. Brush guided the canoe to the river's edge before a shallow, stony ford. Elisha and Professor Tiffin splashed ashore and began hauling packs of stores onto the riverbank. Susette said, "It is not necessary to portage here."

"Why ever not?"

She motioned southeastward. A faint Indian trail cut through the understory, just the barest crush of leaves disappearing into the forest. "This is the end of the canoe. Now we go on foot."

The men paused. Somehow the moment had arrived, inevitable but unexpected. A shiver moved through Elisha as they unloaded the stores on the grassy riverbank, reloaded them into four massive packs bound with leather straps. "Proceed slowly!" Mr. Brush called. "You must move slowly until your body is accustomed to the additional burden!" As one they hoisted the packs with a huff, Tiffin and Susette shuffling under the load, the weight bending Elisha nearly double. He slipped the strap over his forehead and slowly straightened.

"Shall we begin, then?" Professor Tiffin gasped.

They stared at one another: shirts frayed and torn along the seams, stained with soot and deer grease and blood; faces suntanned a deep reddish-brown, the color of ore; leather straps like Native jewelry across their brows. This was the expedition's true beginning, Elisha realized. This was where his greatest efforts would be needed. This was where their hardship would begin.

They set out into the forest.

The Indian trail ran through rolling country of white pine and sugar maple and yellow birch, the soil mealy and black, the hills too low to yield a vista. Sunlight winked through the canopy. Susette set a measured pace, pausing only for Mr. Brush to count timber or mark a blaze. Apart from the man's called-out measurements no one spoke. It was as though a fog had settled over the party, left each unaware of the

others' existence. When Elisha caught Susette's eye her expression was
as blank as an empty page.

And so the boy passed the hours in solitude. Despite this he felt
surrounded by life, a million indifferent eyes regarding him. Wood
beetles creaked and catbirds mewed and wind pushed through the tall
spruces, their limbs stirring restlessly. That first afternoon, Elisha
glimpsed a dark shape gliding through a forest opening, and his chest
tightened: the bird was as large as an osprey, though with a long,
straight bill and a harrier's broad wings. He scrabbled for his fieldbook
but the bird had vanished. Elisha sketched the silhouette from memory, wondering all the while if he had imagined the creature.

On the second morning Professor Tiffin could not rise from his
bedroll. He lay on his back, moaning, his feet swollen and raw. Elisha
and Mr. Brush hoisted him upright, but when they released their grip
the man collapsed with a whimper. Elisha examined Tiffin's footwear:
the soles of his Hessian boots were worn through, the thin leather
gouged and split. Mr. Brush turned away in disgust. The boots were
more suited to an evening at the theater than a tramp through the forest. Susette cut a trade blanket into strips and wrapped the man's feet,
bound them with hide thongs then doused the shoepacks with water.
Tiffin rose with a whine and started gingerly forward. "My dear
madame," he mumbled. "My dear, dear Madame Morel . . . "

That third afternoon the party paused to rest in a clearing beside a
silty stream. Elisha sat on a windfall pine and it crumbled beneath
him, beetles swarming over the rotten trunk. He trapped one between
his palms and shook the insect still. A ground beetle, *Pterostichus
melanarius,* common as dirt. Still, he opened his fieldbook and described the beetle's antennae spreading like metallic antlers from its
angular head, its shiny, grooved thorax. He described its jointed legs,
the undersides fletched with shaggy hair, the tips cloven into pincers
for gripping prey.

Elisha lay down his pen and flipped back though the fieldbook: its
pages were filled with descriptions of beetles and boulders and

wildflowers, sea crows and sugar maples and swamp cabbage. For what purpose? He'd discovered not a single new species, recorded not a single unique observation about an existing species. His descriptions were as hazy and imprecise as gossip. Elisha let his eye travel over the sentences, pausing at an occasional phrase: *The tranquil sublimity of the scene. Shyly displaying its surpassing beauty.* In form and tenor they resembled the secret diary entries of a lovelorn young girl.

He recalled with a note of melancholy the days spent in Alpheus Lenz's house on Woodward Avenue, his desire to see Lenz's shelves filled with every species from Alabama to Africa. It had been so beautifully simple: the natural world arriving on his doorstep in wooden crates, preserved in jars and phials and pouches. As though every living thing could be captured and cataloged, inscribed on a page as large as a tobacco field. And now here he was among the ground beetles.

That afternoon the party made camp in a clearing, Susette taking a trout net to the stream while Tiffin reclined on his bedroll with a Hebrew lexicon. Mr. Brush gathered a rock hammer and specimen pouches and compasses, then gestured for Elisha to follow him into the forest.

The pair hiked along a southern bearing through white pine, the canopy pierced by columns of sunlight, the terrain mounded with moldering trunks. Mr. Brush leveled the solar compass and called out a measurement for Elisha to record, then repeated the measurement with the magnetic compass. Brush was clean-shaven, his hat and jacket tattered but brushed. Beside him a deer skeleton lay atop a litter of pine needles, saplings sprouting among the gray ribs. A bear's leavings, slowly being consumed by the forest. Mr. Brush tapped the instrument's face. "It is happening again!"

"What is happening?"

"The compass needle—I am recording deviations from the true bearing. We are standing in a valley of iron!"

Elisha smiled weakly, too distracted to share the man's enthusiasm. He said, "Could you repeat the solar compass measurement?"

"You are not concentrating."

He jerked back to the fieldbook. "Four degrees, two minutes. Is that correct?"

"I would expect my counsel to be unnecessary."

"Yes sir."

"About the squaw, I mean."

Elisha turned to the man. "She is not a squaw."

"The half-breed, then. Susette Morel." Mr. Brush snapped shut the compass lid. "Not that I blame you entirely. Half-breed women are legendary cockteasers. And Madame Morel is a pretty enough piece of quim."

Elisha turned back to the fieldbook as a flush blossomed on his cheeks. "I admit that she's been occupying my thoughts. Her behavior—it's been purely awful. She nearly abandoned us at the fur post, halfway through our journey!" Elisha lowered his voice. "I will tell you something in confidence, sir. I had severe concerns, like yourself, about the wisdom of engaging a woman. Especially a half-breed, and a Catholic at that."

"You are lying."

Elisha held the man's gaze but said nothing.

"My boy." Mr. Brush sighed, and shook his head. "My boy, you have been blessed with a rare opportunity. Do you understand? You have been granted a means to improve yourself, through practical training and diligent self-instruction. And yet it is increasingly evident that you aim to squander this opportunity."

Elisha felt a familiar, desperate urge toward apology. It was a feeling he'd experienced countless times as a child, perched on a comfortless pew in the damp meetinghouse.

"You seem to believe that knowledge is absorbed by proximity, like water into cloth! That you might bellow a few stanzas of Shakespeare and diddle a squaw, and return to Detroit in August with something nearing an education. Is this true?"

"No sir. It's not true."

Brush bent forward until his forehead nearly touched Elisha's. The man's eyes were watery and pale, a child's eyes in a man's weathered face. The sight froze Elisha. Brush said, "If you are not careful you will end up like Professor Copper Knob, with a veneer of knowledge over a thick plug of ignorance. And I know you do not want that."

The man's tone made Elisha uneasy. "No sir, I don't."

"This nation does not advance under men like him."

"I'm sure it doesn't."

"Then!" Mr. Brush clapped Elisha on the shoulder. "My own education was begun just this way, on an expedition with practical men. This was in Ohio, near Zanesville. I was sixteen years old, as you are now." Brush grinned stiffly. "I daresay you could do worse than to learn from yours truly, my boy."

"Yes sir. I'm sure that's true."

"I studied their example! I obeyed their instruction! I *learned,* my boy. And by summer's end I had quit calling them sir."

Elisha forced himself to smile. "Well, Mr. Brush. I will surely try."

They tacked northward through the remains of the afternoon. As the day's light shaded toward violet they heard a man's faint whistling, and then they came into the clearing. Professor Tiffin lay near the cookfire, the Hebrew lexicon held before his eyes. It was as though he had not stirred since lunch. Susette was nowhere to be seen; then she emerged from a tent, twisting her damp hair into a braid.

Elisha dipped a mug of lukewarm stew and retreated to his own tent. Sleep, he thought, is what this day deserves. But as the boy lay on his bedroll he sensed Mr. Brush's stare. He dragged himself upright and unpacked an ore specimen, threw open his tent flap to gather the firelight. Elisha opened his fieldbook and wrote:

July 5, 1844

This mineral specimen is highly soil-like in nature, possessing a reddish-black color and leaving a beautifully rich maroon streak when touched to paper. It is capable of deflecting a magnetic compass needle (strongly suggesting a partly ferrous composition), and its density appears similar to that of pyrite. It crumbles fairly easily at the pressure of a thumbnail, with a consistency similar to that of week-old panbread. Quite astonishing, when one considers that such a ductile ore is refined into railroad tracks and musket bores and cannons, the stiffest, brutest elements of civilization.

Despair crept over Elisha as he reread the passage. For why was the specimen maroon, instead of coal-black or yellow? And what was the primary cause of its magnetism? Each observation yielded a question, and though he might answer one question a thousand others remained. Was the specimen's heaviness due to the presence of iron, or the iron's magnetic attraction to the earth? And would a greater degree of iron make the specimen firmer, or softer? Elisha stared at the neat sentences. It was as difficult to understand a lump of dirt as it was another human being.

He lined through the passage and turned the page. Raindrops tapped against the tent like idle fingernails against a desk. At last Elisha wrote:

> Her skin is reddish-brown, the color of hematite. Her hands are as rough as ore. Her clothes are torn and tattered, without beads or stitching. Her hair is grown shaggy and long, blued like a gunstock, oiled to a gunstock's gleam.
>
> And yet she possesses a beauty that is unmistakable: a gemstone glimmering in the black night.

That night Elisha dreamed he was a prisoner in a grand Victorian manor. The house's doors were locked but he scurried like a mouse through gaps in the baseboards. Each room was crowded with tables of roast beef and cheese and smoked ham, champagne and cherry pie and lemon pudding, all of it coated with ash. Elisha ate daintily but unceasingly.

He was dressed in Alpheus Lenz's silk opera hat, wearing the man's smoke-colored spectacles. His lips were smeared with greasy ash.

But even as he slept Elisha understood that he was dreaming, and he was irritated by the dream's naked logic—for surely the food represented knowledge, or wisdom, qualities he hungered for but dearly lacked. He tried to steer his dreaming self toward the locked front door. Something magnificent, he was certain, lay just beyond the door.

He woke to a hand on his shoulder. Susette was kneeling beside him, her face masked by darkness. She laid a hand over his mouth, then without a word guided him from the tent.

He followed the woman along the stream, ducking beneath low pine boughs. Crickets rasped in the undergrowth. The water's moon-lit surface was like a trickle of quicksilver through the forest. They reached a small opening in the pines, and Susette turned and offered Elisha a pained smile. "I am sorry to wake you. I wanted to speak without the others."

"I figured you'd grown tired of speaking to me," he whispered. "That, or you were fixing to run off again."

She nodded stoically. The cookfire's glow was just a glimmer through the trees. "You think I am cracked. A cracked half-breed woman who cannot decide what to do."

"I expect you know precisely what you want to do, but you won't reveal the full measure of your thoughts. Which I suppose is admirable."

"I have been cruel to you. I am very sorry."

Elisha sighed with frustration. He wanted to kiss the woman but could not bring himself even to touch her. Susette laid a hand on his arm and he pressed toward her but the woman leaned away. In an instant his desire soured. He said, "So, then. Explain what you want from me."

Without looking at him she said, "I need your assistance. A small help."

"I offered my help. You said you didn't want it."

"The place we are going, the image stones. There is no such place."

"I don't follow your logic."

She would not meet Elisha's gaze. "My husband lied to Professor Tiffin, to gain commission as a guide. When I heard Professor Tiffin's story I understood. My husband would guide him into the forest and receive payment, then he would desert him. There are no image stones."

Elisha was suspended between confusion and disbelief. For an instant he wondered whether he was the butt of a strange prank; then he saw tears rimming Susette's eyes. "Then where are we going?" His voice tightened to a nervous hiss. "Why are you guiding us to a place that doesn't exist?"

"We will arrive soon at a hill. This is the place my husband described to Professor Tiffin—but there are no buried tablets or scrolls, nothing from Midewiwin. It is where Chippewas collect flint for their muskets. Near the hill there is a waterfall. The river above is very narrow and quick."

Dread stirred inside Elisha. He said nothing.

"When we reach the hill I will receive payment. We will make camp. Then I will go alone to the waterfall, with only a fishnet and some food, and I will depart. You will say that I went over the waterfall and was carried away. That I died."

"You don't need to do that. Mr. Brush and Professor Tiffin won't care a whit if you leave."

"It is not them you must tell. It is my husband."

Elisha squatted at the stream's edge. He wondered if the woman's every action during the past weeks had been inspired by this single request. The thought sickened him. He said, "I have to tell Professor Tiffin."

"No, you don't."

"I have to tell Professor Tiffin that he's wasting his time! That this entire expedition is a danged ruse!"

Susette clutched the boy's hand but he pulled away. He said, "You shouldn't do this! You shouldn't cause your husband to mourn a death that never occurred! No matter the circumstance, you shouldn't injure a man that way!"

"My husband will not mourn me if I die." Susette's voice quavered hysterically. "But if he knows I am alive he will track me. He will track me like a dog to the end of the country."

"How do you know?"

"He has promised me this many times. *Please!* He will track me like a dog and he will hurt me."

Susette laid a hand on Elisha's neck and liquid warmth flowed through his body. She knelt beside the boy and hugged him tightly about the chest. "You must help me, Elisha. Please, you must help me. You are the only one who can help me."

He sat silently as the woman wept against him. He wanted to ask her, Who will believe your story? Who will believe you were carried away by a rushing current? Not your husband. Nor Mr. Brush, nor Professor Tiffin. And when you arrive in a new town, who will believe you are who you claim to be? It was a story from a fable, or a myth: the woman borne away on a wave's crest, set down among strangers in a distant land. Yet in the fable she returned home after years of travel.

It doesn't matter, Elisha realized, if no one believes her story. She needs only to believe it herself. If she believes she has died, she can begin a new life.

"I believed you. I believed you about the image stones." Elisha shook his head. "I wanted Professor Tiffin to make a great discovery. I prayed he would."

Susette moved to touch the boy's face but he turned away. He said, "Where will you go now? Back to your mother in Canada?"

She paused, as if scrutinizing the meaning of his words; then her expression softened in relief. "There is a town I have heard of— Milwaukee, in Wisconsin Territory. I have been told that the land is free and the soil is good, and there is fishing and hunting and the winters are not so cold. And the streets are dry and broad, and there are apple trees all through town, and there is work for anyone who wants, man or woman. I will go there. I will find work as a hired woman or laundress and I will live there."

"I expect you might even find a theater in Milwaukee."

She laughed, a sharp sob. Tears spilled down her cheeks.

"Well. In another world I might have joined you."

Susette nodded. "In a better world."

The party came the next morning into a burned-out region of gray, limbless pines, the ground humped with charred logs, the air flecked with ash. The landscape was drained of color save for shoots of pink fireweed. They continued without pause, finally cresting a rise to see white pine rolled out before them like a rich green carpet. A river cut through the forest then abruptly disappeared near a low hill. They made camp in a stand of blackened saplings, and when the fire was kindled and the cookpot set on to simmer Susette said, "It is there, that hill near the waterfall. The image stones."

Silence; then Professor Tiffin turned to Susette. "My dear woman. What are you saying?"

"Atop the hill, where there are few trees. That is our destination."

Tiffin scrambled to his feet. "My jay! Why didn't you tell me we were so near?"

"I did tell you, yesterday. I said we were near."

"Near!" The man fumbled with his pack, jammed on his ragged hat. "Good gracious, near indeed!"

Tiffin stumbled down the slope, startling a flock of sparrows into flight. "We have arrived!" he shouted. "By the grace of God we have arrived!"

They watched the man disappear among the pines. At last Mr. Brush tossed his tea into the fire and shouldered his pack. Elisha struck the tents and kicked dirt over the cookfire, and they started after the man, toward the hill.

Two

He had paced the steamer's foredeck since their sunup departure, drinking coffee and watching Detroit's wharfs and storehouses and church steeples slide away. The city dwindled to muddy flats dotted with rude plank shanties, a few solitary figures casting for trout. As Reverend Stone stared, one of the fishermen staked his pole and trotted down the riverbank apace with the ship, then raised both hands as the steamer slipped behind Hog Island. Reverend Stone returned the wave, his chest tight with excitement. The *Queen Sofia's* signal cannon fired, a flat blast that brought a cheer from the steerage deck. Ringbilled gulls wheeled and shrieked along the ship's bow.

But as they entered Lake Huron a scurf of sooty clouds skated overhead and the waves thickened to a chop. Reverend Stone stood at the railing, bent against the wind. Ahead, the lake rolled to the horizon, as boundless and menacing as the Atlantic. Cows belowdecks lowed above the shouts of Irish deckhands. The air smelled richly of loam.

He remained on deck until he felt the first cold pellets of rain, then stepped into the gentlemen's cabin and ordered a glass of cider, took a seat beside a grimed porthole. Behind him, a trio of soldiers argued the merits of various beer halls in Detroit. Waves crushed against the steamer's hull. The wind gathered itself, then rushed forward in huge, soft buffets. Like a child puffing on a milkweed pod to keep it aloft, Reverend Stone thought. The soldiers hooted raucously.

He understood, suddenly, why some sailors loved the sea. It was the embrace of helplessness, the temporary surrender of will. And with it a grateful shucking of responsibility. Reverend Stone recalled a sermon he'd once delivered, directed toward the congregation's worldlier members: that a life of sin was like a solo sail into an endless ocean, rootless and undirected. Now he sensed the comparison's truth. The *Queen Sofia* hovered, then bottomed sickeningly into a trough. The soldiers' laughter hushed.

Reverend Stone drew a tin from his trouser pocket and thumbed out three tablets, swallowed them with the last of the cider. Then he set the glass on the bar and yanked open the foredeck door. The barman said "Hey" as Reverend Stone stepped out into the wind.

Rain stung his face and neck. He clutched his hat and hurried beneath an awning, braced himself against a pair of stanchions. The ship pitched, riding a swell down and then up in a twisting lurch. Reverend Stone thought he might be sick. The awning snapped like a carriage whip. It seemed impossible that they were sailing on a mere lake.

He swallowed two more tablets then closed his eyes and waited for warmth to melt over him. His fingers began to itch, the sensation accompanied by a hint of familiarity, an odd tang of childhood. He opened his eyes: the lake was gathered into slaty, frothing peaks. The ship's timbers howled. Had his father ever taken him on a sailing ship? Certainly not. In his memories the man was a tiny, stooped figure in a distant tobacco field, or a wrinkled old gentleman scowling at a thirty-cent Bible. Or a steep black shadow on the minister's bedroom wall. Reverend Stone felt touched by the anxiety that had forever accompanied his father's image. He'd been a silent man, spending words like they were gold dollars, repeating a few favorite expressions throughout Reverend Stone's childhood. Now the minister heard his faded Surrey accent, clear as yesterday: *You know who you are when you know what you fear.*

The old fellow would be proud of me today, Reverend Stone thought.

He shrank against the stanchions as the steamer rolled. He felt enveloped by dense, coarse fur. That was why he'd entered the ministry, he knew: to escape his father's dour stare. He had never been drawn to preaching and counseling, weddings and baptisms and funerals. He had lacked the necessary patience. As a young man, though, he had possessed a talent for prayer. Praying, his thoughts would slow to a crawl, the physical world falling away; then he would feel himself rising into calm joy. He felt humbled, bodiless. Over time the sensation had faded, until lately he'd had to convince himself that it was not a dream. And now, what? Reverend Stone wondered. Where did he find calm? In a tin of tablets. His backdoor entrance to ecstasy. His sinner's version of grace.

A deckhand staggered past, gripping the railing for support. His glance lit on Reverend Stone and the man cackled. "Shite day for sightseeing, friend-o!" The minister smiled weakly. He was struck by the absurdity of their endeavor: a few planks of oak nailed together against a roiling lake. Forgive us, he thought. We mean no offense, certainly none at all.

After a while the rain softened to a patter. Reverend Stone shifted against the stanchion, and as he did he felt a knot against his chest. He fished in his vest pocket and withdrew a tarnished chain linked to a loop of scored leather. Adele Crawley's talisman. He murmured, " 'The Lord shall preserve thy going out and thy coming in, from this time forth and for evermore.' " The familiar cadence soothed him. Reverend Stone pressed the leather scrap to his lips, then moved to the railing and dropped it over the side, watched it disappear without a sound into the dark lake.

The *Queen Sofia* was a ramshackle side-wheel steamer, its railings warped and brass fittings dulled, its carpets scuffed down to shiny brown mats. Built to haul pine timber around the lakes, Reverend Stone figured, a homely cousin of the pleasure steamers on Lake Erie. Whey-colored paint bubbled over the tin ceiling. In the gentlemen's cabin, groups of soldiers and businessmen sat in quiet conversation around copper-topped tables, below a film of steel-blue smoke. The cabin smelled bitterly of vomit.

He sat at the bar until his stomach had settled, then walked a circuit of the steamer in the sour-tasting air. From the steerage deck, fiddle strains skirted above an accordion's chords, the pair harmonizing in a fast, droning reel. Germans, Reverend Stone suspected, in good spirits despite the squall. He was ravenously hungry. In the dining room he lunched on broiled trout with white gravy and applesauce, then retired to his stateroom and lay straight-armed on the narrow bunk, his joints aching, his swollen cheek tight and warm. He closed his eyes but sleep eluded him. Instead he lay listening to the steam engine's thrum.

He rose near dusk and stepped into a quiet corridor. The gentlemen's cabin was empty save for a pair of Irish deckhands. A handlettered notice was tacked beside the bar.

FOR THE EDIFICATION AND DIVERSION OF ALL PASSENGERS

AN ADDRESS BY JOHN SUNDAY (OR, O-KON-DI-KAN)

ENTITLED

TRUE NARRATIVE OF THE CONVERSION TO CHRISTIANITY

OF THE SPEAKER, A FULL-BLOOD OJIBWAY INDIAN

TO BE DELIVERED IN THE DINING ROOM AT 8:00 PM

~ ADMISSION GRATIS ~

Reverend Stone passed through the cabin into the dining room. The tables had been pushed to the room's rear, and two dozen men and women sat in rows of straight-backed chairs, staring at a man behind a low pine lectern. He was dressed in a store-bought gray suit and twill shirt but his hair was long and blue-black, his skin the color of weak coffee. John Sunday, the minister assumed. The man's voice was an insistent whine.

"This was at a camp meeting near Saline. I went to sell my liquor to the many people. A preacher named Josiah Stevens spoke, and I listened. He spoke of the dark place, the underworld, and I felt like I would die. I felt sick in my heart. I knelt by the roots of a very large pine tree. I did not understand how to pray, you see? I thought God was too great to listen to a red Indian. Presently I saw a light like a small torch. It appeared to come through the pine tree. My heart trembled. The light came upon my head and spread all through me. How happy I felt! I was as light as a feather. I called in English, *Glory to Jesus!* I felt as strong as a lion yet as humble as a poor Indian boy. That night I did not sleep. The world was new to me, and exciting. That was the beginning."

The man seemed astonished by his own words. His fervor gave rise to an embarrassed silence in the room. A woman coughed dryly.

"The next morning I began my work. I went to the Stony Creek tribe. I told them, *Jesus, my all, to heaven is gone.* Jesus ish pe ming kah e zhod. I told them, *Oh, how hard is my fate.* Tyau gitche sunnahgud. This they understood. They understood the language of loss. But it was difficult. For a smoke of tobacco they would be baptized. For a meal they would come to a prayer meeting. They said if I brought them whiskey, they would become preachers. Yet I continued for now eleven years, in Michigan and Ohio and Canada. I will never tire." John Sunday paused. "Every day thousands of white souls are saved, but how many Indian souls? How many Indians will be risen up on the last day?"

It was true, Reverend Stone realized. His own vision of salvation was that of a great crowd assembled in a rolling valley, white men and Negroes and Chinese and Irish with their faces turned to heaven, rapturous, their varied names for God a mere detail of translation. The idea was near to heresy but there it was. Yet where were the red Indians? The minister recalled reading in Catlin that Natives imagined the afterlife to be similar to life on earth, though with more plentiful hunting and fishing. The idea had struck him as pitiful: it had seemed a fundamental failing of the race.

"And this is why I now ask for subscriptions. So I might continue to work among Natives. So I might continue to bring light into darkness. It is through your subscriptions that I eat and clothe myself."

A man in the front row removed his bowler and with a flourish dropped a banknote into the crown. A twinge of dread rose in Reverend Stone as the hat passed among the chairs. "I thank you sincerely," John Sunday said. "Now I might be as Jonah and go unto Nineveh, and preach unto it the preaching that I bid thee." The minister rummaged in his trouser pocket, extracted a half-dime. When the bowler arrived he dipped his fist into the crown, and at the same time gave the hat a jingling shake. A ruse learned from his own congregation, from the skinflints in the rearmost pews.

He looked up to find John Sunday fixing him with a grim stare. Reverend Stone reddened. He nodded to the man then rose quickly, passed out into the gentlemen's cabin then onto the foredeck.

Outside it was warm, a breeze unfurling the steamer's flags, the sky pebbled with pewter-colored clouds. Reverend Stone leaned over the railing and watched foam ribbon past the *Queen Sofia*'s bow. He drew a deep, calming breath. Where were they? Twelve hours north of Detroit. Nowhere. Yet he was certain they had crossed into a blank space on the map, into a shared unknown with his son. The thought was vaguely comforting.

The gentlemen's cabin door opened, and four soldiers stepped onto the deck holding tumblers of flip. As one they began a round of "Oh, What a Charming City," motioning for the minister to join the chorus. The door opened again and John Sunday appeared. He removed his hat and rubbed his forehead, unbuttoned his collar with a grimace. Reverend Stone moved beside the man and offered a conciliatory smile.

"I am sorry I couldn't aid you further. I've a wealth of admiration for your labors."

John Sunday shrugged. "I was in London in August. I spoke on the need for Christianity among the Natives. I was received at the summer home of the earl of Essex, given many gifts and much money. And when I return to America I must beg like a pauper."

"The British are a pious people. They feel the injury of every lost soul, even those in faraway lands. They are also quite rich."

"There is greed in this country."

"I have begged myself, of late. It is the nature of our vocation."

John Sunday appraised him wearily, his gaze lingering on Reverend Stone's bruised cheek; then his expression softened. "I am sorry. I am very tired. I become tired and open myself to unkind thoughts. It is a weakness." He rubbed his forehead again and sighed. "What is your work in the north?"

Reverend Stone thought to explain, then said, "A pleasure tour. And I shall visit the Indian agent, a man called Edwin Colcroft."

"Colcroft." John Sunday spat over the railing. "Chippewa scratch all day at Colcroft's door, they say, Kittemaugizze showainemin—I am poor, show me pity. They rub onion beneath their noses to bring tears. They call him Nosa, my father. I tell them God is their father."

"There are white men in my own congregation who would make quick use of that onion trick."

"I wish for the day that Natives are like whites. I have much work to do."

"This country—" Reverend Stone paused. "There is a strange desperation among white men these days. A great thirst for meaning, in any form. They live together in colonies and phalanxes, they invest faith in charlatans and wild-eyed zealots. They change denominations like they are changing their hats. They prepare for the last day as if for a Sabbath-day picnic. It is as though Natives possess too little faith, and white men possess too much."

"An abundance of faith can be channeled. But it is hard to quicken faith when the talent for it does not exist."

"Both problems are symptoms of confusion. Of turmoil."

John Sunday grunted. Beside them, the soldiers' song dissolved into laughter, a solo voice stubbornly holding the melody. Then it, too, fell into silence as the soldiers drank. Night had arrived as a starry black sky, salt crystals on a scrap of velvet. To the west: a forest's bristly silhouette. To the north: an invisible horizon, a border between nothings.

After some time John Sunday said, "Do you know what is the saddest phrase of the Bible?"

Reverend Stone shook his head. " 'Jesus wept.' "

"It is from John, chapter one. 'And the light shineth in darkness; and the darkness comprehended it not.' "

They reached Mackinac Island at dawn, the *Queen Sofia*'s signal cannon echoed by a blast from a gun at Fort Michilimackinac. Deckhands' shouts merged with a clang of bells and hoot of whistles as the ship angled toward the pier. Reverend Stone shaved and prayed, then sipped a cup of weak tea in the gentlemen's cabin as the steamer tied up and a dozen soldiers trudged down the gangplank. Twenty minutes later the ship cast off, and at three they arrived at Sault Ste. Marie.

The town was smaller than the minister had expected, just a belt of dirt bordered by a saloon and mercantile and bowling parlor, a leather goods shop, a row of cabins and shanties, two whitewashed hotels. Sharp black shadows lay across the empty road. A mud wagon rattled along the straits. A true frontier town, Reverend Stone marveled, a place to make Newell seem cosmopolitan by comparison.

Three half-breed stevedores and a hotel drummer holding a smudged placard had gathered to meet the ship. Reverend Stone secured a room at the Johnston Hotel from the drummer then paid a stevedore a nickel to deposit his new canvas bag. Then he started through town toward the fort.

Fort Brady was a small, neat encampment surrounded by pickets, its flagpole bearing a weathered Old Glory, its blockhouses monitoring the Canadian settlement across the straits. Chippewa lodges were scattered along the fort's perimeter, their cookfire smoke tinting the

air. At the picket gate Reverend Stone asked for directions to the Indian
Agency; the soldier nodded toward a gable-front house bordered by a
pair of elms. The minister climbed the porch steps and rapped on the
door frame. The shutters were latched as if against a thunderstorm.
Two rain-grayed rockers bobbed in the breeze.

A tall, spindly man with a bald dome and sideburns opened the
door. He was dressed in Sunday clothes, a pink silk waistcoat and
black trousers, a boiled shirt yellow with age. He squinted at Reverend
Stone through iron-rimmed spectacles.

"Edwin Colcroft?"

The man seemed confused by the minister's presence. He said,
"You have called during the tutoring hour."

"My apologies. I have just arrived on the *Queen Sofia* and come
straight from the pier. My name is Reverend William Edward Stone of
Newell, Massachusetts. I'd have left this call for tomorrow, but my
business is fairly urgent."

Edwin Colcroft hesitated; then he opened the door wide. "Come
in at once, Reverend. Please."

Reverend Stone thanked the man and removed his hat. Inside, he
followed Colcroft to the rear of the dim house, waited as the man
ducked through a closed door. A moment later two half-breed girls
wearing identical blue dresses burst from the room, giggling. They
froze when they saw Reverend Stone; then they curtsied and scurried
into the kitchen. Colcroft opened the door and motioned the minister
inside.

Bookcases lined the walls, leather and cloth and pasteboard volumes crammed floor to ceiling, stacks of books on the side table and
windowsill and along the baseboard. The room smelled of pipe
smoke. Beside the window stood a small oak secretary, the desk strewn
with papers, the shelves above filled with mineral specimens and glass
jars. The jars were filled with gray liquid and the vague, shadowy
forms of animals.

"My girls," Colcroft said. "I am teaching them Hebrew, to aid my

own study of the Chippewa tongue. Did you know that the two lan-
guages are curiously similar? For example, the name of God is
Yohewah in the Native tongue and *Jehovah* in Hebrew. The word of
praise is *halleluwah* in the Native tongue and *hallelujah* in Hebrew.
The word for heaven is *chemin* in the Native tongue and *shamayim* in
Hebrew. And et cetera."

Reverend Stone smiled absently. Colcroft followed his stare to the
secretary, said, "Ah!" He took up a jar and raised it to the window.
Sunlight glared through the liquid, illuminating a ghostly pink orb.

"A jellyfish from the South Pacific island of Mohotani, faultlessly
preserved. It is invertebrate, entirely lacking in skeletal structure! That
next jar contains a specimen of oyster from Tokyo Bay. If you look
closely you can see a germinated pearl. The last jar contains a fish that
is half embryonic gar pike, half frog. Note the small leglike appendages
in the ventral region. *Quite* remarkable. The only such specimen in the
world, I'm fairly certain."

"Fascinating. Your cabinet of curiosities would be the envy of
Detroit."

Edwin Colcroft emitted a pleased murmur. Reverend Stone was
struck by a vision of the man as a young boy, his hair a black shock, his
trousers rolled to the knees as he waded in a molasses-colored stream.
His hands slowly closed around a water strider. And then later, alone
in his candlelit bedroom, mumbling softly to the insect as it stumbled
inside a killing jar. The boy soothed it to a lifeless sleep.

"I am primarily interested in diluvian geology," Colcroft said. "In
my view the fundamental question of the age is, Do the natural sciences offer external evidence of the truth of God's word?"

"An important investigation. I have recently discussed the very issue with a fellow minister in Newell. His position was that science and
religion are two translations of the same text—however he feared that
a scientist's innate skepticism might open him to doubt."

"But surely the opposite occurs! Surely scientific explanations of
nature's truths cause us to farther admire their divine Author! For

example, here." Colcroft took up a whitish mineral specimen and offered it to the minister. "You recognize this, of course?"

Reverend Stone turned the stone over in his hands. "It is sugar quartz."

"Actually, limpid hexagonal quartz—extracted in Springfield, Massachusetts, in fact. But note: precisely identical specimens have been found on every continent of the earth—as though scattered from a single source by an immense flood!" He took up a second specimen.

"Ah. Puddingstone."

Colcroft chuckled politely. "Septaria. The patterning is far too regular to be puddingstone."

"My apologies. I am not a naturalist."

"Yes. Then." Colcroft hesitated, then returned the specimen to the secretary. He sat opposite the minister on a faded blue wing chair. "Now, Reverend. How might I be of service?"

"I am searching for my son, Elisha Stone. He has joined a scientifical expedition that departed Sault Ste. Marie some weeks ago, under the guidance of Mr. Silas Brush and Professor George Tiffin. I believe they aim to study the region's mineral and timber evidence."

Edwin Colcroft snorted. "Tiffin."

"You know the man?"

"I have read his recent monograph—*Language and History of the American Indians,* or somesuch. His conjectures are *quite* speculative. You see, though there are many curious similarities between the Indian and Hebrew languages, there is no direct proof that the races are anyhow related. Phrenologically, physiognomically, scripturally—not a scrap of proof. I suspect Tiffin is something of an . . . enthusiast."

"I'm afraid I am unacquainted with Professor Tiffin, or his theories." Reverend Stone drew Charles Noble's map from his breast pocket. "I have obtained a coarse map of the expedition's route. I had hoped that you might assist me in improving upon its accuracy."

"Of course, direct proof of the unity of the red and white races would be an *immense* discovery. Imagine, proclaiming to the world that Natives are not soulless savages, but are instead wayward sons and daughters of Abraham! However, direct proof..." Colcroft leaned forward, grinning. "You see, Reverend Stone, as a general rule, the more profound the conjecture, the fainter the possibility of obtaining direct proof of its veracity. In such instances, reason and deduction are the thinking man's weapons. In fact, even—"

"The map," Reverend Stone said. "If you please."

Colcroft froze; then he accepted the map and adjusted his spectacles. His lips moved wordlessly as he scanned the annotations. After some time he said, "Well. That is interesting."

Reverend Stone said nothing.

"I believe I know the destination of Tiffin's expedition. The image stones—it is a bedrock outcrop containing significant flint deposits, a geological curiosity. It is also rumored to be a sacred location for the Chippewa Midewiwin medicine society."

A description from the Catlin book rose in the minister's mind: men pierced through the flesh with sharpened splints, then strung up from leather thongs in an orgy of pain. Braves painted vermilion and white, like demons, or covered in bearskins and daubed with mud. Catlin portrayed medicine rituals as a savage form of mummery, a grotesque revue. Surely it was an exaggeration. Reverend Stone said, "That destination seems appropriate, considering Professor Tiffin's interests."

"Indeed, indeed. There is rumored to be a profusion of pictographic rock paintings in the area." Colcroft appeared momentarily abashed. "I've not visited the region personally, however I have heard detailed descriptions from a voyageur who has."

"I pray you can assist me. I would like to engage a guide to escort me to the image stones—perhaps one of the Canadian-French paddlers who is familiar with the region."

Colcroft squinted, fingering his sideburns. "Mightn't you rather await the expedition's return to Sault Ste. Marie? Certainly that would be more...comfortable for you."

He sees an old man, Reverend Stone thought. An old, ill man stumbling through the forest. He said, "I bear urgent news for my son. I've not seen him in three years."

Edwin Colcroft rose and paced to the secretary, speaking as if to himself. "I suppose it is likely that Tiffin will spend several weeks investigating the image stone site. If you travel rapidly you might intercept them."

"Then."

A shriek emanated from the hallway; then a drumming of footsteps on the creaking stairs. Colcroft bent toward the closed door, his expression one of restrained glee. He took up a silver-framed print from the desk. "We had a traveling daguerreotype artist pass here en route to Chicago last month. The girls could not remain stationary, of course. A shame. Though in a way it makes the image more beautiful. More truthful, somehow."

He offered Reverend Stone the daguerreotype. Colcroft's daughters stood hand in hand before the fort's flagpole, dressed in identical white pinafores and hair bows. Their eyes and mouths were smudges of motion, and their entire bodies were blurred, as though viewed through tears. Only their shoes were clear, tiny gray moccasins patterned with flowers.

"I believe I can assist you," Colcroft said. "Your son's expedition has engaged as a guide the wife of one of my interpreters, Ignace Morel. Monsieur Morel was not pleased. He accused me of brokering the arrangement, when in fact I had no involvement in the matter. He became quite incensed—Monsieur Morel can be somewhat petulant."

"He can escort me to the legend stones?"

"Image stones. Yes. I can arrange his services, if you'd like. I have some experience in negotiating a fair price with the man."

"I would be indebted. I might also ask your advice on obtaining provisions and equipment. I'm afraid I am not an experienced woodsman."

Edwin Colcroft smiled, his eyes hidden by the glinting lenses. "I envy you, Reverend Stone. A jaunt into nature, breathing fresh forest air and drinking the coldest, purest water. It will be a tonic! And you need not harbor any fears—the Chippewa propensity for violence against whites has been exaggerated by newspaper editors desperate for lurid copy."

"I had prayed as much."

Colcroft burst into whinnying laughter. "Then! I suppose the only thing to do is wish you a bon voyage!"

The straits at midnight were an oily black slash, moonlight spilling across the rippling waves, the water's rush like a congregation's restless whispers. A northerly breeze brought thunder and the crisp scent of Lake Superior. Woodcocks whirred in the nearby cedar thicket. From town, an angry shout was followed by a door's slam, then a dog's frenzied bark that melted to a whine. Then silence.

Reverend Stone reclined on a mat of beach grass near the water's edge, the Catlin book splayed beside him. As he watched, a wash of greenish light shimmered from the polestar down past Ursa Major. Without shifting his gaze the minister slipped a tablet under his tongue. The book's pages riffled in the breeze. The light darkened and pulsed, a delirious vision, a mirage of color. He gazed up into the night sky.

Earlier that evening the straits had been crowded with tourist canoes: ladies with white parasols beside gentlemen in silk hats, a Native steersman sitting high in the stern. They streaked past the rocks, the parasols' jouncing accompanied by shrieks of amazed laughter. By dress and inflection Reverend Stone figured them to be moneyed Easterners, seeking a whiff of the exotic on their summer excursion. The sight had surprised him; then on reflection he figured there must be tourists on every scrap of the wide world. Air and water and earth and tourists, everywhere.

Later, after darkness had fallen, the minister had returned to the Johnston Hotel and taken a late supper of tea and broiled whitefish. A note was tacked to his room door: a message from Edwin Colcroft, written in a crabbed hand. He had arranged the services of Monsieur Ignace Morel, for a fee of ten dollars payable upon return, to guide Reverend Stone to the previously discussed site. He had taken the liberty of provisioning and equipping the voyage, courtesy of the United States Agency for Indian Affairs. Monsieur Morel would meet him on the beach the next morning at dawn. He hoped this arrangement was acceptable. He wished Reverend Stone Godspeed.

Despite himself the minister laughed aloud. He kissed the note, then from the hotel porter ordered a celebratory glass of cider. He felt humbled by his good fortune. The drink finished, he walked the town's length, searching for errands to complete before his departure; then he realized there was nothing to do but wait.

Now it was dark and the straits were deserted. Reverend Stone rose and shook sand from the Catlin book, paced impatiently along the riverbank. Pebbles glistened like gemstones in the glossy moonlight. He felt wonderfully vigorous, as though the lake air had remedied his illness. He had not coughed in several days.

What would he say when he saw his son? He would explain his presence, of course: his receipt of the boy's letter, then his journey to Buffalo and Detroit and the Sault, his encounters and struggles and sights. He would pass on news of the congregation, of Newell, of Corletta and his childhood friends—everything and nothing, the fascinating mundanity of life. And then? Reverend Stone was tempted by the thought that words would not be required, that the truth about Ellen would be palpable; but that was foolish, an idea distilled from cowardice.

They had spoken continually about Elisha, when she was ill. She'd lay beneath a log-cabin quilt in their bedroom, sipping milk steeped with hyssop and paging through old issues of the *North American Review*. The boy had been gone only a month yet she spoke as if she knew he would not return. She hoped he'd found work, in a timber camp or shop or even a dairy farm. She prayed that his new congregation was gracious and hospitable. She wondered if he'd met a girl, maybe a cheery Boston girl to balance his seriousness. Ellen's eyes flickered with remembered joy, her fingers worrying a bloody rag. She took up a charcoal portrait of the boy and pressed it to her lips.

Reverend Stone stopped walking. He understood, suddenly, why his son had left home: because he had not wanted to see his mother die. Because he was too frightened to accept the fact of her absence. And so Ellen was yet alive, to the boy. She was alive in his memories, alive in his prayers and thoughts. Reverend Stone felt touched by grief and a strange, shameful envy. She would be alive to the boy until he learned of her death.

He sat heavily in the crusted sand. A familiar ache grew in him, anger tempered by guilt. Elisha had left his mother lying beneath a log-cabin quilt in a shut-up bedroom, her lips the color of ash; yet she had forgiven him. How could a person forgive such an act? Yet one must forgive, just as Christ forgave. One must. A father must place a robe about his son's shoulders and a ring on his son's finger, and forgive.

Yet he should be the one to ask forgiveness, of his son. Reverend Stone soberly recognized the truth of this notion. He had shut the boy away from Ellen as she lay on her sickbed. Why? For her health, he had told himself, as though he might preserve her in a room un-touched by the world, untouched by time. He had not wanted to share his wife's love with the boy. He'd wanted to focus it on himself as though through a lens. Greed, then, or gluttony, or a sin unnamed in Scripture. He had loved her so much that nothing remained for his son.

He woke sometime later. It was dawn; a cold mist lay along the beach. His skin was pebbled with gooseflesh. Reverend Stone rose and coughed roughly, spat between his feet. Ignace Morel was nowhere to be seen.

He waited until he guessed the time to be near eight o'clock, then returned to the Johnston Hotel and breakfasted on cheese biscuits and sausage and tea. He asked the sleepy proprietor for directions to

Monsieur Morel's house. The man shook his head, then said, "Oh—Morel. That one's living in a shanty down along the pickets."

Reverend Stone hurried past the saloon and leather goods shop and Baptist mission house, the road quiet, the buildings darkened and closed. The town seemed abandoned, as though by people fleeing an approaching army. Outside the mercantile a pair of filthy trappers sat hunched on flour barrels, smoking long clay pipes. Reverend Stone nodded to the men as a vision of Detroit's empty alleyways rose in his mind. He quickened his pace toward the fort.

Two dozen pinewood shanties stood among a cluster of Native lodges along the pickets, some with their doors thrown open and smoke rising from a makeshift chimney. Chippewa women worked at racks of dried whitefish; beside them a throng of half-naked children was engaged in a game of tag. Their shouts broke the morning's silence. Reverend Stone spotted a half-breed girl carrying a basket of clothes toward the straits; he approached her and repeated Ignace Morel's name until she mumbled a string of rapid French, pointed at a tumbledown shanty near the water's edge.

Reverend Stone approached the dwelling and tapped at the splintered door. He called, "Monsieur Ignace Morel?" He knocked again then paced around the shanty's perimeter: it was a small, weather-grayed hut, the seams chinked with rabbit fur, the lone window hung with oiled parchment. The minister peered through a gap between the warped planks.

A man opened the door and Reverend Stone jerked upright. "My apologies! Ignace Morel?"

He stared at Reverend Stone.

"You are Monsieur Ignace Morel, correct?"

The man scratched his nose. "Oui. Yes." The word slurred to a hiss.

"I am Reverend William Edward Stone of Newell, Massachusetts. I believe Mr. Edwin Colcroft, the Indian agent, has engaged you to escort me for the next several weeks."

The man said nothing.

"We were to depart this morning at dawn. Yes? I have been awaiting your arrival on the beach."

Now Morel's gaze drifted past Reverend Stone. He was a short, thick-chested voyageur with shaggy black hair and a stubbled jaw marked by a scar. He was dressed in deerskin leggings and a red cotton shirt, a purple sash tied about his waist. The shirt had been mended so many times that it resembled patchwork. He stank of whiskey. Behind the man a heel of bread sat on a table beside a fiddle's bow and an overturned bottle. A wooden crucifix was nailed to the wall above. Typical Catholic, the minister thought, then immediately reprimanded himself.

"We go tomorrow." Morel's accent was thickly French. "Tomorrow is better to begin."

He moved to push the door shut but Reverend Stone shoved his boot inside the frame. "I would like to depart now. That was the agreement arranged by Mr. Colcroft. So, if you please."

"Twenty dollar."

"Pardon?"

"My fee. To escort you. Twenty dollar, you pay me now and we go."

Reverend Stone was momentarily speechless; then his confusion flared to anger. "The agreement was ten dollars—I have it in writing from Mr. Colcroft. Twenty dollars is an outrageous sum."

The man rubbed his jaw theatrically, as if considering the argument. "Twenty dollar."

"You must honor your word! You must escort me, as you promised."

Morel said nothing.

Reverend Stone clenched his fists to still their trembling. A surge of heat rose to his face. "Listen to me, Monsieur Morel: I will pay you fifteen dollars, when we return. Let us go, now, immediately."

"Twenty dollar, now. Before we go."

"Fifteen. Half now, half when we return."

Ignace Morel opened the door and moved beside Reverend Stone, his chest brushing the man's arm. He was shorter than the minister but powerfully built, his neck and shoulders corded with muscle. A faint smile curled his lips. He said, "You are American, so you do not want to pay. You think I am a black nigger slave? No, I am white. You must pay."

Reverend Stone said nothing. He turned away from the man and drew a fistful of coins from his pocket, counted out ten dollars. Morel stifled a yawn. A whistle sounded from the straits and the voyageur squinted, then raised both hands, laughing. He shouted, "Bonjour mon gros poulet! Bonjour!" Reverend Stone thrust the coins at the man and said, "There. Ten dollars. And ten more when we return."

Ignace Morel shrugged. "So. We go."

The minister waited as Morel stepped into moccasins and knotted a tobacco pouch to his sash, gathered a blanket and spare shirt and canvas fiddle case into a gunnysack. The voyageur made a circuit of the encampment, ducking into shanties and Native lodges, calling out farewells in French and slurred Chippewa. Reverend Stone felt anxious and confused, somehow distanced from himself. He followed the man toward town.

At the mercantile Morel stepped inside to a welcoming shout. A trio of chattering tourists strolled past, bearing picnic baskets and silk parasols; they greeted the minister with cheery smiles. A moment later two Natives emerged bearing large canvas packs, followed by Morel bearing a smaller pack and a five-gallon keg. Whiskey, no doubt. Reverend Stone thought to protest but held his tongue.

The voyageur's canoe was nestled in a swath of beach grass at the straits' western tip. It was a Chippewa craft, its birch-bark hull bound with roots and tarred with spruce gum. A red fiddle was painted on the hull. Morel dumped his pack and hoisted the vessel over his head, carried it to the water's edge and set it gently afloat. He shouted a command to the Natives. They waded hip-deep into the straits, muttering as they arranged the packs in the canoe's middle. Morel trudged up the beach and dropped to one knee beside the minister. He motioned toward his back. "Come. Now."

Reverend Stone hesitated. The voyageur glanced up at him; then he circled behind the minister and with a huff bore the man up on his shoulders. Reverend Stone cried out. He clutched the man's head for balance. Morel staggered into the shallows, then lowered the minister into the canoe's bow, atop a slender birch thwart. Reverend Stone gasped, "Thank you. My goodness." The craft jiggled like a cork in the current.

He is attempting to help me, the minister thought. The man is coarse but he will help me. He will protect me. He must protect me.

Ignace Morel boosted himself over the gunwale. He settled into the stern and took up a stubby wooden paddle, called to the Natives in Chippewa. The Natives laughed scornfully. Morel dug into the straits with a grunt. The canoe jerked forward as though tugged by a rope.

They set off.

Three

The image stones were plum-sized nuggets of flint scattered across the hilltop like windfall fruit. A lone black spruce stood at the hill's summit, near a crumpled lodge frame and a cookfire's charred remnants. Beside the fire pit lay a heap of animal bones. It was an old Chippewa campsite, Elisha realized, just as Susette had claimed. He took up a stone and rubbed it to a greasy luster, brought it near his face. A ghost of his own image appeared.

"This is the site?" Professor Tiffin asked. He was stalking around the fire pit, hands steepled at his chest. "These are the image stones—this is the site's entirety, here on this hilltop?"

"This is the site my husband described," Susette said. "It is not large."

"And where, pray tell, are the image stones themselves?" He took up a specimen of flint and thrust it at the woman. "Are these the image stones? *Yes?*"

"This is where Chippewas gather flints for their muskets. The flints become shiny when you polish them—that is why they are called image stones."

Tiffin flung the stone away. "But where is the pictography? Where are the Midewiwin narratives etched on stone tablets, as your husband described? Where are *they?*"

"The tablets with picture writing are buried nearby. I don't know where. The Midewiwin bury them, then dig them up when there is a ceremony."

Tiffin closed his eyes and sighed, an expression of supreme relief. "Of course! Of course that is precisely what they do, my dear madame! We are standing atop the tablets at this very moment!" He hugged Susette about the shoulders as the woman stiffened; then Tiffin turned an exhausted smile on Mr. Brush. "The image stones are buried nearby! Did you hear that, my skeptical friend?"

"Buried treasure. I am only surprised there was no yellowed map to plot our route. Perhaps a one-eyed crone to ferry us across a river."

Professor Tiffin laughed. "You shall be part of history, my friend! Despite your best efforts to the contrary, you shall be remembered as a member of the Tiffin expedition!"

Brush ignored the man and turned to Susette. "I expect you would like your pay. Half due now, half due upon return was the agreement, I believe."

The woman nodded.

"Then come with me." Mr. Brush offered Professor Tiffin a sarcastic tip of the hat then started down the hillside.

But Susette hesitated, and Elisha realized she was frozen with fear. She met the boy's gaze and he understood her expression as a plea for help. He offered the woman a barely perceptible nod. Her fear seemed to dissipate. She started after Mr. Brush, and as she passed Elisha she touched her hand.

She said softly, "My sweet boy."

They made camp beside a gnarled old hemlock at the hill's base, Susette fetching water while Elisha staked the tents and gathered firewood. Mr. Brush stood with his arms folded, watching the boy work. He said gruffly, "That wood is filled with sap. And those tent lines are loose as whores. Stake the damned things tighter. We may be here a few days." Elisha knew better than to respond. At last Brush snatched up his fieldbook and compasses. The boy said, "Do you need my assistance?" but without responding Brush started southward into the forest.

Susette fried some pork belly with wild onions and lamb's-quarter, added water and rice and set the cookpot on to simmer. A rich, gamy aroma rose from the stew. A short while later Professor Tiffin appeared, his hands coated with soot. He dipped a mugful of stew and puffed over it as he untied his pack. He withdrew three oilcloth-wrapped parcels.

Elisha recognized the parcels: Sault Ste. Marie, the Johnston Hotel. He had seen the parcels when he'd entered Tiffin's hotel room and investigated the contents of his steamer trunk. Now the man opened an oilcloth to reveal a tiny, gleaming rock hammer, a hand spade, a paintbrush and set of calipers and heap of silk specimen bags. Professor Tiffin laid the tools on the grass before him, arranging and rearranging them like a child with toy soldiers. Finally he gathered them into his arms and started up the hill.

"Do you need my assistance?" Elisha called. The man did not respond.

And so it was the two of them alone at camp. The boy busied himself with cutting pine boughs and banking the fire, gathering a second load of firewood, restaking the tents. Susette sat silently beside the cookfire. When at last he paused in his labors she stood and said, "Elisha."

"Well! I suppose it's time for you to think about departing."

He was disgusted by the false cheerfulness in his tone. Susette had laid out a trout net and knife and tin of matches, a spare mug and rice and lump of grease: the barest necessities for an afternoon's fishing. The remainder of her pack lay undisturbed in her tent. She tied the stores in a bundle and hoisted it to her shoulder, surveyed the camp dispassionately. Then she motioned for Elisha to follow her.

The boy felt as though he were carved from wood. He trudged behind the woman on an eastward bearing that dipped into a damp, leafy swale. She turned northward, pausing for Elisha to mark a blaze, then continued for some time until they arrived at a river. It was a narrow channel rushing over jagged rocks, twigs swirling in the current, a fallen maple lodged at the water's edge. Elisha could not gauge the river's depth. Deep enough, he thought numbly, to carry a woman away. They hiked downstream until he noticed a dull thrum that quickly grew to a roar: the waterfall. Ten yards ahead the river disappeared. It was as though the water simply vanished into the hazy sky. Susette dropped her bundle on a spit of sand and turned to Elisha.

Her jaw was clenched but her eyes were wide and bright, her expression that of a woman on a steamer deck awaiting a ship's departure. She's excited to leave but does not want to show it, the boy thought. She does not want to hurt me.

"I feel how I did the morning I left my mother's house in St. Catharines. I am afraid to go."

"I was afraid when I left my father's house. Sometimes I'm still afraid. Sometimes I wish I were still there, in my bed with the quilt pulled up." Elisha turned away, embarrassed by his admission. "It's not easy to start anew. But you will be fine. A beautiful woman is always fine."

Susette smiled tightly. A breeze rose from the river and she shivered as if against a winter chill. "I hope you will forgive me."

"Professor Tiffin is the one who should forgive you, not me. He's the one injured in all this."

She nodded. "He will be disappointed. I know that. I feel awful for the man."

"But not awful enough to stay, and tell him the truth."

"No. Not awful enough to stay."

Elisha watched the woman draw a breath then slowly exhale. He knew how she was feeling, fear and exhilaration and guilt twisting a knot in her stomach. She had likely lain awake the previous night, struggling to draw comfort from the night's calm. Convincing herself yet again that she would be safe on her journey, that she would succeed in a new town. That she would be forgiven by those she was leaving.

"You shouldn't feel guilty for leaving," Elisha said. "You shouldn't let those feelings follow you. And you shouldn't feel guilty for what happened with us—that was my fault and mine alone."

She shook her head. "You say that because you are young. When you are young you believe everything is your fault. But you will not be young forever."

"Well. I don't believe you."

Susette blinked as though fighting tears. "I have never been farther than Fond du Lac. I have never been to Milwaukee. I have heard the town is mostly white people—is this true? I have never lived in a town with mostly white people."

"Fond du Lac is nearly as far as Milwaukee—if you've been to one you've practically been to the other. And don't worry about white people. They are like Chippewas, only less honest."

She laughed, and the boy heard a note of relief in her voice. He said, "American cities are everywhere the same. There are masses of people and everyone in a hurry. The smells are terrible strong. The streets are dust in summer and mud in winter. The carriages are loud and the rooming houses are filthy and on every street corner there are ladies in silk dresses standing beside the poorest rag peddlers. There are Irish and Chinese and Italians and Negroes and nobody knows one another and nobody cares. There is everything imaginable in the world, except clean air."

Susette nodded. "That is what I want."

"Then you shall be happy."

She moved close to Elisha, and the woman smelled of smoke and hair grease. He was struck by the fineness of her form, the bones no sturdier than a bird's, the tendons as fine as string. A delicate creature yet a marvel of strength, one of nature's beautiful mysteries. Susette took Elisha's hand, and then he recognized what would happen. A shiver passed through the boy. He laid a hand against her neck, felt her skin's warmth beneath his fingers.

She whispered, "My sweet boy."

Her eyes, which Elisha had thought to be dark brown, were deep hazel-green flecked with gold. When the sun clouded over they became greener yet, the color of a forest pond, and as Elisha leaned close his reflection grew as if on a pond's surface. Her palms were smooth and calloused, veined with fine cracks, and he traced them with his thumb as though following rivers on a map. Two Hearted River, Miner's River, Yellow River, Train River. A vanished country. Elisha was filled with reverent pleasure.

When he figured enough time had passed he moved atop her again, but Susette placed a hand against his chest. Elisha sensed in the woman a shiver of regret. He closed his eyes and nudged forward, and at last she relaxed beneath him. He was clumsy with excitement but could not slow himself. Susette watched him, mouth open, her breathing rising to jagged gasps. Elisha kissed her ear, her temple, her nose, her jaw, sweat dripping from his chin into the hollow of her throat. Pleasure billowed through him. Susette touched his stomach and the boy heard himself whimper like a pup. She giggled wickedly.

Afterward they lay on the riverbank beneath a white sky. Elisha felt deliciously attuned to the world's sensations, a whiff of pitch and the current's soft clap, a tickle of wood lice beneath his bare legs. This is what I require, he thought indulgently. Regular treatments to invigorate my senses. An image from a dream rose in the boy's mind, of himself in a Victorian house before a food-laden table, consumed by hunger. In an instant he grasped the dream's true meaning: his hunger was for thrill and desire and pleasure, for a woman's damp warmth. Of course.

Susette began to speak about her mother. The woman's name was Marie Beauchamp. She had been to Boston once as a young woman and forever after repeated an account of the visit until it was as legend, or prayer. The visit was in August of aught-three. She'd bought a Chinese silk shawl with a faint yellow print on Summer Street, a pair of Italian leather gloves from a vendor on Kingston. She had eaten the sweetest blueberry tart from a bakery on Tremont Street. On Milk Street she'd seen a gentleman wade into a fountain to fetch a lady's parasol; then he'd presented it to the woman with a deep bow, his trousers dripping. Summer Street, Kingston Street, Tremont Street,

Milk Street. The mayor's wife's handmaid had smiled at Marie Beauchamp. There were Negroes wearing silk hats. A Chinaman owned the city's biggest tanning works and a half-blood Native owned the Cameron Hotel.

Susette stopped speaking and it was very quiet. Elisha felt touched by melancholy joy, the way he imagined old lovers must feel. He moved to kiss the woman, but she rose and slowly donned her skirts and leggings and moccasins, hoisted her bundle to her shoulder.

"I love you," Elisha said suddenly. "My dear. I love you more than I can express. I will always love you, *always*. My dear Susette."

She knelt and brushed a lock of hair from the boy's forehead, kissed his cheek. She laid a finger against his lips. Susette said, "Tell my husband I have died." Then she rose and started upstream along the riverbank. Birch limbs shivered as she passed, then fell still.

He let the cookpot remain empty through the afternoon, then finally Elisha poured in a pail of water, added handfuls of peas and lyed corn and a thick chunk of pork belly. It was the same stew he'd watched Susette prepare countless times. Toward dusk Mr. Brush emerged from the forest and nodded a greeting, pulled off his boots and set to copying notes in his fieldbook. A short while later Professor Tiffin shambled into camp. His shirt was unbuttoned, his chest and arms streaked with dirt. He lay down on his bedroll and tipped his hat over his face.

Mr. Brush set down his pen. "So? The scientific world awaits your pronouncement."

"I wish I had a whiskey cocktail."

"Come now! Surely you've unearthed a mislaid gospel. At the very least a few spare psalms?"

Tiffin's flat voice emanated from the hat. "I have excavated nearly half of that damned hilltop. Susette offered no hint of where to concentrate my search." He sat up and the hat tumbled away. "Madame Morel!"

"She's gone fishing up near a waterfall, some ways east," Elisha said. "I expect she'll return soon."

A brittle silence lengthened; then Elisha said quickly, "Her pack is here. There's no food missing. No cooking gear or matches, either."

"The deceitful scut," Tiffin said. "She has abandoned me again!"

"Mind your language," Brush said sharply. "You will not speak of a lady in that manner."

"She is not a lady!" Tiffin scratched up a fistful of dirt and threw it into the cookfire. "Look for yourself—there is nothing here! She has deceived me, just as her husband deceived me. I will reach Peking before I unearth a buried tablet!"

"She's gone fishing for trout at a waterfall," Elisha said. "She said she'd return before dusk. I fear she may have come to an accident."

Mr. Brush scoffed. "More likely she is five miles distant, counting her coins like a merry Jewess! It is no coincidence that she vanished immediately after being paid."

Elisha said nothing.

"Nonetheless. If she has not emerged by tomorrow noon we will conduct a search."

Professor Tiffin slumped forward with his face in his hands. "The deceitful scut. I have excavated nearly half of that hilltop. The damned deceitful scut."

"Perhaps you're not digging deep enough," Elisha said. "Or perhaps the tablets aren't here at all—perhaps they were moved by the Midewiwin."

Tiffin offered the boy an exhausted stare. To Elisha his manner seemed strangely stiff, a second-rate actor at rehearsal. "They *must* be here. There is an energy, a *potency* in the very air—do you not sense it? It is similar to the energy present at the Grave Creek mound in Virginia. The sensation is undeniable."

"That is only your hunger." Mr. Brush leaned over the cookpot and inhaled deeply. "Let us eat."

Clouds had knitted into a dirty gray quilt and now lightning flickered to the west. The men shifted beneath the fly tents as thunder rolled overhead. A few fat raindrops hissed in the cookfire. Elisha imagined Susette huddled beneath a sugar maple, slowly recognizing the depth of her isolation as darkness closed around her. But no, no: she understood the forest's solitude. She had understood it all along. He wondered if she might be headed back toward camp then immediately realized she was not.

Professor Tiffin sat staring into the cookfire, his plump face pinched like a knot of dough. With a sigh he opened his fieldbook and began to write. Notes from his excavations, Elisha figured, or a letter to his wife describing the day's disappointment. Confessing his fear that the expedition would yet fail, promising her it would not. Revealing the solemn, secret hopes that until now he'd hoarded like a miser. And so Mr. Brush was right: Tiffin was nothing more than a dreamer, pursuing a dream that had never existed.

"Professor Tiffin?"

He started at his whispered name.

"Best of luck with your excavations tomorrow."

The man smiled sadly, his eyes glistening in the firelight. "Young fellow," he said. "Luck is for fools."

The forest southeast of camp was pure white pine spread across a low, flat valley. Mr. Brush spent the morning measuring trunk diameters and crown heights as his excitement grew. "First-quality pinewood," he marveled. "Enough to construct one thousand homes—this single stand, here—frame to shingle!" Elisha recorded Brush's measurements in a neat hand. As they hiked he scanned the forest from floor to canopy, waiting for a flash of motion and the queer, subtle conviction that he'd observed an unknown species.

But his thoughts meandered to a vision of Susette sitting cross-legged before a cookfire, a tattered *Godey's Lady's Book* on her lap and a flush risen to her freckled cheeks. Elisha willed his attention back to the present. A true scientist, he thought, would glance at this forest and recognize an unknown species like a stranger in a roomful of friends. But to Elisha the scene appeared infinitely complex, as anonymous and confusing as a city of thousands.

He recalled with a note of embarrassment his hope that the expedition would be like a long, lazy afternoon at the creek behind his father's house in Newell. There he had understood the seasons' habits, the arrival of bloodroot in April and warblers in May, the water's gradual thickening as it was gripped by November's cold. But here nature's customs remained stubbornly hidden. Elisha moved slowly among the towering pines. Despite his disappointment he did not feel wholly discouraged; for there was beauty enough to soothe any regret. Nature's great consolation, he thought, was its beauty.

They came into the swale after lunch and followed it northward, the white pine dwindling to a thicket of cedar. Sometime later they heard a rush of water, then they stepped out along a slow, rocky river. Eighty yards upriver was the waterfall. It tumbled down the ridge face in a rippling arc, settled into a foam-covered pool. Elisha figured the drop to be fifteen yards.

But as they drew nearer he realized he'd underestimated the falls' vigor. The cataract churned into a boiling white chute then smashed down against a spill of black rocks. Cold mist shimmered in the air. Black spruce and tamarack and white cedar overhung the pool, their trunks bearded in velvet moss.

"An ideal site for a lumber mill!" Brush shouted, above the water's roar. "A large mill operated by an ambitious young fellow might cut today's pine in two winters! Tell me, boy: what would you estimate the hydraulic power of this waterfall to be?"

"I don't know."

"Think! Consider the height of the drop then estimate the quantity of water falling at a given instant. It is a simple calculation. Think now!"

Elisha squatted at the pool's edge, struggling to recall the proper formula. At last he said, "Ten horsepower. Perhaps twelve."

"Twelve horsepower? With a drop of fifteen yards and rate of flow of, say, seven hundred cubic feet per minute, I would estimate a gross power of twenty-five horsepower. Perhaps thirty. A surplus of power for operating multiple saws."

"Yes. I underestimated the rate of flow." Elisha scattered a handful of pebbles into the pool then wiped his hands on his trousers. "We should search the upper river. Susette might have fished the upper river after she'd finished here."

Mr. Brush stared at the boy for several long moments; then he started toward the ridge face.

The upper river ran quick and deep until it surged against the falls' rim in a sort of weir. Boulders loomed like massive fish beneath the water's surface. Upstream the river vanished toward the horizon, a wedge of glimmering water cutting through the forest. Two fat porcupines waddled through the brush at the river's edge.

"Your manner troubles me," Mr. Brush said quietly. "When I pose a question your inevitable response is, I don't know. You do not attempt logical analysis of the problem. You do not attempt even a reasoned estimate of the solution. Your response is only, I don't know. Like an idiot child. I don't know."

"I'm sorry. Sir."

"Luckily, logic and analysis are skills that can be learned. That *must* be learned, if you are to be engaged in a practical art."

Again Elisha felt an urge toward apology. The feeling exhausted him.

"However." Mr. Brush took up a pebble and scratched at it with a thumbnail. "My proposal is in earnest."

"Which proposal?"

Brush spread his arms wide. "A lumber mill, of course! A large, modern mill sawing every stick of white pine in the region, with an ambitious young fellow at its command! You could be that young fellow."

Elisha said nothing.

"We have been blessed with a rare opportunity, my boy. You must understand that. This is supremely rich territory. However it is only as rich as we report."

"I don't follow your logic."

Brush laid an arm around the boy's shoulders and gestured toward the surrounding forest. "We are humble scribes, Elisha. We are recording details of this magnificent creation. And while iron ore and pine timber and hydraulic power might be present in this territory, they shall not truly exist until we have *recorded* their presence. Do you understand? And when this territory has been surveyed and made available to the public—why, a gentleman with capital, such as myself, might purchase a goodly number of prime lots. And an intelligent young fellow—such as yourself—might command the subsequent enterprises."

For a moment the man's words refused to coalesce; then a shock raced through Elisha. "You are proposing to misreport the quality of the land. Declare the finest lots worthless to speculators, then purchase them yourself."

Mr. Brush winced as though he'd been stung. "Not at all! I am simply explaining that we possess knowledge of this territory's vast riches—and that we might draw on this knowledge for the nation's benefit! You see Elisha, this country's unique genius is that the good of the individual is always allied with the good of the nation."

Elisha toed a bough of driftwood. An image of the man's house on Lafayette Street in Detroit rose in his mind: the broad double doors, the Negro hired girl, the oak bookshelf filled with leather-bound volumes. The marble mantel and rosewood clock and gold Roman coins displayed on red silk. So he is nothing more than a thief, the boy thought.

"I am not interested in your proposal."

"Well!" Mr. Brush smiled thinly. "That was a rather hasty verdict."

"I'm sorry. I don't want any part of such a scheme."

The man cleared his throat, a pinched smile frozen on his lips. He seemed startled by the boy's response. "You mean, rather, that you are not interested in learning a meaningful trade. You are not interested in becoming a practical young man. In certain ways, my boy, you remind me of your paramour Mr. Tiffin. Did you know that he is married to a nigger?"

Elisha said nothing. He could not look at Mr. Brush.

"And here we are, this very moment, searching for sign of the red nigger he engaged as a guide! Who has obeyed her defective character and vanished for a second time! My only surprise is that she didn't attempt to collect the balance of her payment—I have yet to know a savage who passed an opportunity to wrangle money. It is inherent in their nature."

Mr. Brush edged forward until his chest touched Elisha's shoulder. Despite himself the boy leaned away. Brush said, "You must be troubled by Madame Morel's disappearance. Stricken, even."

His voice held a mocking tone. Elisha said, "Of course I am troubled."

"Of course. And yet I sense—" Brush strode a few paces downriver then immediately turned back. "Tell me, my boy: How does a half-breed become lost in the forest in which she was reared? How does she become lost *twice* within a matter of weeks? It is incomprehensible—unless, of course, she intended to become lost."

"I don't follow your logic."

"Of course you don't. And neither do you know if she has gone back to the Sault with her pay. Or if she is watching us even now. Or if she has arranged to meet you in Detroit in one month's time, far from the inconvenience of her husband's gaze."

Elisha began to respond but Brush raised a hand. "Consider my proposal, my boy. That is all I ask of you."

Mr. Brush started downriver. As he approached the falls' edge the man paused; then he waded into the river, the current rippling against his back. He braced himself against a boulder and bent over a driftwood limb wedged against the rim of the falls. From the web of branches Brush tugged free a sodden scrap of fabric.

It was a fragment of a woolen dress. Elisha immediately recognized the dress as Susette's. The boy cried out, a strangled gasp that he prayed sounded sincere.

Mr. Brush stared at the fabric, then turned to Elisha. He slung the scrap over the falls' edge. "Well," he said dryly. "May the Lord have mercy on her poor soul."

Four

"How is it possible that the Father, Son, and Holy Ghost share the same indivisible essence? Have you never wondered? Of course the Trinity's oneness is a profound mystery—but what wisdom are we, mere humans, to reap from such a paradox? For surely it would be easier to admit, say, the presence of three distinct deities. Yes?"

Ignace Morel grunted in response. Reverend Stone glanced over his shoulder: the man sat high in the canoe's stern, glaring at the horizon, his cap pulled low against the sun. An unlit pipe was tucked behind an ear. The minister's vision wobbled, then steadied. He was exhausted to the point of nausea.

"Of course, the relegation of doctrine to mystery is very convenient—theologians have been doing it for centuries. Yet it seems an admission of failure, does it not? A failure to honor God's effort in sharing his Word."

He realized that he was jabbering but could not seem to stop himself. He said, "I suspect the root of the issue lies with language. You see, we interpret the word *person* to mean an individual being; however the original translation springs from the Greek *prosopon*—the mask that theater actors wore during performances. So you see—"

"You must paddle. If you talk you must paddle."

Reverend Stone sighed as he turned back to the fore. Before him, the sun was a painful dazzle on the lake's surface. He bent away from the sight.

"So you see, a more useful translation might be *persona*, which suggests a role we play in a certain circumstance. Yes? One actor and three roles, the essence shared but the guise adapted to circumstance. A marvelously rich concept. A bit near to Sabellian heresy, I'm afraid, but rich nonetheless. Please, if you would be so kind."

The voyageur hissed, then slapped a wash of spray over the bow with his paddle. Reverend Stone groaned at the water's coldness. He dipped a mug over the canoe's side and swallowed a draft of lake water, poured a second mugful over his sun-blistered neck.

"Now, you are thinking, An interesting point, but hardly revelatory. Certainly not equal to the profundity of the Trinity. Perhaps merely . . . practical." Reverend Stone twisted back toward the stern. "I suppose I know of no better instruction for contemplating the trinity than Augustine's dictum: Vides Trinitatem si vides caritatem. You see the trinity when you see love. Yes? This is paradoxical, yet it feels true. It feels somehow . . . complete."

"Enough! Paddle."

Reverend Stone smiled unsteadily. "Of course, you Catholics wouldn't agree with many of these points, but our friends the Unitarians seem to get the gist." He dropped the paddle and pressed a hand to his face. "I am sorry. We must stop."

Without a word Morel angled the canoe toward shore. Reverend Stone drew a tin from his pocket, then reclined in the canoe bottom and tipped his hat over his face. He slipped a tablet into his mouth.

They had been paddling three days through airless heat, along thin stony beaches and cedar swamp and scraggly jack pines, the lakeshore's monotony suggesting that they hadn't gained a league. That first evening they'd camped on a spit of rocky sand, Morel staking a tent and gathering deadwood for the cookfire while Reverend Stone fetched a kettle of water. He'd set the kettle on then slumped down on a bedroll. He woke the next morning unable to move, his arms petrified by fatigue, the slightest gesture causing pain to knife through his shoulders. Despite himself he'd cried out. Morel hooted, clapped the minister's back. "Allons, mon vieux!" Reverend Stone swallowed a pair of tablets then hunched before the cookfire until his muscles softened to butter. He'd hauled himself into the canoe. His paddle raised and dipped like a tailor's needle into an endless blue sheet.

That second morning the pain had deepened to stiff, frozen cramps. He swallowed three tablets then lay motionless, his breathing shallow. Paddling, he attempted to focus on scenery: sunlight haloing a stand of birches, plover and goldeneye squabbling on the beach. A white-tailed deer standing frozen at the lake's edge. When they put ashore Reverend Stone collapsed in the sand like he'd been shot. He coughed; then his stomach turned, bringing mucus and a thin rope of blood. The voyageur watched him silently. Reverend Stone shoved sand over the mess and closed his eyes.

Now it was midafternoon on the third day and they were encamped at the tip of a swampy beach. Morel had lit greenwood smudges to drive away mosquitoes, then prepared a stew of salt pork and lyed corn seasoned strongly with pepper. The minister accepted a mug and set it aside to cool. His hands were sunburned, his skin as dry as parchment.

"What is wrong with you?"

Reverend Stone shook his head. "A touch of croup. I'm not accustomed to this variety of labor, you see. Mine is of the spiritual variety, rather than the physical."

Ignace Morel uncorked the whiskey keg and poured a careful measure. "That is not croup. This is croup." The voyageur coughed, a hoarse bark from the back of his throat. "Now, this is yours." He coughed again, a wet spasm that rose from the bottom of his lungs.

"It must be a miasma disturbing my lungs. I didn't expect this region to be quite so damp. Or so warm."

"You bring blood. That is not croup." Morel stirred the cookpot, then puffed on the spoon and licked it clean. "We have no croup here in the north. God does not send us croup or consumption or flux. He does not send any of these. Only sometimes the shakes."

"That must be due to the pure forest air. That, or your pure hearts."

The voyageur smiled as he swallowed a mouthful of stew. "Yes, our good, pure hearts. We are good people, good Catholic hearts."

"I had never suspected otherwise."

Morel's smile lingered on Reverend Stone. He leaned toward the minister and whispered conspiratorially. "I know what you are think. You think that we kneel toward Rome, that we worship the pope like God. That the pope will invade New York with his army, capture all the Protestants. That is what you are think."

"That is absurd! You have been reading—" Reverend Stone coughed into his fist. "You have been reading some outrageous pamphlets."

"Or maybe I am reading the truth. Yes?"

"Of course not. All reasonable men know that those pamphlets are nothing but lies. Lies and gross exaggeration."

"And then these reasonable men burn churches. They burn convents. Yes? This is what they do in Massachusetts."

Reverend Stone moved to speak but was gripped by a cough. He bent double as tears sprung to his eyes. He glanced apologetically at Morel. Slowly, the voyageur took up a flask and removed the cork, offered it to the minister.

"I know what you are think, but I do not care. You pay me, and I do not care."

"You have been reading some outrageous pamphlets." Reverend Stone blinked away tears. "I have the greatest respect for your faith. Believe me."

Morel watched the man drink, a smile frozen on his lips. "I know what you are think. But now you need me."

He lay awake past midnight, the taste of blood on his tongue. Despite the night's heat he was touched by chills, his hands trembling like a drunkard's. Reverend Stone brushed the mosquito netting from his face, took up the flask but found it empty. He tipped the last drops of water into his mouth.

The voyageur lay sleeping before the dwindling cookfire, a line of saliva glistening on his cheek. Reverend Stone studied the man in profile. Despite the tangled hair and scarred chin he was handsome, his jaw angular and strong, his brow blunt but expressive. A half-wild Adonis weathered by drink.

That evening after supper Morel had scoured the cookpot and mugs, sipping whiskey all the while, then rooted in his gunnysack and withdrew a canvas case. He'd carefully removed a fiddle, frowning over the instrument as he fingered the tuning pegs, rosined the stubby bow. Reverend Stone had glanced up from the Catlin book. The fiddle was small and blackened, with a scored belly and short neck, a pair of ragged soundholes. Morel positioned the instrument low against his breast. His left hand curled awkwardly around the fingerboard.

He'd raised the bow with a flourish, then launched into a jerky, rollicking hornpipe, stamping loudly on the beat, the bow rocking and bouncing over the strings. The fiddle's tone was coarse but powerful, tuned sharp to pierce a tavern's din. Morel's eyes fell to slits. Reverend Stone found himself tapping the Catlin book's cover. At last Morel quit stamping and pinched the tune into a quick trill, then stretched the last, low note out to silence. Reverend Stone cried, "Wonderful!" The voyageur nodded gruffly. He said, "Now, 'La Belle Susette.' For my wife."

He began a song that was slow and sugary, played with long bow strokes and intricate fingering, a complexity more suited to a chamber violinist than a tavern fiddler. Ignace Morel frowned in concentration. Reverend Stone stared through the man, the song's melody bringing an image of a rainy night in Newell, a lit-up temperance hall. Smell of whale oil and damp wool, groan of floorboards beneath a fiddle's whine. A social dance sponsored by the Young Men's Society, during the first month of his courtship of Ellen. Two dozen couples waltzed across the muddy floor, their faces agleam with sweat. A Negro fiddler stood on a stool beside the hearth, playing "Shady Grove."

Courtship: the word had seemed part of another language entirely.

Reverend Stone had paced in the room's corner, in his mournful black suit, sipping spring water and grinning stiffly at the young men and women. Ellen was nowhere to be seen. One by one the couples approached, offering a moment's conversation about the weather or the previous Sunday's sermon before returning to the crowded dance floor. Reverend Stone looked up to find the fiddler regarding him with a piteous smile. He realized how ridiculous he appeared: a minister at a dance, awaiting a woman half his age—for what purpose? She no doubt viewed him as a kindly chaperone rather than an ardent suitor. As a father or friend, rather than a husband or lover. Reverend Stone nodded to the fiddler then drained his glass.

Outside it was cool and the evening's rain had softened to mist. Crickets filled the air with a mocking singsong. Reverend Stone thought he had never felt as miserable. He turned up his collar and stepped down to the road; then he heard the distant snap of a coachman's whip. A Concord wagon appeared at the far edge of the green. It rattled past the meetinghouse then turned toward the temperance hall, and before it rolled to a stop the door opened. Ellen stepped from the coach, wearing a maroon overcoat trimmed with fur, matching maroon slippers.

She looked like she'd just run a footrace. Her cheeks were flushed, mottled by a rime of powder, and as she fumbled with her bonnet the color rose to her forehead. A startled smile flickered on her lips.

Reverend Stone spoke without thinking. "A foul evening. I was just fixing to leave."

What a fool he was. He began to correct himself but Ellen said, "I've just arrived from Worcester. I'm dreadful unsettled from the ride—we were nearly overturned outside Springfield. The coachman drove clear off the turnpike to avoid a broken-down chaise. Though I admit I'd begged him to make top speed."

Reverend Stone allowed himself a note of hope. He said, "Your shoes."

She glanced down: the toes of her velvet slippers were smeared with mud. Ellen groaned, then broke into a nervous titter. "I suppose it will be worth the loss if you'll assist me."

She presented herself like a waltzing partner. For a moment Reverend Stone stood motionless, puzzled; then he grasped Ellen about the waist and hoisted her onto the temperance hall porch. She giggled again. "My gracious! It was dry as a bone in Worcester."

Now Reverend Stone marveled at the memory. The feel of her ribs, intricate and fragile beneath his grip. The hint of lilac water on her neck. Heat had rushed to his face, his breathing sharpening to a gasp that he'd masked with a dry cough. He'd felt shocked by the intensity of his desire.

It was a miracle, Reverend Stone thought now, yet at the same moment realized that their love was not unique. His emotions were identical to those of a million other men, on a million other nights. An ordinary miracle, then, as natural as sunrise. The notion was comforting, an affirmation of God's grace.

But the thought gnawed at him as he fluttered toward sleep. It was impossible that their love was ordinary. There had been one autumn night, seven months after the wedding, when they'd lain huddled in bed beneath a layer of quilts. Ellen was pregnant with Elisha. The white heat of courtship had cooled. She'd been singing songs from her childhood in Boston, wicked ditties the minister had never heard.

> *The pudding is hot, the milk is sweet*
> *The children cheer a welcome treat*
> *Then off to bed, off to sleep*
> *Soon father's bed will bump and creak.*

Ellen snorted with laughter, clapped a hand over Reverend Stone's mouth. He was suffused with a strange greediness, as though a lifetime with Ellen could never be enough. Then she had described her vision of love.

"It's like an invisible light," she said, "a light within light. Like the shimmer above a candle flame, invisible but radiating warmth." Ellen paused, weighing her words. "And the light is present everywhere, but becomes stronger when it's reflected between two people. It becomes like sunlight through window glass, a certain intensity of warmth. And that is love, that concentration of light." She touched her forehead to Reverend Stone's chest. "Did you ever consider the thought?"

"I have indeed," he said, unable to conceal his astonishment. "And I would describe it identically: light within light, and warmth. Yes."

She had murmured contentedly but said nothing. Soon she was asleep. Reverend Stone lay awake for some time, filled with desperate gratitude. Tears welled in unpredictable surges. The feeling was unbearable, yet he did not want to sacrifice it to sleep. Only toward dawn did he close his eyes.

That, then: a shared vision of love. Surely it was rare. Surely such miracles were far from ordinary.

Now Reverend Stone jerked awake: a rustle from the forest, followed by a sharp hiss. Lynx, or perhaps raccoon. He edged closer to the cookfire. Overhead the sky was gray-black, a moonless, starless shroud. Reverend Stone whispered a prayer, that his wife's soul might be at rest. He recalled Adele Crawley's claims at the séance in Detroit: that Ellen was consumed with love, that she yearned for him, that she awaited his arrival in heaven. He prayed that the girl was correct.

They traveled only fifteen leagues in four days, Reverend Stone paddling for short stretches then reclining on the canoe's bottom to rest. White sand hillocks and pine forests and sandstone cliffs slid past in the deadening heat. On the fifth day he stirred from a drowse to see tiny wooden houses set on a grassy rise. The minister wondered if he was hallucinating. The houses resembled half-breed shanties sized in miniature, as though for dogs. He asked Morel the dwellings' purpose. "Cemetery for Chippewas," the voyageur said, "to keep away animals."

Reverend Stone felt a prickle of shame at his initial speculation. He murmured a blessing as they passed.

Ignace Morel spoke little as he paddled, instead singing simple chansons to mark his pace. He was like a wondrous machine, the minister marveled, muscle and bone in place of crank and pinion. An engine designed expressly for pushing wood through water. In the evenings Morel landed the canoe then pitched the tents, kindled the cookfire, set on a stew. Supper finished, he scrubbed the cookpot, then took up his fiddle and played a string of hornpipes and reels, each night ending with "La Belle Susette." Only after he'd stowed the instrument would the voyageur engage in grudging conversation.

He'd been born in Montréal, Reverend Stone learned, and came to Sault Ste. Marie as a young engagé of the North West Company, paddling through Canada during spring and summer and resting at the Sault during fall and winter. In those days their canoes were overloaded with peltry. Any fool could kill a beaver by skipping a stone across a forest pond. When the North West Company failed he joined the American Fur Company, and when the American Fur Company failed he joined the Hudson's Bay Company. But slowly their canoes became lighter and fewer, the beavers became young and scarce. Now the furred animals were mostly killed. Voyageurs argued over petty, worthless jobs. Some days Morel worked as an interpreter for Edwin Colcroft, other days he ferried American tourists down the straits. Other days he did nothing at all.

Morel related his tale without bitterness or distress. Reverend Stone recognized the man's character: unambitious but not lazy, unschooled but not slow-witted. Pious but unconcerned with doctrine or Scripture. Searching for comfort and pleasure in every aspect of life. In truth, the minister reflected, it was a difficult philosophy to refute. Hellfire and damnation were a preacher's best strategies.

One evening after Morel had finished fiddling Reverend Stone said, "Your wife, Susette. Did you meet her in Sault Ste. Marie?"

They were encamped on a strip of stony sand at the edge of a dense spruce forest. The voyageur was silent as he returned the instrument to its case. At last he said, "Yes, at the Sault. Five years ago."

"She must be a fine woman to have inspired such a lovely song. May I ask if you've been blessed with children?"

Ignace Morel grunted. Reverend Stone could not decide if it was meant as a yea or nay.

" 'Children are a heritage of the Lord, and the fruit of the womb is his reward.' Yes? I have often admired the wisdom of that passage. I recall my son Elisha, as a very small child, reaching for me and calling, *'Abba.'* Abba! What a beautiful word! It translates as father, of course, but its true meaning is richer, and more affectionate. Part of parenthood's reward is how profoundly we begin to know ourselves through our—"

"No. We have no children. Do you know why?" Morel leaned toward Reverend Stone. "We have no children because she does not give herself to me. My wife. She tells me I smell like vison, like mink. She pushes me away. You understand? And I do not strike her, I tell her what she is—la sainte Susette. Susette the saint. That is what she is! She pushes me away, like a proud chienne. I tell her to go to her mother. She never goes! So. We have no children."

Reverend Stone was silent.

"I know Scripture. 'The head of a woman is her husband'—that is Scripture. It is she who does not know Scripture."

"You suggest a narrow interpretation of the verse. Elsewhere husband and wife are described as a single flesh. Man is called to love his wife as his own body."

Morel scoffed as he reclined on his bedroll. "You are right. She is a fine woman—that is why I write the song. But she is not without fault."

"No woman is without fault. Nor is any man."

The voyageur turned away. Reverend Stone waited, his body taut, as the voyageur thrashed and twisted on his bedroll. Finally an airy snore rose from the darkness. With a sigh the minister drew his Bible from his jacket pocket. He thought to search for the passage Morel had quoted, but instead let the book lay closed on his lap. Perhaps I have misjudged the man, he thought. He wondered what this latest error might cost him.

Mosquitoes, sand flies, thunderheads, heat: July on the lake. Yellow warblers and blackbirds twittered in the violet dawn. Fog hung over the beach, then vanished as the sun splintered across the horizon. They paddled through the morning then rested during the noontime heat; to Reverend Stone's surprise he felt strong enough to paddle into the afternoon. Evenings, he reclined on a bedroll while Morel performed his meticulous routine: supper, washing, fiddle, "La Belle Susette." The minister said little, swallowed a pair of tablets then opened his Bible at random, like a diviner. The remaining tin of tablets was but half full. Reverend Stone acknowledged the fact but refused to consider its implications.

One day after lunch he unfolded Charles Noble's map and traced his finger along Lake Superior's south shore: the coastline ran from Sault Ste. Marie westward to a squarish bay, then undulated toward a horn-shaped peninsula. Reverend Stone presented the map to Ignace Morel. "Will you please tell me where we are?"

The voyageur glanced at the map, jabbed at a point just beyond the bay.

"Then! We are making a tolerable pace."

"We should be here." Morel indicated a region nearer to the peninsula. It was where Noble predicted the expedition would turn inland.

"Well, there is nothing to do but persevere. I am feeling stronger of late—I am better able to contribute to the paddling. You might have noticed."

Morel grunted but said nothing.

They set out that afternoon in a warm drizzle, their paddles' clap and drip muffled by the hush of rain on the lake. Near four the rain paused and they came into a region of strangely colored cliffs. Reverend Stone stopped paddling. The cliffs were knobbed sandstone faces streaked with orange and green and yellow, the colors as garish and blurred as a child's first watercolor. He said, "Spectacular! How do you suppose the colors were formed?"

The voyageur did not respond. Reverend Stone twisted around to find Morel staring past him, his lips moving over a silent chanson. The minister resumed paddling.

Toward dusk they came to a strip of sand nestled among the cliffs. There were Natives encamped at the beach's far end. Three canoes lay overturned near the forest edge, beside a pair of cookfires surrounded by figures. Chippewas heading to the Sault, Reverend Stone thought, most likely to beg for annuity payments. The canoe yawed slightly. He dug hard to correct the tack; then he realized Morel was steering them shoreward.

"What are you intending? Trade?"

The canoe surged forward on a swell's crest. Now a group of Natives stood watching at the water's edge: three tall, barefoot men dressed in deerskin and ragged broadcloth. The voyageur called out in Chippewa.

"Do you know these Natives? Answer me!"

Morel swung over the gunwale as the canoe slid into the shallows. He splashed alongside the bow, seized Reverend Stone beneath his shoulders and hoisted him into the freezing water. A cold shock gripped the minister. He stumbled onto the beach as Morel dragged the canoe ashore. The Natives hurried forward, took up packs of stores as the voyageur hoisted the canoe. From up the beach a child squalled.

Four young braves had approached from the Native encampment; now they stood prodding the bundled stores, their flintlock muskets laid in the sand. The smallest brave was staring at Reverend Stone. Morel greeted the Natives, then addressed a light-skinned Chippewa with fine, Roman features. The minister edged beside the voyageur and adopted an amiable expression. An odor of broiling whitefish wafted over them.

"Please tell me what you are saying," Reverend Stone said quietly.

The handsome Native addressed Morel, then called over his shoulder. The young braves paused, listening. The smallest brave responded with a single word.

"You must tell me what is happening. Please!"

Ignace Morel addressed the young braves, motioning to Reverend Stone. The smallest brave nodded solemnly. He was short but muscular, his chest and arms as thick as a pugilist's, his hair drawn back by a fillet of yellow beads. He was listening intently to Morel. He motioned toward the minister and spoke; Morel responded and the boy smothered a bashful grin.

"These two, good fellows both of them." Morel motioned toward the smallest brave and a second, taller boy. "They will help us paddle— we make a good pace. You pay them."

"What is this? To what business are you are engaging these Natives?"

"We paddle too slow. Your son will soon be gone. So will my wife, you understand? You pay these fellows one dollar each for five days' paddle. Very little money."

"I cannot pay even a dime! I have no money."

It was the truth: he had spent his last dollar at the mercantile in Sault Ste. Marie. His pockets contained a Bible, the Catlin book, a week-old *City Examiner,* and a tin of toothache medication.

"Of course you will pay. One dollar each for five days' paddle. If you don't pay, we take ten days. Twelve. Your son will be gone."

Reverend Stone studied the second brave: no older than fifteen, with knobby wrists and a calm, hungry stare that reminded the minister of a boy from Newell, Byron Wills. He was a shy, pious child who had one morning walked into his father's stable and shot six horses dead with a Colt revolver.

"Are they trustworthy fellows? Will we be safe?"

"Safer than with me." Morel clapped his hands twice. "You pay and we go, tomorrow."

"Eighty cents. I'm afraid I can afford no more."

Ignace Morel laughed. He spoke a long, rapid phrase in Chippewa and the Natives grinned. The handsome Native nodded and the group started back up the beach.

"Come, we eat now. Tomorrow we go."

"And the pay?"

Morel smiled. "One dollar."

That night they took supper at the Chippewa camp, Reverend Stone sitting cross-legged between Morel and the handsome Native, a mug of stewed whitefish before him. Children dashed, squealing, through the ring of seated braves. The food was delicious but the minister had little appetite. Through Morel's interpretation the handsome Native asked Reverend Stone about his home, but when the minister moved to speak his lungs convulsed in a wet cough. He wiped a bloody palm on his trousers. He looked up to find the handsome Native regarding him with a contemptuous expression. Reverend Stone smiled at the squaw tending the cookpot, then moved into the darkness.

He spread a bedroll beside the canoe and lay carefully on his side, concentrating on breathing. He refused to cough. Chippewa phrases floated over him, their rhythm soon merging with the rasp of his exhalations, the surf's surge and pause. Reverend Stone sensed for a moment the utter vastness of the lake, its weight and pull, its gravity. The breakers crumbling against sandstone cliffs. The black swells pushing out to infinity. He felt sick and alone, as insignificant as a shadow. He said a prayer for strength and closed his eyes.

Five

He had found that sleep was the only remedy for his illness, so Reverend Stone willed himself into a constant drowse, perched on the canoe's slender thwart, his head nodding forward until it touched the Native paddler before him. He woke to an unchanged shoreline: maples and bluffs and outcrops and beaches, nature stuttering on a word. The canoe skimmed over the glassy lake. When he turned to the horizon Reverend Stone felt distracted by wonder, a familiar tickle of amazement. The sensation never failed to drag him toward sleep.

Nights he sat awake, exhausted but alert. Ignace Morel lay beside the canoe, his pugilist's face softened by sleep. The Native paddlers sprawled on pine boughs in the darkness. Reverend Stone hunched beside the cookfire, his Bible or the Catlin book tipped toward the low flames. Both volumes had been drenched near the Sault, and now the covers were splayed over thick, wrinkled pages.

On their third night from the Chippewa camp Reverend Stone sat searching through Catlin for a passage describing the Native conception of heaven. Again he was plagued by chills, his arms puckered with gooseflesh. The night was moonlit, silent. He found himself engrossed by a discussion of Native morality. Catlin's writing had taken on a hysterical tone, as vehement as any abolitionist.

I fearlessly assert to the world, (and I *defy* contradiction,) that the North American Indian is, in his native state, a highly moral and religious being, endowed with an *intuitive knowledge* of some great

Author of his being and of the Universe. He constantly lives in appre-
hension of a future state, where he expects to be *rewarded* or *punished*
according to the merits he has gained or forfeited in this world.
Morality and virtue, I venture to say, the civilized world *need not* under-
take to teach them.

A pity, Reverend Stone thought, that such outrage was required—
for surely there were as many virtuous Natives as there were dissolute
whites. He flipped to the frontispiece and studied Catlin's portrait:
thin, sloping nose, pinched chin, eyes drawn down in modesty or fatigue. A noble, melancholy countenance. The minister wondered if
Catlin had taken a Native bride, then immediately was convinced that
he had. The fact seemed written overtop the man's angry words.

Reverend Stone glanced up to find the small brave watching him.
He smiled at the brave; then the boy rose and paced around the cookfire, sat against a humped boulder beside Reverend Stone. He was
short but thick-chested, his skin tanned nearly black. He whispered a
slurred string of syllables. After a moment the minister realized his
words were English.

"English? Do you speak English?"

"Small Throat," the brave said solemnly.

Reverend Stone frowned, waiting; then he understood the phrase
to be the boy's name.

"William Stone. That is my name."

The brave nodded.

"Perhaps you were taught English by a gentleman named John
Sunday? Do you know the fellow—John Sunday?"

The brave's gaze fell, his lips moving silently over the words.

Reverend Stone waved a hand as if clearing away smoke. He
pointed at himself. "Father, William Stone. Son, Elisha Stone."

"Father. Big Throat. Son. Small Throat."

"Yes!" Reverend Stone grinned, struck by the name's literal-minded
poetry. He supposed his own Chippewa name would be Coughing
Stone. "My son—have you seen my son? Elisha Stone?"

The brave glanced uncertainly toward Morel's sleeping form.

"No, no." Reverend Stone gestured toward the surrounding forest. *"Son."*

Small Throat whispered a phrase in Chippewa and glanced hopefully at the minister; then the boy's expression faltered. The cookfire crackled, sparks swirling like gnats into the black sky. Reverend Stone shivered, a fever chill.

"Elisha Stone," he pleaded. "Have you heard the name?"

As if in response Small Throat took up the Catlin book. Reverend Stone recalled reading that books and newspapers were considered medicine by some Natives, the pages viewed as magical talking leaves. Small Throat opened the book to its middle: an illustration of an Osage named Ee-tow-o-kaum dressed in a pink beaded jacket and headdress, Psalter in one hand and cane in the other. On the facing page was a Native named Waun-naw-con. His hair was clipped short, like a white man's; he wore a black frock coat and white shirt, a black cravat knotted beneath a high, stiff collar. The portrait was unfinished, the Native's face and shoulders watercolored but his torso a hollow sketch. Small Throat pointed at the image. "Son?"

Reverend Stone felt overwhelmed by fatigue. He seized the book and tossed it aside, then immediately regretted his brusqueness. He touched the boy's wrist. "I am sorry," he said, "you must excuse me. I am very tired."

But instead of retiring to his bedroll he rose and trudged toward the lakeshore. Small Throat's hopeful gaze followed him. As the minister passed the camp's perimeter he was consumed by darkness: a familiar bodiless confusion, the world gone black then mellowing to coal-gray shadows. Beach sand skittered around his feet.

A grudging calm moved through Reverend Stone as he paced along the water's edge. He had always thought himself happiest in an empty meetinghouse, alone with sunlight and silence and his own tranquil thoughts—yet here he was among strangers, sickly but exhilarated, surprised by life. How amazing, to learn such a thing about oneself, at such an age. Like meeting a foreigner on the street and finding him your brother. With a nudge, Reverend Stone realized, I might have been a missionary among these people, a Catlin portrait with Psalter and cane, dressed in buckskin and beads and cravat. The thought was unsettling, both attractive and deeply strange.

He sat at the lake edge and trailed a hand through the cold water, wiped his face and neck. Lake Superior was flat calm, a runny pane of glass. A low howl rose from the forest. He turned toward camp to see Small Throat bent over the Catlin book, his face lit by firelight. The boy slowly turned a page.

Better, perhaps, to have remained ignorant of all this, Reverend Stone thought. I do not understand this life.

They passed quickly along a stretch of marshy cedar flats, the weather hot and clear, the sky dotted with hawks circling for prey. Mosquitoes swarmed their campsites. Ignace Morel burned moss in smoky smudges, but this only provoked the insects' attention: Reverend Stone's face and hands were soon speckled with tiny red welts. He looked like he'd been shot with a load of pebbles.

One afternoon they landed the canoe to find a bald eagle perched on a deadwood log near the forest's edge. The bird regarded Ignace Morel as the man furiously charged his rifle. At last the eagle unfurled its enormous wings, rising in a slow flutter as the voyageur shouldered his gun and tracked the bird's ascent. The rifle's blast echoed as the eagle tumbled with a splash into the shallows. They fried the meat with wild onions, ate it with wedges of smoking panbread. Reverend Stone thought he had never tasted anything more delicious.

That next afternoon they did not put ashore at all, instead coasting slowly while they chewed strips of smoked venison. The Native paddlers were as tireless as voyageurs, pausing only when Morel withdrew his pipe to smoke. They encamped that evening exhausted but cheery, Morel pouring gills of whiskey for the Natives and a half-pint for himself. Supper finished, he took up his fiddle and twisted the tuning pegs, then began a driving reel that was nearly too fast for dancing.

Reverend Stone clapped with the tune's rhythm as the braves chuckled with bemused pleasure. Finally Small Throat rose and began an awkward, shuffling jig. The second brave cackled with glee.

On the fifth morning from the Chippewa camp Reverend Stone woke from a nap to see black strings of smoke rising along the beach. He squinted through the lake's glare: it was a Native village, two dozen lodges like overturned bowls along a river, a few figures moving among the cookfires. A group of braves was dipping for whitefish at the river's edge. The party's canoe angled shoreward. A pair of skinny, fox-like dogs trotted up the beach, barking; then the braves dropped their nets and ran into the village.

"Chocolate River band," Morel said. "They are fools and drunkards. We leave the paddlers then continue on the river. Half-day paddle, then we go on foot."

"On foot for how long?"

"Four days." A moment's pause. "For you, maybe more."

"Yes. Perhaps five."

They coasted toward the beach. The Natives swung overboard and guided the canoe to the lake's edge, then Morel stepped out and hoisted Reverend Stone onto his back, lowered him gently onto the shore. Small Throat and the second Native hefted packs of stores and dropped them on the riverbank, past a sandbar blockading the stream's entrance. Morel hoisted the dripping canoe over his head and set it beside the stores. "One pipe," he called, untying his tobacco pouch. "One pipe and we go."

Reverend Stone drank a mugful of lake water then poured a second measure over his head. He swabbed his face as a group of Native women emerged at the village edge, chatting merrily, bearing a gutted deer carcass on a travois. They paused to stare at the minister; then they dumped the carcass beside a tanning rack and set to work. Curious, Reverend Stone thought, that there exists no square or meeting place in Native villages, no attempt at order among the lodges. He wondered what it might suggest about their society.

Small Throat and the second brave were standing a few paces up the beach. With a start Reverend Stone realized they were awaiting their pay. He approached the pair, palms outspread to suggest patience and goodwill.

"One moment, please. Yes? Wait here?"

He hurried past the braves as Small Throat nodded uncertainly. At the river's edge, Ignace Morel was squatting on a flour keg, scraping his pipebowl with the tip of a clasp knife.

"Monsieur Morel."

The voyageur did not look up from his work. His hat was tipped sideways, his hair raked forward in a lank black veil, obscuring his eyes. The sight inexplicably irritated Reverend Stone.

"Monsieur Morel, sir. I seem to be in a difficult position. I must pay the braves for their labors, however my coins and banknotes have vanished."

"Your money is gone."

"My money is gone. Yes. I suspect the coins must have fallen from my pocket while boarding the canoe, or perhaps while I was asleep—"

"You think the Chippewas steal?"

"Of course not! The coins were simply lost—they fell from my pocket, or something equally ridiculous."

"You think I steal?" Ignace Morel rose with the pipe clamped between his teeth. "You think I steal, maybe when you sleep I take your coins?"

"No, no—certainly not!" Reverend Stone heard a note of irritation in his voice. He drew a calming breath. "My money is gone. I must pay the braves for their labors. I hoped I might borrow a small sum from you."

Morel worked the pipe between his wet lips. He smelled powerfully, of onions and sour wood smoke. "How much do you want?"

"Two dollars, to pay the braves. You would be doing me an immense service."

The voyageur seemed amused by the minister's proposal. He drew sharply on the pipe, folded his arms over his thick chest. "No."

Reverend Stone nodded wearily. "If you loan me two dollars now, I will pay you four dollars when we return to Sault Ste. Marie. The additional two dollars will serve as interest on the loan."

A flicker passed through Morel's eyes, like a wave beneath a lake's surface.

"You will earn two dollars in but a few weeks, without labor or risk. I will repay you the moment we return to the Sault—I have a standing offer of credit from Edwin Colcroft."

A lie. One easily made true, but a lie nonetheless. He had lied when hiring the braves and now he was lying to pay their wages. Sin in service of sin. Sweat slid down Reverend Stone's neck.

Ignace Morel untied his pouch and pinched a wad of tobacco, thumbed it into the pipebowl. A grin twisted his lips. At last he said, "No."

Despite himself the minister chuckled. Ignace Morel looked up with a furious expression and Reverend Stone rubbed his face to quell the laughter. "My apologies," he said. "It does not matter, I suppose. I could offer you ten dollars and you would not assist me. Would you?"

"You think I steal."

"Of course not. Monsieur Morel."

"You think I steal because I am Catholic, and this is how Catholics are. Yes? Now who is the thief? You go pay the paddlers with air, you see who is the thief! You pay them with Scripture, you see who is the thief!"

"Monsieur Morel."

"You think you know how Catholics are? You are wrong. You will burn in hell as a thief. You will burn in hell while I am fiddling in heaven."

Reverend Stone gestured aimlessly. "I apologize if I have offended you."

Ignace Morel's jaw tightened in a clench; then he glanced away. "We leave in ten minutes. Go."

Reverend Stone turned away from the man, suffused with a

strange lightness. He had taken a risk, and failed; now he would face the consequences. It was nothing more than fair. For the first time in weeks the minister felt utterly calm.

Small Throat and the second brave were watching him from the beach. Reverend Stone approached the pair and grinned stiffly.

"I believe it is time to pay you fellows!" He patted his jacket pocket. To Small Throat he said, "No coin. Not this time."

The brave stared at him.

"Do you understand? No coin. No dollar."

"No dollar." Small Throat murmured a phrase in Chippewa, and the second brave nodded gravely. They seemed neither angry nor surprised.

Reverend Stone withdrew the Catlin book from his jacket pocket: *Letters and Notes on the Manners, Customs and Condition of the North American Indians, Written During Eight Years' Travel Amongst the Wildest Tribes of Indians in North America.* The pasteboard cover was creased and stained, the pages corrugated by rain. Reverend Stone held the book in both hands, and with a bow offered it to Small Throat. He said, "Please accept this volume as payment for your labors."

The spine crackled as Small Throat turned back the cover. He gazed at an illustration of a Mandan chief in an eagle-feather head-dress and ribboned tunic, posing stolidly as Catlin painted his portrait. Braves and squaws and children crowded around the half-finished canvas, their expressions equal parts fascination and dread. Small Throat carefully turned the page.

Reverend Stone stared past the braves. He had purchased the book for one dollar, and now he was bartering it for two—a modest profit in Indian country. Despite the logic he felt despicable. Better, he realized, to give the boy his Bible. The Bible, at least, contained genuine medicine. White man's medicine, but medicine nonetheless.

Small Throat shut the book. He glanced at the other brave; then he nodded expressionlessly. The sight took the breath from Reverend Stone.

"We go now!" A gravelly scrape rose from the riverbank as Morel shifted the canoe. "Allons-y! We go!"

"Take this also. Please." Reverend Stone drew a carrot of tobacco from his jacket pocket. He'd acquired it the previous evening from Morel's stores, while the man was gathering firewood. "Take it—I pray this is acceptable. I apologize sincerely if it is not."

Small Throat accepted the tobacco, and before the brave could speak Reverend Stone clapped him on the shoulder and hurried toward the voyageur.

The river was a sluggish brown channel lined with silver maple and box elder and slippery elm, trees the minister recognized from Newell. Sunlight filtered through the canopy and fell like copper coins on the water's surface. A surge of enthusiasm moved through Reverend Stone and he took up a paddle, but within an hour he felt feverish and weak. He reclined in the canoe bottom and tipped his hat forward. The elms waved past like vague, fond memories.

He woke sometime later to a cooling breeze: the sun had fallen below the treetops, the river darkened to a chocolate hue. The air smelled thickly of moss. They encamped on a grassy fringe and Reverend Stone fell immediately into a dreamless sleep. He woke before dawn, ravenous and full of strength. Morel prepared a hasty breakfast and they started forward, and near noon the river narrowed to the width of a corridor, white water rushing through a maze of stones. The voyageur steered the canoe to the river's edge. He stepped into the knee-deep water and tossed a pack of stores ashore, then with a grunt lifted the minister onto the riverbank.

A canoe was overturned on the grass a few yards upriver. Reverend Stone said, "Whatever could that be?"

"Their canoe. Your son."

"The expedition's canoe?" Without waiting for a response he hurried to the craft. It was a white man's canoe, the planks caulked with spruce gum, a yellow moon painted on the hull. An empty gunnysack lay near the canoe's stern. Reverend Stone took up the sack and flour sifted down to the grass.

"They have been here!" He snapped the gunnysack and a chalky cloud billowed into the air. Reverend Stone laughed, a taste of flour on his tongue. "He has been here, on this very ground! My son!"

A tremor grew inside the minister. He bowed his head, blinking against tears. He saw his son hauling the canoe onto the riverbank, his mouth set in a thin line, cheeks pink with exertion. His shoulders slumped beneath the canoe's weight. Reverend Stone crushed the empty sack beneath his chin.

But no, no—the image was wrong. For in his mind's eye Elisha was a boy of thirteen, not the man of sixteen he was today. For a moment Reverend Stone wondered if his presence was a grave mistake, a gesture rooted in a reality that no longer existed; then he realized the question was meaningless. Mistake or not, he thought, I am here.

He returned to where the voyageur was bundling their stores into packs. Reverend Stone said, "They have been here very recently—I found an old sack with the flour still dry."

Ignace Morel cinched a leather strap, shook it roughly to gauge the tautness. "This is for you."

"To carry?"

The man cinched a strap on a second pack, then kneeled and adjusted the pack between his shoulders. He slipped the strap over his head, leaned forward until it stretched taut above his eyebrows. The man rose with a grunt. "Like this. Come."

Reverend Stone squatted before the voyageur. He heard Morel hoist the pack; then he was thrown forward onto his knees and elbows. Reverend Stone gasped. The pack was like a millstone on his back. Morel dragged him upright, his hands scrabbling over the minister's forehead, and then the strap was pinching his skin as the weight settled into his spine. He staggered sideways as though on a rolling ship, steadied himself against a sugar maple.

"You are ready now?"

"Yes," Reverend Stone wheezed. "I am ready. Let us begin."

Morel clapped his hands twice and started forward. He sang, *Jamais je ne m'en irai de chez nous, j'ai trop grand peur des loups....*

A song about wolves, the minister thought, for me. He believes I am frightened, the poor fellow. Or he wishes to frighten me.

He followed the voyageur into the forest.

They moved slowly through the dim, lofty woods, hiking for twenty minutes then resting for ten, Reverend Stone sliding into a ragged sleep at each pause. His dreams were skewed childhood visions, which when he woke melted into memories: a gangly, sunburned boy tramping through a maze of hickories. Smell of deadwood and sweet fern, choking August heat. A warbler's call like a child's restless chatter. He was ten, eleven, twelve years old. He would hike all morning, past the last familiar brook or outcrop, until he felt a tingle of panic at having gone too far. He was enthralled by the forest's beautiful menace: its saplings and dried bones, its whiffs of earth and death. He would lean against a hickory and unbutton his trousers, tunnel within himself until the world vanished into hot, white light. When it was finished he'd run homeward, aloft on currents of pleasure and guilt. And then a distant voice, *Will-iam,* two long, sloping syllables. His mother calling him in for the evening: even now Reverend Stone heard her voice with aching clarity. He supposed it was a sound no man ever forgot.

He staggered through the afternoon, befogged by memories. A girl stepped from the shadows: thick, freckled arms, feral eyes, white-blonde hair yanked back in a braid. Was she real or had he imagined her? She crouched behind a hickory, watching the boy through a V in the branches. And then a second memory, of the girl in a blue linen dress, hair loose and speckled with burrs, standing a dozen paces before him. Her name was Elizabeth Grady. She was a hired girl at Carroll's. Her Saturday frolic, alone in the forest. They said nothing, their hands working, their eyes half-shut. Then the searing light, the choked cry, the gasp—and he opened his eyes to find her vanished. Surely he had imagined her.

They made camp that evening in a stand of white pine, Morel setting on the skillet while Reverend Stone reclined gingerly on his bedroll. Immediately he was asleep. He woke in a velvet dark, numbed by chills, his clothes damp with perspiration. Hunger gripped him; he uncovered the skillet to find corn mush jellied in grease. The minister raked up a handful and ate greedily. The food tasted thickly of blood. He could not be sure if the sensation was real or imagined. Reverend Stone wiped his hand on the grass and fell back on the bedroll.

And then he was blinking toward wakefulness. It was morning; sunlight was needling through the canopy. He was afraid to move, lest he upset the delicate balance that existed inside him. Finally he shifted, and bile surged to his throat. Reverend Stone lay very still. It occurred to him that he might yet be asleep, moving through a vivid dream; then the thought faded sickeningly.

"Drink this."

Ignace Morel stood over him, offering a steaming mug of tea. The man had kindled the cookfire and pitched a pair of tents; his rifle lay on an oilcloth for cleaning. Birdsong cascaded from the surrounding pines. The voyageur said, "Today we stay here."

"Why ever would we do that?"

"You are too weak. You cannot continue." Morel thrust the mug at him. "Drink this."

Reverend Stone took the mug and set it on the ground. He struggled to his feet. "We must go on. I insist."

"Sit," Morel said angrily. "You cannot continue. You must rest."

"I have rested all night and much of the morning. Let us begin."

The voyageur spat in the dirt. "You are a stupid old fool."

"I insist we continue! Now, I am paying you to escort me, so you must escort me!"

Morel took up the mug and flung the tea into the cookfire. The embers sizzled. He unbound the minister's pack and yanked out a cookpot and sack of beans, shoved them into his own pack. He tossed the lightened pack at Reverend Stone's feet. Then the voyageur pulled up the tent pegs and folded the oilcloths into a parcel, grabbed the rifle and hoisted his own pack. Without a word the man started into the forest.

The pair continued on an eastward route through the morning, Reverend Stone concentrating on each footstep. Colors blurred before his eyes, greens and browns and bright, piercing blues. He was unable to assemble a thought. At some point he glanced up to find a fist-sized blaze hacked into a pine trunk, the exposed wood white as cream. He called, "Ho! Have you seen this?"

"Their mark," Morel called. He was some thirty paces ahead of the minister. "They have been here not long ago."

"Then we are following the correct route! Wonderful!"

Reverend Stone hugged the pine for support, breathing shallowly. He started forward and his knees unstrung, and he fell heavily onto his side, the pack rolling away.

The minister lay motionless on a soft mat of needles, inhaling their balsam scent. Yes, he thought, this is all I need. A week's rest at the parsonage, in my bed, the sheets blued and crisp. Corletta in the doorway with a glass of molasses water and bowl of gruel. Faint lowing of cows from the Geary farm, murmur of voices from the meetinghouse: Edson leading the congregation in prayer. Yes.

Ignace Morel appeared above Reverend Stone, a scarlet weal from the portage strap marking his forehead. "You see now, you old fool? You are too weak, you see?" Morel squinted at the minister; then his expression clouded with concern.

Reverend Stone felt suddenly afraid. "You were right. We should rest for a while. For one hour."

With a huff Morel set to making camp. He kindled a fire then put on water for tea, gathered an armful of balsam boughs, pitched a tent. Reverend Stone lay on his side, watching the man. From his trouser pocket he withdrew a battered green tin and read the label.

MCTEAGUE'S PATENT TOOTHACHE MEDICATION
UNSURPASSED FOR SOOTHING PAIN AND DISCOMFORT
IN CHILDREN AND ADULTS
~ A BOON FOR ALL AFFLICTED ~

He opened the tin to find six tablets. The minister placed two under his tongue then offered the container to Morel. The voyageur regarded it suspiciously. Reverend Stone rattled the tin. "Go on. They are a boon for all afflicted. And we are all of us afflicted."

Morel squatted beside the minister and placed a tablet in his mouth. He squinted at the tin's label. A few moments later he glanced up, as though listening to a distant sound; then the voyageur closed his eyes.

"I see strange visions lately," Reverend Stone said. "Clouds of color hovering about people's bodies, like they've been captured in daguerreotype but moved during the exposure. Or . . . or like they are draped with haloes. Do you know the word—halo? It is a ring of light about a man's head, like an angel in a Renaissance painting, or a . . . I don't know."

"You see haloes."

"Yes. Yours is black."

Morel spread his right hand and turned it over, formed a fist. He grunted softly.

"For a time I believed it showed the color of a man's soul—the halo's lightness reflecting his purity, I suppose. But now . . ." Reverend Stone gestured vaguely. "I've encountered men who I believe to be virtuous, you see, enveloped by soot-colored haloes. And lost souls with haloes the color of chalk."

"It is because you are ill." Morel took the tin from the minister's hand, shook the last three tablets into his mouth. "That is why you are see things. Because you are ill."

"Perhaps. Yes."

"Of course yes. You are very ill."

Reverend Stone felt a surge of anger that slowly faded to nothing. The man was right: he was very ill. Even now he sensed a coldness moving through his veins, slowing his blood and stiffening his limbs. Thinning his lungs to wisps of flesh.

He was ill and might never recover. Reverend Stone considered the fact numbly. Ellen had brought blood on the third Sunday in March; on the fifteenth of September she lay motionless on the parsonage bed, her eyes fixed on the open window, curtains stirring in the breeze. Reverend Stone had been ill now eleven months. Yet what was there to fear, after all? He did not believe, as his father had, that a man's fate was immutable. The rewards of the next life were surely a product of the deeds of this one. Reverend Stone imagined the experience as a sense of profound companionship with all humankind, his love for Ellen magnified a thousandfold. A thousand times a thousandfold. Yet even as he considered the notion a current of dread passed through him.

He wondered for the second time if he should never have begun his journey. He could have awaited Elisha's return to Newell. He might have reached some understanding through prayer in the empty meetinghouse, his lungs soothed by the sweet Massachusetts air. Tears welled in Reverend Stone's eyes. Cowardice, his old companion. And yet it occurred to him that a stranger might mistake his journey for an act of courage.

He rose, and Ignace Morel glanced up at him, blissfully calm. Reverend Stone said, "How much farther?"

"Three days. Maybe four."

"So, then. Shall we continue?"

Without waiting for a response Reverend Stone hoisted his pack and started eastward into the forest.

Six

Professor Tiffin had begun working through the night, the hilltop lit by a ring of sapwood torches. From the campsite at the hill's base Elisha watched the torches wink and flare like fireflies. Tiffin appeared at breakfast, his lips moving in silent conversation, sipped a mug of tea as he gathered food for an afternoon meal. The man's fingernails were bloody, his face scaled with black dirt. Without a word he started back up the hill.

The man continued his routine through three days of smoky heat. Elisha spent mornings gathering wood sorrel and wild onions, sketching gray jays that flitted through camp. Afternoons he followed Mr. Brush on timber surveys into the vast tracts of pine, returning at dusk with a brace of hare or grouse. Elisha prepared supper while Brush completed timber density calculations, a contented frown on his lips. He said nothing about Susette or his proposal at the waterfall. Elisha wondered if he had somehow misunderstood the man.

On the morning of the fourth day Tiffin did not appear at breakfast. Elisha had fried a lumpy panbread and strip of pork belly, watched Mr. Brush eat with gusto. The man swallowed a last scrap of greasy bread then clapped his hands. "Well! I suppose it is time we investigated our esteemed colleague's doings!"

Brush whistled a jaunty melody as he started up the hillside. He was the sort of man, Elisha realized, who was truly happy only when others were miserable. Or when others' good fortune paled in comparison to his own. A shout rose from the hilltop and Mr. Brush paused. A grackle croaked; then a second shout that trailed to a long, jagged wail. Brush jogged back down the hill to his tent, snatched up a rifle and slung a shot bag over his shoulder. Elisha took up the other rifle, his chest gone tight. The shout repeated itself, falling to a chatter like a woodpecker's report. With a start Elisha realized the sound was laughter: queer, low laughter in the empty forest. Mr. Brush broke into a run.

They reached the hilltop to find Professor Tiffin sitting cross-legged amidst a scatter of freshly dug holes. The man was barefoot and hatless, his scalp sun-blistered, his hair a wild crown. He was cradling a broad, flat stone like an infant. Tiffin was laughing. He smiled beatifically at the pair, his eyes brimming with tears.

"You have arrived at last! And so you are my witnesses!"

The tablet was the size of a Bible, sheared flat on its face and etched with faint symbols. The symbols ran in curving rows above a crude drawing of human figures linked arm in arm about a spiraling column: a bonfire or whirlwind, or ray of light. Above the column was an engraving of a star, or the sun. Tiffin scratched at dirt in the column's grooves.

"It was buried beneath an ornamented bear skull! I had unearthed the skull two days ago, expecting it to be a vessel for a scroll, or a small tablet. When I found the skull empty I abandoned the site. Today I decided to delve deeper! I was desperate, you see—I have studied every grain of dirt on this hilltop! Look at this."

Tiffin took up a silk specimen bag and withdrew a pinch of flour. He sprinkled flour over the tablet then wiped away the excess. The symbols were illuminated in bright relief, like chalk marks on slate.

"I was desperate, you see! I reasoned that the bear skull was not a vessel, but rather a notice to Midewiwin elders, that they were excavating the proper location! I was correct!"

Elisha was frozen, confused. Susette had claimed that the buried tablets did not exist; yet here was a buried tablet.

"Of course it is entirely logical that they employed stone rather than birch bark for such an artifact—stone is impervious to rot, which would be a significant concern for something stored in the earth for fifty years, or five hundred years—for five thousand years, even! The ancient Natives must have understood that moisture—"

"You are jabbering like an idiot," Mr. Brush said. "What do those symbols represent?"

Tiffin touched his brow, momentarily overcome. "I do not know. Many of the symbols are unfamiliar to me. But these, here, are traditional Chippewa pictographic symbols. And these others—they resemble Hebrew characters, that with very few exceptions—"

"Tell us what they say."

Tiffin chuckled nervously, glancing from Elisha to Brush. Again Elisha sensed stiffness in the man's behavior, a rehearsed quality in his gestures and tone. Tiffin said, "It appears to be a description of a journey—a very long journey from a warm sea through a narrow strait, then into an immense, violent ocean. There is a character representing some sort of fish, or turtle. Then an account of many days travel on a river among a multitude of islands, and finally an arrival here, at the shore of this lake. There is a symbol of—what *is* it?—of a large, horned animal, a moose or perhaps a buck. There are many symbols that indicate natural features, which I do not understand. There is much that I do not understand."

The man bit his lower lip to stop its trembling. "This warm sea— surely it is the Mediterranean. And the narrow strait must be Gibraltar, and thus the ocean is positively the Atlantic. It *must* be the Atlantic Ocean! This tablet describes a sea route taken by a band of Israelites, many hundreds of years ago, to this very region. It is an artifact of the ancient Christians, who begat the Chippewa race that exists today!"

"Bollocks!" Mr. Brush poked Tiffin in the chest. "You have delayed this expedition far too long with your asinine pursuits! You have done nothing in the past weeks except fart and read Shakespeare, and now you stand here with this, this *rock,* claiming it as a Rosetta stone! You are—"

"Jealousy! You are jealous! And you are terrified of losing our wager!"

Brush flinched, a flush risen to his cheeks. He chuckled hollowly. "You are nothing more than a charlatan and a goddamned liar." The man snatched up his rifle and stalked away.

But his voice held a hint of wariness, and indecision. Of fear. Professor Tiffin stared after the man's retreating form. At last he exhaled, and laid a hand on Elisha's shoulder. When he spoke his voice was filled with wonder.

"My dear boy. Now our work begins in earnest."

Elisha gathered his fieldbook and pens and executed a careful drawing of the tablet's markings, working through the afternoon as Tiffin paced about the hilltop. The man muttered quietly, pausing to glance over the boy's shoulder. When Elisha had finished Tiffin tore a blank sheet from his fieldbook and laid it atop the tablet's face. He fetched a flask of water and soaked the paper, pressed it with his fingernails into the symbols' grooves. Then he mixed a thin gruel of flour and water in a mug and poured the mixture over the wet sheet.

A recollection gnawed at Elisha as the man worked: that first afternoon in Sault Ste. Marie, at the Johnston Hotel. He had entered Professor Tiffin's room and found a fieldbook, a wedding portrait, a squarish parcel wrapped in oilcloth. He struggled to recall the parcel's precise size and heft: it had been heavy rather than light, perhaps as stiff as stone, perhaps the size of a Bible. A chill moved through the boy.

"When the cement has dried," Tiffin said, "the symbols and characters will emerge in relief on the paper. It will form a precise replica of the tablet's engravings, to complement your drawing!"

Elisha said nothing, his gaze fixed on the tablet.

"I will transport the tablet to Detroit, and you will transport the replica and drawing—we will go on separate ships, as an extra precaution." Professor Tiffin smiled wearily. "We are poised on the very verge, my young friend—a moment between time before, and time after. Do you sense it? We will mark this moment together, you and I."

"With the aid of this tablet."

"The tablet is *enough,* my boy! This country is confused—we believe the human race to be divided and divided again, into black and white, Christian and un-Christian, superior and inferior. But of course we are equals before the Lord. We are a solitary, beautiful race. We shall make this country whole, every man and woman equal, black and white and red, young and old, free and owned. With this very tablet!"

"Please excuse me," Elisha said. "I'm not feeling right."

Professor Tiffin called after the boy as he hurried down the hill. At camp, Mr. Brush sat against a hemlock, fieldbook open across his lap. When he noticed Elisha he took up a pen and scowled at the page. Elisha fetched the cookpot and started into the forest, moving as if through a fog. He nearly passed the blazed cedar marking the turn northward toward the river. At the riverbank he sat on the overturned pot and covered his face with his hands. He felt a sharp, painful urge to return home.

Home. The word brought a twinge of confusion—for suddenly Newell seemed strange and distant, his memories embrittled by time. He could never return to his childhood bedroom, to the lazy afternoons at the creek behind the parsonage. To Corletta's Sunday lemon custard, to his mother's wry smile as she guided his hand over a half-finished drawing. Elisha's thoughts lingered over an image of the woman, there in her sickroom bed. She was waiting, half-asleep, for her son to return; yet he could never return. He was as a ghost to her, or a memory.

And he could not return to face his father. He had left the man's house without even a farewell, his heart choked with bitterness; even now his father's memory brought a sullen ache. Elisha longed to see the man but not as a homesick boy: instead he would someday drive a fine red landau into Newell, around the town green then up the cider mill road, draw to a halt outside the parsonage. His father would open the door, and the man's eyes would fill with shame and startled respect. Someday.

Elisha thought, I'll go to Susette. Wait until I'm alone tomorrow, take a rifle and shot bag, some rice and meat and a frypan. In his mind's eye Elisha retraced the party's route through the forest to the canoe, then upstream to the Chippewa village. And then eastward along the coast to Sault Ste. Marie, where he could catch a steamer to Wisconsin Territory. He would meet Susette on the street in Milwaukee, and her first, unguarded expression would tell him if he'd come in vain.

But even as he envisioned the meeting Elisha realized his plan was foolish. Susette had not left her husband to be trailed by a lovesick boy. Her interest in him was as a messenger, nothing more. So where could he go? Anywhere else in the wide world, he supposed: Detroit or Cleveland or Buffalo or Philadelphia. Elisha sat for a long while, staring at the river's dark surface.

Back at camp, Mr. Brush squatted beside his tent, oiling a rifle. The boy raised a fire then prepared a quick stew, and a short while later Professor Tiffin emerged from the forest like a soldier entering a conquered city. The man had washed his hands and face; he was cradling the tablet and fieldbook and whistling a tuneless rendition of "Sweet Mary May." He leaned over the cookpot and inhaled theatrically as Mr. Brush's expression tightened. Tiffin dipped a mugful of stew and sat beside the cookfire. As he ate the man traced his finger over the tablet's symbols, an occasional grunt escaping his lips.

"Are you planning to share your findings?" Mr. Brush said finally. "Or will you simply groan all night like a mongrel in heat?"

"Fragments—mere fragments as yet! I am attempting to interpret the meaning of the scene in the tablet's center. It appears to be an illustration of a ceremony. There are human figures surrounding a column, and there is an image of the sun, or a star. I suspect the scene depicts an astronomical measurement of the passage of time. Or perhaps it describes a particular event, to fix the year of the tablet's creation."

"And on the tablet's reverse I suppose you have found a recipe for the transmutation of horseshit into gold."

Tiffin giggled around a mouthful of stew. "Fret not, my jealous friend! You have played a critical role in this expedition: that of the shortsighted naysayer who was overcome. Many great advances have occurred in spite of such individuals. They are nearly de rigueur in narratives of great discoveries!"

"Great discovery or no, you have spent enough time at this site. By the expedition's charter we must return to Sault Ste. Marie by the end of August. To accomplish this we must depart on the day after tomorrow."

"You are attempting to provoke me," Tiffin said quietly. "But alas, my jealous friend, the fair hand of science cannot be rushed. She is a bashful maiden, shy as the dawn. She does not reveal her secrets according to the clock."

"You may remain alone, as you wish. Elisha and I will depart at dawn."

"Elisha and I have made a prior agreement. He will remain here to assist me in further excavations."

"This is not my affair," Elisha said. "I want no part in this decision at all."

Mr. Brush had finished oiling the rifle and now snapped the hammer shut. "True! This is not the boy's decision—it is yours alone. You, who will not admit the true purpose of your investigation."

Professor Tiffin was momentarily bemused. "And what is my true purpose?"

"It is simple. Your wife is a nigger, and you are a nigger kisser."

"Watch yourself," Tiffin said roughly. He struggled to his feet and pointed at Mr. Brush. "You watch your damned mouth."

"And you would like to believe that the nigger you are kissing is fully human."

Tiffin strode toward the kneeling man, and Brush uncoiled like a spring and struck Tiffin's jaw, the sound like a cane rapped against a fence slat. Tiffin whirled backward, his hat tumbling to the ground. He threw a high, looping punch that Brush ducked with a blow to Tiffin's ribs. The man's breath escaped in a huff. He fell to a crouch and skittered away like a dog. Blood welled in a gash below his right eye.

"Quit now!" Elisha shouted. "Both of you danged quit!"

Mr. Brush stepped forward with his fists balled at his jaw. With a groan Tiffin lunged at the man, and Brush sidestepped the rush then pounded Tiffin with both fists between the shoulder blades. Tiffin sprawled like a drunk in the dirt. A whine rose from his prone form.

"Quit!" Elisha took up a rifle and tore open a cartridge, set the charge. He shook the rifle at the men. "Quit now, both of you! Please!"

Professor Tiffin heaved to his hands and knees, gasping; then Elisha realized the man was laughing. A wheezy chuckle shook his shoulders.

"You have won!" He shuffled to his feet, grinning. Blood seeped in rivulets down his cheek. "You are an expert pugilist! That I concede!"

Mr. Brush spat, pacing in a tight circle. The man's hair was disheveled, veins throbbing on his sweaty brow. The sight terrified Elisha.

"Please accept my apology," Tiffin said. "It matters little, all of this matters little. Please." He dribbled a string of blood, then wiped his mouth and offered a hand to Mr. Brush. The man regarded it warily.

"Come now," Tiffin said. "Behave as a gentleman."

"I am a gentleman." Brush stepped forward and took the man's hand, shook it roughly. "And you are a son of a bitch."

Tiffin gingerly touched his brow. "Swelling already. A souvenir of my discovery, I suppose."

Mr. Brush hissed disgustedly and turned away.

Professor Tiffin dove at the man and wrenched his head down in a clinch. With his free hand he hammered Brush's face, his fist moving like a piston as Brush's hand searched for Tiffin's neck, twisted the man's collar. Professor Tiffin grunted, his face gone crimson. Mr. Brush scrabbled between the man's legs and Tiffin screamed, a sound like a wounded fowl.

Elisha shied sideways toward the pair then grabbed Tiffin's arm and pried it from Brush's neck. Tiffin shrieked *Elisha!* as Brush stumbled free. Blood flooded from the man's nose. Tiffin faced Elisha, his eyes wild; then Mr. Brush was upon him. He jabbed the man twice in the face and Tiffin stumbled. Brush yanked the man's collar and struck him across the nose with a sound like crumpling paper. Tiffin fell again, covering his face with his bloody hands. Brush drove a punch along his ear and he curled into a ball.

Elisha pointed the rifle skyward and pulled the trigger. A flat blast echoed against the hillside. Mr. Brush jerked backward.

"You shit of a boy!" Brush stalked toward Elisha and wrenched the rifle from his grip, threw it aside. "Are you with him, or with me? Tell me now, you worthless shit of a boy! Are you with the nigger kisser, or with me?"

Elisha staggered backward. "Please, Mr. Brush!"

Professor Tiffin rolled to his side with a groan. Brush dragged a hand across his bloody mouth and pointed at Elisha; then he turned to Tiffin. "This expedition will depart the day after tomorrow! So help me God!"

Night came on but no one moved to retire. Professor Tiffin sat beside the cookfire poring over Elisha's drawing, scribbling notes by the dim firelight. The man's eye was swollen, his ear like a loaf stuck against his head. Mr. Brush sat in darkness, an occasional shift in position betraying his wakefulness. It was as though neither man wanted to sleep in the other's presence.

At last Elisha grew exhausted by the standoff, mumbled his good nights and stretched out on his bedroll. He fell asleep listening to a screech owl's distant call; then immediately he was awakened by a shake. Professor Tiffin was kneeling beside him, his hand over the boy's mouth. The man's breath smelled of whiskey. He whispered, "Do not say a word, not one. You must come with me."

Elisha was struck by a sense of familiarity that quickly gave way to dread. Tiffin pulled at his shoulder. "Come, now. At once."

The boy dragged himself upright and followed Tiffin along the river trail. The night was cool and cloudless, birch bark glowing white in the moonlight, a hint of rain in the air. Tiffin stumbled through the shadows. Some fifty yards from camp he turned to the boy and placed a finger against his lips. They were near enough to camp for Mr. Brush to hear their conversation, Elisha thought, were the man awake.

"I must apologize," Professor Tiffin whispered, "for the behavior of Mr. Brush and myself. I pray you will forgive us. Our conduct has been inexcusable and entirely ungentlemanly."

"That's why you woke me? To apologize?"

The man leaned close to Elisha. "You must remain with me, my boy. You gave your word at the Chippewa village. You must keep your word! We shall complete the excavations, together, no matter Brush's efforts against us."

"This is not my affair. You and Mr. Brush must come to an agreement—I'll abide by whatever's agreed. This is your quarrel, not mine."

Tiffin attempted to smile but the effort seemed to pain him. "If you remain with me you will share in the discovery's glory! Do you recognize what that means, my boy? You will be welcomed in Boston and New Haven and Philadelphia and Charleston—your name will be known to Gray and Silliman and Morton. Elisha Stone! Your name will be on volumes for sale at every print shop!"

"I want no part of your conflict with Mr. Brush," Elisha said. "I want nothing to do with any of it. Please just leave me be."

Tiffin grasped the boy's arm, and Elisha tried to pull away but the man tightened his grip. "You must keep your word! I will complete the excavations with your assistance, and then we will return to Detroit! We will share in the discovery's glo—"

"There is nothing to discover!" Elisha twisted away from the man. "Susette told me the truth before she vanished. The hilltop is not a sacred site! There is nothing there, at all!"

Professor Tiffin leaned away, his face veiled in darkness. He chuckled haltingly. "But of course it is a sacred site—it contains the image stones! We have unearthed a sacred Midewiwin tablet, my boy! Madame Morel was confused!"

"There are no image stones. Ignace Morel deceived you. He planned to drag you into the forest then abandon you, but he missed you at the Sault and Susette took his place. Ignace Morel only wanted your money. There are no image stones."

"My dear boy," Tiffin said gravely. "It is you who have been deceived. The Midewiwin tablet is proof. As the scientific world will soon recognize, this tablet—"

"I saw that tablet in your room at the hotel, in Sault Ste. Marie. Before we departed."

Professor Tiffin was silent for a moment; then he shook his head vigorously. "No. *No.* You are mistaken!"

"I am not mistaken. I entered your room when you were out, and I saw your belongings laid out on the bed, and the tablet was among them. I'm very sorry for that."

Tiffin stared at Elisha with pained incomprehension. "You entered my room at the Johnston Hotel?"

"I did. I'm very sorry."

He said miserably, "But why ever would you *do* such a thing?"

"I'm truly sorry. I wish I had never done it."

Professor Tiffin appeared suddenly exhausted, nodding to himself, and Elisha sensed that the man was no stranger to disappointment. The boy felt an impulse toward charity. He's a charlatan, Elisha reminded himself. A fraud and a sinner against science. He said again, "I'm truly sorry."

"You must listen to me now," Tiffin said calmly. "There are certain theories that we know to be true, but cannot prove. We see the truth as clearly as the noon sun, but we lack physical evidence of its veracity— and so we must *create* evidence, create *facts,* in service of the truth. The truth is more valuable than any individual fact!"

"You're justifying a lie, is all. A lie is not a fact."

"Elisha, my boy, my dear boy." Professor Tiffin's breathing wavered, then convulsed in a sob. "We were stripped of our church pew, do you understand? We cannot enter a church together. We cannot dine at a restaurant together. She is a nigger, and I am a nigger kisser. That is what we are, do you understand? Do you *understand*?"

He took the boy's hand and Elisha pulled away, then Tiffin grabbed his shoulders and shook him roughly. "You must help me! You *must*! The truth is more important than any fact—facts are like rocks, Elisha, but ideas can grow! They can grow to be greater than any of us!"

Elisha jerked free and stumbled toward camp. Wildness surged through him. "Your consumption cure," he said, "the one you sold in your pamphlet in Detroit. Was that fact?"

Professor Tiffin paused, bewildered. "My boy—why, that was a mere root remedy! It was folly! This is the *truth*! The two are as distinct as sun and moon!"

"Your cure was not folly to those who tried it, and found it false. They prayed it was the truth. It wasn't."

"But it was! It was! My *boy*—"

"Listen to me now. I will not say a word against you, to anyone. But neither will I help you. Do whatever you're planning to do, but do not ask for my assistance. Do not ask for my assistance at all, ever again."

The man nodded. He moved to speak then touched a hand to his mouth.

"This is not my affair," Elisha said, then turned and started through the forest toward the darkened camp.

Part Four

One

The two men came into a region of skeletal black trees and charred brush and parched, airless heat. Reverend Stone shuffled through mounded cinders, head bowed, his throat clogged with ash. The sun was a dim glow against the white sky. Near noon they paused to rest, and when the minister leaned against a tree bough it crumbled in his grasp, left his hands streaked with soot. The air smelled bitterly of smoke.

He had begun to doubt the reality of the scene around him: the spidery trees, the air aswirl with ash, the cinders. The absence of color and sound. The heat. It was a fatigue-addled vision of heaven, he thought, or a delirious image of hell. He was hallucinating or he had died.

"There. Over that hill, then another hill, then we are arrived."

Ignace Morel's voice seemed to rise from a great depth. Reverend Stone turned to the man: his moccasins and leggings were gray-white, his face coated with ash. It was as though he was being consumed by the forest, slowly transforming into one of the burned trees. Tendrils of hair curled like twigs around his face.

"Arrived in hell, you mean."

"Not to hell. To the place of your son." The voyageur moved before Reverend Stone and peered into his eyes. "Drop your pack."

"Of course not. Let us continue."

Morel moved behind the minister and hoisted the pack, slid the portage strap from his forehead. Reverend Stone staggered under

the weight's absence. "You are a gentleman," he said weakly. "I am indebted."

They encamped for lunch beside a stony river, Morel raising a fire
and staking the tents then stepping into the stream with a trout net.
Reverend Stone reclined on a quilt of cinders, dazed by exhaustion.
He jerked awake to the voyageur's fiddle: "La Belle Susette." He was
suddenly, sharply aware of the branches bowed over him, the wind
sighing through the canopy, the particles of ash tickling his brow. It
was all very beautiful, like a blind man's dream of a forest. Ropelike
cramps gripped Reverend Stone's legs. He wished he had a single
tablet.

The forest's colors warmed from black to gray to green as they
trudged through the afternoon. Woodpeckers rattled and songbirds
fluted in chorus. Reverend Stone focused his thoughts on an image of
his son's face: the frightened eyes and tousled hair, the slender neck
shadowed by dirt. Elisha smelled of a child's tart sweat. He possessed
his mother's voice, her blue eyes, her chin. Ellen will be alive in the
boy, Reverend Stone thought, when I see him. The notion disturbed
and excited him. It was as if, he realized, he was trying to resuscitate
the past, if only its faintest pulse.

A rhythmic scuffing invaded the minister's thoughts. He stood
very still. Where was he? In Michigan, in the state's northern peninsula, in a strange, endless forest. The scuffing paused, then resumed. It
was the sound of hoeing, of stony dirt being disturbed. Or the sound
of a fox scratching beneath a chicken house. I am in Newell, Reverend
Stone thought, and his heart swooned. I am at the parsonage, listening
to my old friend mister fox. The scuffing paused.

He surveyed the surrounding forest: some ways eastward was an
opening atop a low, treeless hill. At the hill's base a strand of smoke
rose from a fire. A cookfire, Reverend Stone realized. He hurried forward, eyes trained on the site. Around the cookfire a trio of wedge
tents stood like drab flags. Then a flicker of motion: a figure moving
among the tents.

Reverend Stone began to run.

· · ·

Professor Tiffin and Mr. Brush had departed camp that afternoon after lunch, Tiffin to the hilltop and Brush to the stream to bathe, so Elisha gathered a load of firewood and fetched a kettle of water, then lay beside the cookfire and tipped his hat over his eyes. He had no desire to do anything at all, except return to Sault Ste. Marie and collect his pay. A catbird called, then a shovel's faint chuff: Professor Tiffin continuing his false excavations. Elisha tried to sleep but could not.

At last he rose and heated a scrap of leftover panbread. As he ate it occurred to the boy that he had not seen his own image in weeks. He ducked into Mr. Brush's tent, rooted through the man's pack for a pocket mirror. The face in the glass was suntanned and lean, the cheeks marked with fine black whiskers. He recognized himself but there was another man present: a wiry stranger with a questioning gaze. The sight pleased Elisha.

Mr. Brush's fieldbook lay beside his pack. Its leather cover was scratched, its pages thickened by rain. Elisha took up the fieldbook, listening for sounds of movement from the forest. He turned to the entry for June 26, the party's first day at the abandoned fur post. Brush's field notes were scrawled in shorthand on the left-hand pages, translated as terse narratives on the facing pages.

June 26, 1844

Site loc apprx 0.6 mi upstr Muddy River (Bayfield). 46° 29'. Abandoned fur post, six dwell.

Slate in knobs, highly argill (27). Sparse white, gray quartz, slaty hornblende (28). Silic pebbles. No comp defl.

Soil clayey with sandy loam. Poor.

Timber primly wht. pine apprx 6,000 bf per ac. Rec fire, cut. Poor. Unsuitable Ry.

There was no mention of iron ore. Elisha recalled Mr. Brush's breathless account of the compass needle skittering like a beetle, the windfall pine with ore clinging to its roots. The shaly mineral specimen shot with reddish veins of hematite. He read the narrative on the facing page.

June 26, 1844

We ascended the Muddy River some 0.6 miles this evening in a thunderstorm. This river is broad and sluggish, and copper-colored due to the presence of pine resin. We came to an abandoned fur post of six dwellings, around which significant quantities of white pine (*Pinus strobus*) have been cut. The rock formations here are principally slate forming in low knobs, mixed sparsely with white and gray quartz, and slaty hornblende. The soil is poor and clayey with traces of sandy loam. There is evidence of recent fire.

Elisha reread the entry, trying to square his own memories to Brush's descriptions. He turned to narratives from later days at the fur post: the timber surveys seemed accurate, but apart from two mentions of bog iron there was no report of ore. By Mr. Brush's account the region was worthless cutover land.

So it was as he'd suspected, and as Brush had denied: the man planned to declare the iron-rich lots worthless, then buy them for a dollar an acre. A seed of anger grew inside Elisha. He fetched his own fieldbook and pens, set to copying entries from dates he recalled Brush locating ore. I will buy this danged land myself, he thought. I will borrow money and buy this land, then sell it so dearly that Brush won't be able to afford his own swindle. The boy's fist trembled around the pen.

A rustle issued from the forest and Elisha froze. He shoved Brush's journal beside the pack and replaced the pocket mirror, scrambled from the tent. A man was running through the forest toward camp. He was dressed in a black jacket and trousers, a black round-brim hat. Elisha fetched a rifle and tore open a cartridge then stepped forward, squinting: it was a white man, neither Brush nor Tiffin, wearing city clothes and brogans and carrying no pack. The man lurched to his knees and the hat tumbled away.

Later Elisha would remember the light in the forest at that moment: long, slender sunbeams surrounding the man's body, as though he was being delivered down from the heavens. The breath emptied from the boy's lungs. For an instant he stood motionless, waiting for the vision to vanish; then he set the rifle down and raised a hand. The man shouted with joy. Elisha raised his hand higher, then started into the forest toward his father.

He helped the man down to a litter of balsam boughs. Was he dreaming? His father was stiff and upright, chin shaved smooth and breath smelling of licorice; yet here was a man with a sparse, ragged beard, cheeks drawn down to hollows, fingers like brittle twigs. His jacket was frayed and his trouser cuffs torn to shreds. Like a scarecrow, the boy thought numbly, staked in a farmer's garden. The man before Elisha was not his father; yet he could be no one else.

"You are surprised," Reverend Stone said, struggling for breath. "Of course you are surprised. I would have written ahead but I did not have an address."

Elisha was stricken by the weakness of his father's voice. "You are exhausted," he said. "You must rest now, lie down. Let me brew some tea."

"On the contrary, I feel better than I've felt in weeks. The forest air is a tonic. The lake air I found less salubrious."

Elisha could not look away from the man's face. He wanted to touch his brow, to confirm that he was not a feverish vision. His cheeks were marked with pale brown spots, his lips wrinkled and split.

An old man's mask on his father's face. "You're alone," Elisha said. "Did you come here alone, without a guide?"

Reverend Stone peered past the boy into the forest. "My boon companion—he is somewhere near. He is a petulant fellow but indispensable as a guide. We fairly flew across the lake."

Reverend Stone's breathing had not settled. Elisha said, "Hush now—let me fix you something to eat. You are surely starved."

The minister did not object. Elisha set on a kettle of tea and pan of corn mush, moving quickly, his thoughts confused. Reverend Stone watched the boy work. As the food warmed Elisha gathered boughs for the man's pallet, and to his horror realized he was busying himself needlessly. He did not know what to say to his father.

Reverend Stone spoke. He described his final service at the meeting-house in Newell: the pews had been filled to the gallery, the windows lit with sunlight. He had told the congregation of his impending departure, and after the service he'd been showered with prayers for his journey and well-wishes for Elisha—from Herbert Weatherford and James Davidson and Asa Snow, from Corletta and Charles Edson. Reverend Stone told Elisha about his train ride to Buffalo, his encounter with Jonah Crawley; then the steamer to Detroit and the fine sermon by Reverend Howell. The storm's waves like mallets against the *Queen Sofia*'s hull. At last he described his meeting with Edwin Colcroft and his departure from the Sault. "Such wild, beautiful territory," Reverend Stone said. "I pray it is never joined to the civilized world."

The minister took a long draft of tea. Elisha tried to imagine the man negotiating traffic on the Grand Circus, or haggling with a voyageur at Sault Ste. Marie. He could not form the images. His father was grave and deliberate, even-tempered to the point of solemnity; he had no use for passion or haste. The boy recalled his mother once mentioning that he had wept on their wedding day, and Elisha had been stunned. It had seemed a description of a different man entirely.

"I followed nearly the same route, though I traveled overland to Detroit from Buffalo. I worked as a specimen cataloger for a man named Alpheus Lenz on Woodward Avenue. It's why I joined this expedition—because I wanted to discover a new species. A flower or fish or insect, anything."

Reverend Stone offered his son a pensive smile. "You enjoy it—the tramping and paddling and collecting. You enjoyed it always, even as a child."

"I thought I enjoyed it. I suppose my idea of the work didn't precisely match the thing itself."

"That is nearly always the case."

Elisha returned the man's smile. For years he had daydreamed of meeting his father, and had always imagined himself bitter, glaring at the minister while the man mumbled an apology. But here his father was, and Elisha did not feel bitter. Instead he felt a happiness near to tears.

"Professor Tiffin has a notion that all men are descended from Adam, black and white and red. That we're all members of a single species, equal under the eyes of God. He is a fierce anti-slaver. He aims to prove the unity of races, to convince people to free the slaves."

"The unity of races," Reverend Stone said. "What a marvelous notion. It seems elementary yet perhaps it is not. I am no scientist."

"He claims he's found proof—this very week, in fact."

"A wise man told me that the more profound the conjecture, the fainter the possibility of discovering proof of its truth. I suppose science and religion are similar in that regard."

"Don't tell Professor Tiffin that. He is convinced."

Silence stretched between the men, and for a moment Elisha was at the supper table in Newell, as a child, gazing at his empty plate. He wanted desperately to speak but could not find the proper words. He said, "I'm so sorry, Father. For running away from you and Mother— I'm so very sorry. Please forgive me. I didn't—"

"No, *no*—you mustn't apologize. You were lost and now are found, my son." Reverend Stone placed his hand atop the boy's. "You were dead and now are alive. You must never apologize."

A tremor moved through the boy, and Elisha took the man's hand and brought it to his lips. Reverend Stone stared at his son.

"Why have you come here?" Elisha asked.

The minister closed his eyes, as if the question was more complex than it seemed. "Another wise man told me that the spring of all human activity is the unease that accompanies desire. I felt uneasy."

His father's opaque logic had frustrated Elisha as a child but now there was merely the memory of his frustration. "Mother," he said. "She is gone."

"Yes," Reverend Stone said. "Your mother is gone."

Elisha stared into the cookfire's low flames. He felt himself nodding, as though hearing news he had long known to be true. He felt an urge to cup the flames in his hands and pour them like water over his head. The flames would warm him, he was certain. A junco called and the sound was like a squealing hinge. Elisha said, "I do not understand."

"It was just three months after you departed. I would have written but I did not know your whereabouts. I am sorry. My child, I am so very sorry."

Reverend Stone looked away; then his shoulders jerked and a sob rose from his throat. Elisha could not face the sight. He laid an arm around the man's shoulders and stared into the forest. "Father," he whispered, "please."

"She wondered if you had met a girl. A Boston girl, to balance your seriousness."

Elisha was trembling. He felt like a flickering flame about to be quenched.

"I believe that was her primary worry: that you find a good woman to guide you. That you settle yourself with a good congregation and a good woman, and bring your mother a grandchild." The minister laid a hand on the boy's cheek. His expression was grave and tearful, suffused with love.

"I hear her," Elisha said hoarsely. "Sometimes when I am nearly asleep I hear her speaking to me. She is calling me to supper from the creek. She is calling my name."

"Yes."

"But then I awaken and she is gone. Her voice is gone."

"And you strain after the sound but there is nothing. And you pray she will speak again but she does not."

Elisha drew his father to him, and the feeling of the man's body caused something inside the boy to fracture. Tears slid down his cheeks. He heard himself sobbing but could not quiet himself; he felt himself shivering but could not still his hands. He stroked his father's head, comforting him as he would a child.

"Elisha," Reverend Stone said, "my dear son. Let me tell you about your mother."

Reverend Stone was asleep when Mr. Brush returned to camp that afternoon. The man emerged from the forest humming a marching song, his wet hair clinging to his forehead. His humming ceased when he saw the minister's sleeping form. Elisha ushered him aside, describing his father's voyage as Brush's expression moved from wariness to sober admiration. He offered Elisha whispered condolences. Elisha thanked him; then he gestured toward Ignace Morel. The voyageur was sitting beside a cookfire at the clearing's edge, staring at Mr. Brush.

He had entered camp two hours previous. Reverend Stone had introduced the man and Elisha had shaken Morel's hand, smiling to conceal his shock. Ignace Morel was younger than Elisha had imagined, with broad, thick features that looked like they'd been molded from clay. A large pack was perched on his back and a second was slung across his chest. Without a word he'd stalked to the clearing's edge and unslung the packs, set to gathering firewood. He was just ten yards from Elisha and Reverend Stone, but all afternoon Morel had ignored the pair.

Now the voyageur approached Mr. Brush and nodded to the man. "You lead this expedition."

"I do," Brush said.

"My wife is Susette Morel. She is with you here. She is your guide."

Mr. Brush's gaze flicked to Elisha. "Madame Morel was indeed our guide. Another member of our expedition hired her on at Sault Ste. Marie. You say you are the woman's husband?"

"Tell me where she is. She is with you here."

"Monsieur Morel." Mr. Brush paused. "Monsieur Morel, there has been a grave misfortune. Your wife vanished from camp some six days ago—she departed to fish at the nearby waterfall and never returned. We searched for her intensely and found evidence of her clothing but nothing more. We believe she came to an accident while she was fishing, and was carried over the falls. I am profoundly sorry."

Ignace Morel smiled faintly, his gaze moving from Brush to Elisha. "No. I do not believe you."

"I am profoundly sorry—I disbelieved it myself, at first, however I am now convinced. We found a fragment of her dress near the falls, as though she had been swept away by the current. I suspect she became injured and attempted to return to camp, but could not."

"Monsieur Morel," Elisha said. "Please accept my sincerest condolences. I am very sorry."

Mr. Brush laid a hand on Morel's shoulder but the voyageur jerked away. "I do not believe you. You tell me where she is."

"We cannot," Brush said.

"You tell me where she is!"

"Monsieur Morel!" Mr. Brush leaned forward, his jaw set in a clench. "You must behave as a man. Despite this misfortune you must behave as a man. Your wife is vanished. She is likely dead. Now, please accept our condolences."

Ignace Morel paced backward, smiling at the pair. "I do not believe you," he said. "I do not believe either of you."

The man turned and ran to the clearing's edge, then took up a rifle and disappeared into the forest.

Past midnight an aurora in the form of a shimmering green cloud appeared overhead. Elisha sat watching light spread over the starry sky. He had not slept, and the aurora served as a welcome diversion from his muddled thoughts. Dusty purple smudges bloomed at the cloud's edges.

Beside him Reverend Stone lay asleep, his breathing a faint rattle. The man appeared peaceful and calm, as though he had traveled one mile instead of a thousand. How strange, Elisha thought, that even now his father was a mystery. Their years spent under the same roof had meant little. Their meals taken at the same table had meant little. Their prayers spoken together had meant little. What they shared, simply, was love: a deep, unsettling pull.

He rose and paced the camp's perimeter, and as he did anxiety overwhelmed him. His father was very ill. He must take him to the Sault, to be bled by a fort surgeon. Then by steamer to Detroit and a better surgeon, a boardinghouse room with sunlight and fresh air. In his mind's eye Elisha saw himself bringing the man tea in a chipped earthenware mug, smoothing white bedsheets over his bony legs. The notion was so strange as to be unbelievable.

He moved before Mr. Brush's and Professor Tiffin's tents. The men lay but a yard apart, asleep on their bedrolls, their tent flaps open to the night. Elisha touched each man's shoulder, and when they started awake he said, "I'm very sorry to disturb you both. I must speak with you."

Mr. Brush sat up, exhaling in a hiss. Professor Tiffin lay squinting at the lit-up sky.

"My father," Elisha said. "He is not well. I must return with him to Sault Ste. Marie at once."

Tiffin emitted a pleased murmur. "Aurora was the goddess of dawn in Roman myth. Did you know that, my boy? Some ignoramuses mistake the lights for religious revelation—they believe the hosts of heaven are descending all around them. Others believe the lights to be visions of dead warriors, battling in the skies for eternity. Foolishness, of course. Most likely the colors are caused by moonlight, reflecting onto the firmament off of glaciers in the polar regions."

"I am in earnest. I will depart at dawn. I apologize for not completing the expedition."

"You must remain here," Mr. Brush said. "Rest is the best tonic for your father's condition. Surely you recognize that."

"For once he is correct," Tiffin said. "It is widely agreed that rest and fresh, pure air are the most effective treatments for consumptives."

"My father needs to be treated by a surgeon. And he claims there is medication at the Sault that comforts him. Now, I cannot aid him here, nor can either of you. I must get him medication and treatment at Sault Ste. Marie."

Professor Tiffin struggled upright, his nightshirt billowing like a dirty flag. "I have studied this sort of illness in profound detail. Elisha—hear me now! Your father's illness can be soothed by an infusion of pine bark and pitcher's thistle and basswood root. Stay! I will concoct a remedy, and when your father has recovered we can transport him back to the Sault in comfort."

Elisha nodded to conceal his impatience. "We will hike slowly back to the canoe. I will paddle across the lake and he can rest during the journey. But I will not let him lie here in pain. I cannot do that."

"You intend to travel alone with your father?" Brush asked. "Or will you bring Ignace Morel?"

Elisha paused. "I'll need the voyageur's assistance. Of course."

"I forbid your departure," Tiffin said suddenly. "Who will attest to my discovery, if you leave? If you leave you will not share in the expedition's glory!"

"Mr. Brush can attest to your discovery. He can share in the glory."

"Who will cook, and attend to camp? Who will bear the stores?" Professor Tiffin pointed at Mr. Brush. "I will not cook for this man. I will not bear his stores."

"You are welcome to come with me," Elisha said. "I mean that sincerely. Both of you are welcome to quit this charade and follow me back to the Sault."

"You must wait four days," Tiffin said, "until my excavations are complete. I am so very near! You must—"

Mr. Brush seized Elisha's arm and pulled the boy toward him. "Little man, you offered your word in Detroit, which I accepted as your bond. Now. If you depart we will be unable to carry a sufficient quantity of gear and stores. We will be forced to curtail this cursed expedition. And that is unacceptable."

Elisha twisted away as a furious sob rose in his throat. To Professor Tiffin he said, "Your tablet is a fake! You carved it in Detroit and hauled it here, then pretended to dig it up!" He turned to Mr. Brush. "And your survey reports are a parade of lies! You are declaring the richest land to be worthless, so you can purchase the lots yourself! Now listen to me, both of you: Tomorrow morning I will pack some food and cooking gear, and you will pay me full wages for this summer's work. In exchange I will disappear from this expedition, and it will be as though I never set foot in this territory. I will never speak your names, ever again."

Reverend Stone shifted in his sleep and the men froze; then Tiffin said quietly, "Let us discuss this situation. I am certain we can devise a mutually profitable arrangement. You might be the primary author on the report describing the tablet's discovery! And Mr. Brush can—"

"Listen to me." Brush's voice was a cold blade. "Your mind is disturbed by your father's illness—that is why I have chosen to ignore your slanderous allegations. However. Madame Susette Morel is vanished, to where I do not know. You, I suspect, know precisely where she is. You have made a pact with the woman to reunite in the coming weeks."

"No. No, that's not true."

"Madame Morel's grieving widower lies not ten yards distant. I expect he would be powerfully interested to hear the details of her duties on this expedition. By which I mean her service as your half-dime whore."

Elisha felt himself trembling at the edge of control. To calm himself he focused on Mr. Brush's boots, standing beside the man's bedroll: even now they were polished to a black gleam, a scurf of mud coating the heels. He said, "I am not troubled by your threats."

"You should be."

"I'm not, and I don't care what you do! I want nothing more to do with either of you, or this expedition! I wanted to learn to be a scientist this summer and that's all! Now leave me be!"

Silence lengthened between the men; then Mr. Brush chuckled wearily. "To think that I chose you for this expedition because I took you for a frightened young fool. Well. I suppose I am the fool." Brush smiled at Elisha, and for a moment the man appeared genuinely disappointed. "I should never have hired you on in Detroit, my boy. Your jacket was filthy."

"I have never been your boy," Elisha said. "I will depart at dawn."

Reverend Stone lay awake with his eyes closed, listening to wind sigh through the pines, a current of pleasure running through him like liquor. Each inhalation brought a whiff of balsam. For the first time in many days he felt no soreness in his limbs. Beside him Elisha squirmed in his sleep, mumbling a litany of praise: "Good," the boy said. "Good. Yes. Good." Reverend Stone thought to wake the boy then changed his mind.

At the first sliver of dawn his son rose and began unloading his pack. Reverend Stone sat up and sipped from a flask. The water tasted of resin. When Elisha noticed that the man had risen he said, "Fetch your trousers and boots, Father. We are leaving for the Sault."

"Do not allow me to distract you from your work! I will return with Monsieur Morel after a short stay—one day, perhaps two. We will follow the same route we came."

"I've spoken with Mr. Brush and Professor Tiffin. We're leaving this morning—if you're well enough to travel, that is."

"I feel well." Reverend Stone was surprised by his own admission. "I feel better than I have in days. Perhaps weeks."

"Then. We'll depart in one hour."

His son's tone left no avenue for response. Reverend Stone watched the boy parcel out rice and flour and pork belly, salt and matches and powder and shot, then fetch a frypan and hatchet and file. He loaded the stores into his pack. As the boy worked Mr. Brush and Professor Tiffin stood before their tents, stonily observing the scene. Reverend Stone smiled at the men but his greeting was not returned.

When Elisha finished with his pack he followed the same procedure for the minister's, then hefted the bundle with a grunt. He removed a sack of shot and transferred it to his own pack. Then he cinched the leather stays.

"Your companions?" Reverend Stone asked. "Would you like to say your farewells?"

"They do not deserve it."

Reverend Stone waited for the boy to explain his insolence. "Come now, Elisha! Surely they deserve a farewell."

"They deserve each other and nothing more. Believe me, Father."

Elisha helped the minister to his feet. He hoisted the man's pack, then settled it against his back and adjusted the portage strap. Reverend Stone exhaled sharply, steadying himself under the weight. Elisha fixed him with a searching gaze. "Can you continue?"

The minister nodded. He shifted from foot to foot, concentrating on breathing. The burden on his back was nearly unbearable.

"We are soon safe," Elisha said, then gestured to the waiting voyageur and started westward into the forest. Ignace Morel hoisted his pack and followed the boy.

Reverend Stone surveyed the camp: two sagging tents before a cold cookfire, a kettle overturned on a patch of dirt, a worn flannel shirt fluttering from a low limb. Mr. Brush and Professor Tiffin stood like exhausted militiamen, hatless and bootless, arms folded over their chests. Reverend Stone could not decipher their expressions: gloom edged with anger, a sour farewell. *We are soon safe,* Elisha had said. I have arrived in the midst of something, Reverend Stone thought.

He raised a hand to the men then followed his son westward into the forest.

Two

They hiked back along the Indian trail through three long, humid days. Mornings brought black flies and evenings a warm, wisping breeze that yielded little comfort. Elisha and Reverend Stone trailed Ignace Morel, struggling to keep pace, calling out when the voyageur disappeared from view. The boy continually monitored his father's condition. When they paused to rest Reverend Stone fell quickly asleep, his eyes twitching beneath their lids; but when Elisha woke the man he rose without protest and continued forward. He seemed immersed in profound concentration.

Evenings, Morel prepared suppers of game birds stewed with rice and seasoned strongly with pepper. Elisha found himself watching the man. He had imagined the voyageur as a crabbed, ugly gentleman, skin mottled by drink, tongue darting over wet, vulgar lips. But his appearance was nearly the opposite: thickset and vigorous, with smooth, tanned skin and handsome features. His accent when he spoke was a low, rich echo of Susette's. Since their departure he had said almost nothing.

On the fourth day of travel they came into a swampy region cluttered with pepperbush and rhododendron, the ground heaped with deadfall, the air redolent of decay. Clouds of blue-winged butterflies whirled around them. They encamped that evening in a maple grove, and after supper Morel withdrew a canvas case from his pack and from it removed a fiddle and bow.

A cold shiver moved through Elisha. Ignace Morel ran a thumb along the bow, then bent over the instrument and twisted the tuning pegs as he plucked the strings. Reverend Stone woke from a doze and smothered a cough. Morel fitted the fiddle against his chest and raised the bow; then he launched into a fast hornpipe, stamping his foot to keep time.

"Remarkable, is it not? He is surely unschooled in performance, yet he plays like a backwoods Paganini. Like he has bargained his very soul."

"His wife Susette spoke of his playing. She did not admire it."

"He has composed a song for the woman—the title is 'La Belle Susette.' The beautiful Susette. Difficult to imagine that she was not flattered, the poor woman."

Elisha said nothing. The voyageur seemed engaged in conversation with the instrument, scowling as the tune deepened then grinning as it rose to a sharp arpeggio. Sweat shone on his neck. The melody dipped then steadied, a pair of phrases carrying the tune until they disappeared under a run of notes, then emerged in a higher key. Finally Morel stiffened and the song drew to a slurred close. He raised the bow again.

"Ah! Here is 'La Belle Susette' now," Reverend Stone said. "Maudlin, of course, but quite charming in its fashion."

The boy's throat tightened as he watched Morel play. Elisha could not manage to follow the tune. In his mind's eye he saw the voyageur in a cramped, dirt-floor shanty, swaying over the fiddle as Susette lay motionless on a straw pallet. Then he saw the man's livid face move over the woman. Susette's eyes shone with fear. Elisha tried to push the image away but it remained as a lurid tableau.

The song halted in a squeal as Morel jerked the bow away. He returned the fiddle to its case, muttering.

"She spoke of your playing," Elisha said. "Your wife. She spoke of the songs you would play for her, of your skill with the bow."

"She never enjoyed the playing." Morel carefully stowed the bow. "She would sit and say nothing. Or she would ask me to stop."

"I didn't say she enjoyed your playing. I said only that she spoke of it."

The voyageur paused with his hands on the canvas case.

"Answer me something," Elisha said. "If she didn't enjoy your playing, why did you continue at it?"

"That is not a respectful question," Reverend Stone said quietly. "You should apologize to Monsieur Morel."

The boy laid a hand on his father's arm. "And the song you composed for her, 'La Belle Susette': Did you compose it to please her? Or was there another reason?"

"Elisha!" Reverend Stone hissed.

Morel stepped toward the boy, his expression clouded by confusion and fury. He seemed uncertain which emotion the situation warranted. "You understand nothing. I composed the song to please her. Of course."

"Strange, to compose a song for someone who hates your playing. Seems cruel. Seems like something you might do to injure a person."

"Playing a song is never cruel."

"Your wife claimed it was."

A shadow passed through Morel. He stepped back a pace, his eyes like black stones. He said, "I played only when she deserved."

"As a man must."

Reverend Stone struggled to his feet. "Stop this conversation, both of you. Monsieur Morel's wife has passed. His actions during her lifetime matter not at all. We grieve her absence but must take comfort in her new life with Christ."

"You believe she is in hell," Morel said.

"I do not!"

"You believe she is in hell, with every other Catholic."

"Monsieur Morel!" Reverend Stone's voice held a note of hurt. He laid a hand on the voyageur's shoulder. "I know how the world appears to you now. The color is disappeared. You cannot see or hear or taste. It is difficult even to draw a breath. And yet the Lord said that he who believeth, even when dead, shall yet live. And whosoever liveth and believeth in the Lord shall never die. She will never die, my friend. You *must* believe me. She will never die."

Ignace Morel shook away from the minister's touch. "Do not pray for me! I do not want your prayer."

"My friend—"

Morel opened the canvas case and yanked out the fiddle. He played the first slow strains of "La Belle Susette," and Elisha strode toward the man but Reverend Stone seized the boy's arm. The voyageur's eyes were squeezed shut, as if against a cutting wind. He repeated the song's first measures, faster, then faster again as the melody quickened to a frantic pace. His fingers stabbed along the fiddle's neck. He seemed to be trying to condense the song into a single phrase, a pure musical word. A lock of hair fell across his face and Morel whipped it away. He bent double over the instrument, then a string snapped with a twang and the voyageur cursed and flung the bow far into the forest. Reverend Stone started. The bow settled with a soft rustle.

Ignace Morel dropped the fiddle, his chest heaving. He nodded at Elisha. "Now I will play her song no more."

He dreamed of falling. In his dream Reverend Stone tumbled through thin green fluid, neither air nor water, his jacket rippling and trousers slicked against his legs. It was Sunday; he was dressed in a black store-bought suit and boiled shirt, polished black brogans. It was as though he'd been falling for a long time and knew he might never reach bottom. Bits of grass sluiced past his face. He tried to speak but could not utter a sound. The feeling, he at last decided, was oddly pleasant.

The sensation faded as Reverend Stone surfaced to wakefulness. Immediately he was gripped by alarm. His shoulders ached. His lungs felt empty, useless, like a pair of gashed bellows. He tried to return to sleep but his mind was filled with sharp white light. Reverend Stone rose to an elbow, breathing deeply.

My good Lord, he thought, preserve me. Wood smoke drifted over him, then Elisha said, "Father? Are you awake?" The boy's hopeful tone filled Reverend Stone with dread. More than anything, he realized, he did not want to disappoint his son.

He forced himself upright and accepted a mug of tea. He was sweating and his tongue was filmed with iron. Reverend Stone leaned against a pine trunk and closed his eyes, dimly aware of a rustle of activity. He opened his eyes to find his son kneeling over him, beside a litter fashioned from birch poles and spruce root and Elisha's spare shirt and trousers. Without protest Reverend Stone reclined on the litter, then the pair lifted him and started forward.

They traveled slowly through a blur of pine limbs and sunlight and brilliant swatches of sky, Reverend Stone clutching the litter as it wobbled and jounced. Sometime later they paused for lunch. Ignace Morel sat apart, studying the pair as he ate; the minister thought to address the voyageur but the prospect exhausted him. He accepted a flour biscuit and chewed slowly.

"We're but two hours' hike from the river," Elisha said. "From the river it's two days' paddle to the Chippewa village, and at the village we can hire paddlers, be at the Sault in no time. And then we'll get you a doctor, some medication. A good bed." Elisha's tone was tranquil yet somehow it heightened Reverend Stone's alarm. He managed a smile.

In fact they did not reach the river until the following noon. It was a quick, stony channel, nearly narrow enough to leap across. Downstream, a pair of canoes lay overturned on the grassy bank. Reverend Stone waited as the men loaded the voyageur's canoe, then allowed himself to be eased down into the craft's middle. Elisha stepped in at the bow, then Morel settled himself on the steersman's perch and took up a paddle. With a nudge they started forward.

The river widened and slowed as they floated downstream. Cool breezes rose off the water and set the sugar maples gesturing. Reverend

Stone was struck by the scene's beauty: the cornflower sky, the broad shimmering water, the wind like a pipe organ's note through the maples. Pain needled him and he remained very still until it passed. It seemed wrong to be in pain amid such beauty.

"Not long now," Elisha said. "Just rest, Father. Not long at all, I promise you."

A female wood duck angled toward the canoe from the river's edge. Protecting her nest, Reverend Stone thought. The sun edged behind a cloud, and just then Elisha twisted around, his sun-browned brow creased with concern. Reverend Stone smiled. The boy's expression tightened; then he managed a nervous grin. The wood duck chattered raucously.

This moment, Reverend Stone thought—then the notion dissolved, leaving a swell of emotion so intense that tears welled in his eyes. He could not understand if he was feeling pleasure or pain. It didn't matter, he realized. Reverend Stone said a prayer of thanksgiving and blinked the tears away.

From his position in the canoe's bow Elisha could not see his father, so he listened for the faint rhythm of the man's breathing. Images from the past weeks emerged: Susette tossing a smoking tobacco stub into Tahquamenon Bay; Professor Tiffin declaiming Oberon's accusations, his cheeks flushed with whiskey and pleasure; Mr. Brush bent over the solar compass, calling out a measurement. For an instant Elisha could not recall the expedition's purpose, then he remembered: timber and iron and the unity of races. Suddenly it seemed to matter very little.

They paused briefly for lunch then came into a wide stretch of river bordered by sycamores, the current a fast ripple. They had been paddling for an hour when Ignace Morel said, "I was to guide the expedition. I was engaged by Monsieur Tiffin in Detroit. She was not to go with you at all."

The man's tone was quietly bitter. Elisha thought to leave the remark unanswered, then he said, "You were absent on the day you'd agreed to depart. Professor Tiffin searched all over Sault Ste. Marie. You weren't there."

"I returned two days later—you should have waited! Instead you forced my wife to guide you. Do you know where she is gone?"

"Monsieur Morel," Reverend Stone said. "You mustn't ask such questions. They cannot be answered."

"But she is drowned, yes? That is what they say. Yet she is like a poisson, like a fish in the water. It is impossible that she is drowned."

"No one can say for certain what happened, because none of us were there," Elisha said. "It was a terrible accident and that's all. I'm sorry."

Morel dragged his paddle and the canoe slowly yawed. "Why do you sound strange when you speak of my wife? Is it because you are sad, because you knew her so well? Is that how you know about 'La Belle Susette'? Because you knew my wife so well?"

"You mustn't ask such questions," Reverend Stone said. "Monsieur Morel, you must stop this conversation immediately. You are behaving queerly, even by your own standards."

Elisha turned to face the voyageur: he was leaning forward from the high steersman's seat as if tugged by the force of his words. Elisha willed himself to hold the man's gaze. "I don't mean to suggest anything other than that I am sorry for your loss," he said. "Your wife was a fine woman."

"A fine woman."

"Let us pray together," Reverend Stone said. "Let us pray together, Monsieur Morel, for the soul of your beloved wife. Together we shall pray for her soul's peaceful rest."

Morel dug hard and the canoe jerked crosswise in the current. "Your father hates me because I am Catholic. He believes he will go to heaven and I will burn in hell. But he is wrong. You both will burn in hell. And I will be fiddling in heaven."

"None of us will be fiddling," Reverend Stone said sharply, "and none of us will be burning in hell."

"Except the adulterer. The adulterer burns in hell." Ignace Morel seemed possessed of a barely contained fury. "Your son will burn in hell with my wife, la belle Susette."

"Monsieur Morel! I will not tolerate another word!"

"Ask your son."

"Monsieur Morel!"

"Ask him!"

The voyageur stopped paddling and the canoe drifted in the river's center, twenty yards from the nearest bank. Morel shoved his cap back on his sweaty forehead. His right hand trailed along the canoe's bottom, fingertips touching the rifle stock.

"Listen to me now." Elisha struggled to master his tone. "Your wife told me she was planning to go to the waterfall. She said she would let herself be carried away. I prayed with her to stop but she would not. She let herself be swept over the edge, and she is gone. Your wife is gone."

Ignace Morel's glare wavered. "You are a liar."

"I prayed with her to stop but she would not. She was already gone, in her mind. She said she could not bear to return to the Sault. To return to you."

"You are a liar!" Morel took up the rifle. It was charged but not primed, though Elisha knew that task would take but a moment. Even unprimed the stock would serve as a vicious club. "She is gone because you sent her away! Monsieur Brush told me. You laid with her then you sent her away."

"Stop, please," Reverend Stone said. "I beg of you both."

"She is gone because you killed her," Elisha said.

Morel yanked a percussion cap from his shot bag and cocked the rifle. He jammed the cap onto the weapon's cone as the minister shouted *Stop!* and Elisha grabbed a gunwale and threw himself sidelong. The craft rolled sickeningly, and then they were in the river.

A frigid shock blinded the boy. He opened his mouth to shout and water flooded his lungs, drove him into a thrashing panic. Something heavy nudged his shoulder then tumbled through the cloudy water. He jerked toward a shimmering light. The river seemed as thick as syrup, and for an instant Elisha feared he was sinking; then with a gasp he broke the surface. His father slapped the water before him, eyes white with animal terror. Reverend Stone clutched Elisha's face and shoved him under. Panic surged through the boy. He wrenched away from his father and surfaced, choking, then swung an arm beneath the man's shoulder. A cough exploded from Reverend Stone's bloody lips. In Elisha's grasp he felt weightless and frail, a gunnysack filled with sticks. Downstream, the overturned canoe spun in the current, Morel scrabbling along the bow for a handhold. The voyageur dragged his head above the surface and gasped. He clung to the canoe as it drifted toward the far bank.

Elisha kicked toward the near bank, thrusting his father's head above water. Reverend Stone clawed at Elisha's arm. A pack of stores floated past, made buoyant by some trapped pocket of air, and Elisha recognized it as his own: his cooking gear, spare shirt, rations, tent, fieldbook. He groped after the pack but his touch sent it bobbing away. Elisha thought to pursue it then immediately turned back toward the riverbank.

"Vous êtes damnés de Dieu!" Morel shouted. The man was fifty yards downriver, clinging to the overturned canoe. "Vous êtes morts, vous êtes damnés de Dieu!"

Elisha's boots felt as though they were made of stone. He paused to draw a breath and his father flailed, sent a blinding splash into the boy's eyes.

"You must not struggle. Please! Kick your legs. We must reach the riverbank."

Reverend Stone became very still, his breathing shallow and thready. Elisha jerked toward the near bank. It was just ten yards distant but his efforts brought it no nearer. A wave of fatigue passed through the boy and he sank until his mouth was at the river's surface. His shoulders burned. Elisha went under and his toe scraped a rock, and the touch filled him with desperate relief. He surfaced, choking, probing the stony riverbed. At last he gained purchase and steadied himself against the current.

He dragged himself up a grade into thigh-deep water thick with river grass, then the boy fell to his knees, hugging his father to his chest. Reverend Stone whispered, "My good Lord." Elisha crawled to the river's edge and collapsed on the grassy bank. The water he'd swallowed came up in a gush, rilling back into the river.

A blackbird settled on a cattail and regarded the boy with a cock of its head. Elisha called, "Father?" and the man responded with a groan. The boy waded into the shallows.

Sunlight spangled off the water's surface. Elisha shielded his eyes, scanning the river for any sign of their stores: the cooking gear, rations, tent, fishing hooks, knives, rifle, shot—every necessity for survival. A hundred yards downriver Ignace Morel stood on the opposite bank. Beside him the canoe was pulled partway up the bank. A paddle was snagged in the nearby river grass.

"Sales chiens!" The voyageur's voice possessed a hysterical edge. "I was almost killed!"

"We must make a truce!" Elisha called. "A peace—do you understand? We will travel to the Chippewa village together! They will give us food!"

"The rifle is gone! The stores are gone! Vous êtes de sales chiens, you are killed now!"

"We must travel together!" Elisha tried desperately to calm himself. "If we travel together we can reach the village in one day. If you travel alone it will take three. Do you understand?"

"Offer him money," Reverend Stone said. "That is a language he speaks."

"I will pay you twenty dollars at the Sault! Fifty dollars! You must come to us, now!"

Morel took up the paddle and pushed the canoe into the river, then swung aboard. Without its load the craft rode high and jittery on the river's surface. He steered the canoe into the current.

"Monsieur Morel." Reverend Stone's voice was weak but clear. "You must not abandon us here. You must not do such a thing. Monsieur Morel, please. I know your heart."

"You have taken my wife," Morel shouted. "I take this canoe. A fair trade, yes?"

"You must help us!" Elisha splashed forward until the water reached his chest. "We have nothing at all! We will die here!"

Ignace Morel laid the dripping paddle across his lap as the canoe angled slowly downstream. Elisha watched the craft vanish into the dazzling sunlight. "Monsieur Morel!" he called. "You must help us!" Water trickled as if from a paddle stroke. The sound repeated, quieter, then quieter again.

Sometime later a cloud passed before the sun, and the scene reappeared as an empty river bordered by sycamores.

Three

He had stripped off his wet jacket and shirt and trousers and now sat in his underclothes on the sunny riverbank, trying to ignore his hunger. He concentrated on breathing. When he closed his eyes he was immersed in oddly pleasant memories: a summertime oyster party at the creek behind the parsonage. A ride along the Connecticut River in a borrowed cabriolet. Murmur of laughter and conversation, dull trickle of water. A blackbird's call.

He woke to find his son standing over him. Elisha had been probing the river's bottom with a makeshift sounding pole, searching for their lost packs. He'd found only mud and stones, an occasional flash of trout. Now the boy knelt beside his father, water dripping from his curling hair. He resembled a Greek sculpture, Reverend Stone thought, with his curls and sun-bronzed features, his shoulder muscles carved in wet linen. The product of time spent in the world. The minister was filled with pride.

"The rifle and rations are gone," Elisha said. "So is the fishing and cooking gear. But I've got a pocketknife and a tin of matches that'll dry, and there's porcupine and frogs and birch moss if need be—we'll have little difficulty managing supper."

"Do not trouble yourself with my condition," Reverend Stone said. "I'm not at all hungry."

Elisha winced at the man's lie. "There's a Chippewa village just a short ways downstream—we'll go there and get some food. It's just a day or two on foot, not more. We'll hire Native paddlers and they'll ferry us back to the Sault. We'll be back in town in no time."

"Monsieur Morel will be awaiting our arrival."

"He won't. He has nothing to gain from further trouble."

"Then good riddance. I owe the fellow ten dollars." Reverend Stone attempted a smile. "Monsieur Morel hired a pair of paddlers at the Chippewa village. One boy was named Small Throat. He reminded me of Byron Wills—do you remember Byron?"

"We must start at once. Please, Father. Let's begin."

Reverend Stone was chastened by his son's tone. He rose, sighing to mask his discomfort, then donned his shirt and damp trousers. Without a word he followed his son along the riverbank.

They hiked along the water's edge beneath a clear sky, passing through columns of blinding sunlight. Dragonflies were scattered like colored glass in the river grass. Reverend Stone shivered continually despite the day's warmth. Elisha urged the man onward, pointing out low branches and loose stones, marking distance to their next rest. His tone was gentle but firm, like a farmer guiding an ill horse back to stable.

As they traveled Reverend Stone found himself wondering what Elisha's mother would say to the boy, were she alive. More than anything he wished she could speak a single sentence to her son. It was not impossible, a single sentence, for those who listened at the spiritual world's boundary. Adele Crawley, that extraordinary girl, with her candles and ashen skin—he would bring Elisha to her, the minister decided, when they returned to Detroit. He would bring the boy to Sixth Street, among the Irish and Negroes, and Elisha would hear his mother speak. The thought filled Reverend Stone with satisfaction.

They continued through the afternoon and at dusk made camp at a bend in the river. Reverend Stone built a fire while Elisha departed in search of supper. Hunger gnawed at the minister. Eventually the boy returned with only a few handfuls of birch moss; they ate then Elisha arranged beds of pine boughs beneath a leafy elm. Reverend Stone studied his son as he worked: the set of his jaw and his thick, curling hair—that was Ellen. And his blue eyes, his chin, the quickness of his gestures . . . She was present in his every movement.

But so, too, was he present in the boy. When Elisha spoke

Reverend Stone heard his own voice beneath his son's, a firmness gird-
ing his halting sentences. It was himself speaking many years ago, before countless sermons and blessings and prayers had smoothed his
tone. The boy was his father's son. Of course he could be nothing else.

"I was remembering a ride we took along the Connecticut River in
a borrowed cabriolet—I believe it was Edward Fell's cabriolet. You
were just a child. Your mother had allowed you to pack the picnic basket, and you took the responsibility very seriously. Do you remember
the day? It was autumn, a lovely afternoon. Your mother was singing:
Home, O home, O happy hillside home."

"*Home, O home, O cozy sweet refuge.* It was one of her favorites."

"You remember! I could not be certain the day had actually occurred. I thought I had dreamed it."

"I packed three jars of raspberry preserves, one for each of us, and
some cheese and apples. There was no bread, or meat. We ate the jam
and cheese together and Mother could not stop laughing." Elisha
smiled. "I wanted to drive the carriage home—I begged you to let me
take the team."

"And did I?"

The boy shook his head. "I can't remember."

Reverend Stone smiled at his son. He had denied the boy's request,
of course, and Elisha had cried until Ellen had quieted him with a
song. Surely Elisha remembered. He said, "I meant only to protect
you. I did not believe you were ready."

"I know you did, Father. Hush now. Let's sleep awhile."

Reverend Stone allowed his son to help him down to a bed of
boughs. Immediately he woke to a warm drizzle on his face. It took
him some time to recognize that he was awake, that it was raining. He
was too weak even to raise a cough.

He dragged himself upright and followed his son through a humid
dawn, staggering through the forest as though drunk. In midmorning
Elisha killed an old, slow grouse and started a cookfire. They let the
meat roast for a moment then fell on it like savages. To his surprise

Reverend Stone found he had little appetite. He watched his son eat. The pair rested for a while then started onward, and sometime later Reverend Stone steadied himself against a birch limb; as he did the forest sank into blackness. He blinked awake to find his son thirty yards distant, squinting back through the swampy brush.

"We're nearly to the village!" Elisha hurried back to the minister and took the man's hand. "There will be food, and canoes to take us to the Sault! Father, please."

"I am sorry. We must rest."

"Please!" Elisha kneeled over the man; then his lips tightened and he drew a sharp breath. "Lie down, Father. You must lie here, right this moment."

Reverend Stone slumped to the forest floor. The pain was like a serpent inside him, brushing his lungs and stomach and bowels as it moved. He laced his hands over his chest but his fingers would not stop trembling. He began to feel afraid. Reverend Stone tucked his hands beneath his arms and closed his eyes.

He woke dew-covered and racked with chills. He was lying among spindly white birches beside a cold cookfire. A blackened spit held the remains of what appeared to be a porcupine. Elisha fed Reverend Stone some of the smoky meat, then gestured toward a pair of birch poles cross-laced with roots into a rude travois.

"You cannot carry me that way. The ground is too rough."

Elisha grasped the man beneath the arms and helped him onto the travois. The serpent thrashed inside Reverend Stone, and he gasped. He reclined carefully against the thin struts. With a grunt Elisha started forward, the birch poles gouging the soft mat.

Reverend Stone understood that his body had failed and felt horrified by the suddenness of it all. Four weeks ago he was in Detroit, at the teamsters' saloon on Franklin Street, drinking cider in the guise of a kindly tobacco farmer. The image was his father's, he knew. Something in the memory exhausted the minister. The travois jerked over a root and Elisha cursed.

He had traveled so far to see his son and now he'd said very little to Elisha. Reverend Stone considered the thought helplessly. He must apologize to the boy. He had kept Elisha from his mother as Ellen lay on her sickbed, hoarding her love like a miser with a last coin; then when the boy disappeared Reverend Stone had cursed his memory. Unforgivable, even now. For so many years, the minister realized, he'd spent his days finding niggling fault in others, wearied by their pained confessions, wondering why they could not appreciate life's beautiful mystery. Of course their lives were more arduous than he had ever imagined. His world was as small and false as an oil-painted miniature. He was a country preacher, nothing more. There was so much for which he might ask forgiveness.

He thought, I must reason with the boy about his faith. Elisha was a scientifical boy and would understand salvation's inexorable logic. For surely Edson was wrong: skepticism perhaps slowed one's acceptance of God's love, but the resulting embrace must be all the stronger. The restless heart at last finding rest. And if not his father's faith then another, everyone gathered in a rolling valley on the last day. He must convince Elisha to not surrender, to not close his heart for want of revelation. He must convince him that faith is a thunderstorm but it is also a faint breeze through the grass.

He thought, I must counsel the boy. Tell him that he will pray for guidance and that it will appear in many forms: as a trembling in his lips, or as an angry man's shouted curse. As a cowbird's call on a rain-damp Sunday morning. That he will be like a hart seeking a brook, that he will desire pleasure and companionship and that he should follow these desires. That he will wake alone at midnight seized by loneliness and despair, besieged by whispers, and that he must summon the strength to continue toward an unseen shore. That the shore did exist. The shore always and everywhere existed.

He felt along the travois pole for his son's hand. Reverend Stone squeezed the boy's wrist, and Elisha stopped.

.   .   .

He had assumed it would be the cough that overwhelmed him but this was a simple fever, chills alternating with sweats, his muscles knotted and sore, his throat dry as paper. He felt exhausted to the point of weightlessness. When Reverend Stone closed his eyes his body seemed to rise among the pines; then he opened his eyes and the feeling vanished. Sleep, he thought. What I require is a night's sleep, nothing more.

It was midmorning and he was lying on a litter of boughs. A low fire warmed his legs. Elisha pressed a dampened cloth against the minister's brow, and with a prickle of alarm Reverend Stone realized the boy was doing what he himself had done for Ellen on her sickbed. What was missing was a stack of literary journals, Corletta's low singsong from the kitchen. The meetinghouse's weathered profile in the window. In his mind's eye Reverend Stone saw himself mounting the granite steps and tugging open the front door, entering the coolness and mildew and dim, thick silence. He felt a pang of desire so intense it was nearly painful. The meetinghouse seemed to contain his entire life and now it was only a memory.

He did not want to die but looked forward to the moment with fearful curiosity, as one would to an arduous journey. He touched his Bible and the book's presence comforted him. Reverend Stone felt a surge of strength. He attempted to sit up but his son whispered in his ear; he attempted to speak but his voice emerged as if from underwater. The minister relaxed down to the ground. He coughed, and when he'd finished Elisha daubed the corners of his mouth. Reverend Stone felt moved to pity, as though for a stranger. It's myself I am pitying, he thought, then corrected himself. Not myself. My body alone.

It occurred to Reverend Stone that he had been twenty-nine years old when his own father had passed. Twenty-nine was a man's age, yet he'd felt like a man only during the years after. It was as though his father's presence had reminded the minister that he was a child. He tried to fix a pleasant memory of his father but what emerged was a vision of the fellow standing at the edge of a tobacco field, at day's end, his figure consumed by a long shadow. Reverend Stone had loved his father but had never felt affection for the man. Strange, that the two emotions had never joined. He wondered if Elisha felt similarly about him.

Reverend Stone coughed again and terror gripped him. He was aware of his son's touch. He heard the boy's voice but could not distinguish the words; he heard himself speak but could not be sure of what he'd said. The serpent writhed and gripped his jaw, forced the breath from his lungs. He wished desperately for a single tablet. The pain tightened and Reverend Stone felt something shift inside him. When at last the feeling passed his tongue tasted bitter and he saw that the world had faded to the color of a smoke-filled sky.

He thought, So this is how it appears.

He was breathing shallowly and with every breath felt himself sinking deeper into a thick liquid. He began a prayer of thanksgiving but his thoughts unraveled. Where was he? Elisha was leaning over him, his breath smelling of stale tea; then the boy was grinning at him through a stand of sedge at the creek behind the parsonage. Reverend Stone had never understood the boy's fascination with that creek. The peacefulness, he supposed, the familiar solitude. A child's version of an empty meetinghouse. Then the minister was in a seminary classroom on a cold October morning, half-asleep, soothed by a man's baritone reciting Scripture. Peace I leave with you, my peace I give unto you; let not your heart be troubled, neither let it be afraid. Reverend Stone smiled. Wine-colored thunderheads scattered over the hills east of Newell. Ellen's weary face in the mirror as she brushed her auburn hair. His father's hands, Prudence Martin's watery eyes, the call of a newsboy on Woodward Avenue. Edson's scalp showing pink through his thin yellow hair.

A blackbird called.

Something soft and warm was pressing on his forehead. His thoughts unmoored and he felt himself in a large, empty room. Was he awake or asleep? Reverend Stone began to pray, and to his surprise felt himself rising into a weightless calm. He was apart from the world yet utterly within it, his breathing the rhythm of a tide, his heartbeat the rhythm of footsteps. The sensation was strange yet wonderfully familiar. He remembered as a boy watching the sun set over his father's tobacco field, honey-colored light glazing the broad, wrinkled leaves, transforming the workaday land into a vision of Eden. He remembered wondering, astonished, how it could be so beautiful. It was all so beautiful, and full of light.

It was dusk when he finished and the forest's silence had given way to birdsong, blackbird and thrush and warbler calling from the dim canopy. Elisha's shirt was heavy with sweat, his callused hands soiled and bloody. He cut strips from his sleeve and bandaged his palms, then waded into the cold river. His shoulders ached. His mind was a black slate. Sometime later he returned to the clearing and stripped off his wet clothes. He found a cabbage-sized stone and arranged it at the grave's head, then placed another stone, then another, his body moving as though ungoverned by his thoughts. It was dark when Elisha lay down beside his father and closed his eyes.

Sleep eluded him. Instead he lay in exhausted limbo, listening to the forest's silence. What was absent, Elisha realized finally, was the whisper of water against sand—and with it a notion of time, echoed in the tide's rhythm. Here there was only silence, like a thick fluid among the trees. It was as though they'd descended beneath the lake's surface.

Was it enough? the boy wondered. Is it enough now?

Night animals moved through the brush and Elisha was certain they were circling the dark camp. He knew he should light a fire but could not force himself to move. A lilting inner voice accosted him: You must light a fire, the voice sang. A fire will keep the creatures at bay. A fire will keep the darkness away.

"Quiet now," he said aloud. "You have no regard, none at all."

The voice muttered a dull response.

At the first gesture of dawn Elisha stood beside his father's grave, among white-flowering raspberries, birdsong cascading from the canopy like a Sabbath day chorus. He recited Psalm 23 and John 3:16 and the Lord's Prayer, then placed a final stone atop the grave. The rite was simple but he could imagine nothing more fitting. At the river he withdrew his pocketknife and marked blazes on three tall elms: for his father, for his mother, for himself. The blazes, he knew, would be visible from the river for many years. A great blue heron regarded him from the far bank with solemn indifference, and Elisha felt grateful for the bird's presence. He understood it as a form of benediction. He returned to camp and lay beside his father's grave, his cheek against the cold headstone.

He had failed the man with his thievery and weak faith, his midnight departure without even a farewell; now he had failed to deliver him back to health. His entire life, Elisha realized, he had tried to not fail his father, and the struggle had exhausted him; though perhaps that struggle was a form of love. The boy allowed himself a glimmer of hope.

After some time he started slowly downstream, moving as if in a trance. Guilt pursued him but he did not turn back. When he'd traveled three hundred yards he sat against an old hemlock, weeping, and immediately his thoughts fluttered among vivid, senseless images. You must honor and obey your father and mother, in all things, the voice said. Elisha closed his mind to the sound.

Was it enough? he wondered again. Is it enough now?

Elisha curled against the hemlock and willed himself toward sleep. He woke to a nearby rustle. He withdrew his knife but otherwise did not stir. Around him the forest was a green sheet, as endless as an open lake. A hobblebush shuddered then a fat porcupine emerged, waddling toward a tall beech then clambering up the trunk. Elisha jerked upright and stumbled through the brush. He stabbed at the animal but the knife plunged into softwood, his fist sliding down the blade. He worked the knife free, and as the porcupine skittered along a limb Elisha hurled the blade. It buried itself, quivering, beside the animal. The porcupine snuffled at the knife then turned away.

The boy was consumed by wild laughter that was instantly smothered by fear. He scrabbled at the trunk but could not gain purchase on the slippery bark. He took up a flat stone and gouged a pair of footholds into the tree's base, but again his boots slid away. Elisha hugged the massive beech, panting. Panic trickled like poison through his veins. He thought, I'll head due north toward the lakeshore. Bypass the river's meanderings, save a half day's travel. He would reach the lakeshore then bear west to the Chippewa village, eating gull eggs and hatchlings, waving down any passing canoe. Elisha's breathing settled as he convinced himself of the plan's worth. Above him the porcupine scuttled among the beech's limbs.

But when he started forward Elisha realized he was uncertain of his bearing. The forest appeared identical in every direction. The sun was cloaked in a gray haze. He wandered through the afternoon, finally coming to a silty brook bordered by birches. Moss encircled the trees' white trunks like emerald scarves. Elisha groaned with relief: moss grew thicker on a tree's northern face. He could use the moss's thickness to point his way to the lake. The boy ate a handful of birch floss then built a large fire and curled beside it. He felt afraid of the coming darkness.

A fire will keep the creatures at bay, the voice sang. A fire will keep the darkness away.

At first light he doused the fire and hiked northward, weak to the point of collapse. Or was he traveling southward? Detroit lay to the south. He could hike to Detroit, turn left and continue on to Newell. The boy giggled at the notion's absurdity. The country was a great, endless forest, and a body could emerge at any town, at any moment in history. Elisha staggered, sprawling into a mat of sweet-smelling ferns. He moved to rise then relaxed onto his back. Could he go back to the cabriolet ride along the Connecticut River? Perhaps this time he would remember to bring bread. Perhaps his father would let him drive the team.

A child's cry, of frustration or pain, sounded in the distance. Elisha closed his eyes. The cry repeated, and for a moment he believed he was hearing his own childhood voice; then he recognized the sound as a gull's call. The boy scrambled to his feet. He started forward as the cry sharpened to an angry caw. Elisha broke into a loping jog, dodging the slender birches. He descended into a shallow valley, and when he crested the rise he glimpsed a sliver of indigo through the thicket of trunks. He cried out.

Lake Superior lay before him like a bolt of blue silk rolled to the horizon. Creamy clouds floated above a wide white strand. Elisha sprinted down a dune and a flock of killdeer scattered. He stalked in slow circles, scanning the stony beach, and at last found a nest scraped in the sand. He robbed the spotted eggs and gathered a few sticks of driftwood, built a tiny cookfire. Elisha wept as the eggs warmed. He tapped open the shells with his knife and sucked out the thick fluid. Afterward he lay flat against the searing sand, luxuriating in the sensation as he scanned the lake's margins. Like a farmer at a roadside awaiting a buggy into town, he thought. A chill breeze tickled his neck.

He woke to a nearby presence. The boy turned to find a buff-colored bird two yards distant. It was similar in appearance to a killdeer, though smaller and lighter-colored, with short orange legs and black eyes. The bird cocked its head as its feathers riffled in the breeze.

Elisha wondered momentarily if he had died. The bird was not a killdeer: its bill was as long as a sandpiper's, the banding on its breast nearly absent. He rose slowly. The bird hopped forward a pace then paused, its glassy eyes shifting. It called, and the sound was like a glass bell tinkling. Elisha lunged forward and cupped the creature as it fluttered in his grasp. With a quick pinch he crushed its neck.

The wings jerked then fell limp. Elisha examined the wingtips and bill and scaly, jointed legs as a quiver rose in his throat. The bird was neither killdeer nor snowy plover nor piping plover. Elisha laughed aloud. It was neither plover nor sandpiper nor gull. It was not any species he had ever encountered.

Something new in the world, he marveled. He had no fieldbook or pen, no rum to preserve the bird; yet he did not feel disappointed. With his last matches he kindled a fire, then fetched a greenwood pole. He plucked the bird and set it on to roast. *Charadrius stonus,* he thought. That is your name. Flames licked the puckered skin and the boy's stomach clenched. Mr. Brush was right, he realized. Life is a practical endeavor.

When he'd finished eating he wandered westward along the lake edge, the sun a hot mask against his face. Despite the day's warmth he was overcome by chills. He slept beneath a spray of beach grass then continued onward, the wind stiffening, the sky receding before his eyes. He was certain the Chippewa village was near. At last Elisha sat heavily in the sand and propped his head against his knees.

A man's shout came to him as though across an empty valley. Elisha raised his head. The shout coalesced to a chant, rising and falling like a gentle wave. A song.

Elisha stumbled to the water's edge. A canoe was gliding eastward atop the lake's surface. The paddlers were chanting a chanson in coarse French. He waded thigh-deep into the frigid lake. There appeared to be four voyageurs in the craft, two apiece at the bow and stern, and between them a man wearing a straw hat. Beside him sat a woman in a white sunbonnet. Elisha remained motionless. When the canoe was but ninety yards distant he raised both hands.

"Ho! Please land your canoe! I need help!"

The chanting paused as the craft dragged to a halt. It was a batard canoe with a green calumet painted on its bow, loaded with oilcloth-draped parcels. A white man sat gripping the gunwales, his sunburned face slack with amazement. Beside him a woman reclined atop a makeshift divan fashioned from stuffed sackcloth. She was holding a book in one hand and parasol in the other. Landlookers or prospectors, Elisha thought, though they did not appear to be either; then it occurred to him that they might be tourists. The notion momentarily confused the boy. Tourists, on a long excursion from the Sault.

"Will you help me, please?"

The canoe rolled slightly as the white man leaned forward, squinting. He whispered to the woman and she set the book in her lap, noticing Elisha for the first time. She raised a hand to her mouth and squealed with delight.

She believes I am Native, Elisha thought. My clothes, my filthy appearance. Or she does not know what I am.

"I am American, a scientist! Please help me!"

A mutter of conversation in the canoe as the steersman held the craft steady. The white man took up a small telescope and leveled it at Elisha.

"I am American! I am Christian! You must help me! *Please!*"

The craft swung shoreward and the chant resumed: *Le premier jour de Mai, Je donnerais à m'aime...* The woman withdrew a lace handkerchief and fluttered it gaily. A voyageur leapt into the shallows to guide the canoe ashore, and the white man called, "Dear fellow! What in heaven's name has happened to you?"

Elisha sank to his knees in the lake and closed his eyes. They understood that he was American. He was American, and he was saved.

Epilogue

The salon was on Atwater Street in a shabby frame building set between a barbershop and confectionary. That morning Elisha arrived to a smell of boiled sugar, climbed the narrow stairs to the studio and threw open the heavy drapes to reveal a small, dim room. A half-dozen large wooden crates were stacked beside a bureau heaped with photographic equipment, and in the room's center was a painted black table. Atop the table a sandhill crane stood among tufts of sedge. Elisha took up a chipped pitcher and doused the sedge, tugged loose a few desiccated blades. He was particularly proud of the tableau: he'd gathered the sedge from the bank of the Detroit River, arranged the crane's posture to match a memory from the previous summer. The bird's left leg was raised and its head was cocked, as though listening for a mate's call.

He positioned the camera stand then fetched a photographic plate and sprinkled it with jeweler's rouge, buffed the plate until his image appeared as a clear, dark reflection. He fitted the plate into a carrier and placed it inside a coating box, sprinkled in a few iodine crystals. An acrid whiff rose from the iodine. Footsteps rose on the stairs as he was transferring the carrier to the boxy camera.

Edward Featherstone entered the studio, whistling merrily. He froze when he saw Elisha bent over the camera box.

"Do not let me disturb you! This is a . . . what? A heron."

"Sandhill crane."

"A sandhill crane! Of course."

Elisha adjusted the camera's pose. He drew back the velvet window draperies and contemplated the quality of the day's light, made a quick calculation. Then he uncovered the camera's lens and held the shield aloft to indicate that Featherstone should not disturb him. When he counted sixty Elisha re-covered the lens and slid the carrier from the camera.

"That will be a thumping good image. I can sense it."

Elisha frowned. "The legs—they are too nearly aligned. The rear leg is partly obscured by the front."

"Well, I find it spectacular." Edward Featherstone whistled, a sharp trill. "Thirty half-plates mounted on maroon velvet, at fifteen dollars per set. Or perhaps we should change to quarter plates, lower the price to twelve and fifty. Multiplied by one thousand subscriptions, perhaps twelve hundred . . ." He clapped his hands. "Let us take a refreshment, shall we? Perhaps a good, strong coffee at Naglee's!"

"You go on. I'd like to capture one more view."

The man hesitated. "As you prefer."

Featherstone gathered a stack of finished plates and tipped his hat. The man's footsteps faded on the stairs; then the street door scuffed shut. Elisha frowned at the tableau before him. He shifted the camera stand a hand's-width leftward and captured a second image, then shifted it farther and captured a third. He drew the window draperies and set to developing the plates, circling them through mercury vapors until the crane's form bloomed on the mirrored surface, then fixing the image with hyposulphite of soda, toning it with gold chloride. But the crane was too dark. He had not allowed a long enough exposure. Elisha tacked the plate to the wall, among a collage of stillborn birds. He was sensitizing another plate when the bell at St. Anne's tolled noon.

He had returned to Detroit from Mackinac that previous August and taken a room on Beaubien Street, spent several days writing letters to Charles Edson and Corletta, various kin in Worcester and Lowell and Norwich and New London. As darkness came on Elisha would wander the city's wide streets, past Irish families chattering on porches, whores whistling down from upstairs windows. Italian boys arguing over bowls on the Military Square. Drunks singing and swaying outside lit-up dancing halls. The air held an early chill, and occasionally it would seep down through his chest and touch his heart, and for a moment Elisha would feel overcome by despair. But eventually the chill would pass. The city was too giddy and boisterous to allow it to linger.

Detroit in the autumn of 1844 seemed as optimistic as a city could be. The morning's newspapers held reports of the most recent improvements: a new rail line laid to Utica, a hydraulic waterworks installed on Randolph Street to replace the old reservoir. Plans for a lyceum on Woodward Avenue, with professors from the University at Ann Arbor offering instruction. The opening of an indigents' asylum on Griswold Street, to care for the city's poor. Detroit was not the place for a man to grow old, Elisha figured, but it was a fine city to learn a trade, or find a wife. And that was plenty good enough, for now.

One afternoon in September he had seen notice of an auction of animal and mineral specimens, from America and Europe and Asia, to be held at the Young Men's Society. Elisha brushed his hat and shined his brogans, thinking to surprise Alpheus Lenz with his presence. But he arrived at the Society hall to find that the collection at auction was, in fact, Lenz's own. The man had died of a bilious ailment that previous month; his specimens and library and Danish porcelain and Italian silver were being sold to the highest bidders. Elisha placed the first bid, for thirty dollars, then saw the price rise quickly to seventy dollars, then ninety-five. He watched the auction's remainder in gloomy silence.

Two days later he stood outside a stylish boardinghouse on Howard Street. His knock was answered by Edward Featherstone. The man invited Elisha into a room littered with sawdust and wooden crates, a pair of long tables cluttered with jars of chemicals. He was a businessman, Featherstone explained, recently of Toledo but arrived in Detroit to pursue a scheme: to capture images of animal specimens in daguerreotype, sell them by subscription as the most precise natural history folio ever offered. Despite his enthusiasm Featherstone's voice held a note of desperation. Elisha figured he didn't know a moth from a butterfly. "I was employed by Alpheus Lenz," Elisha told the man. "I was the one who cataloged these specimens, penned those title cards." Featherstone offered him a job without even knowing his surname.

And so Elisha taught himself how to prepare the silvered plates, how to gauge exposure time depending on the day's cloudiness or haze, how to pass the plates through mercury vapors until the images emerged like memories slowly called to mind. To his surprise he found that he enjoyed the procedure's complexity, the interplay of light and time like variables in an equation whose correct answer was an image that precisely reflected the specimen's form. And yet they were not mere reflections: the images were ghostly, ethereal, as though the specimen's spirit was captured in the glass pane.

Now he took up his hat and stepped down to Atwater Street. It was late October but a warm breeze stirred the flag atop the Chippewa Hotel. The street was loud with shouted conversation, the mild weather buoying the spirits of Detroit's residents. Elisha strolled to the Berthelet market and purchased an ear of roasted corn and a *City Examiner. World Without End!* the headline crowed. The Millerites' day of reckoning had come and passed. The article described the previous week's scene in Albany: Reverend William Miller and ten thousand faithful gathered in a fallow bean field to welcome the Lord's arrival on earth. Instead they were treated to a thunderstorm, and the shocked wailing of those who'd sold their worldly possessions. The wages of foolishness is tears, Elisha thought, then realized this was one of his father's sayings. The notion pleased him. He turned to the editorial notice and read:

INSANITY OF OUR SOUTHERN BRETHREN

It is rare in the annals of civilized discourse that a widely held (if absurd) notion can be dismissed in a single stroke. But can right-thinking individuals anymore doubt the fact that every man on this Earth are as brothers, born into a single Human Race? Any doubts on the matter have been dispelled by discovery of the Tiffin Stone (or Tiffin Stele, as some have it) as an incontrovertible link between antiquity and the present race of Red Indians.

The great and ineluctable deduction to be drawn from this discovery concerns the woeful institution of slavery which pervades our states to the South. We ask, How can Christian men continue to hold Negro men, women, and children in bondage with full knowledge of their natural-born equality? For if Red Indians are the white man's brethren—then must not the Negro also be kin?

Without argument, our Southern brethren should follow the example set by the British Parliament and immediately declare a general emancipation. It is particularly ironical that we must ask our countrymen to follow the example of a Nation we so recently and bitterly fought in the name of Liberty and Natural Rights.

Elisha dropped the newspaper into the gutter. Lately he had found himself scanning the paper for news of Mr. Brush and Professor Tiffin's wager—that they would present their findings to the learned men of Detroit, and the man whose work was deemed of lesser value to science would publish an apology in the *City Examiner* for squandering public funds. But months had passed and Elisha had seen no apology. He assumed the men had forgotten about the wager, or more likely settled it between themselves. Or recognized that they had both lost.

He returned to the salon and set to capturing a dozen images of the sandhill crane, drawing out the exposure time as the afternoon's light waned. He found that he could not concentrate. He worked listlessly for a time then draped the crane with a dust cloth, sensitized a photographic plate and loaded the camera. Then he hefted the camera stand to his shoulder and went back down to the street.

Outside it was nearly dusk and the day's warmth had dwindled to a chill. A column of empty farm wagons rattled northward, toward the city's edge. Elisha started toward the river, nodding at the gentlemen who paused to watch him pass. By now many of Detroit's residents had seen the camera, but there were yet a few who would stop in the street, follow him to wherever he was headed. Lately one particular woman had twice appeared as Elisha was leveling the camera stand: she'd been dressed in a yellow cape and bonnet, her auburn hair gathered in a simple plait. Next time, Elisha thought, I'll offer to capture her image. She was not beautiful but he would shift the lens until her beauty was revealed in the swell of her cheek, or her frail, piercing gaze. For in the lens's eye there was beauty everywhere, in a specimen or a plain young woman or the prospect of a sleeping city. To Elisha it seemed a strange form of grace.

On the pier edge he assembled the stand as a knot of onlookers gathered. The woman was there. She was dressed in the same yellow cape and bonnet, her hair drawn back, her pale skin dotted with pockmarks. She looked to be no older than twenty, though with an older woman's grave stare. Elisha stared at her as he fastened the camera to the stand, and when he'd finished he straightened his bowry and discreetly smoothed his shirtfront. As he approached she offered him a tranquil smile.

"I knew it must be you."

He grinned cautiously. "You have me mistaken, miss. I don't believe we are acquainted."

"You are Elisha Stone, son of the Reverend William Edward Stone. I know your face. You have your daddy's brow, that same troubled crease. And your chin, just the spitting image."

Elisha squinted at the woman. He was startled, speechless.

"We traveled together from Buffalo to Detroit, your daddy and I. He came to one of my séances. And then he wedded me to my husband on June twenty-fifth, not five blocks from this very spot. My name is Adele Crawley." The woman curtsied. "I am very pleased to meet you."

"Well. My goodness."

The woman's eyes were large and green, bordered by fine spidery lines that lent her a weary air. Her skin was so white as to be translucent. She was carrying a paper-wrapped packet that seemed to be seeping blood; then Elisha realized it was a butcher's parcel.

"I apologize for startling you—you look bit by snakes. I've been searching for you for a while now. I figured you might come to Detroit."

"My father told you that?"

The woman shook her head. "I have a sense for such things."

Elisha's confusion had given way to melancholy joy, at encountering a trace of his father's journey. He said, "I suppose he explained the reason for his travels. About my mother, and my departure from Newell. He was bringing me a message."

Adele Crawley cocked her head in sympathy. "Your daddy made a great journey in pursuit of you. He loved you very deeply, he and your mother both. He loves you still."

Elisha nodded. He realized that there were scores of questions he might ask the woman: if his father had been ill when she'd met him, or if his illness had grown over time. If he'd spoken about his journey, or his wife, or his congregation, or Newell. If he had seemed alarmed by Detroit's frantic pace. If he had seemed happy.

But instead he simply asked Adele how she'd met the man. She told Elisha about the depot in Buffalo, riding with the minister to a hotel at midnight, then seeing him again the following day on the steamer deck. And then the séance on Sixth Street, the wedding in Anders Lund's saloon. The woman's smile widened as she described the saloon's crimson wallpaper and stained pine floors, the Italian organ grinder with his garlic smell and lovely music. Her husband's blond silk cravat and her own blond dress, her mother's dress. The table laid with pine boughs, their makeshift altar. A flush rose to Adele's cheeks as she described Reverend Stone's gentle tone, his order that they go forth together into the wide world.

"And that is what we have done," she said. "And that is what we shall do forevermore."

Silence lengthened between them. At last Adele stepped a half-pace nearer to Elisha and touched his wrist. "Would you like to speak with him?"

"I don't get your meaning."

"I can converse with those who've passed. I hear them speak, in my thoughts. It is a gift."

Elisha held Adele's gaze for a long time, until he understood that she was in earnest. He felt a sharp pang of affection for the woman. She had helped his father, he was certain. Somehow she had helped him. It was hard to imagine his father mixing with a spiritualist medium; yet there it was. Another thing learned about the man. St. Anne's bell clanged in the distance; then a nearer bell echoed the chime.

"No. No, I don't believe I will. I don't believe I need to."

She seemed relieved by his decision. "You are right. You don't."

Elisha held the woman's gaze for a while longer, then he smiled and tipped his hat. He started back to the camera. When he turned she had disappeared onto Woodward Avenue.

The day's light yellowed and weakened as Elisha sat on the dock's edge. Onlookers lingered then drifted away, frustrated by the boy's inactivity, until eventually he was alone. He let his feet dangle over the river, watched thin gray foam slap and break against the pilings.

A stevedore trundling a barrow of slops came whistling down a gangplank and overturned his load onto the dock, a spill of bloody ice mingled with fish entrails and spoiled vegetables. Elisha moved beneath the curtain and adjusted the camera's pose. The scene's confusion pleased him: the heaped-up crates and barrels and bales, the thicket of masts at dock, the rubbish slicked across the weathered planks. There would be a moment, he knew, when the sun's low glare would set the scene alight, and the soot and mud and grime would vanish into shimmering, golden light, unlike anything else in nature, unlike anything except itself.

Elisha stood beneath the curtain, his hand on the lens shield. He would wait for that moment.

About the Author

KARL IAGNEMMA'S work has won the *Paris Review* Plimpton Prize and been anthologized in *The Best American Short Stories*. He is a research scientist in the mechanical engineering department at M.I.T. His collection, *On the Nature of Human Romantic Interaction*, is available from Dial Press Trade Paperbacks.